D1295407

Also by Gemma O'Connor
and published by Bantam Books

Time to Remember

Farewell to the Flesh

Sins of Omission

FALLS THE SHADOW

Gemma O'Connor

BANTAM BOOKS

LONDON · NEW YORK · TORONTO · SYDNEY · AUCKLAND

FALLS THE SHADOW
A BANTAM BOOK : 0553 812629

Originally published by Poolbeg Press Ltd, Dublin, Ireland

PRINTING HISTORY
Poolbeg edition published 1996
Bantam Books edition published 1999

Set in 11/12 pt Sabon by
Deltatype Ltd, Birkenhead, Merseyside

Bantam Books are published by Transworld Publishers Ltd,
61–63 Uxbridge Road, London W5 5SA,
in Australia by Transworld Publishers,
c/o Random House Australia (Pty) Ltd,
20 Alfred Street, Milsons Point, NSW 2061,
in New Zealand by Transworld Publishers,
c/o Random House New Zealand,
18 Poland Road, Glenfield, Auckland,
in South Africa by Transworld Publishers,
c/o Random House South Africa (Pty) Ltd
Endulini, 5a Jubilee Road, Parktown 2193

Reproduced, printed and bound in Great Britain by
Cox & Wyman Ltd, Reading, Berks.

Acknowledgements

Falls the Shadow was written in memory of my mother, Bess Nolan Fitzpatrick (1909–1993) who, long ago, recounted an incident which inspired this story.

I would like to thank the distinguished bookbinder, Ivor Robinson for describing his wartime experiences in the Royal Navy. Since he also taught me to bind books, I am indebted to him for what I know about the subject. Caroline Sheehan of Horizon International at Heathrow guided me through the freight forwarding business. My sister, Pauline Fitzpatrick, helped with the research and introduced me to the Gilbert Library. Brother Aloysius Shannon and Brother Bernardine Edwards of the Hospitallers of St John of God and Sister Oliver Russell of The Sisters of the Assumption of the Poor clued me in to the social conditions obtaining in Ireland in the forties. Bob Moir, firearms expert of the Thames Valley Police, was wonderfully generous with his time and knowledge as were Sergeant John Duffy of An Garda Síochána Museum and Archives in Dublin and PC Henry Wymbs of Thames Valley Police in Oxford. Gay McGuinness of Domaine des Anges gave me a location for Domaine Garnier and Chris Green suggested the title.

My special thanks, for their unfailing encouragement and help, to Philip MacDermott and everyone at Poolbeg, specially my editor Kate Cruise O'Brien; John O'Connor, Mervyn Evans and Richie Gill of the Oxford Orthopaedic Engineering Centre; Lucien Taylor, Vanessa Goulder, Steven Williams and Ruth McCarthy; finally, Alice and Laura for allowing me to use their cat.

The Ringsend I describe in Falls the Shadow *is based on my childhood impressions when I couldn't distinguish between Ringsend and Irishtown. I hope the residents of both will indulge that memory and overlook the discrepancies they will, undoubtedly, discover. Daedalian Road and the DART railway loop around Lotts Road are entirely imaginary. I trust the estimable Dublin Area Rapid Transport will forgive me for diverting their trains.*

The reader will search Oxford in vain for Drapier or Tradescant College. Nor are there, so far as I know, even among the most ancient colleges, any with either a bindery or a resident bookbinder attached to its library.

For my dear daughter, Emily, with my love

Nobody mourned him. No-one save his son would ever refer to him again except in disgust or fear or with a stifled, shamefaced, guffaw of relief that he had been taken from their midst with so little fuss. If you could call a bullet in the back of the brain little fuss.

At least it was quick, that dispatch. And deadly accurate. That his killer – or killers – had the good fortune to pick the one night in 1941 when neutral Dublin was bombed, was treated with a respect bordering on the divine. The timing of both bombing and murder exactly coincided and, as a result, the murder was sidelined by the greater catastrophe.

The crime was never solved; nobody was brought to justice. Eventually it was forgotten, or so it seemed. But memories are long and retribution is exacted stealthily. Fifty years pass . . .

Between the idea
And the reality,
Between the motion
And the act
Falls the Shadow.

From
The Hollow Men TS Eliot

CHAPTER ONE

My mother was killed on 28 June while I was on holiday in Mallorca. The day was gloriously hot and sunny. I'd just got back from the beach and was racing my boyfriend for the shower when the phone rang. Many times since I have tried to recall that moment. I see my head turn, my hand outstretched, Davis pushing past, laughing in triumph. I hear no words, the message drills into my brain and I spiral down into deep black silence. I do not remember the long drive from Polença to the airport, nor anything about the flight to Dublin. All I see is the policeman taking my hand. No sounds penetrated my despair. I could not conjure her face. But I thought about her all the time.

Even as a child I recognized that my mother was entirely individual. But I only began to appreciate her quiet self-possession as I grew up. That she cared passionately about me I never doubted. What her feelings for my dad were I can only guess. Because he was so much older than her, I don't think he ever saw her as the strong character she was. He was inclined to chivvy her, mostly, I think, because she was so small. I sometimes felt he treated her like a child. But, if she minded, she didn't say.

Though she talked a lot, communication was not her strong point; she kept her thoughts to herself.

When I was younger I thought, arrogantly, that it was because she hadn't a thought in her head. But I eventually perceived that was not the case. Her great quality was that she was there for me. Dependable, resourceful and, when the mood was on her, fun.

She began to put on weight in her sixties, not too much but with her small frame a little was noticeable. Only in her last couple of years did she ever admit to her change of shape. She once told me that it was a revelation to her, for, as her skin stretched to cover the soft contours of her face, the wrinkles eased away and she looked much, much younger. And she was right, she did. So now I think of her as small and stout and stout-hearted. That is how I want to remember her because as she got older she grew more relaxed and content. But she wouldn't thank me for describing her as plump, believe me. She was, and remained all her life, vain and ultra careful about her appearance. She had always been petite and slim and she never thought of herself as otherwise.

I hardly knew her at all. Or, to be more exact, I have learned more about her since she died than I ever guessed at in her lifetime, and that has left me feeling that opportunities were missed and I am the loser. She was a hell of a lot more interesting than I ever guessed. My biggest and most painful regret is that when she was around, the possibility of friendship with her never entered my head. She was my mother and that was it. Her past and present and future were contained in that brief description, that life sentence: Mother. A little older than my friends' mothers; a little louder, more vulgar. The elocution classes never quite worked, she never lost the flat Dublin accent of her origins.

She was almost thirty-seven when I was born and by the time I got to university she was, as she put it herself, pushing retirement. That's when she started gussying up and getting her beautiful hair properly cut. She became quite spirited and I was, with typical youthful disdain, completely embarrassed by this transformation. But my friends thought she was great. About the same time – it was the last year of my father's life – we got our first car. She and I learned to drive at the same time, so we could take turns ferrying him around. Lily was never entirely comfortable behind the wheel and as a result was a bit alarming on the open road. She really only used the car locally and in the country. City traffic terrified her, though probably not as much as she infuriated other drivers; she would insist on keeping to the centre of the road. Thank heavens, public transport is free in Ireland once you reach sixty-five, so she DARTed about quite a bit, otherwise she used the bike.

Funny how you hardly notice your own mother. I thought I knew the parameters of her life. My father was a widower with two grown-up sons when they married. My two half-brothers emigrated to Australia before I was born, so I was, in effect, an only child. The boys were not good at keeping in touch but then my dad wasn't much of a communicator either. A night with his cronies in the pub was what he liked. He wasn't a heavy drinker, a couple of pints was his usual limit, but he preferred, I think, the company of his own age group and his own sex.

Because my dad had retired, for as long as I remember, my mother was the breadwinner. He was a carpenter who never earned all that much. I know now that her earning power was much greater than his. He was sensitive about money so I suppose she felt she had to be discreet. I couldn't have gone to college without her. Though I got a partial scholarship and lived at home, she had to work all the hours God sent, to keep us going. Looking back, I can't believe I took so much for granted. During my college years her dressmaking took on a new lease of life. She stopped doing cheapskate repairs and began to make these brilliant ball gowns and party gear. She smartened up her prices. Smartened herself up as well. I used to think all those bright, primary colours were a bit much, but actually, she looked all right. Cheerful. Some might say eye-catching.

I was an only child but she never clung. That is the quality of hers that I most appreciate now, but I hardly noticed when she was around. She was proud when I did well at school and prouder still when I announced that I wanted to go to university.

'We'll manage,' was all she said. Now I wonder how she did? We lived modestly, in a small semi-detached house in Dun Laoghaire, a sea-port on Dublin Bay, just six miles from the city. She always showed an endearing pride and delight in the house. It was, she said, hers, and that meant more than she could say. I now know why.

At last, I am beginning to get a glimmer of her resourcefulness. My father died during my last year in college. He had his first stroke, a mild one, when

14

I was about sixteen and a much more severe one three years later, when he lost much of his speech and the movement on his left side. She cared for him without fuss and without complaint and, at the same time, managed somehow to beef up her earning capacity. It must have been tough for her but it passed over my head somehow. It seems hard to believe now, how little I noticed.

After graduation I decided to go and work in London. She accepted that too, even though it was shortly after my father died. There was no pressure of the 'you're all I've got' variety. Instead, she chose to see it as a way of expanding her own horizons.

'I've always longed to travel, Chucks, and now I can,' she said. And she was as good as her word. I suppose that's when I began to get to know her as an individual. Her pleasure in her twice yearly visits was infectious. She took to airports the way other people take to the bottle.

'It's an education, Chucks. You see a great variety of people.'

I believe she would have been perfectly happy to spend a week at Heathrow or Gatwick every year and sometimes she almost did. I work at Heathrow Airport. Not on the passenger side but at the back of the main runway where the cargo depots are located. In the autumn of 1991, I became UK operations manager of a German owned, international freight forwarder. During the day-time, while I was at work, she took to prowling around the terminals like an author in search of characters. She wasn't picky. She also liked the rail links to London or Gatwick. I would drop her at Terminal

One on my way to the office and off she'd go. Magic-carpeting she called it. She loved the excitement and bustle of the terminals and seemed to be able to strike up fleeting friendships with a skill which, had she been born later and in other circumstances, might have led to a hot-shot media career. The strange thing is that she was a real loner; she had no close friends of her own. She was always more comfortable with strangers. She could tease a life story out of the most unpromising material but her great skill was in recounting her adventures for my friend Maria and me.

I'd give anything to have those times again. I wish I'd told her how much I admired her courage, her amazing *joie de vivre*. The mindless, heartless, casual cruelty of the way she was mown down, flicked out of the way and left to die, makes me shake with wild, impotent rage every time I think of it. I miss her, sometimes so much it hurts.

It must have been around the time of my move to *Morgen Morgen* that Lily discovered the coach system serving Heathrow. She used it to travel about the country, taking herself off for day excursions. She was thrilled with this cheap way of seeing the beauties of England but I have, since she died, discovered that Ma was a little disingenuous there. She wasn't seeing the country, for the most part she was seeing one city.

Funny to think that it was I who helped set up her little subterfuge. I was struggling to get on top of my new job at the time and uneasy that she was spending so much of her holiday on her own. I'd arranged to meet her at one of the airport passenger terminals one afternoon after I finished work. We'd planned an outing to Windsor for a spot of sightseeing and supper. I was late of course and she wasn't waiting where we'd arranged to meet. After haring around for a frantic half-hour, I eventually found her outside Terminal One watching the steady stream of coaches leaving the bus station opposite.

'They go all over the country, Chucks,' she greeted me brightly. 'I've made enquiries. I can take day-returns to all sorts of places.'

'By coach?' I was trying to catch my breath and control my irritation. I'd just had a barney on the phone with Davis, my boyfriend. He was always a bit of a pillock when Lily was around. She never said whether she liked him or not. She didn't have to. I knew perfectly well he bored her rigid and that, of course, made me edgy and resentful.

'What sort of places?' I asked.

'Oh, everywhere,' she shrugged and held out a sheaf of timetables. 'It'll be great, Nell. You could drop me here on your way to the office and pick me up – whenever.' She grinned in the way she had, with her head cocked on one side. 'And then, Chucks, you can have a bit more time with that man of yours. You won't have to be worrying about me and getting all in a heap. Like you are now.' She linked her arm in mine. 'Come on, I'll buy you a drink and we'll make a few plans.'

I was about to protest, in my uptight way, that I couldn't drink and drive but she held up her hand.

'You can have what you like, Chucks, but I'm for a glass of Guinness.'

So we had one apiece while I worked out an itinerary of the cathedral cities which ran coaches to and from the airport. I remember her delight with the plan and the enthusiasm with which she began her travels. She certainly visited each place on the list once. She'd come back from each outing with a guidebook and regale us with detailed descriptions of the cafes she had stopped in, the people she had encountered. Her pleasure in the great churches she simply could not have faked, but then, she always had an eye for beauty.

Now that I come to think of it, those excursions opened a new chapter in both our lives. I no longer felt responsible for keeping her entertained. They gave us independence and, at the same time, drew us together. I hadn't, until then, realized how much I wanted her to like where I lived. Appreciate England's beauty. Like everyone else at the time, we were saturated with the tensions of Northern Ireland. We might try to avoid the subject, but it was always there, dictating our attitudes. Over the years I had visited many of the places on Lily's list. So for the first time since I left home, we had something new in common, something new to talk about.

'Listen, Chucks, if I can't enjoy myself at my time of life, I'd be a sad case. Would you get on with your life and stop worrying. I'm fine.' She didn't tick me off for treating her as a duty, though she might have done. As it turned out, because she entertained herself so well while I was working, I could even take the occasional day off and not resent it. We both relaxed. From then on her visits were a real buzz. For the pair of us.

It went on like that right up to the end. When she'd worked her way through the list she announced that it was impossible to take in enough in just one visit. Well, she must have been reading guidebooks to those cathedrals with some avidity because she described Gloucester, Bath, Wells, Bristol, Oxford, Lincoln, Salisbury, Ely in fanciful detail and all the time, as I later found out, it was only Oxford which drew her again and again. She was a dark one.

And that, really, is how I eventually began to learn a little about my mother. Though at the time it never occurred to me to wonder what on earth she was up to. How she filled her time. Those innocent-seeming coach trips. The high excitement on her return. The smiling, pink-cheeked, little woman: so cheerful, so enthusiastic, so artless. So what? So secretive, is what. She certainly pulled the wool over my eyes. I have to laugh when I think of it. She was bloody brilliant.

I wish I'd taken more trouble. I wish I hadn't been so preoccupied. I wish.

Oh dear. Oh Lily Gilmore, I wish I'd known you better. But I'm getting beyond myself . . .

1992

CHAPTER TWO

'Watch your step,' the driver droned monot-
onously as each passenger stepped from the coach.
As he counted them off, he checked the number
against his receipts, then realized he was one short.
He strolled slowly back along the aisle. A brightly
dressed, white-haired woman was sitting in the
window seat of the third row from the back. She
was short enough to be obscured by the tall seat
and was staring out the window, a lace handkerchief held to her eyes. When he coughed she turned
and looked up at him, tears pouring unchecked
down her pale, still-comely face. He wondered that
she managed to cry so elegantly, without snivelling
and without the usual blotchy face. He shuffled his
feet in embarrassment.

'We're in Oxford. This is the end of the line,'
he said gruffly. 'Unless you want to go back
to Heathrow? We'll be leaving again in half an
hour. You can sit there if you like, it's up to
you.'

'Oh dear me, no. Thanks very much,' she said,
mopping her eyes. 'Don't mind me. There's
nothing really wrong. I'm just a sentimental old
fool thinking about the past and all the time I've
wasted. I'll be fine in a minute. This is where I want
to be. I'll catch an afternoon coach back.' She gave
a self-deprecating little snort and checked her
make-up. Then she threw back her shoulders and
got to her feet. He was struck by how suddenly she

had sloughed off her sadness. She looked rather like a beautifully turned-out robin. Her flawlessly cut clothes were intended to flatter – as indeed they did.

'It's a lovely place, isn't it?'

'What? The bus station?' he asked incredulously.

'Ah, get on with you.' She waved her hand playfully, flirtatiously almost. 'No, I mean the town. Was that the main street we drove down?'

'Yeah, The High,' he said, as if each word caused him an effort.

'Is that the main shopping street?' she persisted.

'There's the covered market just off it, if you want shopping. There's all sorts in there,' he said, as she carefully perched an absurd little black hat on her neat snow-white page boy. 'Hats as well,' he added, as she preceded him up the aisle.

He picked up his cash box and jacket and followed her down the steps of the coach. She was now fully recovered, sprightly even. She had the air of someone about to embark on a great adventure.

'By the way, can you tell me where the university is?' She squinted up at him. Her voice was as bright and cheerful as her cerise suit.

'It's everywhere, all over the place,' he said impatiently. 'There's nothing you could call a university. Not any one building. It's all colleges here.' He was about to walk away when she cleared her throat. He sighed heavily as he looked down at her.

'Which one are you looking for?'

She stood on one leg, acrobatically propped her large navy-blue handbag on her knee and rummaged through it, before triumphantly producing a scrap of paper which she peered at short-sightedly. The driver read it over her shoulder.

'This one or that?' he asked, pointing at the scribbled writing. She looked up at him quizzically.

'Oh, two? Is that right?' She bit her lip. 'I thought it was all the one. Now, I'm not sure which.'

'No worry. They're quite close together. Now, let's see.' He rocked back and forth on his heels. 'Your best bet,' he advised in a strong Oxfordshire burr, looking at her flimsy high heels, 'is to take a taxi. Not far as the crow flies but it's coming on to rain and it's hard to explain exactly how to get there. Near Merton College, I think.' He scratched his head and smiled ruefully. 'Yeah, best take a taxi. He'll set you right. OK, are you?'

'A taxi will do grand.' The bright blue eyes crinkled attractively when she smiled. 'Thank you very much. I'm fine, thanks for your help.' She popped the scrap of paper back in her bag. 'Now, could you please tell me where I would find a taxi?'

If she had baggage, she'd have me lugging it around the town for her, the driver thought resignedly and stifled an impulse to laugh. He pointed to an empty taxi rank across the square. 'Over there. Just hang about, there'll be one in a minute.' He watched as she teetered across the Gloucester Green cobbles towards the taxi-rank, the peacock feather in her tiny pill-box hat waving in time to the tip-tap of her neat shoes.

The taxi driver, when she asked, took her on a short tour around the town, though he knew almost nothing about the university. Disappointingly, he had only the sketchiest notion of which college was which and, when she enquired, had no idea at all where the libraries were. Indeed he insisted that there was 'just the one' which turned out to be the city library and not the source of her information. She felt in her pocket for the letter and drew it out: The Bodleian Library, University of Oxford, read the printed heading of that courteous note.

As you will appreciate, there are bookbinders and restorers working in many of the college libraries. But I'm intrigued by your description – I should like someone to describe me in such flattering terms. You mentioned Merton Street and The High, so I should start with Tradescant and Drapier College. Mr Garnier of Drapier fits your description most closely. If you have no luck, then drop in and we'll think again. Bodley is on the Broad, beside the Sheldonian Theatre.

'I think it's on the Broad Street,' she said tentatively. The cabman put up a show of resistance, suggested she'd made a mistake but was eventually persuaded to stop outside. He asked if she'd like to go in.

'No thank you. I just wanted to see it,' she answered brightly. Next time, she silently promised, if there was a next time, she would go and thank the nice librarian for his help. If, that is, his information proved accurate.

By the time Mrs Gilmore got to the second college on her short list she concluded that not all the inhabitants of Oxford were as helpful as her librarian correspondent. She had just spent a fruitless hour wandering through Tradescant College library. That it was ancient and wonderful she had no doubt. That it had rare and fine treasures was apparent even to someone as ignorant of scholarship as herself. That it had not contained the treasure she was looking for had, alas, become obvious within fifteen minutes of her arrival there. The rest of the hour had been spent in trying to extricate herself from a guided tour of American academics and one importunate, long-winded, Bostonian professor in particular. It was very nearly two o'clock by the time she walked through the gates of Drapier College.

The porter was young, clueless and professed to know nothing of the library or its staff. Quickly tiring of her questions, he directed her to the college office. The reception there was positively frosty.

'I'm afraid there's nobody free to take you through the college. In any case, the library is not open to visitors, except by appointment.' The bored college secretary looked as though life was a continuous irritant. She studied Mrs Gilmore over half-moon glasses. Mrs Gilmore eyed her levelly while mentally cropping her unsuitably long hair and discarding the floral milk-maid dress. A bit of make-up would improve that disappointed face no end, she thought; from habit, not malice. A decent bra and a well tailored suit, such as I could run up for you in no time, she continued to muse, would work wonders. Mrs Gilmore was a wizard with her needle and earned a good living as a (ladies) bespoke tailor and costume-maker. She was also no mean hand at evening gowns.

'Did the porter not say?' The object of her scrutiny broke into her thoughts brusquely.

27

'The porter,' Mrs Gilmore said, 'told me to come and ask you.' She smiled disarmingly. Miss Irene Spence did not succumb. She did not like the old woman's strange accent, she could not fathom where it came from and did not think of asking. But it was definitely uneducated, of that she was sure. Irene (accent on the final e, please) Spence, who had a rather poor opinion of the organizational abilities of the college dons, thought of herself as a cut above. If she was not actually running the college, she was certainly the person who held things together. She would have words with that new porter. The nerve of him showing this loud, pushy old woman into her office. Common, she looked. And over-familiar.

'Oh, but I have a long-standing appointment,' Mrs Gilmore said, if not accurately, with conviction. She wondered how else she could describe fifty years?

'Then I should have a note of it,' the secretary announced tiredly. 'What is the name?' She looked at her visitor doubtfully, opened a leather-bound appointment book and ran her finger down the columns of several pages.

'Gilmore, Gilmore. With the librarian, you say?' she asked. 'Sorry, I have nothing here.' She closed the book firmly.

'Excuse me. Not the librarian. The bookbinder,' Mrs Gilmore said quietly.

'The *Bookbinder*?' The secretary sounded exactly like Dame Edith Evans enquiring about *the Handbag*? 'We don't have a bookbinder. I suppose you must mean our conservationist?' Mrs Gilmore had not the least idea what a conservationist was. The word put her in mind of jam-making, but she held her ground.

'Yes, that's right,' she said pleasantly.

'Oh well, in that case, I'm afraid you're out of luck. We don't allow visitors in the *workshop*.' Miss Spence's lips curled in a sneer. 'Sorry. Anyway if it's *Mr Garnier* you're looking for, he never sees anyone. Never.' She gave a triumphant little snort. This time she did not look up and thus she missed the look of relief that passed fleetingly over Mrs Gilmore's features.

'He'll see me,' she said pleasantly but with certainty. 'I have come a long way and it's important. So, if you could just show me the way, I'll pop in to see him.'

'I'm afraid, madam, you can't just walk through the college. Alone,' Irene Spence replied frostily and drew in a loud, martyred breath. She picked up the phone and dialled. 'It's engaged,' she said and went back to her typing.

Mrs Gilmore drew herself up indignantly. 'I don't,' she said, impatience overcoming her suddenly, 'I don't see that you have any reason to be so rude to me.' She leaned over the desk and glared into the two startled eyes which were raised to meet hers. 'I'm a visitor to your college and your town, you might try to make me feel welcome and not like something the cat dragged in.' She took a deep breath and continued while she had the advantage. 'Now, if you'll just point me in the right direction, I'll go ahead. I'm perfectly capable of finding it on my own.' She straightened up, her face was flushed and her hat wobbled perilously on her head. Miss Spence looked suitably admonished.

'I'm just doing my job,' she muttered. There was a brief, pregnant stand-off while each tried to outstare the other. The hapless Miss Spence caved in first. 'Oh, well then,' she said ungraciously. 'Go through the first quad and cross over to staircase eleven. It's marked with an X and an I.'

'You don't say? Not an I and an I?' Mrs Gilmore asked sweetly.

'We use roman numerals,' the secretary began before she noticed the mocking eyes. 'Go ahead.' She had the grace to blush. 'I'll try him again shortly and tell him you're on your way, but don't blame me if he gives you a cool reception. He can be very truculent. He doesn't allow anyone up there. He *hates* visitors,' she added triumphantly and peered enquiringly at the older woman. 'Is it family business?' she asked, as if to make amends.

'You might say,' said Mrs Gilmore vaguely and thanked her elaborately for her trouble. She tripped lightly from the room looking remarkably pleased with herself.

When Miss Spence tried to redial the library extension a minute or two later she found the line was dead. It took a full five, harassed minutes for her to locate the cause of the trouble. Somehow the connection on the side of the phone had worked itself loose. Not that it mattered for, when she eventually tried the number again, it went unanswered. By which time Mrs Gilmore had negotiated both quads and was puffing up the long steep stairway to the bindery.

She paused at the top landing to recover her breath then knocked on the heavy door. She tried several times with increasing vigour and, when there was no reply, she depressed the brass handle quietly, pulled back the stout oak door and almost broke her nose against a second green baize door behind it. When she had eased that open, she nervously straightened her hat, tip-toed inside, closed the door softly behind her and stood for a few moments resting her back against it before she set her bag down on a nearby bench and extracted a small canvas roll from it. Then she did a curious thing: she slipped off her shoes and laid them neatly beside the discarded bag.

She looked about her. The room was immensely long and narrow – perhaps forty foot by fifteen – so that at first sight it looked more like a passageway than a great gallery. Patches of light from the stained-glass windows shone on the undulating oak floor. High above, the wooden barrel-vaulted ceiling, which must once have been richly decorated, still bore odd remnants of gold, blue and red paint. Three tall wooden book-presses stood against the white, plastered walls with immense leather-bound volumes clasped between their huge platens. Except for a series of brightly illuminated maps, the walls were quite bare. The smell of leather pervaded the place. She sniffed appreciatively at that almost forgotten memory.

In the centre of the room, backed by the largest window, three refectory tables laden with piles of books formed a U-shaped working area. A lean grey-haired man was working at the central table. He held a decorating tool in his left hand and appeared to be repairing the cover of a large book which lay on a thick mat beneath the light. He did not look up at the intruder's silent approach nor did he even seem aware of her presence. She wondered if he was deaf until she noticed he had a pair of headphones clasped to his ears and realized why he had neither heard her nor answered the phone which had begun to shrill. She stood some way from the bench, out of his line of vision, and watched his smooth and measured movements as he worked. The hand moved effortlessly. A hiss, a sigh. Dreamily, she drifted back to a time long ago when she had once watched almost exactly the same scene. Though not in so grand a place.

He worked slowly, calmly. To his left lay an oblong suede-leather pad upon which gold-leaf had been divided into minuscule squares. A little to his right, a neat row of wooden-handled brasses were warming on a small electric ring. He picked up each one in sequence. The heat of the tool appeared to draw the gold to it and he deftly applied the leaf to the cover where the pattern had been damaged or lost. He must have repeated the movement a dozen times or more before he laid down the brass tool, switched off the hot-plate and drew his hand wearily over his eyes. He pulled off the headphones, pushed back the stool he'd been leaning against, and straightened up. He extended his arms and spread his hands on the bench. His eyes were closed. He remained motionless for a moment then he leaned forward and backwards several times, easing the stiffness of his back. He still appeared not to have noticed her standing silently watching him. As he half-turned to the window, the sunlight shone directly on him. Now, at last, it was possible for her to see his face properly for the first time.

Her heart skipped like a lamb in springtime. He was almost unchanged. The same gentle face. Even after all those years, the beautiful features unblurred by age or fat. His rich, once dark, hair was now as white and as abundant as her own and it gave her pleasure to see that, like her, he was vain about it. It was well barbered. A handsome man.

She thought he hadn't noticed her until he turned slowly, looked straight at her and gave a quiet, characteristic little chuckle. The things she remembered about him amazed her but not as much as her realization that he had been aware of her all the time she'd been watching him.

'Will I pass?' he asked softly. 'No-one could ever stand as still as you, or for so long. Have you had a good enough look?' He chuckled again at her surprise. She did not reply. Instead she moved forward, unrolled the canvas holder she had brought with her and laid it on the bench in front of him. He stared down at his old set of tools; the paring knives and the yellowing bone folders, the brasses, the slightly rusting shears.

'You kept them all this time?' He held out his arms to her.

'Ah, Lily Sweetman.' He shook his head in disbelief. 'You're a sight for sore eyes. How on earth did you find me?'

31 May 1941

CHAPTER THREE

Outside the door, the Buller Reynolds's dog growled menacingly; the child began to scream in rage and alarm.

'Shush, Jimmy, shush. Oh, for pity's sake don't cry now. Don't cry baby, please, please.'

The young girl gently rocked the wheezing child in her arms, holding her tear-streaked face close to his wizened little features. When he let out another piercing yowl, she clamped her hand over his mouth.

'Shush, little one, shush. Please, Jimmy,' she whispered desperately.

Sobbing softly, she laid him on the stained mattress. It took up almost half the dismal box-room which was otherwise, except for a backless kitchen chair, unfurnished. She crouched down beside him, pulled an old grey army-blanket up over both of them and cuddled the snivelling infant to her. In the next room the thumping noises started again and something crashed against the partition wall at her head. The dog's growling grew frantic as it scraped furiously at the foot of the door. The child squawked in terror as he struggled to escape the heat of the blanket and his sister's grasp. His whimpering grew more agitated.

'Oh dotie, dotie, shush. Please, please. Oh please. Help me. Shuuuush, please please.'

She cradled him in one arm and stuck the crooked knuckle of her other little finger in his mouth. Immediately he quietened down and sucked mightily. She held her breath and her uncomfortable position until, after a few minutes, he fell asleep. She eased her deadened arm from under him and lay watching him, marvelling at the sudden peace of his innocent little face.

Rejected by his mother, the care of the child had, almost from his difficult birth, devolved on her and she was fiercely protective of him. She loved his sweet little smile. She hated it when the neighbours called him *simple* and said he should be in a home. He did no harm to anyone, little Jimmy. She lay watching him in the gloom, gently stroking his temples, terrified in case he would start crying again. Even in sleep he was never still, his little deformed body struggled for each breath, hands flailing, useless leg twitching. Every now and then a little tremor ran through him and when she took her hand away he wriggled towards her, cuddling into her as if he only felt safe within her shadow.

She forced herself to remember the words of songs, the nine times tables, half-remembered prayers, the six times tables, anything, anything so that she might not hear the awful pounding noise in the next room, her mother's groans, the growling dog. As the light faded, the room grew darker. The baby rolled away from her, gave a tiny shriek then lay quiet. She knew it must be past ten but it was the end of May and there was still some light in the sky. She knew how it would go now: they'd be quiet for a time then he would get up and shout and clout her ma again. And then he'd be off, taking his terrifying bloodhound with him. To moider someone else. Six times six, thirty-six. Four fives twenty. She had to be quiet then for sure because if she said anything, or Jimmy started crying, her Ma'd go wild. And tonight. Oh God, tonight was the worst. She mustn't think about it. Bad thoughts were a sin. Six sevens, six sevens are, six sevens are . . . She cringed with fear.

Something was dragged across the floor. Heavy footsteps. He was coming to the door. Oh God. Oh God. She stuck her fingers in her ears and lay rigid, her heart pounding painfully. Don't let him in, don't let him in. Please somebody. Don't let him in. He rattled at the door then kicked it and shouted something at her mother.

The lock held. Milo's lock held, she thought triumphantly and breathed a silent prayer of thanks. Jimmy gave a little titter in his sleep and rolled over. She buried her head in the blanket and waited for the sound of the landlord's footsteps going down the stairs. Waited for her mother to start moving about.

She must have dozed off because she didn't hear either of them. When she took her fingers from her ears the house was quiet except for the usual scratching and scrambling behind the wall. She wouldn't look at that gaping hole where the skirting board was missing. She didn't care what anyone said; it wasn't rats. No. No rats. No rats. She eased herself off the mattress. Mice, mice, mice, mice, mice, she sing-songed softly as she crept to the door. She stood with her ear pressed to the flaking paint, listening. It was only mice. She wouldn't think of the rat that once tunnelled its way in from the empty place next door. Or the possibility there might be more. The rat was dead,

dead, dead. Martin clobbered it with a shovel. Mice couldn't harm you, they were too small. They smelt but. Rosie in the flat too floors down said they should get a cat. To protect the babies she said, but the kitten Martin brought home was a wild thing and too small. When the kitten saw the red eyes on the stairs, it streaked out of the house like it was scalded and never came back. Now Rosie was gone away as well. That's what happened to people in this awful house. They got the feck out as fast as they could.

The room was almost completely dark now. She turned the key in the lock, pocketed it, and eased herself out on the landing which also served as a makeshift kitchen. Immediately, at her feet, there was a mad scampering across the tattered lino. She squeezed her eyes shut and slowly counted to ten before opening them. The alarm clock on the shelf said twenty-five past twelve. She must have slept nearly two hours. She peeped around the open door of the other room but it was empty. Her mother was gone out then, not asleep as she'd hoped. She fought back her rising panic and set about tidying the place. There wasn't enough water left in the bucket to wash up, so she piled the dirty dishes in it and set it on the table out of reach. As she bustled around she became aware of a dull low drilling pulse which seemed to come from overhead. Aeroplanes? She stood and stared upwards as if she could see through the roof above. Gradually the noise became so deafening she felt as if the planes would burst in on top of her. The floor under her bare feet vibrated gently. She crept back in to the child but he slept on.

She knelt by the window facing directly on to the street and stared out moodily wondering when her mother would come home.

'Ah poor oul Dicey Reilly
she has taken to the sup,
And poor oul Dicey Reilly
she will never give it up . . .'

She sang the words under her breath. It was the song that bowsey Packey Brennan chanted every time he saw Ma. There was always someone shouting and jeering after her in the street. Lily hummed tunelessly, unable to get the song out of her head.

It was really dark with only a sliver of moon showing occasionally through the clouds. She could make nothing out but the aircraft seemed to be moving off, the sound was fainter. Now and then searchlights swirled around, making patterns high in the sky, and once or twice she heard the sound of gun-fire and a siren. She wondered if it was an air-raid. There'd been a lot of talk of air-raids in the past few weeks but Milo said it was all eejity talk, that Ireland couldn't be bombed because it was neu-something-or-other. Lily half hoped Dublin would be bombed and that her house would be the first thing to go up in smoke. With the Buller Reynolds inside, if possible. The rest of them could run. She wished her mother would get back from the boozer or wherever she was and hoped it wouldn't be long. She was dropping on her feet and her face was sore but she couldn't go back to sleep till Ma got home. Trouble was, sometimes she didn't get back till morning. Or later.

Lily peered into the darkness and allowed her worries to come singly through her head. Like lead soldiers marching in file was how she thought about it. She didn't allow herself big worries about the future: about Jimmy; about the fact that she herself hadn't been to school for more than two years; or what was to become of the three of them if her Da didn't come back. Her lead soldiers were the smaller things which, when she worried about them, grew and grew. No food in the house and no money to get any. Sometimes Milo slipped her a tanner, once a whole shilling. A new thought struck her. She padded silently back into the other room and searched through the scattered clothes and down the side of the bocketty old sofa. Her search yielded two thruppeny bits, a penny and a couple of ha'pence. She rolled the coins carefully in a scrap of paper so they wouldn't rattle against the key, and stuck them in her pocket. Then with a sigh of relief, she returned to her vigil. The road was still deserted. There was no sign of her Ma.

There was a second smaller and higher window in the room which gave on to the garden of the house next door. She had to stand on a chair to see through it and even then it was hard because it was completely covered with creeper on the outside. The great thing was you couldn't see it from the road. Her secret spy-hole. A long time back, when the trouble started, after Ma had Jimmy and her daddy went away, and *he* started coming, she had broken a small pane of glass and made a gap in the leaves big enough to see through. Every now and then she had to move the broken pane and pull away the leaves. From her perch she could usually see *him* coming from Sandymount, where he lived. Then she would take Jimmy and hide. Sometimes, like tonight, he had come from the other, the Ringsend, side and she'd miss him. Nobody knew about the window, not her Ma or even Milo. Jimmy didn't count. If he knew anything, he wouldn't say. Jimmy couldn't talk yet. Ma said he never would. Except she cursed when she said it.

She could still hear the sound of the aeroplanes. Sometimes far away, sometimes very close. Every time she heard them the searchlights came on too, and several times the sound of the guns. She felt more restless than usual, frightened *he'd* come back and her mother wouldn't. Afraid that one night she might go and never come back, just like Da. Then what would they do? She had to stay awake; she had to, you never knew what might happen. She'd been asleep the night Da sneaked away and all their troubles started. She had to look after poor Ma. And little Jimmy.

Thus young Lily Sweetman played her desperate little game each night: if she stayed awake, her mother would come back safe. She arranged her chair, locked the room again, climbed aloft and looked down on the street. Almost all the lights in the terrace were out. As she kept watch, the rest were doused until at last there were just a couple in the next door house, number nine. A solitary lamppost gave off a dim light at the end of the terrace just where the road bent to the left at a sharp angle. There was nothing, and no-one, beyond the bend. The two houses there had almost completely fallen down. There was barbed wire around the doors and notices which said *Danger* with a red sign, like lightning, after the r. Lily could see right down to where the road veered away from the railway line, and beyond that, if she stood on tippy-toes, to Sandymount.

No sign yet of Ma. The mail train rumbled past with the lights out. She knew it left Westland Row at half past midnight and passed by about twenty-to-one. Above, the dull throb of aircraft came nearer, getting louder and louder. She quite liked the rumble. It sounded a bit like faraway thunder but that didn't worry Lily, she loved the excitement of storms.

She was about to climb off the chair and lie down when the door of number eleven edged open. She watched curiously. She could see nothing for a moment or two, then a dark shape emerged, and using the scattered bushes as cover, began to creep down the garden. Jimmy stirred, she turned to check he was all right and, when she looked back, the black shape had gone. She jumped off the chair and ran to the other window to check the road but at first she couldn't see anything, then suddenly she noticed someone else walking on the railway side, coming towards her from the Ringsend direction. He was sloping along in the shadows as if afraid of being seen, and he was holding something clutched to his chest. Even as she watched he suddenly disappeared behind a bush. If she squinted up her eyes she could just about make him out in the gloom.

Two people hiding. She began to get really frightened. She clambered back up on the chair and peered out the high window. Her eyes darted up and down the road, into the gardens, checked the houses. Nothing, except the door of number eleven was still slightly ajar. Then, all at once, two things happened: for an instant she saw the red glow of a cigarette behind a bush in front of number eleven. And a dog barked.

The sound of footsteps. Her heart skipped a beat. Someone was coming from the same direction as the watcher across the street. She could hear the footfall distinctly now, just below the window. She almost cried aloud in panic. Her heart flew into her mouth as she recognized the plodding, heavy step. Oh God, Oh God in Heaven, Buller and his terrible dog. He must have gone down to Ringsend to check on the factory. He often did that after he left them. Her mother wasn't with him. Her first thought was that she needn't have worried; her Ma was safe. But then, without any clear idea why, she knew something terrible was going to happen. Her head swam and she had to clutch the windowsill to stop herself toppling off the chair.

An ambush. Who were they? Why were they hiding? Was it the Buller they were waiting for? Suddenly the planes were back, closer now. The whole house shook. The drone filled her head, deafening her and because of that, everything that followed was like a silent, slow-rolling film, yet it was over in seconds. Her heart pounded painfully but she held on, watching dreamily.

The dog stopped to raise his leg against a broken gate. Reynolds jerked roughly at the lead and dragged him along. They plodded slowly down the terrace, past the first, then the second house, getting closer to the lamppost. Nothing else moved until, out of the corner of her eye, she saw the watcher on the far side of the street come out from the darkness. He kept pace but held back far enough for Reynolds not to be aware of him. She pressed her eye to the gap. He still had something clutched in his hand but she couldn't make out what it was; some sort of small bundle or package, she thought. Nor could she recognize him, he was huddled forward, his face in deep shadow. Suddenly he jerked his head around, glanced over his shoulder and quickly melted back into the bushes. Someone else must be coming. Lily strained her neck but could see nothing.

Reynolds was now walking past the Brennans' house, number ten, the only house on the terrace he didn't own. The shadow in the next garden edged towards the pavement. She moved her eyes off him for a second, trying to keep track of the others, and lost him briefly.

Without any warning a bicycle appeared out of nowhere going very fast straight at Reynolds. The rider was dressed in black from head to foot. But by far the strangest thing: it made no sound. Or, if it did, the thunder raging overhead drowned it completely. Buller was getting nearer the light. He didn't seem to notice anything except the din above. Every now and then he would pause and look up at the sky. The bike came to a stop just before it got to Buller. The rider straightened up, dropped a long, black-clad leg to steady the bicycle and stayed there, still as a statue, right in the middle of the road.

And still Reynolds, his head thrown back, did not notice; but the dog did. He turned and bared his teeth. As Reynolds yanked at the lead again, he too saw the bicycle. His mouth opened in a horrified O as the cyclist swivelled around to him, right arm outstretched, the left hand steadying it at the elbow, a gun just visible against the glow of the streetlight. At the same moment – her eyes swivelling frantically between the two – Lily saw that the figure in the garden had raised himself to a kneeling position. He was holding a much, much bigger gun.

That instant she held for ever, still and shocking, in her memory. Two, three, shots rang out. Buller Reynolds, poised for an instant with his arms half raised, toppled forward. As he did so, there was a huge explosion and the sky turned red. The Buller crashed to the ground, blood gushing from the remains of his head as it made sickening contact with the kerbstone. The dog yelped and tore off down the road with his lead trailing behind him. The cyclist followed. Lily watched in mesmerized terror as they passed the bend and quickly disappeared from view. When she tried to make out where the gunman in the garden was, he too was gone. All she saw was the door of number 11 easing closed. A moment later, windows began to open. The terrace was awake at last.

Above, the explosion swelled and reverberated, the sky ablaze with flashing lights. The second figure had come out of the shadows across the street and stood blinded, frozen. Lily's jaw dropped. As the boy stepped forward, a light came on in the upstairs flat of the Brennans' house directly opposite from where he was standing and the window shot up. He stopped, caught in the instant, one foot on the pavement, one on the road, while a great burst of gun-fire rang out and searchlights once more swept the sky. Holy God, she thought, what is he doing? As Lily began to pound furiously at the window there was another huge explosion. The boy held his hands up in front of his blinded eyes. The package was gone.

Dolly Brennan leaned out her window. Her hair was in curlers.

'Murderer!' she screamed, pointing her finger at him. 'Murderer! I saw you, I saw you. You kilt him. Someone call the guards!'

At last, galvanized by fear, Milo did the worst thing he could possibly have done. He took to his heels and ran for his life.

CHAPTER FOUR

He had no memory of that terrified sprint. Somewhere along the way he must have dropped what he was carrying though he did not remember doing so. Fear gave wings to his feet. He ran up the back lane towards his home and collapsed panting against the back door until he caught his breath. The cuckoo clock chirped twice, though he did not hear it, as he crept through the empty kitchen into the hall. It was then, for the first time, that he became aware of footsteps running up and down the street in front. The night pulsated with sound. As he crept towards the stairs he heard a key turn in the lock. His legs buckled. He sat down heavily and began to tremble.

His sister Hanora stood with her back to the door, smiling. She was wearing an absurdly large hat. He noticed vaguely that her jacket was misbuttoned and the hem of her skirt was hanging down. She glowed with excitement.

'There's been a bomb, Milo. There's been a mighty bomb. On the other side of the city. Somewhere near the Phoenix Park, they think.'

He stared at her dumbly.

'Did you not see the explosion? Hear the anti-aircraft guns?'

'A bomb? What bomb?' he whispered. 'Han, the Buller is dead.'

'Dead? How did you ...' she began then

stopped and looked closely at her brother for the first time.

'You're dressed, Milo,' she said in surprise. 'Has something happened to you? You're in an awful state. Why aren't you in bed?'

'You're not listening to me, Han. Buller Reynolds is dead. I saw him getting shot, the blood, the blood . . . it was pumping out of him.' He trembled violently.

Hanora's jaw dropped. 'You saw what? How, how? Milo talk to me.' She sounded distraught. 'I thought you were joking . . .' The words died on her lips. She took her brother's face in her shaking hands. 'Where?' she gabbled. 'What? How could you? I don't understand. Buller is dead? What do you mean? Did you . . . Milo . . . you didn't . . .'

Her voice was drowned by a loud burst of engine-noise from the street and the sound of running feet pounding past their door. A loud whistle blew. Both froze, then the boy's head jerked around. His face was white and terrified.

'It's the police,' he hissed. 'They're coming. Oh God help me, they're coming to get me.'

'Shush,' she whispered softly and dug her fingers into his. 'For heaven's sake what's wrong with you? It's some sort of alarm. It's nothing, nothing, to do with you.' Her voice sounded less certain than the words. Outside the distant rumble of aircraft returned.

'What happened? Quick, quick. Tell me, what happened?'

'What's the use? You can't do anything for me, nobody can.' He choked.

'Shush. Keep your voice down,' she hissed. 'You'll wake Mother.'

Myles pulled away from her. 'Leave me be, so. It's all confused. Please. You can't do anything.'

'Don't whinge,' she commanded brusquely. 'Quick. Tell me what happened.'

'I was down on the bindery. I stayed talking to old Josh too long . . .' he started.

Hanora grabbed his hand. 'You were out till now? Till two o'clock? Down in that dump? You're mad! That old fellow takes advantage of you. I told you not . . .'

'Shut up,' her brother hissed. 'He doesn't, he doesn't . . .'

Hanora shrugged impatiently. 'Bloody skinflint,' she burst out fiercely. 'You should have been home hours ago. What on earth were you doing?' Myles shook himself free and began to chew his nails.

'I worked late . . . something Mr Handl wanted me to finish. Afterwards I kept him company for a while. He's old, Han. He's lonely since his wife died.'

'I give up. He pays you nothing. You're just lowering yourself . . . at his beck and call . . .' his sister began an old and much practised lament.

Myles glared at her. 'I've had a desperate fright and that's all you can say,' he whispered tensely. She touched his arm. 'I'm sorry, little Milo. Tell me what happened. Please. Reynolds isn't really dead, is he? She drew his face gently towards her, cupping his cold, pale cheeks in the warmth of her strong palms. Her eyes bored into his but she listened quietly enough for the very few minutes it took him to recount his story from the time he'd left the book shop in Ringsend.

'Only the woman saw you? How could she? You said there were no lights, that it was dark. I don't understand what you were doing th . . .'

Her words were drowned out by a most tremendous explosion which was followed, for a breathless instant, by an almost palpable silence. Brother and sister eyed each other in startled surprise. Then, as one, they rushed to the door and yanked it open. The sky to the north was lit by an eerie blue light which, as they watched, turned orange, then red. A huge fire was burning somewhere across the bay. Great flickering lights shot up into the air accompanied by tremendous clouds of smoke. Anti-aircraft lights criss-crossed the sky. To the right and left of them windows and doors opened but as quickly closed at the sound of more gunfire and sirens. The din was tremendous. Someone began to call for volunteers.

Hanora and Myles backed nervously indoors, clutching each other. They crept to the front room window and peered out into the street. At the corner a group of men was beginning to gather. They stood helpless, calling directions to each other. A policeman raced into view. They heard him shout 'On the North Strand!' Four or five men with the armbands of the various voluntary organizations joined him. Within minutes an army lorry, already dangerously overloaded, roared up out of the darkness and picked the group up.

'Milo.' Hanora held her finger to her lips and pulled off her hat, her long brown hair tumbled about her shoulders. She quietly edged open the front door. 'Listen.'

In the distance they could hear the tinny clang of ambulance and police bells. The sky was now totally ablaze, great palls of smoke rose into the reddened sky.

'In the name of God, what's going on?' Their mother appeared at the top of the narrow stairway. Her hair was tousled and she looked confused, as though she'd just woken from a deep sleep. She had little bits of cotton wool sticking out of her ears.

'Hanora, Myles, what are you doing up at this hour? Why aren't you in bed? What are you doing dressed? Have you been out imbibing, Myles?' she asked suspiciously. 'Oh what's to become of me, at all? I never know what you pair are up to. Get off to bed,' she shouted.

'For heaven's sake, Mother, take the plugs out of your ears,' Hanora said impatiently. 'We couldn't sleep. The explosions woke us. We only just got up. I'm going to see what's going on, wait here.'

She was gone for about five minutes and arrived back breathless.

'Dublin's been bombed, Mother,' she announced dramatically. 'They're looking for volunteers to go and help with the rescue work. A whole lot of houses were hit on the North Strand. Myles and I are going,' she added. 'You go back to bed. We're in no danger.'

'You treat me like a fool in my own house. Never pay heed to anything I say,' their mother grumbled. 'Don't think I don't notice. You've no respect for your poor mother. You children must go back to your beds this minute.' She shuffled back into her room. Her children waited until her door was shut.

'Quick Milo, get off your jacket and get a jumper on, it's cold out there.'

'I won't. Leave me alone, I want to go to bed. Please Han, I can't move, I'm exhausted,' Myles began. Hanora pushed him aside impatiently and tore upstairs. She returned a couple of minutes later, wearing a pair of his trousers and carrying a couple of thick woollen jumpers. She threw one at him furiously. 'Shut up and put it on. Buller Reynolds dead. Dead?' she repeated. 'I can't believe it. Are you sure it was him, Milo?'

'Oh for God's sake! I saw it happen. I saw him lying there. Half his head was gone.' He drummed his temples with his fists. 'Of course he's dead. And that blasted woman is saying I did it. I didn't do it,' he hissed fiercely.

'I believe you. Are you listening to me, Milo? I believe you. Of course you didn't do it. I'm trying to give you an alibi, that's all. We have to get out of here.'

'I don't need an alibi! I didn't do anything,' he protested, struggling into the jersey. He sniffed softly, despairingly.

'What will I do?' he asked his sister. 'Oh God help me, what'll I do? No-one will believe me.'

'I believe you, Milo,' she repeated softly. 'I believe you. I'll help you.' She looked at him thoughtfully.

'Do you think that woman saw what you were wearing?'

The boy nodded mutely. His sister considered him for some time, lost in thought. But when at last she spoke her voice was brisk, business-like and unemotional. She was substance to his shadow and in complete charge.

'Right then, we better get rid of your jacket. We'll do it on the way. Dump it.'

Myles began to empty his pockets then patted them frantically. He stared at his sister in horror.

'Oh for heaven's sake! Now what?'

'My tools. The canvas holder has my name on it. I don't have it any more. It's gone. I must have dropped it somewhere. I don't know where it is.' His voice rose in panic. 'Oh God, Han, what'll I do? I'm banjaxed. There's nothing anyone can do now. The police'll have me for sure.'

Before she could reply a lorry drew up outside. Hanora threw open the door.

'They'll have a hard job of it,' she replied defiantly. 'You could have dropped it anytime. Just keep your head. You didn't do anything, remember.'

He nodded.

'Well then, come on,' she said. 'Don't worry, you'll find it. When the coast is clear.'

'I'll go now,' he said making for the door. 'I'll go round to Dolan. He'll know what to do.'

'Would you come back out of that, you dope. The place will be crawling. Look, if we go to the North Strand and help, who'll think of looking for you over there? Come on, Milo. You'll be all right.' She held out her hand to him. 'The fellow I talked to just now said there are thousands dead. The police will have more to do than search for you tonight. Anyway, I'll look after you. Don't I always? Come on. Let's get going.'

She looked like Joan of Arc, transfixed with her own heroics. Behind her the sky was on fire.

CHAPTER FIVE

Echoes of the explosion shook the house as Lily Sweetman ran swiftly and silently down four flights of stairs into the dingy hall where she paused uncertainly, listening. The occupants of the other three flats were stirring but none had yet emerged. She was carrying a baby, or what looked like a baby, wrapped in a grubby blue hand-knitted wrap. She opened the door gingerly and peeped out. A strange silence had descended on the street. She could just see the dead man lying askew on the path. The dark shape she had seen on the patch of ground in front of number eleven was gone. When she craned her neck, she thought she saw its front door slightly ajar. She crept out and stood quietly, in the shadow of the doorway, looking about her. People were leaning out windows, staring upwards, jaws open in amazement. Some jiggled their ears as if deafened by the explosions. Through a billowing smokescreen, the sky was ablaze. They remained frozen in position for what seemed like eternity until Dolly Brennan, still hanging out the upstairs window of number ten, started screaming for the police again.

The neighbours began shouting instructions at each other. It took a few argumentative moments for them to realize that the explosion and Reynolds's death were separate incidents, not cause and effect. Dolly, with the authority appropriate to the only householder among them, emerged from her flat with an old black shawl flung over her nightdress and screamed for the police.

'Why don't you go and get them yourself?' a woman's voice challenged.

'Can't ya see I'm in me night attire?' Dolly screamed back. 'D'ya want me to be arrested?'

'Aha, that's a good one Missus.'

'Where's the nearest telephone?' a more reasonable voice interjected.

'Down the Lotts Road.'

'Sure, that's miles away.'

It was clear that someone would have to go and fetch the guards. Daedalian Road, in the Kingdom of Reynolds, was entirely free of domestic luxuries, especially telephones. Or inside plumbing, some wag added. As she heard them titter, it seemed to Lily that there was an odd air of relief about the scene.

Dolly Brennan positioned herself as sentry to the dead man. There was a further conference.

Nobody noticed Lily. But then, they never did. Because she was small, slight and frail, she seemed like a child and therefore of little consequence. In fact she was almost fifteen and wise and mature beyond her years. But for her own convenience and survival she affected the child-like air. She was poorly dressed and looked half-starved and anxious. If you looked at her closely she was comely, almost doll-like, with huge solemn blue-grey eyes and a mop of dark curly hair which could have done with a good wash. She wore a long grey-green cotton night-shift and was barefoot.

Her sharp eyes were everywhere, darting, searching for the thing she saw drop as the boy ran away; the light from the Brennans' flat or maybe the blaze of the explosion had caught it for an instant as it fell. She hoped Dolly Brennan hadn't spotted it as well.

A neighbour joined Dolly by the dead man. They both knelt down, and with piously joined hands and bowed heads said the Act of Contrition. Lily Sweetman put her face close to the baby's blanket and chuckled mirthlessly. Buller Reynolds would need more than a whispered confession where he was going.

Mr Alphonsus Kelly emerged from the downstairs flat of number twelve, two doors down from the Brennans', wheeling his bike. In his loud voice he instructed the bystanders not to touch the body or anything else. 'I'm off up to Donnybrook to fetch the Gardaí,' he announced. Mr Kelly was a native Irish speaker from Mayo; everyone else called them the polis. Or the guards. A retired and rather self-important railway porter, he habitually wore his old porter's cap. He was wearing it now. He used it to cover his old baldy head, Lily knew, because she had once seen it blow off in a high wind and Mr Kelly never spoke to her again after she had witnessed his discomfort. There was no danger he'd say anything to her now. He pedalled a few yards until someone yelled out a further instruction. Mr Kelly put one foot to the ground to steady himself and turned to listen. The little colour Lily had drained from her face when she saw him stop and swivel around on the saddle to shout something at Mrs Brennan. Her eyes never left him until he had cycled out of sight.

After he'd disappeared, people moved closer to the body but the talk was more of wonder at the explosion than the sight of Buller Reynolds bleeding to death. While they conferred, Lily sneaked, unnoticed, across the road. Other nosy-parkers began to emerge from the flats in her house. These were the ones Lily most distrusted and had to keep clear of. With only one exception, the residents of number eight had no time for Nan Sweetman and her brats. They didn't think much of her way of life and were not slow in saying so. They made out that she brought disgrace on the stinking ruin. As if she could. They made Lily sick.

Dolly Brennan, relishing her starring role, was entertaining the populace. Lily listened for the arrival of the guards. She made it to the other side of the street without being noticed, then edged along the few yards to where a small roll of canvas lay, half concealed beneath a straggly bush. In one fluid movement she eased herself onto the ground and flicked her nightie over it. As she did so, she held the bundle to her face again and made soft cooing noises, her eyes darting this way and that.

By now, the crowd had swollen to a dozen or so, others were hanging out the windows of the five houses nearest the murder site. Their attention was torn between the pyrotechnics in the sky and the body of their landlord on the ground.

'What are ya doing up at this hour of the night, Lily Sweetman? That misfortune of a child should be in his bed,' Dolly Brennan bawled. 'And where's that mother of yours, I'd like to know? Here's one could do with her ministrations.' She laughed raucously and looked around for approval but the others shuffled their feet in embarrassment and looked away.

Down in Slattery's as you well know, Lily muttered under her breath. Or Gerrity's or Nash's. She was saved any further goading by the sound of a police bell. A bull-nosed Morris came slowly into sight. It was followed, at some distance, by Mr Kelly whose legs were going like pistons in his effort to keep up. As the car came to a halt, the crowd surged forward and Lily seized her chance. In the twinkling of an eye, she slipped the canvas holder into the blanket and headed, nonchalantly but swiftly, back across the street and into the house. When she re-emerged three or four minutes later she was carrying her baby brother who was mercifully asleep. Her brief absence went entirely unnoticed.

Two guards stepped out of the car. 'I'm Sergeant O'Keefe,' the older man said and shooed the onlookers away from the body. As the car drove away, O'Keefe and his young companion instructed the bystanders to go back indoors, they were in the way. The people ignored them both. They formed a semi-circle around the two men as they examined the scene.

'Would you keep back!' O'Keefe snapped. But he was paid no attention whatsoever. One or two brave ones edged closer.

Lily sat on the doorstep of number twelve, the last occupied house on the street and the one nearest to where the body lay. She was out of the way of the policemen but in a perfect position to watch what they were doing. The constable raised the blanket and screened the sergeant as he crouched beside the dead man. When they dropped the covering back over the body they drew chalk lines around it. The sergeant took out a measuring tape and made detailed measurements in every direction. They wrote everything down in little black notebooks.

Dolly Brennan never stopped her chatter. It was amazing how very patient Sergeant O'Keefe was. He listened to every word. After a time, with great deliberation and as if on her instructions, he walked very slowly across the street, counting as he went. Lily's heart skipped a beat when he stopped exactly where the package had been. Dolly talked furiously but the sergeant didn't seem to take much notice of her. He walked slowly to and fro, shooing the gawpers aside. He lined himself up with the dead man, then with the Brennans' window, moving from one side of the road to the other, in infuriating silence. He was very, very serious. At last he talked quietly and earnestly to Dolly, then sent her back indoors. She reappeared a minute later, leaning out the window as she had earlier and looking triumphant. Behind her, Lily could clearly hear Mick Brennan roaring his frustration.

'For the love of mike, woman, would ya get in outa that and let me sleep. What are ye doing at this hour of night hangin' out the window without a stitch on ye? They'll think I married ya for yer money!'

Dolly ignored him. She looked down at the upturned faces and then pointedly at the sergeant.

'I'm tellin' ya, Super-intender, I'm only tellin' ya, but I saw him with me own eyes. Standin' there, bold as ya like. Not a second after killing that poor soul down there.'

She crossed herself piously, one or two of the bystanders did likewise. All eyes were now on Dolly and she was so delighted with herself she began playing to the crowd. O'Keefe watched with interest as she moved from side to side, leaning further and further out. He kept asking her to tell him exactly what she saw, was seeing now. Eventually he told her where to move and sent the young guard up to stand behind her.

'Tell me what you see now, Mrs Brennan? Over there.' He pointed to his helmet which he'd hung on a broken railing just beyond the dead man.

'The body of course. What d'ya think I see?' It was plain Dolly could see neither railing nor helmet. Behind her the young guard shook his head. O'Keefe went over to the railing and stood alongside it.

'What's on my head, Mrs Brennan?'

'Your hair.' Dolly, pleased with her wit, looked in the direction of the voice.

'Anything else?'

Dolly leaned so far out the window that she almost went headlong. The young guard grabbed hold of her nightdress and hauled her back in. But Dolly wasn't daunted.

'Your helmet of course. Am I getting warmer?' she asked, as if she was playing hunt-the-thimble. Sergeant O'Keefe strolled into the middle of the road and looked up at her. He was holding his helmet by his side. The light from Dolly's window shone on his bald head.

'Thank you, Mrs Brennan, you've been a great help. Now, if you could just let the garda take a look. Thank you, that's all.'

He was only humouring her, Lily thought. He looked quite pleased as he turned away. Not with Dolly, that much was obvious. With himself.

O'Keefe turned now to the neighbours and asked who else had seen anything. There was a show of hands, perhaps three or four, all women. Dolly Brennan, who was back down in the street, looked disgusted. Lily said nothing. A heated exchange between the volunteers followed. Sergeant O'Keefe hushed them up.

'Did any of you see a young lad? On the railway side of the road, was it, Mrs Brennan?' He spoke very quietly and seriously.

Lily's little sob of fear sounded awful loud to her.

Dolly Brennan let a shriek out of her: 'Come here to me, Sergeant. Ask that young one over there! I see her consorting with all sorts. The cut of the mother, and we all know what she is. Lily Sweetman! Who's that young fella you're always talking to? Now that I think of it . . .'

Lily shrank backwards.

'Hush, woman dear,' said the sergeant. 'Don't be frightening the child now.'

'Child how-are-ye,' snorted Dolly. She kept her eye fixed on Lily, who buried her face in Jimmy's blanket to prevent herself crying aloud. Embarrassed silence descended on the bystanders whose shuffling feet traced imaginary patterns on the ground.

Nobody came forward. O'Keefe's eyes swept around suspiciously. The young guard wrote slowly, laboriously, in his notebook. Once or twice he asked his exasperated superior to repeat what he'd said. At times the older man looked as though he would box his ears.

A big black van arrived. Two men got out. One held a camera, the other, older man a leather bag. They huddled in conversation with the sergeant. The young guard told everyone else to stand away as the doctor opened his Gladstone bag and squatted beside the dead man for about ten minutes or so. When he stood up he talked earnestly to Sergeant O'Keefe while the photographer took a lot of pictures. When he'd finished, the body was taken away. Most of the onlookers had drifted back indoors, now the last stragglers followed them. A couple almost stepped on Lily on the way back to their flat. The man asked what she was up to and told her roughly to be off home about her business.

It was now that Sergeant O'Keefe appeared to notice her for the first time. He looked across at where she was sitting, then allowed his eye to travel slowly from Lily to the chalk mark and even more slowly back again. Then he raised his right hand and beckoned her over with his finger.

1941

Irish Independent

Saturday 31 May 1941. Stop Press:

DESTRUCTION ON NORTH SIDE OF CITY

Planes were heard passing over the city from about midnight, and strong anti-aircraft fire was opened by the ground defence, while searchlights searched the sky.

WHERE THE BOMBS FELL

Three bombs were dropped between 1.55 a.m. and 2.10. The first fell in Summerhill Parade, the second in the North Circular Road near the Phoenix Park, and the third in the North Strand.

ZOOLOGICAL GARDENS HIT

Elephant toppled by bomb blast. Bison Stampede.

CHAPTER SIX

The lorry was full to overflowing with men and women of all ages dressed in a motley assortment of hastily donned clothes. Some of the men carried shovels or pickaxes or lengths of rope. A couple of women were tearing sheets into strips of bandage. They were squashed together, faces here and there pinpointed by the red glow of lighted cigarettes. The smell of tobacco was pungent. Talk was subdued, in whispers. Nobody showed much interest in the newcomers.

'Would yez hurry up if yer comin',' the driver yelled at Myles and Hanora. 'Find a space at the back there. And hang on for dear life.'

Sister and brother climbed up quickly and found precarious space at the very back where they sat with their legs dangling over the platform of the truck, hunched against the wooden side rails. Someone passed them a grey army blanket. They had barely time to wrap it around them before the engine juddered into life.

The journey across the bay was just under three miles. But because of frequent stops and starts it took nearly forty minutes. Myles looked all in, numb with exhaustion, and scared stiff. His thin intense face was deadly white except for a livid spot of colour on either cheek. He hoped Hanora knew what she was doing. She insisted that no-one would believe that the killer would have the gall to go on a rescue mission barely an hour after

Reynolds was murdered. It was at least worth a try, she claimed. He was less sure.

I wish I'd killed him, he thought viciously. I wish I'd had the courage to do it. Stuck a knife in his fat back when I spotted him coming out of the press. I should have left the bastard bleeding on the doorstep. And when I saw him going up by Lily's . . . I should have done it then, instead of skulking in the undergrowth. He was after her. She wouldn't say but I know he was after her . . .

It had been pointless following him. Even at the time he'd known it, though he could not admit it. He couldn't take on someone like Reynolds, no matter how much he wanted to. He was too big, too strong, too much of a bully. Mr Handl had tried to calm him down. That was why they'd sat talking so late. Mr Handl hadn't jeered when he told him that he loved Lily. He hadn't said anything about them being too young. He'd just said, 'Wait until you finish your apprenticeship. I'll see you right, Myles. There's no-one else to take over the business. I have no children, my dear. Another year is not long.' He insisted Lily would be all right. 'The poor child has to learn to be tough, my dear. She is a good girl. I'd back her against that evil man any day. She is quick and she is clever.'

But that wasn't the point, was it? Lily depended on him and he had to look after her. He wanted to make sure the Buller didn't go into her house, that's all. Well, apart from wanting to kill him, of course. What possessed him to carry home his tools? Three sharp knives that could pare a

70

millimetre from a skin of fine calf, that could cut a man's throat like a hot knife through butter . . .

They'd pin that murder on him for sure. The more Myles rehearsed the details of the night the more guilty he knew he must seem. In his heart he had already given up hope of clearing his name. He'd have to get away. If the police found his tool holder . . .

'I've been thinking,' Hanora broke in on his thoughts. 'If you run away, you'll make people think you're guilty. Maybe you should go to the police tomorrow. I'll come with you. It might be better in the long run to tell them exactly what happened. If you go . . .'

'You said you'd help!' Milo whispered desperately. 'You're backing out! Hanora, I was there. I know how it looks. The woman heard the shots, she'll say she saw me do it. Please, don't let them question me. You said you'd help.' He was almost hysterical. 'Who'll believe me if you don't? I have to get out of here. I'm getting off. Now!' He made as if to jump off.

Hanora kicked him sharply and grabbed his arm. 'Shut up, you eejit. Nobody's making you do anything. You don't know how well she saw you, do you? But if they do get on to you, we better have your story straight. That's all. So, go over it all again. We won't get another opportunity. From when you left Handl's. Leave nothing out.'

She stilled the shaking of the boy's hands with hers, clasping them firmly under the blanket. His long narrow fingers felt chilled and clammy against her warm skin. He looked around furtively but no-one was paying any attention and, in any case, they couldn't be overheard with the racket of the engine. They could barely hear each other.

'Now.' Hanora dug her nails into his hand. 'One thing I don't understand. Why did it take you so long to get home?'

Myles glared at her furiously. 'I told you. I was talking to old Josh. I picked up my tools . . .' His voice trailed away, his hand shot to his mouth and he made a second attempt to jump off. He would have done if it were not for Hanora's restraining arm. He leaned against her, closed his eyes and sighed despairingly. 'Oh God. Where did I drop them?'

'We'll think about that later,' she said confidently, but beneath the blanket she crossed her fingers. His name was on it. Poor stupid Milo. But she was forgetting, he could say he dropped them much earlier, or on another day, couldn't he? Or say they were stolen. The old Jew would back him up, wouldn't he? The bombs, surely they made a difference? The police would have more on their minds than the solitary murder of that thug of a landlord. The death of Buller Reynolds would hardly be top priority.

Hanora nudged Myles in the ribs. 'I meant after you left Ringsend. You said it was twenty to one at Beggar's Bush. Why did it take you so long to get to Daedalian Road? It should only take seven or eight minutes. Come on, Milo, just go through it again.'

He held out his left hand palm up. There was a long angry scratch right across it. 'I forgot. The kitten. It was caught in some barbed wire. It took me ages to untangle it . . .'

72

Hanora wagged her head in disbelief. 'Jesus. You're hopeless, little brother, really hopeless. D'you know that? Why didn't you leave the blasted thing alone? Still,' she pondered carefully, 'still it might be possible . . . I'll think about it. Just start from the beginning again.'

'There was an awful lot of aircraft noise . . .'

'Start with Handl. Don't change anything.'

'I'm just telling you how it was,' he snarled. 'Don't you believe me?'

'Shush, of course I believe you, but you forgot the kitten first time, didn't you? I'm only trying to help.'

As the truck bumped its way into the line of assorted vehicles grinding slowly along Pearse Street, Myles went carefully and painfully through his awful experiences again. This third time, as he took his sister through it step by step, he realized just how damning the evidence against him was. Each time he went over it, small details he had overlooked surfaced alarmingly. He should have gone straight home. He shouldn't have been trailing Reynolds. Bad cess to him anyway.

'I just ran and ran,' he finished despairingly. 'Oh God help me, what'll I do? No-one will believe me.'

'Could anyone have seen all three of you?' she interrupted. 'I mean, Buller, the bike and you? Anyone who knows you? Who could back you up?'

'There was nobody,' he said morosely, avoiding her eye. 'Nobody at all. Only that horrible woman screaming at me. There was nobody else.'

'Sure? Nobody else?'

The boy was silent as he relived each terrifying

second, examined each frame of the film he held in his memory.

He shook his head slowly. 'No. The place was deserted. There was no-one else. At first I thought she was shouting at the cyclist, then I realized she was pointing at me.'

'You're certain?' she insisted. 'Could anyone else have seen it happen? Seen you? Or the cyclist? What about the other houses? Do you know anyone along there?'

He stared at her for a long moment. He would not mention Lily. He would not. He knew exactly what Hanora would think about Lily.

'There aren't any houses on the railway side of the road, only bushes. It was dark. The woman's window was very close to the place where he fell. Upstairs room. She must have had a clear view.' He stopped and looked at Hanora in horror, his mouth open. 'The house is just a little before where the road curves off at a sharp angle. The cyclist must have been out of sight. She can't have seen him. She can't have seen him. She only saw the dead man and me.' He panted. 'They'll have me for murder . . .'

After a few minutes Hanora asked: 'Hasn't your pal Dolan a bike?'

'What are you talking about? It wasn't Dolan,' Myles said excitedly. 'Don't you think I'd have recognized Dolan? And his battered old bike? The back wheel is banjaxed; it makes an awful racket.'

'Don't be so stupid. I'm not talking about that bike,' she said dismissively. He could tell she really didn't believe him about the cyclist at all. 'I was thinking of something else. In case you have to get away. I may have an idea. It's the bank holiday on Monday.' She kept her voice to a whisper, quietly outlining her plan. She was clear and precise but she looked keyed up, exhausted.

The lorry juddered to a halt at the beginning of the North Strand. As they jumped down, Myles surreptitiously tossed his rolled up jacket under the wheel of the lorry then lined up beside the others waiting for orders. The first thing that hit them was the terrible stench. But the sight that confronted them was truly stupefying. The destruction was fearful. The bomb blast had ripped up the tram tracks and exploded onto a row of decrepit and overcrowded houses which had fallen like a pack of cards, taking their inhabitants with them. The carnage was indescribable.

There was a vast crater in the road. Around and above it, tangled tram tracks rose crazily in a giant cat's cradle. Rescue work was being carried out by eerie gaslight, which shot strange elongated blue light upwards. The noise was terrible. Babies screeched, dead-eyed little children wandered about, half-naked and bleeding. Dazed women in torn nighties cried pitiably for their children. All along the street, houses were burning. Firemen on ladders leaned heroically against crumbling walls too frail to bear them. People lay scattered: dead, dying or stunned with shock.

Myles's problems seemed unimportant now, trivial. For the following few hours, while he joined in the rescue work, he put the murder from his mind.

At four o'clock in the morning, Lily was still

peering out through the thickly latticed leaves. The undersized frightened girl watched as she always watched. Watched for her mother to streel home in the small still hours of the night. She waited. Steeled herself for the habitual beating she would get for reasons she could scarcely work out. She watched over her tiny brother, whimpering with fear.

CHAPTER SEVEN

Little Shadow, Sergeant O'Keefe called her, but she was beginning to get on his nerves. She seemed to be everywhere, yet he never caught her moving nor did she speak. He was almost certain she was still there when he left the murder scene just before four in the morning. When he returned at a quarter past six he didn't see her but when he looked up after an hour or so, she was back. She'd simply positioned herself on the steps of the house with the best vantage point of the murder site, exactly where she was when he first spotted her. Now, as then, she pretended not to notice him.

The night before, when he'd beckoned her over, she'd turned away like a frightened rabbit, shouted 'Mam!' then shot off down the road to greet the drunken woman who was rolling along, singing tunelessly, as if she hadn't a care in the world. He'd watched with pity as the young girl, struggling with the weight of the child in her arms, nudged at her mother's arm and protectively hurried her indoors, all the time averting her face from the sergeant. What had really struck him, and saddened him, was how the mother did not once look at the girl. Or touch her.

She looked worn-out but she was still minding the child who sat quietly on the step beside her, his head on her lap. He was chewing a crust of bread. He looked about eighteen months, but like herself, he was a puny youngster so he might have been older. Sergeant O'Keefe wondered idly whether she'd slept or for how long? Since he hadn't been to bed himself most of his sympathy was turned inwards or towards those of his colleagues who were still on the rescue mission over on the North Strand. He wished with all his heart that he was with them. History in the making, and he was stuck trying to make sense of a murder that, even at this early stage, he was uneasily aware nobody wanted him to solve. There was no doubt at all about it, those who killed Buller Reynolds had the devil's own luck with their timing.

Or were they, he thought wearily, just fiendishly clever? There had been an unusual amount of aircraft noise over the city for hours before the murder, and anti-aircraft fire. He'd heard sirens, watched the searchlights sweep the sky and had felt a powerful, heavy menace. People had been frightened of attack for weeks, ever since the terrible destruction of Belfast in April, when 700 people were killed. Had the killers gambled that the fear which cleared the streets would give them time enough for their evil work? Or was it a mere fluke? Whichever, their timing was impeccable.

Sergeant O'Keefe sighed deeply as he took in the scene. The place was a disgrace. Neat terraces had once lined either side of the road, now only one short inhabited group of five houses remained, at either end of which stood pairs of much taller, four storey tenements like giant book-ends. Three of these were boarded up and crumbling. The fourth stood fifteen or so feet proud of the rest of the terrace. At either end of the row were stretches of scrubland strewn with dwarf thorn bushes upon which litter clung like rags to a skeleton. The road was pot-holed, most of the street-lights were smashed. The decayed terrace was like a forgotten island in its own wasteland and, from the word go, it was apparent that the brow-beaten tenants had neither regard nor pity for their deceased exploiter.

O'Keefe rubbed his jaw and wondered morosely what he was going to be able to achieve with the fumbling help of one new and, in his opinion, extremely raw recruit. While he offered a silent prayer for patience, he knew in his heart that his chances of solving the murder were remote. If the assassins were as lucky or as smart as he suspected, then they were probably already on their way to the North Strand to make heroes of themselves.

He was sickened. He had no stomach for murder and little experience of it – a mere station sergeant could not be expected to have any. It was the calamity of those terrible bombs which had cata-pulted him to where he was. As soon as the alarm was raised the entire station had rushed forth to help, leaving himself and his hapless sidekick to do the best they could. Still, one thing at least, there were few on the force with as much local knowl-edge as Sean O'Keefe, both places and people. And at this moment what he'd learned of Buller Reynolds, added to what he already knew, was making him extremely uncomfortable. No matter how hard he tried, he could not entirely suppress a faint feeling of approval for his untimely dispatch. But he was trying, he told himself, he was trying.

While he worked, he watched the girl covertly. Her interest, he was certain it was not idle speculation, intrigued him but her impassive stance gave nothing away. She knew something or was trying to protect someone. Probably that useless mother of hers. Once or twice he felt he must go and speak to her but instinct told him that he would do better to let her come to him in her own time.

He felt dreadful. Every joint in his body ached from lack of sleep. He had lain down behind the desk for forty winks but had to give up after half an hour or so and make do with several scalding cups of sweet tea. The station had been buzzing with reports from the North Strand. Some of those who had gone to help had come back around five, punch-drunk with shock and fatigue. It was their first taste of the devastation war could bring and it was terrible. Worse, it felt so personal. Neutrality had lulled them into a sense of false security which had been brutally taken from them. The information they came back with, God only knew from where, was that it hadn't been some devious ploy of the British to lure Ireland into the war. The aircraft had been Heinkels, the bombs German.

Over endless cups of tea they talked sadly, with new awareness, of the huge Irish populations in those English cities being nightly bombarded. Of the legions of Irishmen who had signed up to fight Hitler. Every man jack of them had someone, child, brother or friend, fighting in the British Army. O'Keefe's own two sons had joined up the previous January. The raids which had killed so many in Belfast, in Birmingham, in Liverpool and Coventry, now took on a fearful, immediate reality. And one of the realities – it was unmistakable and universal – was a heavy feeling of isolation. Those cities were being blitzed again and again. In their ruin there was at least a profound sense of solidarity against a common enemy. As he listened, O'Keefe vaguely sensed the first faint rumblings of disquiet. Perhaps neutrality had hidden disadvantages after all?

Sergeant O'Keefe pulled a packet of Craven A from his pocket, lit up and drew in deeply. He picked an imaginary fleck of tobacco from his lower lip and viewed the deserted murder scene through narrowed eyes. Nothing, as far as he could see, had been disturbed since he'd left an hour or so before. Dawn was well advanced, the day was bright, cloudless and very mild; an unusually good start to the Whitsun holiday. Later, he guessed there'd be a rush for the seaside – Sandymount being about the nearest strand to Dublin – but for the moment all was quiet.

Positioning himself by the shape of the figure chalked on the pavement, O'Keefe took a long look up at Dolly Brennan's window and offered a silent prayer of thanks that she was still abed. Not only had she a voice like a corncrake but she was also a desperate know-all and a thoroughly unreliable witness. She was full of notions that she had seen everything and could not be shifted from this view. He shook his head doubtfully and, pretending not to notice his Little Shadow's eye following him, walked over to stand just below the window from where Mrs Brennan claimed to have seen 'the boy' murder Reynolds.

Supposing, he thought, just supposing Buller had his back to 'the boy'? Would the force of the shot have spun him around? Quite apart from O'Keefe's doubts about 'the boy', the fact remained that the back of the man's head had been shot off. Even at this early stage, the boy theory just didn't make sense. Except, perhaps, as another witness. And with this thought uppermost in his mind, Sergeant O'Keefe crossed the street and began a meticulous search of the ground around where Dolly Brennan claimed to have seen the phantom boy. Phantom was right. When asked, she could not identify him except as 'someone she might have seen before'. It would come to her, she said, she had a good memory. O'Keefe's mouth turned down sourly. Strange that no-one else had seen him.

He bent down and searched the ground inch by inch but it yielded nothing. It looked as if it had been – he wasn't quite sure why he thought so – rearranged in some way. On the railway side of the road, where he was searching, there was no pavement, just shrubs beneath which were rough grassy tufts among patches of sandy soil. The soil looked – was he imagining it? – the soil looked as though someone had drawn a broom or perhaps a cloth across it. Sergeant O'Keefe straightened up, stretched his back painfully and allowed his eye to follow the track in either direction. There were certainly signs of movement, a lot of it, and plenty of rubbish as well. Discarded sweet papers, cigarette packets and tin cans. God, but it was a dismal place.

A black layer of soot clinging to the railing and

bushes only added to the general squalor. He looked across at the road. Only those six seedy, overcrowded houses remained of what must once have been quite a handsome row. Everything else had either been boarded up or demolished to make way for a corporation housing project that The Emergency had put paid to. However long the war lasted, the inhabitants of Daedalian Road were doomed to stay put for the duration.

The Reynolds properties were never meant for multiple occupancy; the smaller houses would be hard pressed to contain one family, let alone two or three. The tall house was much larger but it was divided into three flats and four single rooms and listed twenty-three occupants. That didn't count the rats. It was said to be infested. O'Keefe had that on the best authority. It turned out that his young sidekick roomed there. And so, come to think of it, did the Little Shadow.

O'Keefe stood with his back to the railway line and looked around for the girl. She had moved. Now she was sitting on the edge of the footpath, rocking the child on her knee and singing softly. She did not look up, but he was certain she was still watching him. More interestingly, she was edging closer to him.

Ignoring her, Sean O'Keefe looked up and down the road, pulled out his pocket watch, checked the time, shook it, held it to his ear then put it away. The hapless recruit-garda Vavasour was late. He wasn't sure whether to be furious or relieved. The poor lad wasn't much help. Anxious to please and eager to learn certainly but, in the opinion of the good sergeant, he had not the makings of a guard, even of the lowliest rank. However, he might turn something up, he was, after all, local. As well as being burdened by that outlandish name.

'In the name of God, man, where did ye get a name like that?'

'The nuns, sir.' Except he said sor.

'The nuns?'

'Yes, sir, the Little Sisters. They found me in Vavasour Square.' He blushed furiously and added wistfully: 'I wish it had been O'Connell Street.'

O'Keefe was about to crack, 'Well, thank your lucky stars it wasn't Dame Street,' when he checked himself.

'Vavasour Square? That's quite close, isn't it? Did you know Reynolds well?'

'He was the landlord, sir.'

'*Your* landlord?'

'Yes, sir. Number eight.'

The last occupied house on the road, the one furthest away from the murder site and the tallest. But, of course, as luck would have it, Vavasour had been on duty in Donnybrook at the material time. O'Keefe looked at him thoughtfully and, when they got back to the station, tried to pry out of him everything he knew about Reynolds. The poor fellow was half-dead on his feet but he was a good-natured soul and not given to speaking ill of the dead. It took a few minutes to coax him to loosen up, then he let fly with an anger which surprised O'Keefe but made him respect the boy.

According to Vavasour, the landlord was an out-and-out blackguard.

'He owns most of the houses on the row, sir.'

'Most of them?'

'Yes, sir, all except the Brennans'. It was a very sore point with Mr Reynolds, sir. A real torment to him. He tried everything to make them sell up, sir.'

'Offer them a good price, did he, lad?'

'Oh no, sir, Mr Reynolds didn't believe in throwing money about, sir. That wasn't his way.' The young man avoided the sergeant's eye as he continued the sorry catalogue of his late landlord's short-comings.

He did no maintenance, charged the maximum he could, harried his tenants for their rent every Friday night on the dot – woe betide him who was short. The six houses he owned were over-crowded and filthy with no indoor lavatories, much less washing facilities. The only running water came from a tap in the back yard. Most of the men were away, either working in England or in the army or on Essential Work in the country, so it was the women who carried the water. Vavasour, Martin, had to lug his to the second floor of the house and slop out in the outside privy like the rest of them every morning.

It was also the women, by the young man's stumbling account, who had most cause to dread Buller Reynolds. All of them loathed him: his fumbling hands, his lewd remarks, the way he forced himself on them. And there the shy and blushing boy pulled himself up, unable to bring himself to discuss the matter further, or perhaps it was just that at that stage – it was after five – he was barely able to keep awake.

O'Keefe was about to send him home for an hour's sleep when he remembered to ask: 'Your wife wouldn't have seen anything, would she?' *The assassin running off, for instance.*

'No, sir,' Vavasour mumbled, avoiding his eye. 'The wife's away, sir. With her mother, in Dolphin's Barn, sir. She wouldn't know anything about the, er, killing, sir.' He swallowed hard.

'Something the matter between you, garda?'

'No, sir. It's just . . .'

'Something to do with Reynolds?'

The young man's squirming embarrassment was obvious but he didn't reply.

'Was he bothering your wife, lad? Speak up.'

'Trying to, sir. I er, warned him off, sir. And I sent the wife to her mother's, sir . . . We're stuck, sir. We're down for a corporation house, sir.' He drew himself up and stared into the middle distance. 'We've a good chance of getting one. The house we're in is condemned. If we move, we'll lose our place on the list. So we're stuck, sir. That's why I sent her to her mother's place. And,' he hesitated before adding bravely, 'I told Reynolds I'd have the law on him.'

'Did you now?' O'Keefe tried to sound matter-of-fact. 'You'd better tell me about that, son. Did you threaten him?'

'No, sir, I couldn't,' Martin Vavasour mumbled. Tears brimmed his eyes. 'I was afraid of him, sir. He had a terrible tongue. Filthy. I, er, just said that – about the law, sir – but I couldn't tell anyone at the station. I'd be too ashamed.' He bit his lip. 'I didn't touch him, sir. I wish I had. But I swear to God, sir, I did not.'

That was two hours ago. O'Keefe had taken pity on him and told him to go off home and rest. Now the sergeant fixed his gaze on his Little Shadow and walked across to her. This time she waited, her arm around the child who was perched on the step beside her. As he drew closer he noted she was older than he'd thought; beneath the shapeless shift she was quite well-developed. She had a calm pixie face with slightly slanted deep blue eyes. A livid bruise down one side of her face accentuated the white, white skin. There were two bright spots of red on her cheeks, almost as if she was rouged but, when he looked closely, he saw the skin was roughened and raw. O'Keefe stood and regarded her silently but she didn't stir, her calm gaze never faltered.

Properly fed and cleaned-up she'd be a picture. Did she know that? Was she protecting herself with the childlike air? he wondered. With the shabby shapeless clothes? Little mother? he thought, but immediately dismissed the thought. The gossips had it otherwise; the child belonged to the drunken mother. Who the father was, nobody knew – or said. He guessed the girl used the constant presence of the infant as protection, a shield. Sergeant O'Keefe shuddered at the thought of Buller Reynolds anywhere near her. And if what young Martin Vavasour had said about the mother was true, then she had good reason to try and protect herself. Common knowledge seemed to be that Nan Sweetman, for the past couple of years, had been Reynolds's whore.

'Do you know which flat Mr Vavasour lives in?' he asked abruptly.

She looked at him but did not reply. The child turned his little old-man moon-face to the sergeant.

The round pale mongol eyes welled with tears, he burrowed into the girl's lap and began to howl. He had a powerful pair of lungs for such a puny little thing.

'Is that child all right?' O'Keefe asked, his voice more gentle.

'Jimmy. His name is Jimmy, he's me little brother,' she said fiercely. She had a flat Dublin accent. 'What d'ya think's wrong with him anyway?'

'I, er,' started O'Keefe.

Lily Sweetman looked straight at him, daring him to say anything. She lifted the child onto her lap and soothed him tenderly. His undersized limbs were flaccid; one leg seemed to be bent under him.

Lily looked up at O'Keefe without the slightest trace of self-pity.

'Look, mister, he's a bit slow that's all. He had a desperate cold all winter. But he's grand now. He's no bother to no-one.'

'All right, child, I didn't mean anything. He's a grand little lad. Listen to me now. The young guard that was with me last night? You don't know where he lives, do you?' O'Keefe asked.

'Martin? Yeah, I know Martin all right.' He waited but she continued to gaze up at him as if to say, 'What's it worth?'

Two could play that game. He went on waiting.

'Me ma wasn't drunk,' she said suddenly. 'Jus' upset. She looks after us . . .'

So that was it. She was afraid he'd arrest the mother – for what? – loitering, he supposed. He felt unaccountably let down. As if, when his precious oracle had spoken, she gave forth non-sense.

'I'm tellin' ye, mister. She looks after us,' she insisted shrilly.

'I'd say, miss, that if anyone does the looking after, 'tis yourself.' His tone was kindly. 'I'm not after your mammy, child, you don't have to worry.'

'Number eight. The big house down there. Two flights up. Second room on the right,' she said tersely. She picked the child up and moved away from him.

She had an amazing sense of timing, O'Keefe thought, because just as he was about to detain her, a tousle-headed Vavasour appeared at the door of number eight.

CHAPTER EIGHT

'Do you know that young one?' O'Keefe asked softly, drawing the young guard aside.

'Who? Lily Sweetman? Yes, sir.' LS? Little Shadow; Lily Sweetman. O'Keefe felt strangely satisfied.

'Do your tunic up, man. And put on your helmet. This is a murder inquiry,' he said gruffly. 'Know her well, son?'

'Yes, sir. She lives upstairs. On the top floor. She looks after the chisler – when we want to go to the pictures or something.'

'*You* have a child?' O'Keefe was astonished. The boy was hardly more than a schoolboy and his wages would barely support one, never mind three. Small wonder he lived in such a dive.

'Yes, sir. Sean, sir,' he added sheepishly.

'Sean?' O'Keefe repeated stupidly, for the moment not catching the significance of the child's name. 'Sean, eh?' He was pleased.

'Six months old, sir. Grand little fella.'

'The girl, lad, it's her I want to hear about,' the sergeant said gruffly.

'Rose, the wife, sir. My Rose says Lily Sweetman is the best little worker in Ireland. She's grand with the babby. Rose is teaching her to sew, as well. Rose is in the tailoring, she thinks Lily shows great promise,' he added proudly, his earlier terrors forgotten. He drew himself up and stood to attention, a beam of absolute pleasure all over his innocent spud of a face. He looked unassailable; the orphan boy secure in his love for his family. O'Keefe suddenly thought of his own boys, far away in some filthy battlefield. Fighting other men's wars. He had no idea where, their letters did not say, but he hoped with all his heart it wasn't Crete. Even the tight-lipped censored reports in the newspapers could not disguise the fact that something horrific was happening in Crete. Wherever that was. He must look it up on a map.

'Sir?' The young recruit touched his arm.

O'Keefe pulled himself together. 'Right then, lad. Could you go over and talk to her. I want to know what she's up to . . .'

'Ah, sir, Lily wouldn't be up to anything,' Vavasour interjected.

'Well, now, I wonder about that. Just you go on over and ask her why she's been hanging around the whole night, keeping that poor child from his bed. And herself. Sure she's falling out of her standing. There must be some reason for it.'

'She waits up for her mammy every night, sir. She has a hard enough time of it, poor Lily. That's what she was doing last night. Didn't you see . . .'

'Of course I saw, man, do you think I'm blind?' O'Keefe interrupted roughly. He wondered why the innocence of the young man irritated him so much. He almost asked him if Lily Sweetman knew about his dispute with Reynolds, but decided to deal with that later. He took the young garda by the sleeve and walked him towards where Lily was sitting rocking the child.

'But that's not what she's waiting for now, is it?'

he continued softly. 'And while you're at it, find out what time the mother left the house, would you? Reynolds must have only just . . .'

'Oh no, sir.' Constable Vavasour blushed furiously. 'Mr Reynolds had other, em . . .'

'Ports of call? Is that what you're trying to tell me?' O'Keefe couldn't keep the disgust from his voice. God Almighty, he thought, what sort of filth was he?

'Yes,' the younger man muttered miserably. 'There's Mrs Coffey next door and . . .'

O'Keefe held up his hand. He walked away to the small plot of ground – it did not merit the title of garden – in front of which Buller Reynolds was struck down. They were no longer alone. One or two early risers emerged from the houses. The first train of the day trundled past with much hissing of steam and puffing of smoke. Curtains were drawn back and windows pulled up. A horse-drawn milk cart idled slowly by, its steel-rimmed wheels making a great racket as it clattered in and out of the potholes.

A little before eight, an army truck stopped and dropped a group of helpers at the end of the road before continuing, with loud shunting of gears, along Daedalian Road. Just as it reached O'Keefe it stopped. The tailgate was down. Two men climbed down wearily and stumbled towards the houses like sleepwalkers. They were carrying spades, upside down, against their shoulders.

'Were ye over at the North Strand?' O'Keefe asked them as they passed. They nodded slowly, their grimy faces etched with exhaustion, dead-eyed, blank.

'It's terrible. There are children in bits over there,' one of them burst out. His companion went ahead of him into number eleven without speaking. He banged the door shut.

'We were pulling legs and arms out. A head. Someone found a head . . .' The young man wiped his eyes with a filthy sleeve then gestured impatiently with his hand. 'Ah, well,' his voice tailed off. He pushed at the door and, when he found it locked, drew a string from the letterbox and with the attached latchkey let himself in. O'Keefe pulled off his helmet and scratched his head.

As the truck pulled away, its engine cut out. The driver made several attempts to restart it and, having failed, got out of the cab to crank it. When it still wouldn't start, he stood chatting to Sergeant O'Keefe for a few minutes before trying again. With the tailgate down the remaining passengers, sprawled in the back, were easily visible. Hanora McDonagh was lying with her head on her brother's lap, apparently asleep. Myles opened one eye and glanced idly about him. He looked as though he had just woken up and did not know where he was.

Lily watched intently as her beloved Milo began to take in his surroundings. But when his terrified eyes met hers she gave no sign of recognition. She watched as he slid down and pulled a blanket over him. He was a second too late. Just before his head disappeared from sight, Dolly Brennan came out of her house bearing two steaming mugs of tea. The truck moved off before she had time to take proper stock of the occupants in the back. Almost, but not quite. She was about to hand O'Keefe the mug when she did a double-take. She pointed excitedly at the truck's passengers. O'Keefe, Lily noted with profound unease, listened to what she said with some show of interest. But he made no attempt to stop the truck. Instead, to her vociferous fury, he calmly went back to his task.

Martin Vavasour sat down on the kerbstone beside Lily who was trying to see who or how many remained in the lorry.

'Did you hear that? Do you think many were killed?' she whispered as she watched the truck drive slowly off.

'It was a desperate big blast. You heard what the man said. I don't know, Lily. Please God there wasn't too many. Now listen here to me, Lily. Have you been to bed at all?'

Lily pursed her lips and shook her head from side to side. 'I didn't want to wake Jimmy,' she said innocently and looked at him out of the side of her eye.

'Would you stop codding me, Lily, and tell me what you're doing here?'

'Nothin'.'

'Nothing? God between us an' all harm, Lily, but I'm jaded and you're making me feel worse.'

She looked up at him solemnly. His eyes were bloodshot, the lashes thick with tiny yellow globules. His normally pink face was greenish white. But he managed a smile. Martin could always manage a smile even in the worst times, Lily thought gratefully. Rose had told her how upset he'd been about Reynolds. And how he'd told her she'd have to go off to her mother's, out of the way. Lily missed her. Martin and Rose and baby

Sean. Lily's picture of a real family. She let out a huge, slow, sigh. Neither she nor Martin noticed that O'Keefe had ambled over and was now standing close by.

'She won't let us in the bed,' she whispered and brushed her hair back from the bruise on her face. She put her hand to her quivering lips and looked up at him with full, over-brimming eyes.

'He made me watch them. He hit me first, then he made me watch. Then he beat the living daylights out of me ma.' Her voice thinned with revulsion.

'Oh, Jesus Mary and loving St Joseph. Oh, Lily, Lily,' Martin's voice broke. 'He didn't,' he swallowed, 'he didn't touch you, Lily?'

She shied away, twisting her shoulders, a grotesque grimace distorting her features. For that fleeting moment she looked like a sad and tired old woman.

'No. No. No,' she blurted. 'I'd have killed him first. Oh God. Oh God, Martin, I didn't do . . .'

'Shush, shush, Lily dear. Of course you didn't . . .'

'She won't let me back in,' Lily interrupted, her eyes wide with hurt. 'She doesn't want me near her. It's getting worse. I told Rose. I don't know what to do.'

Martin put his arm clumsily around her shoulders and drew her close. She leaned against him and shut her eyes.

Not just young Vavasour then. Lily Sweetman had every reason to kill Buller Reynolds herself, O'Keefe thought grimly. His eyes fixed on the two houses nearest where Buller was killed. Had someone done it to protect her? She looked so young yet so weary; so innocent yet so knowing; as if she knew the worst that life could throw at her. His gorge rose and he had to walk away lest he screamed his rage that not one of those blathering women he'd questioned had mentioned Reynolds's filthy antics or protested at them. They'd turned their backs, just as he was turning his, in case they'd have to get involved. Did they, he thought savagely, did they think they wouldn't have to face it if they didn't mention it, have to confront it? Or were they afraid that if it wasn't Nan Sweetman he was taking advantage of, then another of them might have been at his mercy? Much easier to shun poor drunken Nan Sweetman and blame it all on her easy virtue.

But someone minded. If not about the Sweetmans then about something or someone else. They'd shot him to bits the only night of the year, or perhaps of the century, when they might be able to get away with it. They had known his disgusting habits and his timetable. Known that after the rent collecting he would present himself to the unfortunate Nan Sweetman and take his pleasure or revenge on her and her child. The neighbours must have known what was going on. Yet not one of them, except for young Martin, had lifted a hand to help Lily or her brother. Except the killers, of course. To his mortification, Sergeant O'Keefe felt a huge surge of sympathy for that act of mercy. He tried vainly to batten it down. The world might be well rid of the likes of Reynolds but his job was to find out who'd done it.

He looked around him. Martin still had his arm around Lily's shoulder. She was comforting the bawling child. She looked frail and tiny and utterly lost yet, in his soul, he was certain she knew more than she was letting on. He would be keeping a close eye on Lily Sweetman. And he would waste no more time about it either. But first he would have to go and talk to her mother.

As if on cue, Nan Sweetman came out of the house and stood on the step, looking blearily around for her offspring.

'There's no bread,' she shouted. She held one hand in front of her face but it couldn't hide the violent purple bruising or the swollen eye. 'Why didn't you get the bread, you rossy?'

'There's no money, Mam.' Lily rubbed her eyes. 'But I kept some of yesterday's for you,' she placated. 'It's under a cloth up on the shelf. I kept two slices for you, Mam. I'll fry it for you, Mam. I'll . . .' She started to her feet but her mother was already retreating into the house. Suddenly she stopped and swung around.

'Lily Sweetman,' she screeched. 'What are you doing talking to them polismen?'

Lily handed Martin the child and ran towards her mother who backed away in alarm, both hands in front of her face, as if the girl was going to attack her.

'Buller Reynolds is killed, Mammy. The Buller's killed. Someone shot him dead.'

Nan looked at her for a moment then raised her arms skywards and slowly sank to her knees.

'Oh Lily, Lily. Oh merciful hour,' she said and pulled her daughter towards her.

97

Martin Vavasour walked towards them, little Jimmy cradled in his arms. When he got to the doorway he leaned down and drew Mrs Sweetman to her feet and, without a word to his superior, led the family inside.

O'Keefe turned away almost weeping with pity. He felt too drained to go on but he knew he had no choice. There were so many uncomfortable questions to answer. Somehow he had to find some way of protecting young, innocent Garda Vavasour. And the girl. Soon one of his superiors would be along, expecting more from him than vague theories of phantom boy-killers. And shortly too, Dolly Brennan would be out to him, full of righteous resolve and demands for 'someone in authority' whose ear she could deafen.

He wished he knew a little more about guns. He wished he had a better idea of what exactly he was looking for. Something, anything out of the ordinary. He retraced his steps to where the body had lain and meticulously went over the ground between the chalk mark and the house where his little shadow had kept sentinel.

After some minutes he reached the spot where the pavement edged into the scrubby grass of what had once been a front garden. A huge purple-flowering Hebe remained from a long gone shrubbery. Beneath it the grass was overgrown and coarse with weeds. As far as he could see, it had not been disturbed but a little beyond it, right behind the bush, some tufts were flattened. He was surprised that he had not noticed them before. He hunkered down behind the bush and peered through it at the chalk marks. He grunted with satisfaction, as with flattened hands, he began to move slowly back towards the house behind, number eleven, patting the ground on either side of him as he went.

A small grubby hand touched his face. O'Keefe sat back with a sharp cry of annoyance and looked up. Lily Sweetman was crouched down beside him. She put a finger to her lips and pointed to two small mounds of leaves about five or six feet away. Sergeant O'Keefe got to his feet and let her lead him forward. At the first mound she knelt down carefully. She stretched out her hand and he lunged forward to stop her, but she shrugged him off indignantly. Afterwards he recalled, though it did not strike him at the time, how strong she was and how skilfully she deflected him. He watched silently as she picked up a twig. Her hand hovered above the leaves then very delicately, using the stick, she teased up a little branch, which, as she extracted it, dispersed the rest of the leaves and revealed the earth beneath. And there, gleaming dully in the morning sunshine, was a spent cartridge.

O'Keefe stared at it for a long moment, slowly nodding his head. When he looked up she was running back home and in her place stood Recruit-Garda Martin Vavasour, grinning down at him. For an awful moment O'Keefe saw triumph in that innocent, boyish smile.

His resolve to keep a close eye on young Lily Sweetman hardened. She knew a great deal more than she let on and he was determined to catch her out, make her talk. Poor Sergeant O'Keefe. He might just as well have tried to catch a will-o'-the-wisp.

* * *

There was no mention of Reynolds's passing in the papers that day, the thirty-first of May. Nothing indeed until a brief mention of it appeared towards the end of the following week, on the fifth or sixth of June. Up to then the newspapers were full of reports of the North Strand bombing, the battle raging in Crete and the allied raids on Germany. Strangely, the tragedy did not stop the race meeting scheduled for the Phoenix Park on that very Saturday as the photographs of smiling punters in the following Monday's paper would attest. Perhaps it was simply that in the shocked aftermath nobody thought to cancel it.

City life also continued uninterrupted. The Gaiety Theatre was playing *You Can't Take It With You*, The Peacock: *Any Time For Love*, The Gate – perhaps more appropriately – had Anew McMaster in *Macbeth*. In the Capitol Cinema Judy Garland starred in *Andy Hardy Meets Debutante* with Mickey Rooney and also in *Little Nellie Kelly*. In The Savoy, Don Ameche and Betty Grable starred in *Down Argentine Way*.

It was nearly seven o'clock on Saturday evening by the time the policemen had done with their interminable questions. The minute they were gone Maisie Reynolds dashed upstairs. Free at last from the restraints laid upon her by her overbearing and unlamented husband, she laced her baby's bottle with a liberal dose of gripe-water and gin, tucked him firmly into his cot and took the tram in to the Savoy Cinema.

Don Ameche was one of her most favourite pin-ups, and she just couldn't resist.

CHAPTER NINE

A study of the victim provided the police with a hefty list of possible suspects. Every time poor Sergeant O'Keefe turned a stone, he found some other villainous secret about Reynolds. Trouble was, no one clear suspect emerged and certainly nobody on whom it was possible to pin the murder. That Myles McDonagh – oh yes, the good Sergeant tracked him down and questioned him long and hard on Saturday and Sunday – and Lily Sweetman were shielding someone, he was certain. But not the murderer. He believed, firmly and stolidly, that they hadn't a clue who the murderer was. And, for reasons best known to himself, he held passionately to his belief.

Scandal clings in tight-knit and introspective communities. Too many lives had been ruined, too many innocent victims hoped that death would put paid to Reynolds's disgusting history. Hoped maybe that it would be forgotten and their disgrace with it. The assassination was seen as justice, more divine than rough. Buller Reynolds's tenants displayed a solidarity after his death that they had lacked during his reign of terror. None of them would say a word. Apart from Dolly Brennan, and she was worse than useless, nobody wanted anything further to do with him or his murder. If they kept quiet they knew it would eventually, like his hapless family, go away. And deep in his heart a troubled Sean O'Keefe agreed.

The list of possible suspects grew and grew. Whenever anyone described their dealings with the murdered man they threw up, almost unconsciously, yet more reasons why he should have been disposed of. Reynolds, it seemed, could not cross a single person's path without making a further enemy. Whatever chance the authorities had of pinning this random murder on Mrs Brennan's 'boy in the brown suit' vanished when Lily Sweetman found the spent cartridge for Sergeant O'Keefe. But, for reasons which he kept firmly to himself, O'Keefe never actively pursued the question of how Lily came to know where the cartridge was hidden. She always denied seeing 'the boy', and from that stand could not be budged. When, on the Sunday afternoon, thirty-six hours or so after the murder, he eventually got round to asking her if she knew a Myles McDonagh, she said, quite simply, that she'd never heard of him. And it was true – in a way – she thought, crossing her fingers, for it was the first time she had heard his surname. Up to then she only knew him by his diminutive; as Milo.

She'd seen him first the previous summer on a very hot day when little Jimmy had fallen down in the street in a fit. He'd been sitting on the ground outside Heaney's shop while she was inside buying the milk. She ran out and screamed for someone to help her but nobody would touch him. Until this tall thin boy came out of old Handl's bookshop across the road and picked Jimmy up.

102

'We'll take him to the hospital,' he said, just like that. 'St Ultan's. Do you know it? It's the children's hospital way up along the canal. Will you be able for the walk?' He looked at her old boots doubtfully.

'I will.' She was so full of gratitude she could hardly get the words out.

'We'll have to go and tell Mr Handl,' he said. The old man sitting inside the door of the shop told him to take his leather apron off and get a move on. He promised to lock up if they didn't get back in time. Lily thought he looked very like God the Father, but more smiley.

The boy carried Jimmy the whole way, and it was very, very long. It took well over an hour but they walked along in companionable silence until, just by Baggot Street bridge, he looked down at her and asked her name.

'Lily. That's a lovely name,' he said and she was his for life. 'I'm Milo.'

By the time they got to the hospital Jimmy had come out of the fit. The nurse who examined him said he'd be all right to go home if there was someone to look after him, but he should be brought back for treatment every week.

'You're not the mammy, are you?' she asked. Lily was so ashamed in front of Milo that she went scarlet and prayed for the ground to open up and swallow her.

She never brought him back, of course. She couldn't manage to carry him all that way herself. Anyway, she was afraid if she did they'd want to take him away. Say she couldn't look after him right.

Milo walked them the whole way home that day, right to the very door. She was mortified she couldn't give him a cup of tea or anything. She was too ashamed to have him climb all those stairs and see the awful old place they lived in.

'Look after yourself, Lily,' he said, 'and the little fellow.' He was lovely, she thought, the way he made everything so nice and easy.

'You're not to be minding that bossy old nurse, Lily. You look after your little brother great, so you do.'

That's when she knew she'd love him for ever; because of the kind way he made sure that she knew he believed her. He went off with a little wave that day, loping down the road towards Sandymount. She raced up the stairs two at a time, shoved Jimmy down on the mattress and climbed up to the spy-hole just in time to see him turn left at the end of the road. The exact same way the Buller Reynolds went home.

In the following weeks she plodded off every day in that direction, or to the bookshop, but she never once ran into him. She was too shy to push open old Mr Handl's door and ask for Milo. She had begun to think she'd imagined him, or that he was her Guardian Angel come down from heaven, when he strolled up to her one Saturday when she was sitting outside on the steps minding Jimmy. He was pushing a small little cart with a handle made out of an old walking stick. The box was wood with a little bit of carpet lining the bottom and beautiful red leather padding around the top edges.

'What's that for?' she asked.

'That's for Jimmy,' he said. 'He's too big for you

to be carrying,' and he lifted Jimmy into it. Jimmy squealed with fright at first, but when Lily pushed the little cart back and forth he loved it.

Milo sat on the step and watched her with a little smile on his face.

'And how are you getting on, Lily?' he asked as if he'd only been gone a minute. 'It's a lovely day. I was wondering, would you like to bring him up to Sandymount Strand for a paddle? The sea air would do him good. And yourself.' He grinned. 'I know a great place where there's heaps of little pools, just right for him. It's not too far, you'll love it.'

'In your cart?'

'That's not my cart. That's for Jimmy. I made it for him. It's nothing, only an old butter box with a pair of wheels I found out the back of the shop. Mr Handl gave me the bits of leather for around the top.'

'It's only gorgeous.' Lily could hardly breathe for joy. 'I love red. Jimmy loves it too. Look at him, feeling it with his little hand. He loves it, so he does.'

'I've got something else for you, we had a bit of the leather over,' Milo said shyly. He took a tiny red draw-string purse from his pocket. 'Happy birthday, Lily.' He smiled. She'd put out her hand to take the gift, now she drew it back.

'It's not me birthday,' she said sadly. 'Me birthday's in January.'

'What day in January?'

'Nineteenth. I'll be fifteen years,' she said proudly.

'Well then. We're the twenty-fifth of July. So

happy half-birthday, Lily.' He laughed and put the purse in her hand.

She stroked it lovingly with the tips of her fingers and pressed it to her face. Her cheeks flamed scarlet. 'It's beautiful. I'll keep it always,' she breathed.

'How old are you, Milo?' She loved saying his name.

'Seventeen today,' he laughed. 'Honest.'

'You gave *me* a present for *your* birthday? Oh. What'll I give you? I've nothing.' Her face squidged up with disappointment, then, as suddenly, brightened. She held out the purse.

'It's a great present, Milo. But if me mammy sees it she'll take it. Could you keep it for us? It's the nicest thing I ever had. I'd like for you to use it. For a birthday present, from me,' she added seriously. 'I couldn't bear for to lose it.'

After hesitating for a moment, Milo slipped it back in his pocket. 'If that's what you want? Sure?'

'Really and truly, cross my heart.'

'Right then. Thanks Lily, it's a great present.' He laughed. 'Now, what about the seaside?'

It was easy pushing Jimmy along. Much better than lifting him everywhere. He sat quiet as a mouse, his little smily face peeping over the top edge.

As they walked along, Milo told her all about his work. He said he'd less than a year till he came out of his apprenticeship. He'd started out as a printer and he still did a small bit, but now he preferred binding books. When she asked what that was, he said it was making covers of beautiful soft leather and sometimes putting designs on, with real gold.

He said he liked mending old books as well.

'Sometimes, I like it better. The paper's so nice, and the old print.' He went off into a little dream after he said that. Lily didn't understand what he meant. She thought of books as stories, not as things, but she didn't let on.

After that she saw him lots of times, making sure she was outside Heaney's at the time he finished work. Only once or twice a week though, she didn't want to make a nuisance of herself. One time he let her come in and see the bindery at the back of the shop and the books he made. Lily had never seen anything so beautiful. Mr Handl was working at a clattering old machine thing. He told her it was called a press and showed her the pages he was printing. He wasn't so frightening up close, with his funny accent and little beady brown, kind eyes. He called everyone 'my dear'. The customers even.

It was Mr Handl who told her that the print-works down the road from the book shop, that belonged to Buller Reynolds, once belonged to Milo's family. It had, in some way she didn't understand, been taken off them when his father died. Milo was in the front of the shop at the time and when he heard him coming back, Mr Handl put his finger to his lips and said Milo didn't like to talk about it. She never let on she knew.

It wasn't long before Lily began to see that Milo was almost as much afraid of Buller as she was. She didn't tell him about what the Buller did to her Ma but he seemed to know anyway. He said she was to keep as far away from Buller as she could, that he was a terrible bad man who did an awful lot of harm. When he said he was afraid of Buller as well, she didn't tell him that she knew why. But after that, Lily was careful not to let anyone see her talking to Milo in case someone told the Buller. That's why she wouldn't ever let him come near her house. But unfortunately, before she knew any of that, on the day they went to the strand, Dolly Brennan had, as usual, been hanging out her window. Lily would never forget it.

As they passed, Mrs Brennan had called to her crony Mrs Doyle, 'Would you look at that young one strutting along with the auld chariot! Mark my words, Mrs Doyle, she's a chip off the old block. I can see it coming. The blood's bad.'

They both laughed, Lily went bright red, but she couldn't say a word, she was that upset. When they turned the bend, Milo took her gently by the hand and whispered, 'Just keep yourself to yourself, Lily, and don't be minding those old biddies. A pair of mischief-makers, they are. They ought to be ashamed of themselves.'

She could never, ever do anything to put Milo in the least danger. She wished she could remember more clearly just what had happened to the Buller. He was lying dead before she realized it was Milo on the other side of the road. But she knew one thing for sure. No matter what Milo might have done, or who he might have been helping, she wouldn't tell a single soul about him being there. Not ever. Dolly Brennan could yak till she was blue in the face.

Lily Sweetman sneaked round to Milo's street very early on the Monday morning following the murder. She had to leave Jimmy sleeping beside

Ma even though she was worried he'd wake up and cry. Ma hated the sound of him crying. Lily went before seven because she wanted to give him the tools on his way to work. She'd forgotten it was the Whit Monday holiday.

She waited for nearly an hour, worrying that he was going to be late. Then a big crowd of people on bicycles turned up and stopped outside his house. A lot of them were wearing knapsacks on their backs. She stayed hidden in a doorway a bit down the road and kept peeping out but she couldn't see him.

Someone shouted, 'Milo, for the love of mike! Would you get a shove on, or we'll never get where we're going.'

She gathered that the gang of them was going off to the seaside for the day. Skerries was mentioned. One of the girls said they'd have to go the long way because the North Strand was blocked. One of the boys made a face and said that wasn't the right way anyhow. At last, Milo came running out of the house. He had on a knapsack but it was much bigger than the others had. One of them asked him if he had the kitchen sink in it and they all started jeering and laughing.

Milo said to one of the girls, 'I put in a towel for you, Hanora.' Lily knew by the name that the girl, who was very tall and beautiful, was his sister, so she didn't have to feel jealous. At about the same time another man came around the corner wheeling an old tandem. One of the boys began to sing 'Daisy, Daisy' and one or two of the others joined in for a few bars until Milo's sister told them to shut up. She got on the back and said, 'Giddyup.' They weren't able to ride it very well. Everyone began laughing again and one of them said it should be in a museum. The tandem went off first. As it wobbled along, Milo's sister got a fit of laughing and shouted 'Stop'. The man in front almost fell off but she just sat there like a queen, bursting her sides with laughing and waving the others on. She took a white beret from her pocket and stuffed her beautiful long dark hair up into it.

Lily thought she looked like a film star. She was dressed in a pale pink blouse and floppy navy-blue pants which she asked the man to tuck inside her socks so they wouldn't get caught in the spokes. And he did what she told him, which completely amazed Lily, because he looked too old to be bossed around like that. Some of the others tucked their trousers in like hers or rolled them up. When at last the whole group was up and moving, Milo's sister shouted for him to hurry up.

He was at the tail-end with the stragglers. Lily thought he didn't see her but, as he passed, he fell back a little, turned his head in her direction and gave a little nod. She took the canvas tool-holder from behind her back and held it in front of her, clutched to her chest. The relief that passed over his face was her reward. He gave a little start, his jaw dropped then he looked straight at her and nodded again. She bowed her head and put her finger to her lips. She only hoped he understood. He looked terrible. Frightened and tired. Then it was all over.

She stayed as still as still, looking after them, trying hard not to cry. One of the men came a little way back and circled round Milo, edging him into the middle of the pack. He was quickly swallowed up from her sight. Gone. Lily ran all the way home and hid her precious bundle where she knew no-one would ever find it. She could hear Jimmy bawling as she climbed the stairs.

And so Lily fobbed O'Keefe off with impenetrable innocence, obscuring as much as she revealed about that terrible night. Most fascinating of all, she never said she thought she recognized the dark shadow behind the bush. Who the cyclist was, she genuinely did not know. Nor could she work out what part that strange ghost-like figure had played in the murder. Worst of all, she couldn't work out what Milo was doing across the road. But she knew it looked very bad. Apart from anything else, there were sharp knives among the tools in the canvas holder.

Lily stayed mum because she was smart enough to figure out that almost anything she said would come back on Milo. She didn't care who killed Buller Reynolds. Or why. She was glad he was gone; thankful that he would never plague them again. Milo was her friend and she wanted to protect him. The best way to do that, she knew, was to remain silent.

Myles McDonagh didn't return from that inno-cent-seeming Whit Monday outing. Didn't return at all. It frustrated O'Keefe that both his sister and mother were so blank-faced about his disappear-ance. It wasn't until several weeks had passed that the mother volunteered the information, with her usual ration of hand-wringing and tears, that her darling boy had gone to Belfast and enlisted in the Royal Navy.

'He's going to be killed for certain, Sergeant O'Keefe. You've hounded him away with your questions. A gentler boy there never was. What'll I do, at all, without him? Who'll look after us now he's gone?' She pushed her contorted face into O'Keefe's. 'That boy wouldn't harm a fly. He'll be destroyed, killed.' Her voice rose shrilly. 'Hasn't he only gone and pledged himself for the duration of the war? And God only knows how long it'll last. Oh, oh, oh,' she moaned. 'I'll never see him again.'

And, for the time being at least, that was that. Myles had disappeared knowing some of the facts. Lily knew others, but she wouldn't talk. Between those two there was, had they matched the interlocking pieces, complete knowledge of what had happened. At the time, neither was old enough or experienced enough to fully understand the motives for that terrible crime. And because they could not, its aftermath lived with them for the rest of their lives.

CHAPTER TEN

In the weeks following her husband's death, Wilfrid (Buller) Reynolds's widow, Maisie, realized that the police might seem helpful enough, might make out that they were 'in active pursuance of a line of enquiry', that they'd 'apprehend' someone for the crime shortly, but she didn't believe a word of it. She wished they'd use plain English and stop trying to confuse her with all those long words.

They were all like that, the Irish. Never stopped talking but they said nothing. She hated the Dublin accent which was so thick and flat it was impossible to understand anyway. Worse than Liverpool, in her opinion, and that was saying something. They never looked a person straight in the eye either. That was the worst. For the first time in her life, she agreed with her late husband. Like him she was certain that the Irish were a bunch of liars, cheats, out to protect their own and stupid with it. Stupid but cute. She didn't stand a chance with them. All that soft talk and over-politeness. What was worse they were, she was sure, laughing up their sleeves at her.

She was almost right. The truth was that the victim's lechery was an embarrassment. His ownership of the tenements compounded the insult. His tenants, especially the women, might not have helped their unfortunate sisters but they noticed. Each and every violent and sexual misdemeanour was chalked up against him. Self-oppressed memory is long and bitter. Within the tenements, Buller Reynolds had power over most of those, young Martin Vavasour among them, who should and would, in other circumstances, have been making an all-out effort to help track down his slayer. They dragged their feet. They stopped paying the rent and the Buller's timid widow was much too frightened to demand it.

Maisie Reynolds sat at home in Sandymount too scared to go out. She used to think of the Irish as foreigners, now she felt like one herself. She neither knew nor trusted any of her neighbours. She remembered how her husband had raged about their 'cowardly neutrality'.

'Men should be men and fight for king and country.' Like him 'first time around', during the Great War. Maisie never got over what happened the day war was declared. He'd dug out a bunch of medals – they weren't even his medals, he'd picked them up on a stall along the quays – and pinned them on his chest. Then he put up a flagpole in the front garden and ran up the Union Jack. Their next door neighbour went wild. He came roaring out of the house and demanded that it be taken down immediately. Wilf grabbed him by the coat collar and kicked him up the backside.

'Get back to your fucking rat-hole!' he shouted. 'Hun arse-licker. Too yellow to fight, ain't ya? Bloody scum. Expect His Majesty's Government to feed you and protect this effing cunt-try, eh?' His face contorted with contempt. 'Get it? Cunt-try? Or are you just too stupid, Irish? Lily-livered micks. Won't even fight for their king and country.'

Maisie, cowering behind the curtain, watched with amazement as Mr O'Hara stood his ground. He drew himself up to his full height, which was at least six inches shorter than Wilf's five-ten, and asked calmly whose country he had in mind?

'The Royal United Kingdom, that's what country,' Reynolds sneered. 'God save the king!'

Mr O'Hara dusted an imaginary speck off his lapel and, fast as a cat, leapt at Wilf and landed a stunning blow smack on the side of his nose. He leapt nimbly over the gate while Wilf tried to stop the blood.

'And wouldn't you know all about that, Mister Black-and-Tan Reynolds?' O'Hara shouted loud enough for the neighbourhood to hear. He bolted indoors while Wilf danced about in apoplectic rage, spewing a stream of invective against poxy republicans and their grievances.

Oh, Reynolds knew all about that. What he hadn't taken into his reckoning was that the neighbours did too. They knew exactly how he came to be in Dublin and how he'd spent the years between the wars. Reynolds could hardly open his mouth without giving himself away.

Days slipped by, weeks, then months. Maisie Reynolds, shunned, isolated and increasingly apathetic, prayed that the war might soon end so that she could go back home to Sussex and safety. But that seemed unlikely for the foreseeable future. England at war offered little advantage over hated, neutral Dublin, where, at the very least, there was enough to eat and cheap help for the child. Maisie was canny enough to know that, if she left too soon, she might never retrieve anything of her late husband's considerable holdings. Finding out how to cash in her assets took a little longer than she foresaw.

She started with the tenements. These at least she knew something about. In the first year of her marriage her husband had made her collect rents. It had not lasted long, this task, for he quickly realized how inept she was when faced with whining pleas for deferment from his feckless tenants. Her mistrust of them made her powerless, even if it came a poor second to her self-pity. As soon as she could, she used her pregnancy as an excuse to give up her weekly round of wheedling empty threats. The tenants had reason to miss her when the fearsome Buller resumed the task himself.

In retrospect, she was amazed at how long it took her to realize that Wilf's rent-collecting wasn't just that, that there were other guessed-at attractions attached to that weekly round. Perhaps it was just as well that, by then, whatever small regard there had been between them had been killed by his brutality. Only the child inspired what little tenderness he had. Even that, she noticed with alarm, diminished as the boy grew from baby to toddler and was slow to live up to the robust expectations of his sire.

Maisie Dent had met Sergeant-Major Wilfrid (Buller) Reynolds when she'd almost given up hope of ever finding a husband. She was thirty-five, he was forty-nine. He had fought in the Great War and afterwards volunteered to go to Ireland. He was a keen army man, was Buller, who prided himself on knowing how to keep jumped-up micks in their place. Fighting, he liked to boast, was all he knew. Not quite. While he was in the army he had learned other ways of turning a fast trick. In Dublin he found openings undreamed of for one of his class in his native land. As the British withdrew, both army and civilians, many houses were abandoned. And the good sergeant-major was in prime position to arrange things to his own advantage. He was shrewd and ruthless and invariably got what he wanted. His ambition was to make his pile quickly and by whatever means possible. By the time he was forty, he'd acquired five two-bedroom houses on Daedalian Road. A year or so later he bought another, a three story house in the same terrace, and he had his eye on the rest. He knew the site could, in time, become a gold-mine; so close to the docks and only a short distance from the city centre. In the meantime, there was a tidy income to be had from the rents. Who cared that the houses were run-down and seedy, without indoor plumbing or sanitation? Everyone knew you didn't have to provide such niceties. Those people wouldn't know what to do with them. The sergeant became landlord, the rents rolled in and he began to turn his attention to other ways of turning a profit. And to providing himself with an heir.

He was visiting an old war-time buddy when he met his future wife, in 1933, at the pictures. Maisie was the usherette at the local Odeon. After that he turned up regularly each year. From Ireland, he told her. His pal called him 'Sarge'. She assumed he was still soldiering. She never asked what he was doing or who he was fighting 'out there'. Her knowledge of geography was as hazy as her grasp of history. To Maisie, Ireland was about as foreign as Timbuktu.

Then, one cold December night in 1938, he appeared out of the blue as she was going home and asked her to marry him. He was drunk and maudlin; his pal had just died. He wanted, he told her, to settle down but the trouble was he didn't know many girls. She was so grateful he'd described her as a girl that she accepted. He wooed her, for a week, with boxes of chocolates and lisle stockings – she never really forgave him for not giving her silk. She didn't know many men and those she knew she didn't think much of – hadn't she seen what they got up to in the back row of the Odeon? No-one before had offered marriage. She wasn't exactly delighted but she accepted all the same.

Their wedding was a shabby little affair in the local Methodist chapel. Neither of them was Methodist but the minister was glad of the fee. They caught the boat-train for Dublin as soon as the wedding breakfast was done. For Maisie, and no doubt the good 'Sarge', the journey was endless. The Dublin packet was crowded, the weather foul, the crossing rough. Wilf got drunk while Maisie was prostrated with sea-sickness. It was raining when they arrived and, as far as Maisie was concerned, it had been raining ever since. She hated the city from the moment she set foot in it. She hated the cold and the damp and the wind. She missed her job, her cronies. And because she couldn't understand a word anyone said, she mistrusted the people and made no attempt to find kindred spirits. Which was a pity because, with a bit of effort, she'd have found plenty. With her head full of film-stars and the hit parade, Maisie might have been a bit dizzy but she was never vicious. She was impressionable and easily bullied and in very short order she made her husband's prejudices her own. She had done herself no service at all in marrying the Buller Reynolds.

In the end she resented him bitterly. Had she had any option, or means, or imagination, she would have gone straight back to England. But she had none of those. Until his murder provided her with her opportunity. In the circumstances the bloody war seemed a personal inconvenience. About her own possibilities and the future well-being of her boy, Maisie was a realist. With considerable trepidation she set about discovering what her husband's convertible assets might amount to. She assumed that their main source of income came from the houses. But there was also a printing works in Ringsend. The only thing she knew about it was that Wilf had dropped his partner's name and added '& SON' when Arthur was born. She knew nothing whatever about what they printed or who worked there. Indeed she'd been only very dimly aware of its location until a small party of employees came, ostensibly to 'pay their respects'; in reality to find out whether they still had jobs.

They were led by two tall, dark, rather hard-looking men called Hanlon, who looked like brothers. They introduced themselves as the printers. One of their companions, a gnome-like man called Reilly, was the foreman. She was surprised that they stood aside while the little fellow addressed her. His accent was so thick she could hardly understand what he said. Before they left, the foreman presented her with a printed address of loyalty from the staff. Then the older of the two printers stepped forward, smiled a chilly smile and promised to carry on 'as usual' until he heard from her. For the first time since she came to Dublin she had absolutely no difficulty in understanding what he meant and knew immediately that she would have little chance of taking possession of the business. Not with those hatchet-faced thugs in charge.

She thought about it for a week and decided to sell up and get out while the going was good. She would have to get professional advice about her right to the printing-works. Once that was cleared up, she'd sell her share or, as the elder Hanlon had picturesquely put it, 'come to some arrangement'.

The printers were not her only callers, certainly not the only ones who brought with them a hint of menace. She began to understand that she must do without a good honest solicitor. Wilf had not, apparently, sought the help of professionals in his business dealings. The solicitor she went to pulled out a couple of weeks later.

'I'm sorry, Mrs Reynolds, I don't quite know how to put this, but I don't think I can be of much help.' He smiled vaguely as he ran his eye over her furniture. He made her feel like dirt. She had trouble grasping what he meant with his la-di-dah voice. 'Acquisition not purchase was, I'm afraid, your husband's stock in trade. In my view, his means of acquisition are best left unexplored. To say he has left you on shaky ground, legally speaking, would be putting it mildly.'

All this might have cowed her but, perhaps surprisingly, it did not. It simply got her dander up and made her determined to salvage as much as she could from her loathsome husband. Nobody knew better than she how evil he'd been but she wasn't just fighting for her livelihood now, but for her boy's future as well. She hadn't asked to come to this godforsaken island and she had no intention of staying. But she was damned if she'd leave empty-handed. To hell with the blasted solicitor. As she saw it, whatever she retrieved by her own efforts was hers by right and not a gift from her rotten husband. She'd jolly well sort it out before she went anywhere. She'd get what was owing to her, see if she wouldn't. Bit of a spitfire was Maisie.

There was, however, another problem: she couldn't go home until the bloomin' war was over, could she? The bloody Irish might be in a hurry to see her go, but she had to think of herself for once. With all that rationing and food shortages, why, poor little Arthur would surely starve. And she didn't fancy going back home to Mother. She'd stay as long as it suited her.

Maisie knew where the tenements were and had some idea how much the houses were worth. She wondered if anyone could be persuaded to take them on, especially with sitting tenants. Or how, since she could find no trace of deeds or bills of sale, she could off-load them profitably. She needed advice, and she needed it from a local.

Barely two months after Buller's death, Maisie strapped her twenty-month son in his pram, stuck a dummy in his mouth, and went to call on the only approximation of a friend – and then, only since her husband's death – she had made in her three years in Ireland.

Maisie Reynolds and little Arthur left Dublin in June 1945, a month after VE day. She had enough cash in hand to set herself up as a seaside landlady. She wasn't welcomed by her three married sisters, two of whom had lost their husbands in North Africa. They regarded her as little more than a traitor because she'd sat out the war years 'out there' in Ireland. She had, they accused, gone over to the enemy. Which was a bit rich, really. For six years she'd thought of nothing but home. The city lights, Saturday night dances, Max Miller's side-splitting dirty jokes, fish and chips, port and lemon, Friday night at the Odeon.

She couldn't believe it. No matter how often, or how vehemently, she expressed her contempt for the Irish they wouldn't listen. All of a sudden, she was one of them. She'd sold her birthright for creature comforts. Wasn't fit to call herself an Englishwoman. Didn't deserve to. She was shunned, no longer treated as 'one of us'. It was as if she, Maisie Reynolds, Dent as was, true blue and British, was another unwelcome, despised Irish immigrant.

No matter how much she raged and screamed she couldn't shift them from that point of view. A great gulf had opened. She hadn't shared their grief or their terrors. She hadn't spent cold damp nights in underground air-raid shelters, hadn't worked in the munitions factories, hadn't had to make do with powdered eggs, grey bread, no meat.

She hadn't met all those lovely Yanks either, had she? So when they talked about the blitz or the air-raids or the terrible food and clothes shortages, Maisie tried to look interested when all she was thinking was how much better her life would have been as a GI war bride. When they made sly comments about how rich she was all of a sudden, Maisie shrugged her shoulders and went her own way. She didn't moan on about her horrible mate or the loneliness of those long years, did she? So she had no intention of taking a blind bit of notice of their jealousy. Nor any intention of sharing her ill-gotten gains either.

Little Arthur was not quite so robust. His playmates, taking their lead from the adults, made him the target for their bullying. He had a 'hit me' look they couldn't resist. In their childish war-games he was, for evermore, on the enemy side. The Battle of Britain was re-enacted daily in the school playground when he was safely away from Maisie's protection. Arthur was the entire Luft-waffe, overwhelmed by a dozen little Spitfires who pummelled, biffed, scratched and left him snivel-ling in helpless fury. For years he endured taunts he never fully understood.

'Sticks and stones, Arthur dear, sticks and stones.' Maisie would lick her handkerchief and wipe away his tears. 'Water off a duck's back is what I say, Arthur. They're just jealous. Mummy'll knock their blocks off when she sees them. Get your coat on, kiddo, and we'll go down the picture house. Who's his mummy's boy, then? Don't you worry, I'll look after you, Arthur.'

The routine hardly changed over the years, just the words. Arthur could never quite remember when she switched the words around, but the phrase echoed in his head for most of his adult life.

'You'll look after me, won't you, Arthur darling? You won't ever leave Mummy, will you?' He never understood why the little-girl voice was so compelling.

'Who loves his Mummy, then?'

1995

INTERMEZZO

It was raining the day they buried Lily Sweetman Gilmore. And chilly. The temperature dropped about sixteen degrees overnight; from seventy-five to fifty-nine. The following day, it rose again. In the two weeks before, and the five weeks after, the funeral the sun shone and the temperatures soared. It was the warmest summer on record, some said the warmest for 200 years. The grass dried out. But with the first downpour the green came back, as if the colour had been only lurking beneath the surface, waiting to pop out. Later on, in August, the landscape would become brown and scorched again. Everyone said there was never a summer like it.

The day Lily Gilmore was buried was a brief respite, the one cold, wet day in forty-two. A memorable day in a memorable summer. And not just for the rain.

The cemetery where she was buried was disturbingly beautiful. It lay beside the sea, overlooked by the Wicklow mountains. As Lily's daughter, Nell, took her place behind the hearse at the entrance she looked up at the Sugarloaf and startled herself with the thought that such breathtaking views were wasted on the dead.

The wreaths and bouquets of flowers were laid in a carpet beside the grave. As soon as the two diggers had lowered the coffin into the ground they hauled up the strong flat ropes which cradled it and took them off to the side. Once out of sight of the mourners, the older and more bent of the two furtively lit a cigarette and, holding it lovingly clutched between forefinger and thumb, took a few deep and satisfied drags. As soon as the priest started the prayers, the cigarette was discarded and trodden quickly into the soil. That was when the rain started.

As the grave-diggers waited behind the mound of earth for the ceremony to end, their attention was momentarily caught as a smartly-dressed young man, leaning idly against a nearby head-stone, unfurled a giant black umbrella. He appeared extremely interested in the small group at the graveside where several umbrellas had also sprouted. One was held aloft over the cassock-clad clergyman while three elderly women jostled for protection under another. A little to the right of them, a tall thin, grey-haired man stood alone, his head bowed.

The fine misty rain was almost imperceptible at first but it quickly drenched the straggled congregation. The priest brought the ceremony to a close with practised ease and, after an awkward pause, the mourners began to shuffle towards the gate leaving a slim young woman standing by the open grave. She appeared to be unaware of the rain.

After some minutes Nell Gilmore turned and ran her hand over her wet hair. She looked bewildered, her intelligent face drained and pale. She was about thirty, of medium height, very blue eyes, fair hair tied in a bunch at her neck. She was striking rather than pretty. Her lightly freckled face was tear-stained. She wore a long navy-blue mackintosh

128

with a large floppy hood. Her black pumps were soaked.

As soon as the main group was close to the gates the watcher edged resolutely in Nell's direction but pulled back quickly as a middle-aged man, clutching a golf umbrella, broke away from the group and hurried back towards the girl. The watcher stooped and busied himself rearranging the flowers on an adjacent grave. An elderly grey-haired man limped past the girl. She did not appear to notice him.

'We'll see you at the house, Nell?' the man with the golf umbrella suggested diffidently. He looked embarrassed and spoke with an English accent. The too-small Irish tweed cap perched on his head looked so absurd she almost laughed.

Nell nodded quickly and waved him away. 'Yes, of course. I'll follow, but I have to see the sexton first.'

The man hesitated, comically uncertain whether to risk getting soaked by handing over the umbrella or to turn tail for his car.

The girl suppressed a smile. 'I have my own car, thanks. I didn't ride with the hearse. I'll be all right. You go ahead.'

As he walked away from her, she called after him, 'That man ahead of you could do with some shelter, he's getting soaked. Go ahead to the house. Our next-door neighbour, Mrs Dwyer, will be there. Tell her I'll be along as soon as I can.'

She turned for a last look at the grave and caught a half-glimpse of the watcher before a sudden gust of wind caught her sideways. She bent her head against it and jiggled her hood to release the beads of rain which had begun to slither down her face. Then, hastening her pace, she headed for the little chapel.

The watcher waited until she was safely inside, then he walked swiftly to the gateway and slipped into the back seat of a black Mercedes which was idling at the kerb.

'Well?'

'He was there.'

'More than him,' came the rejoinder. There was a pause: 'Did he talk to her?'

'No, he came back to offer her a lift but she refused, said she had her own car. It's that red Renault Clio parked across the road.'

'Did she know him?'

'I don't think so, she hesitated over his name.'

'How?'

'Oh, you know, Mr, er, er. Like that. I'm pretty certain she hadn't a clue who he was.'

'Mmm. You keeping with her?'

'Yep.'

'That's something at least. What about him?'

'He's gone to the house with the rest of her old cronies. I'll pump the girl.'

'Good. You're certain about Arthur?'

'I don't know. I can't watch both of them, can I? Anyway, if I miss him afterwards, we know where he's staying.'

'Right. You'd better get on, she'll be out in a minute.'

'Nice timing. Look at that sodding rain.'

'Well, then, what are you waiting for? Offer her the sodding umbrella, why don't you.'

'It gives me a good excuse, I suppose.' He laughed.

'Precisely.'

Nell Gilmore was inside the chapel for no more than seven or eight minutes. When she came out she found a man sheltering in the porch. He turned at her approach. The wind had risen and the rain was much heavier. She looked at it glumly. He stepped forward and held out his free hand in greeting.

'Nell,' he said, as if addressing an old friend.

She looked startled for a instant. 'I'm sorry, do I know you?'

CHAPTER ELEVEN

I didn't know him from Adam.

'Arthur sent me back,' he said. 'He suggested you might give me a lift to the house in return for the shelter of my trusty umbrella.'

He shook it out and a shower of spray caused us both to step back hurriedly and bump into each other. He steadied me with his hand and let it linger on my arm. I moved aside, casually.

'Though I'm not sure how trusty it is.' He laughed wryly.

'A good deal better than none at any rate,' I replied briskly. 'It's very kind of Arthur. And you,' I added hurriedly.

I was embarrassed because I couldn't place him. Mind you, I was well aware that in the present circumstances it might well turn out he was related to me. Or possibly Arthur-with-the-funny-hat. Though where Arthur came into the picture baffled me. Another mystery man. He'd introduced himself just before the service, claiming to be an old friend of my mother's. Knowing Lily, that might mean anything.

The funeral was turning out to be more interesting than I expected. I looked at my present companion as blankly as I could. There was a crowd of relatives of my dad's in Kildare I'd met a couple of times as a child. He could be one of them. I wasn't aiming to start a family feud.

'I'm sorry,' he said hurriedly, 'I should have introduced myself. Cormac Hanlon.' His accent was hard to place; certainly not Kildare. Educated Dublin, but neutralized. More like my boyfriend Davis's than mine. I guessed he'd spent time in an English public school.

'Hanlon?' I played for time. It was a common enough name but it rang no bells with me. 'Not a relation, then?' I asked.

He looked amused. 'Afraid not. But the Sweetmans and Hanlons go back a long time.'

Oh really? I was puzzled that he'd used Lily's maiden name. I had a vague, uncomfortable impression that he was expecting some reaction from me. I didn't oblige.

'Your mother was a great friend of the family. Since Ringsend days.' He spoke fluently and fondly.

Ringsend? Lily would have said Sandymount, being something of a snob. Ringsend is becoming quite smart these days, new flats – sorry, apartments – and some of the squares have been tarted up. Young professionals trying to take over. Bit of an uphill struggle, really. They'd be better off planting a few trees. Lily was pretty sceptical about its possibilities. I don't think she could ever see it other than it was when she was a child: depressed, run-down, poverty-stricken. I took another look at my snazzily-dressed companion. I was rather touched that he claimed to share my mother's modest origins.

'Ah, Ringsend.' I was noncommittal because I couldn't think what else to be. I wasn't in much mood for chat. I'd suddenly lost interest. The rain matched my feelings exactly.

He was quick on the uptake, I'll give him that. He held out his free hand. 'Shall we make a run for it?'

He linked his arm in mine and drew me under the umbrella. He was casual and friendly yet somehow managed to stop short of familiarity. Heads bent against the wind and rain, we sprinted like children to my car – actually it was Lily's little Renault – and huddled against it while I fumbled for the keys. A huge, black Mercedes shot past us, sending up a vicious spray. We were both so soaked that our shoes squelched as we got into the car. I hadn't realized how tiny it was until I tried to struggle out of my coat. My new friend kept getting fistfuls of gabardine in his face. It was hopeless. The car windows were misted up and two people in that space was one too many. I was only barely under control, and losing it. Not so Hanlon.

'Hang on a minute,' he said. 'Look, there's quite a good pub nearby. Why don't we dry off there?'

'I can't, not really. I must get back to the house.'

'A quarter of an hour or so won't much matter, will it? At the rate those old dears drive, we'll be back before them.' He chuckled. 'The neighbours will take care of everything. The place will be awash with tea. I don't know about you, Nell, but I could do with a drink.'

It was a cheering prospect. I let out a sigh of relief. 'Me too,' I said. 'Me too.'

'Let's go.'

The pub was empty, which wasn't surprising at four in the afternoon, but there was a roaring fire, which was. The landlord watched without comment as our dripping umbrella and my raincoat sent rivulets of water meandering across the floor. When a large puddle had formed, he straightened himself slowly and roared into the open doorway behind him: "Melda? Floor'll need wiping.' Then he turned down the volume and told us what we wanted.

'Hot whiskies?' He had a real take it or leave it manner. One of the world's great charmers. I almost had a hernia when Hanlon agreed. I could see myself staggering to my mother's wake smelling of strong spirits. I hoped the cloves and lemon would mask the whiskey.

While Hanlon was waiting for the drinks at the bar, I sat back by the fire and took a good look at him. Tall, very. Six-three or four. Generously built, athletic – rugby perhaps – beginning to run to fat though he seemed to be containing it. Nose might have been broken. Well-dressed; discreet navy pinstripe, white shirt, funereal black tie, expensive black (wet) brogues. Tightly barbered dark hair. Face a bit jowly, slightly sulky I'd already registered, but now, as he turned to join me, I revised my opinion. Open smile, dark eyes. Somewhat under forty – thirty-six or seven probably. A businessman by his clothes. Prosperous. I wondered again what his connection to my family might be.

'Will you be here long?' Hanlon asked politely when we'd had the first, long, warming draught.

'In Dublin? Not long. I've a few things to do. A few days at most. I've been here long enough. Ten days. Since the accident,' I said, and immediately began to worry about being away from work and what to do about my mother's house. Everyone had warned me about the dangers of leaving it empty.

'You'll sell the house?' He seemed to read my thoughts. Or perhaps he was only making conversation. My mother's little house could hardly interest him.

'Not sure.'

'It must have a lot of memories for you.'

'Yes.' I didn't elaborate, though I was aware he was trying to probe again. For what? Why?

'Oh. Of course.' An almost imperceptible hint of uncertainty as he backed off.

'You knew her well?' I asked casually.

He smiled regretfully. 'Not well enough. I really met her for the first time when my uncle died, some years ago. They were great friends. I went to see her and, well,' he shrugged, 'I saw quite a bit of her after that. Wonderful to chat to, wasn't she? A real old-timer – I mean, the interesting stories she had,' he added hurriedly.

'Yes.' I suppressed a smile. Lily would have slapped his face for the 'old-timer' quip. Lily wasn't an old anything. She wouldn't thank him for referring to her age. I didn't either. It was not up for discussion.

'I'm sorry about the accident. Dreadful business. It must have been a terrible shock.'

Shock? I almost screamed out loud. Shock? Is that what you call it? I could think of a more graphic description. Like massacre. Like mindless, mind-blowing, violence.

Some idiot hit-and-run driver had mown down

136

my mother and left her to die, alone and in agony, on a deserted road. She was a sprightly, alert, interested and involved sixty-nine-year-old. It should not have happened, everyone said so. She had excellent hearing and eyesight and presented a clear target – unmissable, I'd have said. Though she was small in height, she wasn't all that thin. She also dressed with great exuberance. Bright, bright colours. How could he, they, whoever, not have seen her? That it had happened in broad daylight, on a deserted road, made it worse. Poor Lily lay where she fell for over an hour, the police said, before the howling of her small and terrified dog attracted the attention of the occupant of the only house within a hundred yards. But that hour was critical. Help came too late to save her.

She was killed in Ringsend. On a run-down, deserted road beside the railway line. What she was doing in such a place was anyone's guess. And why she had used her bicycle and not the car was something I couldn't figure out.

'I'm sorry. I've upset you,' Hanlon's apology broke in on my thoughts.

'No,' I said shortly. It troubled me that his name rang no bells. Lily had never mentioned him, I was sure. I couldn't make him out. He seemed nice enough but really, it was quite the most extraordinary chat-up – if that was what it was. While I gave him some credit for ingenuity, I felt uncomfortable with him. It all seemed a little, well not to be priggish, a tad disrespectful.

'Time to go, I'm afraid,' I announced abruptly.

'You won't have another?'

'No thanks. One was good though. And wel-come.'

The rain had stopped by the time we left the pub. He kept up a steady line of chat as we made our way to the car. The traffic was heavy on the main road so I drove home by the coast road which was worse. It seemed to be my day for Mercedes. I was tailed by a creep who clearly thought it was a real gas to ride on my back bumper the whole way. I was stroppy enough not to let him pass. I even slowed down, to really infuriate him. I lost him at the T-junction at the bottom of the Vico Road. I went one way, he accelerated the other. I drove the rest of the way in preoccupied silence. I dreaded the wake. We were almost at the house before Hanlon spoke again.

'I wondered,' he said as I pulled into the kerb, 'I wondered if we could meet again before you leave?'

'Why?' I stepped out of the car.

'I'd hate to think I'd upset you. Please?' He came around and walked along beside me.

'That would be nice,' I said vaguely.

'Nice?' He raised his eyebrows at me. 'Nice? That bad was it?' He put on a look of utter dejection and I found myself smiling at him. I hadn't noticed till then that he was quite attractive. Deadly timing, though.

'I'm sorry, there's too much to do before I go back. Maybe some other time.'

'Tomorrow,' he cajoled, grasping the advantage. 'How about lunch? I'll call for you around twelve. You have to eat sometime.'

'Oh. All right,' I smiled. Curiosity got the better

of me. 'It'll have to be somewhere local though, in Dun Laoghaire, I've a lot to do.' I drew a deep breath, bracing myself for the wake. 'Oh lor,' I huffed. 'I'm dreading this. Thanks for the drink, it's given me Dutch courage.'

'Pleasure.' He stretched out his hand and shook mine.

'Oh. You're not coming in?'

'I'm sorry, Nell. It's much later than I thought, I'm afraid I have to get back. An appointment I'd almost forgotten. I'm sorry.' He strode away, leaving me slightly stunned. I watched him until he turned the corner. I noticed his dark suit had picked up a mass of white dog hair from the car. I crossed the road and let myself into the house.

I was engulfed the minute I stepped in the door. There was an amazing crowd packed into the front room. I glimpsed Arthur (who *was* he?) a couple of times during the next couple of hours but each time he was out of reach. When I was ushering out the last of Lily's old neighbours, I noticed him boarding a city-bound bus.

'I thought Arthur had a car,' I said.

'Arthur who?' They didn't know him, they said.

Nor did anyone else I questioned. Somehow it didn't seem all that important and I quickly forgot about him.

CHAPTER TWELVE

I didn't have lunch with Cormac Hanlon the day after the funeral. The rat stood me up. At the time I was furious; later I was glad. My life was too complicated for casual emotional baggage.

I'd been engrossed all morning in trying to restore order to my mother's house. It had an agitated, disturbed appearance as if she had gone out without tidying up the day she was knocked down. It was the first thing that struck me when I walked into it after I identified her body. Though disorder is probably stretching the point. Anyone else would probably not have noticed, but it surprised me. My mother was extremely house-proud and neat and she'd passed her finickiness on to me. In the ten days of neglect since then a layer of dust had settled over every surface, like a shroud. The wake had added to the mess. I was tempted to call in a professional cleaner but I knew she would have hated strangers clearing up after her. In any case I wanted to do it myself.

I started very early because I had decided to get back to London that night. By midday I was bushed. I finished off by emptying the fridge and sluicing down the kitchen floor. Her little West Highland terrier, Spud, eyed this activity sourly from his basket. He'd spent much of his time since Ma's death with the next door neighbour, Mrs Dwyer – I never did know her first name – where things were obviously more to his fastidious taste. When I began to wield the mop he got into a frenzy and started snapping at my heels. I tried the cuchie-coo tactic and cravenly put out a friendly hand to him. He had a go at that as well. That did it. I tucked him unceremoniously under my arm and went next door.

'He's only pining,' Mrs Dwyer said. 'Aren't you darlin'? Come back to auntie for a little bone?' Darling put on his playful act. The one my Ma found irresistible. He sat with his head cocked to one side with his little pink tongue stuck out lasciviously. Then, when he had her in the palm of his paw, he disappeared under the sofa. To my relief, Mrs Dwyer found this performance personally flattering. The implication was that she understood our four-legged friend while I, smart as I was, did not. She had already agreed to keep an eye on the house until I decided whether I wanted to keep it. It was not an easy decision and I thought it best to give myself some time to mull it over. Now she asked if I'd like her to look after Spud as well. I almost fell upon her neck with relief.

Spud very kindly came to the door to see me out. He sat gazing up at her, wagging his tail. He looked quite cute. Really. But to tell the truth, since the accident I couldn't stand the sight of him. He had survived; my mother had died. The suddenness of it all had knocked all emotion out of me, I really didn't know what or how I was thinking. It was a bit like being smothered in cotton wool. I was left blind, deaf and gasping. I needed to get away. I thought I would come back in a few weeks and sort through her belongings, but for the moment I found it almost unbearable to be in the house alone. Handling or discarding anything as intimate as her clothes was more than I could bear. Nor could I touch the huge wadge of stuff that arrived from her bank. I put it straight in my suitcase to sort out when I got home.

I had just about done when I remembered to check her sewing room where I found five orders neatly hanging on the coat-rail waiting to be collected. Her tailoring was immaculate. I ran my finger over the neat seams and almost wept. She was punctilious about keeping her books up to date, we were alike in that, so I knew exactly what to do. I managed to contact four of the five clients and arranged for a courier to make the deliveries. On the final finished gown and the pile of outstanding work I simply closed the door.

Of course all that took much longer than I hoped and it well past one o'clock when I suddenly remembered my lunch date with Cormac Hanlon. I gave my face a quick splash and changed out of my jeans, then hung around until a quarter to two when hunger got the better of me. I stomped down the hill to Dun Laoghaire for a glass of Guinness and a ham sandwich. As usual it was made with indigestible soft white factory bread. I don't know why I eat that stuff. Every time. I don't seem to be able to resist. I suppose it reminds me of the sandwiches Lily used to make when I was small, with moist bread almost hot from the bakery. I swear the yeast keeps proving in your insides, hours later you still feel bloated. And a bit sick. I didn't mention that she was the world's worst cook, did I? She loved food when someone else cooked it, but she never got the hang of buying good or fresh ingredients, she always went for the cut-price 'bargains'. I know more about mouldy vegetables than most.

I was skulking in my dark corner, contemplating a cup of the pub's disgusting coffee, when a stranger slid onto the bench opposite me.

'Miss Gilmore, isn't it? I wonder if I could have a word?' He struck me as rather creepy but when I looked closer I recognized him as Arthur. I sat down again and ordered coffee for both of us. He didn't say anything until the waiter had gone back to the bar so I had time to take a good look at him and I knew I had never in my life seen him until the day before. I suppose if I were asked to describe him I'd say: Average. Middle height, middle-aged, middle everything really, except that he had a slight cast in one eye which made it impossible for him to look straight at you and had the unfortunate effect of giving him a rather sly, underhand look. He was dressed conservatively in a single-breasted navy-blue suit and white shirt, but spoiled the effect by wearing a floppy red bow-tie which looked much too theatrical for him. He was rather like a small boy in grown-up clothes. He had greying hair with a rather peculiar lock of much darker hair plastered over his balding dome. His steel-rimmed glasses put me in mind of a politburo apparatchik. I was very relieved he wasn't wearing a raincoat.

'We're not related, are we?' I said more out of politeness than anything else. After all he was at the funeral, but I didn't think I wanted him as a relative.

'No such luck.' He had a nervous, embarrassed smile.

'I thought not. I couldn't place you.' I shrugged. 'What did you say your name was?'

'Reynolds.' He spoke in a hoarse whisper, glancing furtively around as if he was afraid of being overheard. It was rather unsettling. 'Arthur Reynolds. Did your mother mention I'd been in touch?'

'Nooo.' I shook my head. 'Should she have?'

'I wondered. I saw her a few weeks back. She knew my father. A long time ago, in Ringsend. Wilfrid Reynolds.' He sat back as if he expected me to comment on this disclosure but since I could think of nothing to say, I just waited for him to continue.

'I'm not from Dublin,' he said. He made it sound like a virtue.

'I'm sorry about that.' I meant it ironically but he took it quite seriously. I hardly knew whether to laugh or cry.

'Oh no. I know I was born here but I don't count that. Mother took me back to Sussex when I was four. She never liked it here.'

Top marks for tact, Arthur, I thought.

'Your parents were English?' For some reason I felt compelled to join in this surreal conversation.

'Yes. From Brighton. Or at least Father was from Brighton, Mother was born in Hove. She died last year. She was a great age; over ninety. And a widow for fifty-three years.' He was about to ramble in the way people who live alone tend to, given an opportunity, but I quickly cut in.

'You looked after her?' That's it, I thought, he's

144

lonely. Been looking up his old mum's friends. Wants a chat. And Lily would be just the person to draw him out. Yet for some reason I had a vision of Lily doing a flyer when he hove into sight. Friendly she might have been, but she gave the seriously weird a wide berth. Time to go, Nell, I thought.

'Yes. She ran a boarding house in Brighton when I was a child. After the new university opened she turned it into student accommodation. I worked for the DHSS. Until she died, that is. Very depressing it was, all those layabouts looking for something for nothing. I took early retirement. Now I've got time on my hands, I've been trying to trace people who knew her in Ireland.' He pronounced it 'island', which always irritates me. 'And my father. Bit of a hobby really. I never came over until six months ago, now I've been four times. Isn't that strange?'

'Very.' Poor Lily. I bet she called him the Brighton Bore. He was very twitchy. He kept looking over his shoulder. I became more and more uncomfortable. I couldn't see where he was leading or what it had to do with either my mother or me. Besides, time was running on, I had calls to make and a plane to catch.

'I'm trying to find out a bit about my father's life in Dublin.'

'I'm sorry, I don't know anything about your father.'

'No, of course not.' His voice became an overpatient whine. 'How could you? My father died in the war. He was a soldier.'

'Oh. Then what . . .' This was getting nowhere

fast. 'Look, Mr Reynolds, I'm afraid I have a lot to do and a plane to catch . . .'

Of course I realized that was a mistake the moment I said it. He immediately suggested that 'If it was more convenient he could come and see me when we both got home'. Well, I wasn't having any of that. I tried to remember if I'd mentioned where I lived. I didn't want this weirdo knocking on my door one dark night. So I did the only thing I could think of. I ordered us both another cup of coffee and asked him, as firmly as I could, what exactly he wanted to know. (Apart from my address, of course.) I mentally allowed him another five minutes to get to the point. After that, I promised myself, I was out of there.

He edged towards it crabwise and I let him ramble on. It was not a good decision. I should have gone when I had the chance.

'When I say my father died in the war, I don't mean he was killed in action, though that's what I believed. I always had an idea that he was killed in France, on a battlefield. Heroically. There were a lot of medals in the house. But when Mother died . . . Oh, I'm sorry, I don't mean to upset you mentioning death like that and so soon . . .'

I brushed that aside as politely as I could and began to wish that the mighty Mr Hanlon was entertaining me. At least he didn't talk in that awful nasal whine. Now that Arthur had at last started along his peculiar track there was no getting him off it. I was well and truly stuck. I hoped someone was chalking up my reward in heaven.

'Like I said, when I was going through the house

after Mother's death – did I mention I intend to sell up and get something more convenient? No? I thought of buying a little antique business. Well anyway, as I was saying, I came across some newspapers from the nineteen forties, and some other things to do with my father's various business interests. They were Irish newspapers.' He sat back and waited for my reaction. But he'd lost me. I stared at him blankly, completely mesmerized as his wall-eye yo-yoed back and forth.

'Irish newspapers?'

'Yes. And the funny thing, there was a little bit about him in one of them. That's how I discovered he didn't die in action. Mother hadn't been quite straight about that. Why, he wasn't even in the army by then. He died here in Dublin. On the 31st May 1941. There was also a big article about a German bombing raid on that night so I naturally assumed he was killed in that . . .'

'And was he?'

'No. I've been doing some research in one of the libraries down in the city. Pearse Street, is it?'

I began to get interested. The Gilbert Library in Pearse Street has an excellent newspaper archive. I nodded.

'Dreadful slum. He wasn't anywhere near the place where the bombs fell. I looked up a map. Mother stayed until the end of the war and then we went home. Mother was a Dent, from Hove. Things weren't easy for her. People were very nasty, even her family. That lot wouldn't have anything to do with us. Jealous, they were. Said she'd sold out, living in the lap of luxury out here while they starved. Said they'd heard my father owned half of Dublin. But it wasn't like that. Mother said she only got out barely enough to buy the house in Brighton, and I, for one, believe her. Whatever she made later, she did it by her own efforts. Very thrifty was Mother. An astute businesswoman in her way.

'The abuse went on a long time. She would have moved if she'd been able to get a decent price for the house. Made a fresh start. But it wasn't easy to move, things were pretty tight in the fifties. I had a terrible time of it at school. They called me a conchie. I never knew what they meant till I grew up. There was very strong feeling about Ireland's position during the last war, I can tell you.'

Oh dear, I thought, he's been looking at too many VE Day commemoration programmes on telly. All this had been thoroughly dredged up in early June during the 50th anniversary celebrations. As a matter of fact, one documentary had prompted me to think, for the first time in my life, about Ireland's neutrality.

'Yes, I know.' I just stopped myself saying that I lived in London so of course I knew. 'I read history at university,' I substituted, then felt ashamed at my own pomposity. Arthur Reynolds was an unprepossessing specimen but he had an insidious way of eliciting sympathy. I don't know what stopped me running off except that I was beginning to find his lack of tact hilarious. He exerted a peculiar fascination. I suspected that he was the kind of bloke who always ended up having his face punched. How right I was.

'I don't see what all this had to do with my mother,' I interrupted. 'Did she know your family?'

'She knew my father. She must have done. She lived in one of the houses he owned. On the street where he died.' The song they left out of *My Fair Lady*; I almost started humming.

'He owned a lot of property at one time. But it didn't pass on to Mother or me. Mother was cheated.'

'And you spoke to my mother about this?' I didn't bother to keep incredulity from my voice. He didn't reply. He stared into space as if he was trying to sort something out in his mind.

'Would it have helped to talk to her?' I persisted.

'Yes, I think it would have done. But I didn't get a chance.'

'Oh? I thought you said . . .' By then I could hardly recall what he'd said, it was such a rigmarole. But I sensed he was implying something unpleasant about my Ma.

'My mother,' I said fiercely, 'was a completely honest woman. I hoped you're not suggesting my mother had anything to . . .'

'I didn't,' he interrupted waspishly, 'want to talk to your mother about the property. I was just telling you how she knew my father, that's all. Filling in the background.' He reminded me of a rather nasty little terrier. For some reason this show of spirit made me see how the weak become the most terrifying bullies. But he didn't frighten me, I glared at him over the rim of my cup. His next remark made me spill my coffee right down my front.

'My father was murdered, you see. I believe your mother knew something about it.' He stared straight at me, glassily, without blinking.

'I think your mother was murdered too,' he hissed.

That did it. I pushed the bloody table right into his middle. His mouth opened like a goldfish as he tried to get his breath.

'How dare you say such a terrible thing? I've just buried my mother. What do you think you're doing making nasty allegations like that?' I stuck my face right against his and spat the words at him. 'My mother died in an accident. You think you know more than the police? Who the hell do you think you are?' I burst into tears and rushed out.

I didn't stop to see what happened to him; I didn't care. I was half-way up Patrick Street by the time I was calm enough to slow down. People were staring at me. The front of my shirt was drenched with coffee. I held my bag over it and rubbed my eyes.

The man was completely weird. I wondered if he made a practice of insinuating himself into funeral parties. Probably how he got his kicks. I was making too much of the encounter. The man was pathetic, sad. A freak. I'd heard of people who crashed weddings. Happens all the time, apparently. Perhaps this was a variation on the theme. I forced myself to stop hyperventilating and was almost rational by the time I reached the house.

Then I really saw red. Cormac Hanlon was leaning against the hall door smoking a cigarette. He was wearing a pair of linen slacks and a pale blue shirt with the open cuffs turned back. Dead cool. He had a large bunch of white roses under his arm. He straightened up when he saw me and blithely held out the flowers. I looked through him.

'Nell, I'm terribly sorry, my car was clamped in town. Outside Buswell's. I was only inside for a few minutes. Officious bloody traffic-warden. It took ages to sort it out. By the time I got here you were gone. I've been driving all over Dun Laoghaire looking for you. I'm really sorry. Come and have a cup of coffee, please?'

I cut him off. I was in no mood for him or his flowers. In bright daylight he wasn't nearly so attactive as he'd seemed beneath his expensive umbrella the day before. In any event, the thought of him using poor Lily's funeral as an excuse for a chat-up seemed grotesque and I was thoroughly ashamed that I'd encouraged him. I felt crass. Worse, I felt used and dirty. I pushed past him.

'Some other time,' I snapped. 'I'm leaving shortly.' I opened the door and stepped inside.

He shot a piece of paper with a telephone number scribbled on it through the gap. I ignored it and made to slam the door.

'Will you let me know when you're next over? Please?' he cajoled. 'Please. I'm so sorry about lunch. Am I forgiven?' He put his head winsomely to one side. 'Please?' He looked a right eejit. So did I.

'I'll be in London next week. Could we meet then?' he said, pressing his advantage. Some innate caution made me give him my business rather than my home phone number. I didn't want to go out with him, but I was mystified as to why he should seek out my company. I wanted to know why. I wasn't flattered; it made me extremely uncomfortable. When he left, I sat quietly in Lily's bedroom for a long, long time.

Eleven days had passed since that awful accident. I'd been summoned to Dublin on the twenty-eighth of July, which was the third day of a two-week holiday in Pollença, on the north-east coast of Mallorca. We'd just got back from the beach and were racing each other for the shower when the phone rang.

'You get it.' Davis, my partner, laughed as he pushed past me. 'Bet it's your bloody office. You never learn, do you? If you're on holiday, be on holiday. Delegate,' he shouted through the bathroom door.

He's quite right to be annoyed, I thought as the phone shrilled again. Strangely, I was reluctant to answer it as if, at some level, I recognized its portent of evil. In my memory, its ring was sharp, laden with threat. I actually laughed with relief when I heard Maria's voice. Maria Walker is my closest friend. She and her husband Steve had recently moved into the flat below mine. Apart from the office and my mother, she was the only person to have the hotel number. I thought she just wanted to chat, so I said, 'Hang on a moment,' grabbed a towel and settled on the side of the bed before picking up the receiver again.

I was in a catatonic daze when Davis came out of the shower.

I remember him standing in the doorway, drying himself with a pale blue towel. His hair was dripping down his tanned face but I couldn't seem to remember who he was.

'Shower's free. Get a move on, I need a drink. Come on, Nell, what's wrong with you?'

I couldn't answer. The words were jumbled in my head, I couldn't get them out.

'Nell?'

'My mother . . .'

'What about your mother?' He threw the towel on the bed and began to dress. I stared at him, wishing I tanned as easily. His undershorts were striped, blue and white.

'I have to go home.'

'Oh for heaven's sake, why do you have to go home? You're forever running after her. What's wrong with her anyway?'

'Nothing any more. She's dead.'

He came and sat beside me on the bed. He tried to look sad but it came out all wrong.

'What happened?'

'She was knocked down. I have to go home.'

'Oh, poor Nell. When?'

'Now. Tonight.'

I managed to get a stand-by seat on a direct flight to Dublin, but I was in bits when I got there. A tall silent policeman stood close by my side as I looked down on her dear face, disfigured by an awful gash from temple to chin. She looked shrunken, vulnerable, like a dead bird.

I hadn't cried for her then or at any time since, except briefly at the graveside, but I began to weep after I'd seen Hanlon off, and I could not stop. After I packed, I stood at the doorway of each room, placing her. Now in a chair, now whisking around with her ridiculous red feather duster. Poor old Lily, even the damn duster had to be bright and gay.

It was as if my ghastly encounter with Arthur Reynolds and my anger with Hanlon had released the numbness in my soul and heart. The house was full of her. Because she'd been poor for so long, she cherished her possessions in a way I understood for the first time. It almost broke my heart. Nothing she had was really valuable, but my father had made his best pieces of furniture for her and, over the years, Lily had put a patina of pure silk on their surfaces. She didn't keep things from greed, she kept them from love. Now I noticed that the brass handles of her bedroom chests were dull and unpolished. And I had no time to clean them.

I turned to go when a thought popped into my head and lodged there uncomfortably: both Reynolds and Hanlon had mentioned Ringsend. Yet Lily herself rarely talked about her childhood and then only in passing references to her dead brother. I didn't even know what street she lived in. As far as I could tell Ringsend was a place she didn't want to remember. I had always put it down as one of her little snobberies. Strange as it may seem, up to that moment Ringsend had not appeared to have any particular significance except that it was a very long cycle from home. But it struck me now all right. Lily was knocked off her bike in Daedalian Road which ran between Sandymount and Ringsend. The newspaper reports of the accident had all mentioned it.

And that, I now decided, was how both my

154

horrible pick-ups had manipulated me into believing they knew her. They had simply fed me that scrap of information gleaned from the newspapers. Nasty, perverted, ambulance chasers both of them, out for weird, weird kicks. Conmen. I was sick at them and at myself for being so gullible, so stupid. They didn't know her at all. Those two fine boyos were probably casing the joint and I, like a perfect ninny, had told them precisely what they wanted to know: that the house was going to be empty.

I unpacked my suitcase and rang the office before contacting the local Gardaí. They took my fears seriously and in doing so somewhat restored my battered self-esteem. I felt as if the strange lethargy that had overtaken me since Lily's death had begun to lift. I could make some rational decisions, sort out her estate before returning to my own life. Try to come to terms with her death.

CHAPTER THIRTEEN

'You mean Davis isn't with you?' my friend Maria squawked down the phone. 'I don't believe it!' I held the receiver away from my ear and counted to five.

'I didn't want him to come. It was his first break for ages, he was absolutely exhausted. As you know. Anyway he never really got on with my mother . . .'

'I don't think that's the point, Nell, I can't believe he's not with you. He should be with you. If I'd known, I'd have taken the time off. Why didn't you ask?' Maria sounded hurt. Or annoyed, I wasn't sure which, but I was getting fed up with her diatribe. It had been going on for at least ten minutes.

'Please,' I said. 'Don't let's argue. I just rang to say I'm staying on for an extra week or so. My holiday wasn't due to end until Monday anyway, and Dieter says I can take as much time as I like. Jen will make sure that Roger doesn't get too fond of my office.'

Dieter Ross was the UK director of *Morgen Morgen*, and my immediate boss. *Morgen Morgen* guarantees next-day delivery world-wide, hence the name. I was their operations manager. Dieter and I got on extremely well which was more than I could say for Roger Mason who had been angling for my job for the last year or so. But as long as Dieter was in charge the status quo would survive. Apart from anything else, he was well aware that another company had been trying to tempt me for the past few months. He didn't want to lose me so he didn't balk when I asked for compassionate leave. Besides, August was our quietest month. As for Roger, I could rely on my assistant, Jen Harper, to protect our interests and keep me informed. We'd agreed that if I were to go, so would she.

'Nell, are you listening? How long are you staying?'

'I'm not sure. A fortnight in the first instance. But I'll keep in touch. Maria, will you do something for me?'

'Yeah, sure. Pencil at the ready. Start dictating.'

'Milk, butter, bacon, bread. Enough for breakfast. Would you do that? The flight doesn't get in until midnight.'

'Hold it, hold it. Didn't you just say you were staying in Dublin?'

'Not me. Davis. The flight from Mallorca.' This was greeted with complete silence.

'Maria? You still there?'

'Yes, Nell, I'm here all right. You mean to tell me that bugger stayed on holiday while you went off to your ... I'm speechless. I can't believe what you're saying. I thought at least he came back with you to London.' Her voice spluttered to a stop.

'I flew direct to Dublin. There wasn't any point in us both losing our holiday.' I didn't add that Davis had been completely racked off by the whole thing. By now, I knew he would be thinking of all sorts of treats for making it up to me. 'Look, if you don't want to do it, just say, Maria.'

'Did I say that? Did I say I wouldn't? Sometimes

I just don't understand you, Nell. The man's a shit. I offered to come with you. Why didn't you let me?'

'For the same reason I didn't want Davis with me, Maria, I wanted to do this on my own. Honestly, it's nothing personal, it's just, well, it was sort of private. I don't know how else to put it. You've got the list?'

'Yeah,' she said wearily, 'I've got the list.'

I left the phone off the hook for a couple of days. I told myself it was because I didn't want Hanlon hustling me. Which goes to show how muddled my thinking was. Or perhaps I was simply deploying my self-protective antennae. At some level I must have decided to put my relationship with Davis on hold. He could always manage to talk me around. I didn't want Maria banging on at me either. She'd touched a raw nerve.

The heat wave, which had broken for the funeral, resumed next day with a vengeance. My old room was tiny and stifling so, after a couple of nights of tossing and turning, I moved into my mother's room. During those hot nights Lily haunted me. I had a curious, feverish feeling that I was letting her down in some way I couldn't define. Sometimes I felt that she was long gone or just part of a half-forgotten life. By day, I could not believe how quickly she was fading from my mind. I had to close my eyes and concentrate hard before I could conjure up her face or her walk. But at night it was different. I could see her clothes but they waltzed down my dreams with no-one inside, the empty sleeves flapping like bat's wings, skirts swirling. A chance sighting of a TV ad for Persil, depicting a line of colourful washing dancing in the breeze, became my nightmare. Each article clothed her dead body, hanging limp, battered.

Thus barely nascent doubts about her death began to grow as memories of that hideous whispered accusation pounded at my head: 'I think your mother was also murdered.'

One day I rang the local garda station, and, on the pretext that I was researching hit-and-run accidents for a magazine article, questioned them about how they would go about their investigation if such an accusation was made.

'With difficulty,' was the reply, 'and extreme caution, unless there was very good evidence to support the claim or there were witnesses.' I rang off when his questioning became more focused and my answers grew more and more feeble. I knew then that the heat was getting to me, that it was ridiculous to allow the ramblings of a madman and a would-be crook to play on my mind. Hit-and-run didn't seem to me to be all that different from premeditated murder. The effect was exactly the same. A life carelessly snuffed out. I wanted to murder whoever did it myself.

Who would want to kill Lily Gilmore? An ordinary, elderly, suburban widow who had lived an uneventful life, modestly but with style. Who enjoyed a game of whist with her cronies, sheltered behind a wind-break on Killiney beach, a little primus stove brewing the tea and a noggin of whiskey at the ready. Who adored going to the pictures and had a cassette of every American musical known to man, in the house and her car. Who never paid one visit to a shop if she could spin it out to three. Who went devoutly to Mass every Sunday. Or nearly every Sunday. Who bought her lottery ticket every Thursday. Who cycled for miles on a natty pink bike with Spud, trembling with pleasure, in the front basket. Who terrorized every passing motorist when she took to the road in her beloved little red car. As a life, it mightn't appear to amount to much, yet Lily lived every moment with a zest which grew with every passing year. They had no right to take it away.

Before she died, I thought I fancied something secretive about her smile, as if she had been hugging some delightful, private thought. But really it was just her way. Old age didn't faze or discourage her, each year seemed to increase her enjoyment. The independence of widowhood suited her. Then in one brutal moment it was over. Smashed. Gone. Some careless lout had ploughed into her then taken off without a thought of what we'd lost; Lily, me and poor old Spud. When I thought about it, as I did increasingly, I almost exploded with rage and frustration. My uncertainties about Davis simply highlighted my loss.

Whatever that weird duo Reynolds and Hanlon were up to, they did not appear to have designs on the house because there were no break-ins or even attempted break-ins. Oddly, that did nothing for my sense of security. Or belonging. Sometimes I felt that Dublin too was receding in importance. If I wanted to continue having some contact with my native city, I would have to find other, more personal, realities there. I knew that when I sold the house, it would be a long while before I could comfortably return.

CHAPTER FOURTEEN

Spud refused to leave Mrs Dwyer. Every time I dropped by we eyed each other suspiciously. He had always considered me a rival for his mistress's affection; loss did not improve his filthy temper. Before her death it used to take days of craven cajolery before he'd deign to come near me. Now, no amount of tugging and pulling or downright bribery would induce him to shift from Mrs Dwyer's best sofa. She complained long and loud but I could see she was pleased at his unmistakable preference. When I threw myself on her mercy and asked her what we should do with him she said, as if there was no question of anything other, that she would quite like to have him permanently.

'He's a grand little watch-dog and great company,' she said, 'if you handle him right. Sure, he's only pining.' Silly me.

'The way he looks at me sometimes, you won't be upset now, the way he holds his little face, cocked to the side. You know, honest to God, it reminds me of your poor mother. The Lord have mercy on her.' She crossed herself piously.

Crafty old Spud knew which side his bread was buttered. I could no longer stand the sight of him. I handed him over with profound relief. I even gave him a parting gift of a new red collar. Mrs Dwyer favoured brown in fashions and furniture; I didn't want him to lose his colour sense.

With the dog out of the way I concentrated on my most pressing task; the sale of the house. It was situated off Patrick Street, a long and steep incline which runs from the centre of Dun Laoghaire up towards Sallynoggin. It's about six miles by road from Dublin or about fifteen minutes by the DART (Dublin Area Rapid Transport) train. Though Dun Laoghaire is a town and port in its own right, it has pretty well been gobbled into greater Dublin. From my bedroom window, if I stood on my toes and craned my neck, I had an excellent view of Howth Head across the bay. On summer days when the sky is blue and the water is filled with little white sails, Dun Laoghaire is pure magic.

The house itself was pretty ordinary. In 1906, a small dairy farm at the top of the hill was cleared to make way for Swift Terrace. The six pairs of cottages would probably have been described as artisan's dwellings. They started off with two rooms up, two down, before the later addition of kitchen and bathroom. There are a great number of such terraces scattered all over Dublin, many built as railway or tram cottages, though these are usually single storey. They are attractive, stoutly built and, if the rooms are few in number, they aren't mean in size. Our house was at the end of the terrace, so we had a pretty wrap-around garden which my mother loved tending. It was full of colour since she favoured the varieties of flowers sneered at by 'real' gardeners: petunias, geraniums, candytuft, begonias, phlox, stock and antirrhinum. Blue, pink and red were her favourites, the bolder the better. She planted haphazardly but what she achieved had a wild and vibrant splendour about it. The houses were built of a wonderful dark, rich red brick with lintels of glittering Dalkey granite. Above each door there is a name carved. Ours was Slievenamon but we just called it number twelve.

Though I'd always liked the house, I no longer felt comfortable there. I knew that if I ever came back to Ireland it would be to where we went on holidays, further down the coast in County Wicklow, near Brittas Bay. I decided I would keep only a few cherished pieces, most of the furniture could be sold with the house. Before I began to dismantle it, while it was still looking attactive, I had the estate agent around. Patrick Ryan was an old pal. We'd gone out, briefly, when we were at college and since he worked locally, we often met up for a drink when I was home. I told him about my prowlers and said I wanted the house sold as discreetly as possible, without advertising. He suggested that he started the sale process at once, so it could go through once probate was granted. It seemed an excellent idea. He named a rather higher price than I expected and assured me he'd produce a buyer in no time.

I went swimming at Sandycove every day and each evening walked Spud, for old times sake, to the end of Dun Laoghaire pier. Mrs Dwyer wasn't as nimble on her feet as my mother, her idea of a walk was a slow amble around the block. Spud was feeling deprived, I think, because his attitude to me became slightly less grudging when I offered to take him out. Once or twice I imagined I caught a glimpse of Hanlon but always, when I turned, he wasn't there. Of Reynolds, thank goodness, there was no sign. My mother's friends and neighbours

163

called to pay their respects; once or twice I ate out with friends. The one thing I didn't do was go through my mother's things.

Four or five days later the estate agent turned up with a young couple who fell in love with the house at first sight. They made a generous offer which included some of the furniture. I accepted. I could no longer postpone sorting through the contents. I had a sudden feeling of panic at the awful finality of what I was doing.

It was about ten days after Lily's burial when I started. I watched the BBC news as I dawdled over breakfast. The run-up to the fiftieth anniversary of VJ day had just begun. An interview with some survivors of the Japanese prisoner-of-war camps held my attention. I was saddened at how close in age those veterans were to Lily – within ten years at most. Somehow it opened up another gap between us, especially when one man began to describe them as the forgotten survivors. He spoke bitterly about how they hadn't been allowed to speak of their experiences. I felt an enormous pang of distress that I knew so little of Lily's origins and had been, well, almost ashamed of what I did know. We'd been separated by more than age, she and I, and by more than the normal distance between parent and child. We had been most effectively separated by education. That 'leading-out' had closed my mind.

I started with the sewing room. A friend of Lily's, Sinead Flynn, had offered help and now I rang her. Sinead's mother, Rose, had taught Lily her trade. She died about the time I went to secondary school and though I couldn't remember her, Lily spoke of her so often I felt I knew her quite well. If I ever asked her to explain why, for instance, she cut things on the bias, or did complicated double seams, she'd say:

'That's how Rose Vavasour taught me to do it.'

In Lily's eyes, Rose was the goddess of the french-seam and the most gifted cutter in Dublin.

'Actually she was a bit of a tyrant,' Sinead laughed as we piled the sewing machines and bales of cloth in her van. 'She built the business in Wexford Street out of nothing. Mind you, none of us ever had a chance to do anything else.'

'Don't you like it?' I asked.

'I do, but Isobel, my daughter, would have preferred a bit of independence. Not to mention my poor old Dad.'

'What did he do?'

'Deliveries,' she said and turned her mouth down.

Both her parents were dead. Sinead now ran the business with her second daughter.

'Isobel got a Morrison visa and escaped to Boston,' she laughed.

It was only when she'd gone that I regretted not asking her if she knew how and where Rose and Lily had met. I might have rung her but I felt I didn't know her well enough. Perhaps the real reason was that I was ashamed of showing an acquaintance how ignorant I was of my mother's past.

By now there was only one gown, I couldn't describe it otherwise, still waiting to be claimed. It was long, elaborately draped and in the most splendid gold and dark green silk. Unusually, it had no note pinned to it, nor could I find a trace of it in the work-book. I bagged it up and set it aside. Someone, I was certain, would turn up looking for it. The fabric alone was much too expensive to be abandoned. And if it wasn't claimed, I fancied it myself. I tried it on, and apart from being much too long, it fitted beautifully. I rather hoped nobody would call about it, and they didn't. This wasn't altogether surprising since I rarely answered the phone. Then, when I returned from my swim one morning, Mrs Dwyer dropped by.

'A woman called looking for something your mam was making for her. She said your phone is out of order. She wrote down her phone number and asked would you ring her?' She thrust a scrap of paper into my hand.

'Did she leave a name?'

'I don't think so, now let me think ... D'you know, Nell, I can't remember. My poor head is going.' She sucked at her lip, making a series of complicated gummy noises. To no avail. 'Sorry, darlin'. She must have said her name, mustn't she? Hang on, now, she said the dress was green and something.' She beamed at me triumphantly. Damn.

'That's OK,' I assured her. 'I know the one. Green and gold. I'll give her a ring. Thanks Mrs Dwyer.' I slipped the number in my pocket, went and had a shower and promptly forgot about it for several days.

I could not keep any of Lily's own clothes even if I'd wanted to, they were far too small. I stand five seven in my stocking feet – a good six inches taller than Lily. Our colouring was different as well; she was dark-haired, I am fair, like my father. I shut down both mind and memory as I filled two large suitcases to overflowing. Some small person was going to have a bonanza in the local charity shop. I delivered the first lot, came home and refilled the case. I left the old suitcases behind the second time and immediately felt curiously liberated. At least now I could walk around her room without being disturbed by the whiff of her perfume.

'Chanel No 5, Chucks,' she'd say with a characteristic wink. 'What's good enough for Marilyn will do me fine.' Now I wouldn't have to risk brushing against a favourite suit or dress. Her fabrics were like her garden, a blaze of colour. Her despair at my adolescent preference for unrelieved black was, that hot afternoon, matched by mine.

There were two small chests of drawers, both made by my father, on either side of her bed. One chest was entirely taken up with underwear and stockings. When those last intimacies were bagged and binned, I called it quits for the day, walked down to the coal quay and bought some crab-claws for supper. When I got back it was already dusk.

The mind plays odd tricks, doesn't it? The house was, to all appearances, exactly as I'd left it yet, as I cooked and ate my supper, a faint suspicion that it was somehow different grew more and more persistent. I checked every room but could find nothing to justify my fear. One or two things, letters I'd been writing to the Gas and Electricity Boards asking for final accounts and my diary, might have been disturbed but so slightly that I thought I must be imagining it. I told myself I was a complete fool. I was still unhinged by the peculiar shenanigans of Messrs Hanlon and Reynolds. I sipped a glass of wine and forced myself to think about those incidents rationally.

If they were conniving with each other, then they were casing the joint.

'If that is the case then there must be something to steal,' I murmured out loud. For some reason, the sound of my own voice had a calming effect. I walked through the house, looking to see if anything struck me. There were plenty of nice things but nothing of any great value apart from the television, video and hi-fi, but these were usually the target of youngsters looking for drug money. Neither Hanlon nor Reynolds looked particularly hard up. The whole thing was definitely absurd. A figment of my imagination. Oh. So what *did* they want? What had they been up to, I asked myself? I could think of no answer to that but at least I had talked myself out of the fear of being knocked on the head by maddened drug-fiends.

I was washing the dishes when the phone rang. I froze, listened to its shrill pulse, ten, twelve times. When I picked up the receiver, the caller had already clicked off. I cradled the receiver and was on my way back to the kitchen when it rang again.

'Nell? Where the hell have you been? I've been trying to get you for days.' Davis didn't sound too pleased. 'Why don't you answer the phone? Nell? Are you there? When are you getting back? Nell? Are you listening to me?'

'I'm afraid Miss Gilmore isn't here.' I amazed

myself with my very best Cork lilt. 'Can I take a message?'

'I'll ring back,' was all he said, so I knew he'd recognized my voice. I sat reading for a couple of hours waiting for him to ring again but he didn't. Nor were there any other disturbances. I drank a couple of long cold glasses of lager and, by the time I went to bed, I'd convinced myself that it was only the day's activities which had disturbed me.

It was quite late when I woke. The sun was streaming in the windows as I lay quietly, thinking: this is what my mother saw when she woke up each morning. We'd decorated the room together. The walls and matching carpet were fuchsia. I'd scoffed at her choice but I had to admit she was spot on. It worked. The paintwork and ceiling were brilliant white. The sash window, which was in three sections, was not particularly large but she had made full-length, tightly gathered curtains out of white kitchen-muslin which covered the entire wall. The soft suffused light which came through them was magical.

The bed took up a good third of the room. Its cover was an old, rough linen bedspread and she'd made a headboard from the same material. The only picture in the room, apart from a zillion photographs on the mantelpiece, was a reproduction of Luini's smiling *Vergine Santa* which I had brought back from the Pinacoteca Ambrosiana in Milan, some years before. Trying to impose some sort of restraint on her taste, I had framed it simply, but Lily had subsequently found a heavy, ornate, gilded frame for it somewhere, which suited the print much better. I resolved to take it back with me with the two chests of drawers. I wondered idly if I should try to reproduce her colour scheme, then dismissed the idea; Davis would have a fit.

I scanned the jumble of photos on the narrow mantelshelf. They were almost three deep, I knew them all. The milestones of my life: toddling, walking, laughing, Christening, First Communion, Confirmation, graduation. In the sun, the snow, blue with cold at the seaside, my chattering teeth almost audible. There were one or two of my father. Lily herself was camera shy. There were none of her, I knew. That's when my eye came to rest on a small silver frame I had never seen before. The only thing I could make out was Lily's distinctive white hair. I leapt out of bed too quickly, tripped and stubbed my toe against something concealed by the floor-length curtains. An agonizing jab of pain shot up my leg. I sat on the floor, rocking back and forth, until the pain subsided, then leaned forward and pulled aside the curtain and laughed with pleasure.

It was the chariot. When I was little, I used to push my cat around in it. It was small and square with wheels on either side and made out of an ancient butter box – or so I was told – with worn red leather padding around the edges. I used to pull it along with a bit of string. The cat wasn't so enthusiastic. He hated it almost as much as he hated being dressed in doll's clothes. He left home eventually, and never came back.

The wheels were gone. I bent down to pick it up. The curious thing about lifting a familiar object is

170

that you exert just enough leverage to match the weight. But the box didn't budge, and my hands flew up with nothing in them. I lifted the little cushion which fitted snugly into the top space and found a wooden lid had been recessed a couple of inches, precisely fitted, beneath the leather padding. Two brass screws held it firmly in place. I tried to rock the little seat, but it didn't move.

The phone rang while I was searching, vainly, for the screwdriver. A rather imperious voice commanded that I deliver the gold and green dress ASAP. When I demurred, she mentioned her fruitless journey of three days before, suggesting that I owed her a quid pro the quo. I was so taken with this quip that I jotted down her address and promised it by the morrow. She didn't thank me.

'I should think so too. It's already paid for. I always pay in advance.' She rang off without leaving a name.

I abandoned my search. The only screwdriver I could find was a tiny electrical one – not nearly strong enough. The local ironmonger was a good ten-minute walk away. I went back upstairs to dress. Oddly enough, in the excitement of finding the chariot, I had, for the moment, forgotten the photograph. As I slipped on my blouse, I found myself staring at it again.

It showed Lily and an unknown companion, taken within the past three years. It was easy to date because she'd had her hair cut in a bob about then. They were outside a cafe whose name was cut off. I thought it might be somewhere in Richmond, but I had to admit it wasn't anywhere I recognized. She was sitting sideways to the camera, shading her eyes from the sun and smiling across the debris on the table at a man wearing a Panama hat. One hand was shading his face, making it impossible to identify him. I took the photograph out of the frame but there was nothing written on the back. I looked at it carefully, trying to figure out where it was taken. The background gave very little away. Just a hanging basket of flowers against the outline of the cafe window. I must have stared at it for half an hour before I copped on to the reddish blur of a double-decker bus, reflected in the glass. Irish buses are usually green.

What upset me most was the man. He was clearly not one of Lily's loony chance acquaintances, the scene was too relaxed and intimate. It was the only photograph of herself that she'd either kept or displayed. Her wedding photo was missing. I felt terrible. She looked radiant. I got dressed and went down to Dun Laoghaire to buy a screwdriver.

CHAPTER FIFTEEN

A couple of tiny leather tabs had been attached on either side of the lid so that it lifted easily out of the box. Beneath it, a small knitted blanket was neatly folded to fit snugly against the edges. I laid it on the bed and then pulled out the brown paper package which filled the remainder of the space beneath. It was about eighteen by twenty-five centimetres and, for its size, surprisingly heavy. The stout black tape which bound it was tightly knotted which necessitated another frenzied search for something to cut through it. Since I had already given away Lily's dress-making shears, I made do with a kitchen knife which reminded me that I had made no decision about what I should do with my mother's kitchen equipment. This kind of distraction had rather overtaken me since my decision to stay on in Dublin. I found it hard to concentrate. One minute I would rail against the fates, the next panic about what was happening in the office – Jen's last couple of phone calls had hinted that Roger might be up to something. Most irritating of all, I would tackle some urgent task then drift away to do something entirely unnecessary. I'm not normally so scatterbrained and it infuriated me. There were a million things to do before I went back to London, and all I could do was skulk in the bedroom.

I settled myself on the bed and, in some

anticipation, cut the tape, pulled open the wrapping and revealed a small white cardboard box in which were two thick leather-bound books, elaborately decorated with gold. I could not have been more surprised. Books? Lily never read much. Magazines and newspapers yes, books no.

'I just never got in the habit, Chucks,' she'd say, shrugging her shoulders. More to the point she never had time. I always wondered how her eyes held out with all the sewing. Perhaps because she didn't further strain them with extensive reading? I sat staring at the books for minutes while my hands caressed the beautiful smooth leather, following the intricate indentations of gold with the tips of my fingers. As I traced the centre motif, I gradually realized that it was an interlocked L/M.

Why did I hesitate to open them? Books are for reading. Surely the natural thing would have been to turn the pages? But I found I could not. The neat way they had been parcelled up and hidden proclaimed the intentions of the concealer. If she went to so much trouble to hide them, had I the right to violate her secret? As objects they were quite stunning, the rich, mellow colours of the skins wonderfully complementing the gold decoration. Deep rich red and blue. Her favourite colours. I laid them side by side on the bed then picked up the blue. As I stared, a little grouping of letters crowning the initials swam into focus: *MCMXL* 1940. The red was dated *MCML*.

I rotated the blue book edgewise in my hand. All three sides were gilded. For the first time I fully appreciated the word *tactile* in reference to books and saw why such bindings were valued. Why, before the advent of paperbacks, people could sit for hours smoothing these pleasing objects with their hands until they were burnished by time and affection.

My heart pounded as I opened it, turning each page gingerly as if I was afraid it would explode at my touch. *Incomparable Lily, the first ten years*, read the dedication on thick, smooth, creamy paper. Inside the leaves were quite different. It appeared to be a diary, the fragile pages written in different hands; sometimes sprawling and childish, interleaved with neat italic. The paper was marked and worn, the writing blurred. Where the ancient creases had been carefully smoothed, there were tiny cuts and tears. The state I was in, I did not try to decipher a word but turned the flimsy pages to the end. It was cheap, copy-book stuff whose edges had been trimmed, sometimes cutting into the words. The last entry was dated 31 May 1951 yet the date on the cover just said 1940. I flicked through looking for other dates, but those I found followed no notable pattern. I came back to the dedication: *The first ten years*.

I shut my mind. Its implications were too momentous for me. My mother was, after all, my mother. The diary ended with a blank page dated 31 May 1951. Odd, I thought, wondering what it signified. The other diary ended 31 May 1961. It was both intriguing and baffling. Somewhere at the back of my mind a faint bell tingled. I dropped the book on the bed and wept.

I don't remember lying down but when I woke up I was burrowed into the pillows and my eyes were puffed and smarting. It was past two o'clock and I had promised to deliver the gown to my mother's demanding client at three. I parcelled the diaries up carefully and was about to return them to their hiding place when my fears about the house being watched irrationally returned. I do not think that at that stage I had allowed the significance of the cache and Reynolds allegations to merge. Indeed I do not think I even half admitted that something of extraordinary significance had been going on in my mother's life for over fifty years. I did not allow myself to think at all. But thank goodness, my instincts held true.

I fixed the box back to the floor and screwed down the lid. Next, I returned its cushion and redraped the curtains around it, just as I'd found it. It was not visible from any angle and unless you fell against it, as I had, it was effectively concealed. I took the books downstairs, found an empty shoebox, padded the sides with newspaper and wedged the two books into it. As an afterthought I slipped the photograph of my mother between them. Then I parcelled it up in brown paper and addressed it to myself at *Morgen Morgen*. Before bringing it to the post office, I made a quick phone call to my PA, Jen Harper.

'A registered parcel, Jen, it's marked personal. Take it home with you, will you? For safe-keeping. It's important.'

'Sure. No problem. It's not fragile or anything, is it? You don't want me to open it to check?'

'No. Just keep it safe. Were you able to sort out the Predergast contract? And Hallsteins, have you managed to follow th . . .'

'That is very kind of you, Mr Morrow.' Jen's

pinched 'we're being overheard' tone cut me off. 'I'll pass on your compliments to Miss Gilmore, she'll be very pleased . . .' Her voice dropped to a conspiratorial whisper. 'Psst, Nell. Bloody Roger's snooping. You didn't call a meeting with Dieter on Friday, did you?'

'No. I talked to him a few days ago. Everything was fine. What meeting? Tell me what's going on, Jen?'

'Friday, ten a.m. . . . Look I'll ring tonight,' she broke off and laughed merrily. 'Why thank you, Mr Morrow. Oh? Felix then, you're very kind.'

Jen should get a job as scriptwriter, she's that good. She's not a bad actress either. Her message was clear enough. Roger Mason was obviously trying to undermine me. I closed my eyes and swayed back and forth. I could feel stress rise up my body, like toothpaste up a tube, squeezing the breath out of me. I would have to fly over first thing on Friday morning, unless I sorted it out privately with Dieter. On the other hand, it would be nice to spike Roger's guns by turning up unannounced . . .

I picked up the package and tucked it under my arm. I was not going to let Roger Mason best me, but, for the moment at least, I was more concerned with the diaries.

I realized I was behaving peculiarly. The simplest and probably the most honourable thing would have been to destroy the diaries. Unread. I stored that possibility at the back of my mind for future consideration and took myself off to the post office.

CHAPTER SIXTEEN

Upper Mount Street runs in a straight line from Merrion Square to the Pepper Cannister Church, which was once embraced by the curving arms of Mount Street Crescent. When one arm was amputated it was replaced by a modern office block which is too imposing, the wrong shape and built of a vile shade of red brick. But it's not irredeemable. On the pavement outside a bronze urchin forever maypoles the bronze lamppost. I was about to call out a greeting when I realized it was a sculpture.

I parked my car by the canal and strolled across Huband Bridge. The heat was stifling, the reflection of light on the water was almost blinding. The passing cars made a wet, sticky sound as the tarmac melted under their tyres. It felt more like the south of France than Dublin. I could not remember ever having rivulets of sweat running down my body from the exertion of a slow amble.

It was years since I had passed that way. When I got to the church I sat for a while on the steps in the shade provided by the tall Greek columns. Stretching before me was probably the finest street in the city. In the bright sunshine it was at its best. I could see right down past the greenery of Merrion Square to Leinster House. What astonished me most was the tranquillity. There were few passing cars; an occasional pedestrian. The only constant was the hum of distant traffic.

I wondered if Lily had ever sat looking at the same scene. I suppose it was then that I felt most clearly how very little I knew of her day-to-day life. The business she had built up in the years since I moved to London seemed very different from the work she used to do when I was around. Which meant, of course, that I had no knowledge of her customers or how she dealt with them. I don't know where the thought came from, but something told me that she would not have delivered her work herself. Curiosity had led me to Upper Mount Street; a desire to see at least one of the faceless ladies who wore her clothes. I wanted to catch a glimpse of Lily in professional mode, to round out my impression of her, to add another dimension to already fading memories. She had become elusive, as if her death had released her from the straitjacket of my cosy, harmless, domestic image.

The discovery of the diaries and the photograph still upset me. I was torn between wanting to know and not to know what they implied. I was afraid, even then, that I might not like what would turn up, that a little time-bomb was ticking away under me. I also knew that the real reason for posting them to Jen was not that I feared they'd be stolen but that I was simply not ready to tackle them. I didn't want to be tempted to sneak a look.

I must have sat there for quarter of an hour, letting my thoughts drift idly from the past to the future. One day, I vowed, I would come back and set up my own business. Then, in the way you do, I began to choose which of those glorious houses I would like for my own.

The one I fixed on, as chance would have it, turned out to be my target. It was the last house on the east side of the street, before it curved into the crescent. It had the advantage of south-facing windows on the gable end from which, I guessed, it would be possible to see the canal. It was in immaculate condition, imposing Dublin Georgian at its best. Lily had certainly gone up-market. I stood up reluctantly, dusted down my skirt and tripped down the steps.

A car passed just as I was about to cross the road. I stepped back and, as I looked to my right to make sure all was clear, caught a glimpse of a man disappearing around the back of the church. I had not noticed him passing and it disturbed me. Was there something vaguely familiar about that back view? Or was I just seeing things again? Hanlon and Reynolds were never far from my mind. Whenever I looked around quickly, I thought one or other of them was there, just out of vision, tailing me. It was nonsense, my nerves playing up. Feeling a complete fool, I forced myself to follow in my spectre's footsteps. There was nobody there of course, there never was. I threw back my shoulders, crossed the street and took the steps of number seven at the double.

The woman who answered the door was over six feet tall. Her age was unguessable; anything between sixty and eighty. She had strong features with huge, slightly protruding, flecked hazel-green eyes. Her steel-grey hair was pulled severely into a bunch and held at her neck with a soft black ribbon. She stood erect, excessively thin and dressed in a long, black, diaphanous skirt topped by a matching over-shirt with high neck and sleeves buttoned tightly at the wrist. Two abnormally long, narrow feet, sheathed in brilliant purple, silver-buckled, shoes protruded from beneath the skirt. I was mesmerized as much by the length and flamboyance of the shoes as by the matching sheer purple stockings which encased the thin ankles above them. My own feet, in shabby old sandals, felt like knuckles of ham. She was cool, poised and faintly amused and she had me at an immediate disadvantage.

'Who did you say you were?' she asked imperiously, as if she had not made the arrangement for me to call.

'I'm Mrs Gilmore's daughter, you called about this dress.' I indicated the black plastic coat-cover I was holding. But I didn't hand it over. I didn't think she deserved Lily's work.

'You rang me last night, if you remember. Perhaps you made a mistake? I really don't know who you are or if this really is your property.' I must have sounded as rude and as cross as I felt because she drew herself up to her full height in such a menacing way that I inadvertently ducked as if to avoid a blow.

To my intense irritation, she laughed. 'I'm not going to eat you, child,' she said, though she looked exactly as though she might. She raised her eyebrows mockingly. 'I think you'll find it's mine. The green silk Mrs Gilmore was making up for me is from the Fortuny factory in Venice. It's hand-blocked in gold. There. Does that satisfy you?' An amused chortle came from deep in her throat. 'Now, won't you come inside and show me what you've got and perhaps you'll tell me your name.' It was an order rather than a request. I did not respond.

It was the most perfect hallway, with a stunning curved staircase rising from it. Soft down-light came from an elliptical dome in the roof high above. A deep rich emerald carpet snaked from the door as far as the eye could see. The clotted-cream walls were hung with huge old gilt-framed maps. An exquisite Burmese cat licked daintly at his paws at the foot of the stairs. On the first floor landing a tall grandfather clock chimed the hour.

'How beautiful.' I couldn't help the gush. It was heavenly. I turned to hand over the dress. To be honest I felt pretty silly. And shabby. Some people have that effect; make you feel uncomfortable. Lesser. This woman, I felt, was into power. Being so immensely tall, she dwarfed me. I wondered how my poor five-foot-nothing mother dealt with her.

'Your dress. I must go, I'm afraid, I'm in rather a hurry.' I held out the dress but she ignored it.

'So soon? Don't you want to see the rest of the house?' To my discomfort, she took me firmly by the arm and led me into the drawing room. 'I was just having some iced tea. Perhaps you'd like some?' She looked me up and down. 'I find it cooling.'

There was another cat on the red sofa, a huge white Persian. The room was as beautiful as the hall but more sombre. The walls were hung with faded red silk, with matching half-drawn curtains which almost entirely excluded natural light. As my eyes became accustomed to the gloom, I saw that at least four other cats were elegantly draped around the room. They gave an unsettling impression of coiled menace. I did not like their basilisk stares which matched that of Madame as she sat before her samovar, pouring pale tea into a tall slim glass. She floated a slice of lemon and a sprig of mint on top, then slipped the glass into a silver holder.

'Sit down, sit down, my dear. Tell me about yourself,' she commanded, handing me the tea. I perched on the edge of a winged armchair, still clutching the garment bag. I was afraid I'd squash one of her moggies if I moved too far back.

'Does, did, my mother make many things for you?' She seemed surprised, faintly amused by my question.

'Over the years, yes. Rose Vavasour recommended her, if I recall, oh about twenty or more years ago. Did you know dear Rose?' She looked at me sharply. 'Or perhaps you're too young?'

'Not too young, but I only met her a few times.' I unzipped the bag. 'I believe she taught my mother to sew.' I eased out the dress and held it out to her. Her long slim hands smoothed the soft, beautiful fabric. She took the dress from me and held it against her face so I couldn't read her eyes.

'Then the pupil was better than the teacher,' she said. 'How,' her voice was quiet, muffled, 'how did your mother come to know Mrs Vavasour?' One of the cats chose that moment to leap into my lap. It gave me such a shock I dropped the tea on the carpet. I jumped up and stared at the spreading stain and then at my hostess who, ignoring my agitation, repeated the question.

'I've no idea,' I said. I had not got on in business by being gullible; something about the way she persisted warned me that an important question had been asked. It seemed innocent enough, but I was on my guard. If she was that interested, why hadn't she asked Lily? Perhaps she had. If Lily had barracked her imperious interrogations then Lily must have had good reason.

'Do sit down, my dear. I shall get something to mop up the tea. Pour yourself another glass.' She pushed open the double doors to the room beyond and disappeared.

After a few minutes' silence, I tiptoed over and peeked in. The room, as bright as the sitting room was dark; duck-egg blue and a lot of white woodwork. On a gleaming mahogany table in the centre of the room, a large tabby lay dozing. There was another stretched out beneath it. I shivered.

I was back in my seat when the 'something to mop the floor' came in, with a small plastic bucket in her hand. Without acknowledging me, an elderly maid knelt down and rubbed vigorously at the carpet after which she left as silently as she came.

'What do you think?' Madame was back, gowned in green and gold. It was a stunning dress, clearly Lily's modified copy of a Jean Muir. Naomi Campbell couldn't have modelled it better. She'd changed her shoes. They were in a slightly darker shade of green than the dress, soft suede sprinkled with tiny faceted gold studs which twinkled in the light. She noticed me staring and girlishly flicked the skirt.

'Like it?'

'I wished it were mine,' was all I could manage.

'Your mother was clever,' she said and raised here eyebrows archly. 'Very. Did she make many things for you?'

'No, not many. She needed to earn her living. I have a few things, that's all.' I laid my glass on the table.

'I suppose we didn't really pay her enough,' she spoke slowly. She watched my reaction closely. 'She will be hard to replace.'

Oh, poor you! What on earth will you do without your little dressmaker? Don't mind me, she was only my mother.

'I expect you'll be taking up where she left off?' she asked lightly but her eyes didn't blink. They bored into me. I think my mouth must have opened and shut like a goldfish.

'No. I don't sew. Will you excuse me, Mrs, er Mrs . . .'

'Hanrahan. Hanora Hanrahan. Alliteration is such a bore, isn't it? I'm usually called HC. My second name is Constance.' She inclined her head graciously. 'And yours? Ah, Nell? Nell Gilmore. I like it. My dear, don't go. If you don't sew, what do you do?' She smiled enquiringly.

'I work for a freight company.'

'Surely not as a driver?' she asked archly.

'No. The office.'

'Oh? How nice. So you inherited your mother's nimble fingers after all!'

'Sorry? Come again?'

185

'Typing, you know.' She merrily jigged her long red-nailed fingers on the arm of her chair. What made me think she knew perfectly well that I was not a typist? I glared at her stonily.

'Something like that,' I replied smoothly.

'Oh, of course. All you young people use those thingummies these days. Computers. So clever.' She made it sound like an unpleasant personal habit. There was a moment's awkward pause before she leapt to her feet.

'Come, my dear. Wouldn't you like to see the rest of the house? You seem to have an appreciative eye.' She struggled to flatter but I could see it was out of character. What game she was playing I could not begin to guess. Perhaps she was amusing herself at the expense of m'dressmaker's daughter? If so, she had underestimated Lily and she certainly underestimated me.

'I'm sorry, but I have a lot to do. Some other time perhaps?' I held out my hand. 'The dress is really beautiful, Mrs Hanrahan, Lily would be delighted, she appreciated fine things.' I deliberately fed her own words back at her. I wondered how many times she'd invited Lily to view her domain?

To my surprise she laughed and said inconsequentially: 'You know, the best dressmaker I ever had, apart from your dear mother of course, was Rose Vavasour and she had the dullest taste imaginable. Your mother was, er, slightly more colourful but then poor Rose came from the slums of Ringsend . . .' She grinned toothily. 'As I did myself, my dear, or at least quite close by.' She paused to enjoy my gob-smacked expression.'

'Funny,' she continued, 'I never did know where your poor mother came from.' She raised her eyebrows quizzically and her tone was light, but she'd overplayed her hand.

'Why on earth would you be interested?' I asked rudely, wondering if all my mother's customers were so damned patronizing.

'I just wondered. I read about the accident in the papers, it seemed such a coincidence.'

'Coincidence? How?' Déjà vu. Why was everyone so damn interested in Ringsend? 'Well, yes. As I said. I lived near there, as did Rose. I just wondered . . .' She shrugged.

'My mother was killed,' I said as quietly as I could, 'by a hit and run driver. What could be more random than that? The fact that it was Ringsend is neither here nor there. She certainly wasn't born there, she came from Sallynoggin. You know it? It's not far from Dun Laoghaire.'

It was the first place that came into my head. The truth was I hadn't a clue where Lily was born, she'd only ever said 'Dublin, Chucks, I'm a real jackeen,' but I wasn't about to offer hostages to fortune. Lily obviously hadn't confided in her customers; if she maintained a little air of mystery about herself, it was OK by me.

'I'm so sorry, my dear, I had no thought of upsetting you. I was away when the accident happened which was why I didn't attend the funeral.'

She was lying. For some reason she was lying. Or perhaps she was only being polite? In London a person would not be expected to attend her dressmaker's funeral. In Dublin, however, they would. They did. I'd met two or three old customers at the church. Or at least that is how they introduced themselves. But Mrs Hanrahan clearly hadn't thought it worth her while. Why then was she rabbitting on?

'I only heard about it three days ago from Sinead Flynn. You know Sinead, of course? Hasn't quite the talent of her dear mother . . . Or yours,' she said, in a voice which sounded like Mrs Thatcher at her most insincere. 'I hope you'll forgive me for not being there?' She held out her hand and grasped mine, drawing me slightly towards her. I felt I was being embraced by a Praying Mantis. Though preying seemed nearer the Mark.

'Promise you'll come back? I give some good parties. In the autumn? When the Dáil is back in session. There'll be lots of interesting people. And a pretty girl is always welcome. Do say you'll come. I'm sure you'd enjoy one of my Thursday evenings. When will . . .'

She was off. But then, so was I.

'I'm sorry,' I said. 'I don't live in Dublin. I'm going back home in a few days.'

'Oh. Well, next time perhaps?' she said vaguely as if she'd already lost interest. We murmured our goodbyes. I shook a limp hand. As I followed her into the hall she turned so abruptly I almost crashed into her.

'You forgot to collect payment.'

'But . . . I'm sorry, I don't understand. You said your account was up to date. When you phoned last night.'

'Did I? Heavens above, I must have been dreaming. I have it all ready. You just wait, my dear. I won't be a moment.'

She disappeared up the stairs leaving me standing like a beggar waiting for a handout. She wasn't just into power, the bitch, she was into humiliation. I had my hand on the door-handle when she called me back. I turned and looked up as she sauntered down the stairs, gently slapping a thick white envelope against her wrist. Her strange unblinking eyes never left mine as she handed me the envelope.

'Final payment then, my dear?' She leered toothily, the arched eyebrows mocking, mocking. Almost as if the payment was for *me*, not Lily. Or was this yet another of my paranoid fancies? I blushed scarlet but couldn't bring myself to thank her.

'I shall miss your dear mother's little visits. And, of course, her beautiful sewing. I don't know what I shall do without her. Goodbye, my dear. So good of you to deliver my beautiful dress so efficiently.' She laughed gaily. 'But then, you are in the freight business, aren't you?'

I felt like treading on her long elegant foot and grinding it into the ground. But I kept my dignity. I was almost at the bottom of the steps when she called after me. 'My dear! You forgot to give me your address. For my party.'

I looked up at her and gave her my most dazzling smile.

'I'm sorry, Mrs Hanrahan, I don't have my business card with me.' I waved at her jauntily and legged it before she could come up with anything else. For the life of me I couldn't think what she wanted my address for. Parties, my eye.

I sat with the car door open for several broiling minutes. Even with the fan turned on full, and the windows down, the heat was stultifying. I went over and over what madam had said. I sensed a hidden agenda but I hadn't a clue what it was. She'd said she'd settled her account, so why had she produced the envelope? I opened it and counted the crisp ten pound notes and was amazed to find they came to five hundred pounds.

Oh God. I leaned back and closed my eyes, hot with shame. I had misjudged her. She was, however back-handedly, trying to be kind. She must have thought I'd not been able to meet the funeral expenses. One or two of my mother's other friends had shuffled anxiously around that vexed question until I reassured them. So why not her? Perhaps the heat was getting to me but, during that fraught visit, I'd had the distinct impression Mrs Hanrahan disliked Lily. Or did not quite trust her. Which made us quits because try as I might to dismiss my suspicions I had to admit that I both disliked and mistrusted Mrs Hanrahan. Was it simply that I hated being the recipient of what I saw as charity? Perhaps, after all, she had meant what she said. That, having checked, she realized that she still owed my mother a whopping five hundred pounds. It seemed rather a lot for one dress, however beautiful. Still, it would be easy to check. The bank had sent on my mother's statements and her accounts book was still in the house. I thought I

190

might spend the evening doing a little detective work.

Then, as I turned the ignition, I had a brainwave. Or to be exact, two. I did a neat U-turn and headed in the direction of Ringsend.

CHAPTER SEVENTEEN

Daedalian Road yielded me no answers, at least not that day. I still couldn't understand what had drawn my mother to such a dismal place, unless she'd simply been using it as a short cut between Sandymount and Ringsend. Or vice versa. I did not know, nor had I thought to ask, in which direction she was travelling. I suppose the policeman must have told me, but I could not remember exactly where on its length she'd been knocked off her bike.

It's a long road which starts at the Dodder River at Newbridge Avenue. It crosses Londonbridge Road before ending at Bath Street which is between Irishtown and Ringsend. The railway line runs along it, making a loop between Landsdowne Road and Lotts Road stations. I drove along slowly and estimated that I clocked-up just over a half mile. At the Sandymount end there is a row of ten or twelve mean, utilitarian, houses dating from the fifties, then some lock-up garages. The road undulates gently but has a sharp turn in the middle section where there is a triangular development of low-level office blocks, all of which were empty and vandalized with For Sale notices plastered all over them. They looked as though they also dated from the fifties, monuments of crumbling grey concrete with rusting, thin-framed metal windows, painted the inevitable green. Even on such a bright sunny day they looked deeply depressing. With so much concrete, grey was the predominant colour. I could imagine what it looked like on wet days: Grey skies, grey rain, grey sea, grey roads, grey buildings. Really cheerful. After the deserted industrial estate there was an apology of a playground where a couple of youngsters were sharing smokes in the shade of a stunted sycamore. After that the houses deteriorated steadily into Ringsend. Only one side of the road was built upon, the railway line ran almost the full length of the other.

I parked my car close to the playground and walked slowly, first in one direction then in the other. Trains passed constantly, Lotts Road Station was close by. Dun Laoghaire station, on the same line, is no more than a seven minute walk from our house. Since my mother was something of a DART enthusiast, and since, as a pensioner, she travelled on it free, it seemed very perverse of her to have cycled five or six miles. She must have had some pressing reason for using her bike.

I was aware that the kids in the playground had been watching me. I walked back to them and asked them if they knew anything about the accident. They stared at me sullenly without answering. Then, as I turned away, one of them shouted after me, 'D'ya mean when the auld one was knocked off her bike? She was lying there for ages, me Da said. We wasn't here at the time,' he added as if I might accuse him.

'Do you know where it happened?' I asked.

'Yeah.' His companion stood up. 'There. In front of them factories, me Da said. Near the lamppost.'

She pointed to where the road curved off to the left.

'Thank you.' I could hardly speak for the lump in my throat. They came towards me, suddenly interested. They looked like clone stick-men, the two of them in scruffy black jeans and Doc Martens. The only difference between them was that the girl's dyed hair had several strands plaited with beads and her dark eyes were caked with kohl. Cheerful they weren't, but they still managed to look good.

'Did you know her, miss?' The boy looked at me curiously. I nodded, not trusting myself to speak.

'Would ya like a smoke?' Crossing my fingers against plagues and diseases, I took the butt-end from his outstretched hand and let him light it for me, then all three of us sat, companionably inhaling, on the edge of the pavement. It was the first cigarette I'd had in ages.

'Do you come here a lot?' I asked.

'Yeah. Nuthin' else to do . . .' They exchanged guilty looks and laughed.

'I just wondered if you'd ever seen her. The woman who was killed. She had a little white dog. Sometimes she drove.' I pointed at the Renault. The girl, who looked about twelve or thirteen, got up and walked around the car. She stood in front of it for a long time, swinging her leg back and forth. Then she shook her head a little uncertainly.

'She wore very bright clothes. Not like an old woman. Red, blue, pink,' I called. She didn't respond, instead she continued to walk solemnly around the car.

'Here, Pete.' She beckoned her companion, they

stood closely together, whispering. Then, with a great peal of laughter, she opened the driver's door and settled herself at the wheel. At which point I remembered I'd left the keys in the ignition. I shouted at them to stop. Pete, who was hopping up and down with glee, punched the air with his clenched fist.

'Yeah. Nice one, Jackie!' The girl jumped out of the car and they did a little dance in the middle of the road. She laughed as she dropped the keys in my lap. 'Ya wouldn't want to be doing that around here, miss,' she said. 'Nice car but.' She laughed again. 'I wasn't going to rob it, honest. I can't drive.' She seemed to find herself hilarious.

'You didn't answer my question.'

'Sorry, miss. We never saw the old lady. Nor the car neither.' She shrugged, her voice a little less sure on this last point.

'We might have,' the boy added kindly, 'but we don't remember. Does it matter?'

'I don't suppose so ... I just wondered,' I started.

Jackie, who was still staring at the car, suddenly grabbed my arm. 'Hey, hey! I remember. She drove right in the middle of the road, didn't she?' She spoke triumphantly and did another of her little dances. 'Nutty. White hair, like the dog. Oh, sorry miss. She had white hair?'

'Yes. Cut like this.' I described a page-boy with my hands.

Jackie nodded vigorously. 'Yeah, yeah, yeah. 'Member, Pete? It's ages ago. It was teemin' down with rain. Yeah, come on, 'course you remember. The dog was sittin' in the front seat. He had his

paws on the side window. He was lookin' out.'
They giggled at the memory.

Pete said: 'Ah right, right. Yeah. Right. I remember now. It was nearly dark. We were shelterin' from the rain. She stopped for a minute under the light there. That's when we saw the dog. We fell over with the laughin'. Drove him bananas. He started barkin'.' He turned to the girl. 'Did we ever see her again, Jack?'

She bit her lip while she considered that but then slowly shook her head. Pete made an expressive, plaintive gesture with his hands. 'Sorry, miss.'

'Hang on a second.' Another thought struck me. 'Was she looking at a map or anything?'

They thought about that a long time as well. Jackie squidged up her eyes as if she was trying to visualize what she'd seen. Eventually they turned to each other and like a pair of Siamese twins, shook their heads.

'Don't think so, might have, but she seemed to be jus' sittin' there lookin' up the road.' Pete pointed in the direction of Sandymount.

After that we all three fell silent. I stood up to go, then Jackie thought of something. 'She did the same as you.'

'What?'

'The day we saw her, she got out of the car and walked up the road, past the turn, then she walked back again.' She shrugged. 'We never saw her after that. She jus' drove off. Middle of the road.' She giggled again and looked at me for approval.

I gave them a fiver and a lift down to Irishtown, then took myself off for an hour's walk along the wet, cool sand of Sandymount. I headed for home when the tide turned. No matter how many times I turned it over in my mind, I could make no sense of Lily's preoccupation with Daedalian Road. It was a dump whose fascination for her was impossible to fathom. Nor could I figure out the significance of that other visit; by car. I tried to tell myself that she had merely used the road en route to somewhere else. To a customer? It was at least a lead I could follow through her appointments book or her accounts. I teased that out for a few minutes but it didn't wash. It troubled me that the children had seen her stop at almost the precise spot where she had subsequently been killed. It was just too much of a coincidence that I had instinctively stopped at the same place. Chilling even. Perhaps the policeman had told me where the accident had happened, but I could dredge up no memory of that at all.

I was idling at the level crossing at Merrion when I surrendered to my second brainwave. I crossed the line, headed back towards the city and turned left at Ailesbury Road for Donnybrook Garda Station.

Detective Inspector Moran passed me as I pressed the Enquiries bell. I didn't recognize him at first but he turned his head when I asked for him at the desk. He did a sort of double take, as if he was mentally running through his files, then he came back towards me and held out his hand.

'Miss, Miss, er, Gilmore? Isn't it?'

'Yes. Inspector Moran, I wondered if I could talk something over with you. It won't take long.'

'Is it official?'

'No. No. Just something I'm a bit worried about.

I really only want to put my mind at rest.' Talk about not knowing what you think until you hear what you say. I shied away from the realities that were crowding in on me. To my relief, Inspector Moran didn't seem to notice.

'In that case why don't you join me in Kiely's? It's quiet this time of day and I could murder a Guinness. My office is like a furnace. No fans.' He grinned and steered me to the exit. 'The heat's desperate, isn't it? We're just not used to it, are we?'

He asked me what I'd like to drink. I ordered a soda. My tongue was hanging out for a long, long cold gin and tonic, but I didn't want to be arrested for drunk-driving by my drinking companion. He held out his cigarettes and, when I declined, he lit up and inhaled pleasurably while I marshalled my thoughts. He was as silent as he'd been the day I identified my mother's body. I found it hard to judge his age; somewhere in his fifties, I supposed. He must have been quite handsome once but now his face was mottled and slightly bloated. Blood-shot, opaque, brown eyes. His grey hair receded well back from his forehead which gave him a rather kindly, quizzical look. But his still quality was hard to resist. Which was why, when he'd told me my mother's death was an accident, I had believed him so firmly. I assumed that if he had doubts, he would have done something about them. Now the unkindly thought passed through my mind that his silence might indicate no more than indolence; the man might just like a quiet life, fag in one hand, pint of Guinness in the other.

'I'm worried that my mother might have been

killed,' I said abruptly. He jerked his head back in surprise and raised an eyebrow. 'Intentionally, I mean.' He took that aboard for rumination. I was already feeling a bit of a fool when, after a considerable pause, he sighed. His enthusiasm wasn't exactly overwhelming but he was, at least, polite.

'How so?'

Now it was my turn to keep quiet but only because I wanted to tell it simply and in order. I didn't want to sound deranged. I didn't believe he'd give me a second chance. 'Several things: A man accosted me the day after the funeral and said he thought my mother was murdered.' Sergeant Moran's eyebrows rose again and I thought I detected a slight twitch of his lips.

Then he surprised me. 'You said several things,' he said quietly. 'Just tell me what you're most afraid of, tell me what's made you believe your mother was, er, murdered. That is what you believe, is it?'

'I'm not sure I'd go as far as belief,' I said slowly.

He took a long draught of his stout before he spoke again. 'This is informal, right? You're not accusing anyone, are you?'

'No. I just want to sort things out for myself.'

'Well, then. Just tell me what happened to you. Just say it as it comes.' He smiled. 'I'm a good listener.'

He was. I told him as simply as possible about Arthur Reynolds and Hanlon and my suspicions that one or other of them, perhaps both, had been nosing around the house. When I mentioned that once or twice I had the vaguest feeling, and I didn't put it stronger than that, of someone being in the house when I was out, he asked about my neighbours and suggested, mildly, that it might have been Mrs Dwyer looking for something for the dog. After all, she had a key, hadn't she? Because he was slightly brusque I censored the references to Reynolds's father and his claim that my mother knew him because it all sounded such gobbledy-gook. Nor did I mention the diaries; they didn't seem immediately relevant and they were private, though even then that half-familiar date was nagging my memory. I could justify the omission because I hadn't read them. At that point I also held back on Mrs Hanrahan. Instead I described my journey to Daedalian Road and what the children said. He sat up at that all right.

'You're driving, are you?' He drained up his glass. 'One drink will do you no harm. What would you like?'

I asked for a gin and tonic. With ice and lime. He threw back his head and roared with laughter. 'Tell you what, if they have a lime in the house, Miss Gilmore, I'll get you a double. Would you be content with lemon otherwise?'

'Now. What are you not telling me,' he asked quietly when we were both settled with our drinks. When I started to protest he held up his hand.

'Your mother was seen in Daedalian Road, exactly where she was killed. That is a big coincidence. It's worth thinking about, at the very least. But it's only one thing. We'll get back to

Hanlon and Reynolds in a minute. Was there anything else?'

I told him then about my visit to Upper Mount Street and tried to put into words the feeling I had that Mrs Hanrahan had been probing me for information. It all sounded pretty lame. That's where I lost him.

'Ringsend? She asked you about Ringsend? About your mother's accident?'

'No. That's what was so peculiar. She seemed to be just making small talk, asking me where my mother was born. I don't think I would have noticed it except that Reynolds and Hanlon did too.'

'Did what?' he spoke impatiently.

'All of them mentioned Ringsend. In reference to her childhood. Not her death. With Hanlon and Reynolds I thought they were trying to make me think they knew her ...' Our eyes met and I saw my own doubts magnified. 'I'm not making much sense, am I?'

'Not a lot. But it's not an easy time for you. Sudden death is a desperate shock in any circumstances. It takes us different ways.' He sucked at a back tooth and regarded me steadily. 'Ringsend isn't the worst place in the world, you know. Not nowadays. And your mother didn't do too badly from it, did she? So why are you reacting to it so strongly? Did she not like to be reminded of her origins? Is that it?'

I counted to ten before I replied, but I couldn't control a spurt of annoyance at the amateur psychology. 'We're not talking about what my mother did or didn't think, Inspector Moran, we're talking about me.'

'Quite.' He pulled deeply on his cigarette and squinted at me through the smoke.'

'Are you saying I'm over-reacting?' I was almost relieved but my voice must have bristled.

'Calm down, Miss Gilmore, calm down. Look, you're worried, your mother isn't long dead. You're still very upset.' He held up his hand against my only half-stifled protestations. 'I've had a lot of experience of death. People don't feel comfortable with it. Often, they say the first thing that comes into their heads. They knew your mother came from Ringsend, she was knocked down there. A horrible coincidence. Nervous, that sort of thing makes people nervous. Honestly.' His tone had softened, he seemed genuinely concerned.

'A friend of mine,' he continued, 'had a heart attack the other day. Now, what do you suppose was the first thing I said, when I went to see him in hospital? "I nearly died of a heart attack on the bloody stairs." The man is dying.' He raised his eyes in despair. 'Nerves. And guilt. He's dying and I'm on sixty a day.' He stubbed out the cigarette. 'Do you see what I mean?'

'Yes. I see what you mean.'

'But you're not buying it, eh?'

'I'm not sure,' I said. It was at least partially true. He had planted a doubt. My reactions were all over the place, My highly organized life was in tatters. Perhaps I was looking for someone to blame for Lily's death? Trying to make sense of the senseless?

'Look, it's no wonder you're worried with strangers hanging around.' Moran broke in on my

202

thoughts. 'I *would* worry about *that*. I'll see if I can find out anything about those two buccaneers. You're probably right about them. There's been a terrible spate of burglaries recently. Associated with deaths. Sometimes when the actual funeral is going on. It would only disgust you. There was a case up in Terenure last month when a removal van turned up and the place was stripped bare while the family were at the graveyard. You'd scarcely credit it, would you? That's why we recommend someone stays behind in the house. What about your mother's place?'

'I'm selling it as soon as I can. Most of the furniture as well. It's in the hands of the auctioneer. I live in London. It would be impossible to look after it properly.'

'It's for the best,' he mumbled. 'You did well to get their names. Now can you give me a description of them?'

He took notes in a tiny notepad and nodded encouragingly when he slipped it back in his pocket. 'Excellent, excellent. I wish everyone was as observant as you.'

'God,' I burst out. 'I can't believe I was so gullible.'

He patted my arm avuncularly. 'Easily done, easily done.'

'They looked so respectable.' Even as I said it, I knew I didn't really believe his explanation. My head told me he could be right but my gut said otherwise. I think that might have been the moment that I started knitting all those maverick little incidents into some coherence. I became so preoccupied that I didn't notice he'd started talking again nor did I immediately catch the drift of his remarks. I just noticed that his voice had hardened.

'. . . so be careful what you say about Mrs Hanrahan. You've been abroad a long time, haven't you? I can tell from your accent. Maybe you've forgotten what it's like here. Dublin can be surprisingly small, you know. And defensive. Everyone knows everyone. She's a respectable businesswoman, well known, very successful. She's got a lot of influence where it matters. She's involved in every major charity in the country and half the government is in her pocket. A big noise, she is. You didn't know that?' He sounded somewhat incredulous.

'No.' What else could I say? It sounded like a warning, however mildly expressed. I'd obviously put him in an awkward position.

'Did your mother know her well?'

'She sewed for her. I didn't get the impression it went further than that.'

'No. I can quite see that. I've come across her myself, once or twice. Unfortunately. An imperious bitch, if you'll excuse the expression.' His conspiratorial grin didn't restore my confidence. We both sat in silence until I offered to refill his glass.

'No, thank you. I'm afraid I have to push on.'

He looked at me as if he wanted to make amends. 'Miss Gilmore, I know this is very painful for you but let me just make our position clear. Your mother's death is still under investigation. The car that hit her was damaged, there was some debris around the scene. I don't have to tell you that it takes a long time to contact every repair shop in the country but if we have to do that, we will. So far we're concentrating on Dublin; we started those inquiries immediately. We take hit-and-run deaths very seriously indeed. But it's not a murder investigation, at least not yet. I take note of your doubts but, quite honestly, I don't think you've given me anything remotely substantial. Now,' he leaned towards me, emphasizing his remarks by repeatedly stubbing his finger on the table, 'if you can come up with more supporting evidence, anything, anything at all, then you must get in touch. *Immediately*.'

'I'm sorry for wasting your time,' I muttered.

He looked at me sadly. 'If I've made you feel like that, I'm sorry.' He spoke earnestly, perhaps even a little apologetically. 'You are perfectly right to distrust those two fellows, I've already promised that I'll see what I can dig up on them. I have their names and you've given me a good description.' It must have occurred to us both, at the same time, that the names might not be their real ones because we turned to each other, wide-eyed, but neither of us said anything.

We parted at the pub door, he hopped on a passing bus heading into the city while I joined the traffic streaming out of it. It might have been the gin but I was certainly calmer. I drove home slowly and with as much concentration as I could muster, pushing away the thought that I was being taken for a stranger in my native city. I felt like getting the hell out, not just going to London for a few hours, as I intended to do next day, but permanently. I resolved to get my business finished as quickly as possible and do just that.

I stopped to pick up a pizza in Monkstown and it was almost seven-thirty by the time I rolled into Swift Terrace. By now the effect of the gin had worn off, I was feeling absolutely jaded and thoroughly disgruntled. I picked up my greasy package and pushed open the gate and only then took in the tall, dark-suited figure leaning against the door, his face coyly hidden behind a huge bunch of roses. A frigging re-run. Except this time they were red.

'Hi darling.' Davis Marcham, my best beloved, sporting a glorious tan, kissed me fondly on the lips and held out the flowers. I shoved them straight back and dumped the pizza slap against his Armani chest. He stepped back, protesting vehemently. I ignored him.

'Hold that,' I said rudely, 'till I find my key.'

He followed me into the kitchen, threw the pizza box on the table and went back to the porch to collect his overnight bag. Gucci, wouldn't you know. I stood looking at him, as he strode into Lily's pristine kitchen and saw him, really saw him, for the first time. The petulant mouth, the gorgeous, handsome, sexy body, the intelligent face, smiling in anticipation. Poor sap. The surroundings were wrong for him, he didn't look right. At least he didn't look right for me. I wondered, not for the first time, what the hell I was doing with him.

'Now, my darling,' I said sweetly, 'perhaps you'll explain why it took you so long to come and pay your respects?'

'My what?'

'Not your respects? Sor-ry. What then?' All of a sudden I was seething.

'Nell! What is this? Stop arsing about. Aren't you pleased to see me?'

'That's usually my line,' I countered, ironically. Sexy beast. 'As a matter of fact, I'm not. Not in the least pleased to see you, Davis. Specially since I have to catch the first flight to London in the morning.'

'London? You can't do that. I've only just arrived.'

'Afraid I must, old love. No choice. I have a fight on my hands with Roger Mason. He's trying to muscle me out of my job. I need to sort him out. As well.' He completely missed that crack. I've always been too subtle for him.

'But I'm here for the weekend. I took the day off tomorrow, specially.'

Big bloody deal. But I couldn't bring myself to comment. I just stood staring at him, thinking of my own agenda for once. I hardly took in what he was saying.

'You're having me on, aren't you? You can't go back. I was really looking forward to it. Come on, Nell, I've missed you, sweetie. Come here.' He took me masterfully in his arms. He did feel heavenly. Well, excited anyway. Which made two of us, the bastard could turn me on at will. God, the humiliation. I broke away and stood leaning against the table, considering. He watched me, a half smile on his handsome mug. He was very sure of himself, was Davis.

'Why didn't you tell me you were coming home, Sweet? I needn't have come. I could have booked a nice weekend for us somewhere. Had a relax.'

'Tell you what. Why don't you do that? You can

come back on the early flight with me. My meeting will be over by noon.'

'OK.' He began to cheer up. 'OK. Where would you like to go?' I did mention he's a stockbroker, didn't I? Money no object. And of course, he lives in my flat so his living expenses are on the low side. But he's great for treats. Funds are for fun is the motto. Terrific for Sundays, just not so hot for the daily grind.

'Sorry. Not me, darling. Just you. I have to come straight back here for a while. I'm selling the house. But I think you should have a nice contemplative weekend. Alone. Sorry, love.' I grinned bitchily, loathing myself. Being good at sarcasm doesn't make it likeable, even to oneself.

He began to laugh until he realized I was serious. I enjoyed watching the anger rise in a deep flush from the edge of his collar until it reached his forehead.

'You're a complete bitch sometimes, you know that? Why didn't you ring? Have you any idea what the air-fare to this bloody country is? I've just spent a fortune getting over here. I thought I'd be a help . . .'

'A fortnight late? Really? A help? Wow. How *did* I manage, all this time?'

'Oh, come off it, Nell. You can't lay that on me now. I offered to come. It was you who insisted, *insisted*, that I stay on in Mallorca.' He held his head on one side and simpered: '*Oh Davis, darling. No need for you to come. I can manage.* Or are you going to deny it? No? Well then.' He glared at me furiously.

'I admit it. But I thought . . . oh well who knows

what I thought? That you'd just come anyway? That you'd be here for me? I was upset! I don't know what I expected or wanted. Not this, anyway.'

I felt like bursting into tears. I wanted to be strong, to break free. Or better still to make a fresh start on more equable terms. Trouble was our relationship was based on sex, otherwise we lived totally separate lives. Those were the rules. But we'd both made them. Now I wanted to change them unilaterally. I could see trouble ahead, no doubt of it.

'Why don't we have a meal and talk about it?' I asked in a small voice.

'Not that bloody mess!' He slid the greasy pizza box across the table at me.'

'No, not that,' I said in a more reasonable tone. 'There's a good fish restaurant about five minutes away, down at the pier. We'll go there. But Davis, we've got to sort things out.'

We didn't, of course. We drank too much and fell into bed at about midnight. I woke up at four with an unmerciful thirst and a great naked hunk sweating all over me. I got up and showered, made a pot of tea and sat for a couple of hours preparing for the meeting with Dieter and thinking about how best to shaft Roger Mason once and for all. I was in just the mood for a fight.

We flew to London together next morning with very little resolved between us. The meeting went well though, Roger got a bollocking and I flew back to Dublin on the one o'clock flight. Triumphant, but alone.

I drove straight to the Gilbert Library in Pearse

Street and spent the afternoon browsing through old newspapers. The man who brought the huge bound volumes to my table was a real old Dub. Full of chat and a fair deluge of information.

'There ya are now, miss, last week May, first week June 1941. Never a week goes by without somebody or other wanting to know about the North Strand bombing.' He looked very pleased by my startled expression. 'That's what you're looking for, isn't it?' he said with a wink and a broad grin. 'That's the lot. Y'll be grand there now.'

I got so completely absorbed in the reports of the bombing that I almost forgot what else I was looking for. The first three pages or so of each of the national papers were completely taken up with reports and pictures of the catastrophe. There were no familiar names among the dead. I had turned to page four of the *Irish Press* for the second of June 1941 when a short, boxed item caught my eye.

MAN STRUCK DOWN IN SANDYMOUNT. Following the shooting of a man in the early hours of last Saturday morning in the Sandymount/Ringsend district, the Gardaí at Donnybrook request that anyone who might have witnessed the incident or knows anything about it to come forward.

I spent a frustrating couple of hours searching through the papers of the following ten days but found nothing further.

I tried to tackle my mother's accounts that evening but I was too tired to make much sense of what I found. I finally gave up and went to bed at about one in the morning. I immediately fell into a dreamless sleep and didn't wake up until the phone rang at eleven the following morning. It was a rather distant Davis who, without much preamble, announced he was going to Hong Kong on business for a couple of months. Immediately. He sounded as if he wanted me to talk him around but I didn't. We had one of those awful conversations talking about everything but what we both wanted most to say. I think we both knew that some sort of Rubicon had been crossed but didn't feel like admitting it, or couldn't. There didn't seem to be anything between us suddenly.

'Nell? Can we sort all this out when I get back?' he asked, finally. I grunted. I still wasn't sure what I wanted.

I made a late breakfast and went back over Lily's accounts. Both sets. My mother had a rather better income than I had realized. That surprised me. She wasn't paid, as I'd expected, piecemeal. For nearly fifteen years my mother had had a regular bi-monthly income. It wasn't vast, but by comparison with her sewing charges it was quite startling. Separate account. Five hundred pounds every two months. A lot, especially since there seemed to be no explanation of it. And besides those payments there were regular, if variable, cheques which were neatly recorded, logged against items of tailoring in her accounts books. My mother had tidy amounts squirrelled away in four separate building societies, two of them in London. All in all, I was about eight thousand pounds better off than I'd realized. Which was, you might say, a rather generous widow's mite.

There was one other small surprise. Though it took me a little time to home in on it. I was closing out the utility accounts when it occurred to me to ask the telephone company if they could let me have an itemized print-out of her last couple of bills. It might help to know who she was in contact with, apart from me. She had left no clues in the house, no notes, no letters, no scribbled doodles on the phone-pad.

'We don't do it as a matter of course. It isn't coming in as a normal service till next year. There'd be a charge.'

And a few days delay, wouldn't you know.

'We'll send it out on the twenty-fourth. You should have it a couple of days after that.'

'If I came to the office now, would you be able to let me see it?' I gave her a breathless spiel about urgency and about my mother's death, I'd have thrown in the dog had I thought it would help. She let me warble on.

'Certainly,' she said politely when I'd run out of steam. 'All you had to do was ask. Bring some identification.'

I looked over the print-outs for the previous three quarters, which took me right back to the beginning of January. Lily was, as I knew to my cost, frugal with the telephone. She made very few international calls. All were to my number, except two. I checked them both. One was to Australia – her annual call to my step-brothers. The second, a long expensive call – they must have kept her hanging on for ages – was to the coach terminus at Heathrow. What to make of that was anyone's guess.

The long list of local numbers, I set aside to work through later. I sat staring into space, wondering why it didn't add up. As a rule, I rang

Lily at least twice a week. She was very careful about her phone bill. Whenever I stayed with her, I used my mobile for overseas. The firm picked up my phone bill so why should Lily pay? But in eight months she'd certainly made more than the dozen or so calls listed to my number. I could only assume she used public phones more than most. Frugal or careful? Or afraid? Or was I jumping to more conclusions?

On the evidence before me I certainly was.

At the end of the following week *Morgen Morgen* shipped my bits and pieces of furniture back to London. I put the car into the garage for servicing. When the mechanic asked if I wanted to sell it I told him I'd think about it. My last call was to the estate agent, where I left the keys of the house. I flew home on Tuesday evening. I thought it was about time I read the diaries. It was August the 21st.

CHAPTER EIGHTEEN

'I don't know what I'm supposed to be looking for,' my pal, Maria, grumbled. She turned the photograph upside down and squinted at it, shook her head then turned it right-side up again. 'It's great of your mother though. Who's the guy?'

'I've no idea.'

'Oh. Know where it was taken?' She grimaced ruefully at me as the penny dropped.

'That's what I'm trying to work out,' I answered impatiently. I took the picture from her and studied it again. 'It's not around here, is it? We'd recognize it if it was somewhere in Richmond, wouldn't we?' I asked. We nodded at each other.

'Why? Is it important?' she asked again.

'Yes, I think it might be.' I shrugged my shoulders. 'I don't really know why.' I avoided her sceptical eyes.

'OK then,' I caved in, 'I have a reason. Hang on.' I went up to my own flat and fetched the diaries. Maria had cleared away the dishes when I got back. She swooped on the beautiful bindings, turning them sensuously in her hands.

'Nell, they're gorgeous!' She made to open them but I laid my hand on hers and stopped her.

'They're her diaries. I'll let you see them some other time. Sorry.'

If I'd upset her, she was too good a friend to say. But then, she'd been humouring me since I'd got back the previous evening. And I have to confess it wasn't all that easy. I was something of a liability: moody, irascible, weepy and, worst of all, aimless. I couldn't motivate myself back to work and it made me miserable. Goaded by my friend, my latest resolution was to give myself the remainder of the week plus the weekend to pull myself together and get back to the office bright and early on Monday while I still had a job. Over supper I had, at last, managed to confide some of my worries. With her usual no-nonsense practicality, she congratulated me on Davis's departure and urged me to talk. But my feelings about Davis were still too confused and anyway I was never much sold on 'talking things through'. Instead we went back to my mother.

'Is it somewhere near your place in Dublin?' Maria asked, picking up the photo again.

'No.' I must have answered more sharply than I thought.

'OK. Don't bite my head off. Why not? Isn't it more likely if she had a friend, it would be there? Anyway,' she added curiously, 'what's wrong with her having a friend?'

'Nothing at all. I'd just like to know something about him, that's all. And it's not in Dublin.'

'How can you be so sure?'

I drew her attention to the reflection in the plate glass of the restaurant window behind my mother and her bel ami. 'See, a double-decker bus,' I said. 'Red.'

Maria drew back a little and stared at me. 'You've lost me,' she said.

'Most double-deckers in Ireland are green.'

'Like everything else,' we chorused and laughed.

'I see. Right. Good sleuthing, Nell.' She cocked an eyebrow. 'That go for Northern Ireland, too?'

'That's a point.'

'So we have only NI and the UK to worry about. Well, that narrows the field a bit, doesn't it.' She giggled. 'What about her travels, Nell? She was all over the place. Couldn't he just be one of her pick-ups?' I looked at her scornfully and she peered at the photo again. 'On second thoughts, forget it. They do look like old buddies, don't they? To say the least.' At last, her interest was fully engaged.

A second bottle of Valpolicella and about an hour later, we somehow contrived to link the man in the pictures with the diaries. There was, or to our bleary eyes, there appeared to be, a package on the table between them. We also thought we could make out something written on the side of the bus, where the long ad usually is. I don't know at what stage it was decided to get the photo enlarged but when I woke next morning there seemed to be no doubt in my mind that I must do so.

I had a half-formed idea that the man in the photo might have had some connection with my mother's death. Once the thought was lodged there it stuck; I was boiling over with 'what ifs?' There seemed to be a growing number of unanswered, uncomfortable niggling little inconsistencies in Lily's way of life. Not to mention her death.

I strolled across the street to Instaprint as soon as I was dressed. Mark, the boy who runs the small photography department, is a dab hand at enlargement. He has an amazing laser machine which colour copies in about two seconds flat. I told him to keep doubling up until the images got too blurred to be useful, expense no object. Ten minutes later, I had a sheaf of copies from six inches square to half-poster size. I went home, made myself a pot of coffee, spread the copies on the table. Then I lit my second cigarette in six months and studied them closely.

I was 50 per cent successful. The writing on the bus became more, rather than less, blurred so that was no help. But my second question was answered: it wasn't a package on the table, it was the two diaries lying on their open wrapper, with the man's hand pointing to the design on the cover. Or perhaps the date? His face was shaded both by his hat and the cup he held to his mouth. But even so, with every enlargement, the look passing between Lily and him was more and more unequivocal. Their attitude, the body-language, as they sat forever in the sunshine, spoke volumes. Not just friends; lovers. Or at the very least about to be.

Yet I couldn't recall having seen him at the funeral. Which could mean, giving him the benefit of the doubt, that he did not yet know she was dead. The death notice had been in the Dublin papers but even so most of the mourners had been contacted either by neighbours and friends or by me. Surely somebody knew the mystery man? Another possible explanation was more disturbing: he knew and chose not to turn up. Because why? Because he – slowly, slowly – because he was in some way connected with her death. It was a quantum leap but the indisputable fact was that there had been no letters from him, no personal letters at all for Lily all the time I was in Dublin.

Nor any phone calls. Did this mean the mystery-man knew she was dead and was making himself scarce because he was implicated?

I sat back, closed my eyes and rocked to and fro. Reynolds? Could he be Reynolds? I grabbed the enlargements but the thought died even as I picked them up. Reynolds was no more than five eight or nine and quite stocky, flabby almost. The man with Lily was thin and elegant. I tried to calculate his height by comparing them. He looked rather tall. But then compared to Lily almost everyone looked like the Empire State building. Still, leaving aside his height, there was simply no similarity between the two men. Thank heavens, I thought, as I set aside the photographs.

I was going to have to find Lily's pal, that much was clear. My motives were still fuzzy, my ideas as to how to go about it even more so. So I did what I'd been postponing since I first found the diaries. I made a fresh pot of coffee, lit another wonderful, amazing cigarette, settled down on the sofa and read them from cover to cover.

CHAPTER NINETEEN

The Diaries
1941–1951

No. 8. The blood was everywhere. Bombs dropping out of the sky. Dolly Brennan was screaming
her head off. I couldn't hear her, but her big gob
was wide open. My heart flew into my mouth
when I saw who she was pointing at. He didn't do
it. There were two of them with guns. The fella in
the garden, and the one on the bike. They were the
ones plugged him. Bad cess to him. I saw the guns.
I tried and tried to shout at M to run, run and then
he did. I prayed to God that old bitch Brennan
didn't notice he dropped something. I got it later.
Before the polismen got there. The old one keeps
watching me. His name's O'Keefe. I'll be careful of
him, he doesn't miss much. Martin is his helper.
Martin's no trouble. He'll look after us.

*Portsmouth 1941. It was a nightmare from begin-
ning to end, as if someone read my mind. He'd
been after Lily. She wouldn't say, but I know it.
The brute. She's only small. He'd kill her. The
bully. I was only going to warn him. Not that he'd
have taken much notice of the likes of me. He*

knew he'd destroyed us already. He just laughed when I said I wanted to work in the press after Father died. He said, 'Just you try, boy, and see what you get.' He laughed. Then he opened that filthy mouth of his once too often. 'Send that good-looking sister of yours, why don't you? I'll give her what she wants.' I can still hear his cackle when I lunged at him, he caught me by the wrists and shoved me away as if I was a bit of dirt.

No 8. I showed Mr O'Keefe where the bullet was. Now he keeps asking me questions about the 'boy in the brown suit Mrs Brennan saw'. I said I never heard of him.

I went around to the house again today. I hid in the porch of the lock-up shop where I was the morning he left. I saw his sister. She was with a man. He was very big like her and skinny. She didn't look a bit sad. I don't think she misses him at all. Or maybe she sees him every day? Maybe it's only me he doesn't want to see.

Portsmouth. The harbour is jammed with ships and craft of all sorts and sizes. And thousands of servicemen. I've never seen so many people in my life. Everyone looks the same in uniform, I can't tell what age people are. They all seem to know what they're doing. I wish I did. I'm terrified I'll run into someone who knows me. Knows about Buller. There's a lot of Irish. We sleep in hammocks strung up on the deck heads, close together. You can never get away from people and noise.

No. 8. Two whole months. I know I'll never see

him again. I was there watching. I didn't think any of them saw me but when he rode off he nodded his head like he was saying I'll be seeing you Lily. But I know he won't. He's gone for ever. I know it, I know it.

Mrs Reynolds has hair like a film star, all gold, with Marcel waves down over her ears and lovely red lipstick. When she came for the rent me Ma wouldn't come out of the room. She said I was to bring Jimmy down with me. I said he was too sick but she made me. I think she knew that poor little Jimmy would frighten the life out of Mrs Reynolds or that she'd feel sorry for us and not ask for the rent. She was right too. Isn't that funny? The woman took one look and said I was to bring it around to her next week, when the child was in bed. She meant Jimmy so I think Ma was right.

Portsmouth. I didn't think about sea-sickness. But then I didn't think, did I? I just went into the first recruiting office I saw and signed up.

'Any experience of the sea, sir?' the officer at the desk asked me.

'Well, I live close to it.'

'Just the ticket, sir.'

Now I'm in the navy. Sick as a dog. Sea-dog.

Old O'Keefe stopped coming asking questions. He kept it up for weeks and weeks but I never said anything. I seen him once or twice near their house but he didn't see me. I think. You never know with him. He sees more than he lets on. The last time he came around he gave me a shilling. I still didn't say nothing. But he knew anyway. I know he did. He said I was brave and that he admired the way I looked after Jimmy. I said why wouldn't I? Maybe he thought a shilling would get something out of me. But it didn't.

HMS Collingwood Fareham. This isn't a real ship. It's a land based ship, if you ever heard of such a thing. I'm being trained for wireless telegraphy – in between drills, helping the local farmers to pick spuds. It's wet and muddy but I like it. You get to be on your own. You can see who's coming. I wish I hadn't joined up. I could have just come and worked on the land. They're very short of people . . .

Nobody's collected the rents. All the people are saying that the Buller's missis is afraid of her life of coming around here. Mr Doyle in number ten says he'll give it to her if she shows her nose in the place. Fat lot he'd do, afraid of his own shadow, that fella. Lyrics Cotter is full of old chat. 'Not a penny piece will she get outa me,' says he. 'I'm tellin' ye. We better get ourselves orgorized,' says he. I think he means organized. You wouldn't be sure though. He's just like the rest of them never said boo to old Buller. Just yes mister, no mister kiss me arse mister. Easy for them to be brave now when it's only a woman against them. They're all old talk. But none of them talk to us.

Scotia, Ayr, Scotland. More training this time in a converted holiday camp. Thank God. I couldn't wait to get away. Out of the frying pan . . . There's a man from Dublin here. He's from Irishtown. I

222

avoid him. I've only made one friend from home.
Not from Dublin, from Achill in the west. His
name is Peader but he's called Pete. He's a native
speaker. He's trying to teach me Irish. The weather
is beautiful, so is Scotland . . .

They think I'm stupid, but I'm not. Mr Byrne was
jiggling the change in his pocket while they were all
talking. A half-crown fell out. Lyrics was shouting
at the time so he didn't notice me picking it up. I
brought it down to Mrs Heaney. She said she'd
start a slate for us. She gave me some bits of bacon
and three spuds free. Said I should make some
soup for Jimmy, that he looked half starved. Mr
Handl's shop was still closed and the blinds down.
Mrs Heaney said he was took bad with his heart a
few days after the bombing. Maybe he's gone away
too?

  Me mam won't get up. She says there's nothing
for us now that poor Buller's gone. Poor Buller
how are you. He terrified the life out of us all, now
she's pining after him. It makes me sick, so it does.
She was grand for the first few weeks. One day she
came with us to Sandymount to paddle. Jimmy
loved it. She asked me where I got the chariot but I
wouldn't tell her. I said Martin found it for me.
Martin's afraid of me Ma so he won't say
anything. She says he's soft in the head being with
the polis. She took the money I made for sewing
hems for Rose. I get sixpence for each one.

HMS Malaya . . . The holiday camp is over. This
ancient old battleship was in the battle of Jutland –
First War. Noble old thing. Bloody uncomfortable.

*The seas are huge, terrifying. I pity the poor sods in
the engine rooms. There are some Irish on the ship,
mainly from Belfast. I avoid them. They're mostly
Prods. I've a feeling that whatever they were,
they'd say they were Prods – they don't want to
be associated with us from the south. You'd
have thought that fighting for the same cause
might unify us, but it doesn't. I never thought
that Catholic could be a swear word, but it is.
Papish. I had 'Fuck the Pope' chalked on my
locker one day. Lucky it wasn't paint. You just
rub it away and say nothing. That about sums up
my life – say nothing. I've become the man from
nowhere.*

Mr Handl's dead. That's what Mrs Heaney said.
Died up with a relative in Terenure. I'm that sorry.
He was a lovely old man. There's nothing in the
house to eat and Jimmy has another cold. I think I
might be able to sell some of the ration coupons to
Lyrics. He said the butter ones were the best. We
can't buy butter anyway, so it makes no difference
to us. I told him a penny a coupon wasn't enough.

Mrs Reynolds came around two Fridays ago.
She had a little boy with her, sitting up in his pram.
He was all dressed in blue with a big sausage curl
on the top of his head. But he's not as nice as
Jimmy. He has a cast in his eye. If Jimmy had
clothes like that he'd look great. Mrs Reynolds said
his name was Arthur but she called him Baba all
the time. She said she couldn't leave him so we'd
have to pay our rent out on the steps. Rose said
she'd mind him for a few minutes but Mrs
Reynolds didn't like that, she looked as if she

thought we were going to give her nits or something. Rose said not to be minding her, that she was only afraid of us all and why wouldn't she after what happened to her man? I hadn't thought of that. That she might be afraid of us.

Sea-sick every day. I'm getting skinnier and skinnier. Thank God I don't have to look at myself. They call me Stringer. I don't mind. They give you a desperate time of it if you have any sort of unusual name. When I signed up the recruiting officer said 'Take my advice, son, call yourself Jack.' Good advice. So I'm either Stringer or Jack. I hate shipboard life. People on top of you all the time. I haven't touched a book in months. I'm terrified. Ships are so damn noisy, people everywhere. I'd give anything to sit in a green field. Alone. There isn't room to fart in peace, much less anything else. I'm terrified of talking in my sleep. I have awful dreams.

I felt too terrible to even write it. I've been working for Mrs Reynolds. At first I hated it in case she said anything about Ma. Now I just hate it. I keep myself to myself. She thinks I'm half-witted. I heard her saying that one day. I didn't mind. It left me off. There isn't much harm in her, really. And she hated old Buller, the way she talks. The house is massive. Full of furniture. She has so many pots and pans she doesn't know what to do with them. I go after dinner. At half past one. She goes in to the picture houses in the city. The Capitol or the Savoy or the Tivoli. She lives for the pictures. She's always talking about Betty Grable and Errol Flynn. She says she'd die for Errol. She leaves Baba. I'm supposed to look after him while I clean the place. It doesn't need much. I think she just listens to the wireless. I only left Jimmy with Rose the first few times. Until I got to know Mrs Reynolds's routine. She always gets home at ten past six. I leave Jimmy in his chariot in the next door garden till she goes, and put him out again just before six. I have to give Baba his boiled egg at half past five. She says he can't do without his egg, the fat lump. He can. I save as many of the eggs as I can for Jimmy. I reckon Baba can manage all right. Anyway he prefers warm bread and milk. So I'm doing him a favour. Mrs Reynolds isn't bad. Lyrics Cotter says she's a dizzy dame. He would. But I'm not going back to her. Jimmy's too sick.

Old Josh must be dead. Must be. He wouldn't let me down. His heart was bad. I have no contact. I cadged an Irish newspaper off one of the lads who'd gone to Dublin on leave. It was a week old. He says he'll always get one. If I'm interested. But then he asked me why I didn't go over on leave myself. I said my sweetheart was in London. And my family was dead. Never a truer word.

I found a great hiding place for the tools. In a little hut at the back of the empty house next door. If you climb out the skylight on the first landing you can get out on the back roof and drop down on the shed roof next door. The house is empty, all boarded up but the coal house isn't too bad. I loosened a brick in the wall and pushed the tools in. I had them all wrapped tight in newspaper and an oily rag to keep them dry then I pushed the brick back in and made a little scratch L to mark it. I should never have looked in that window. God between us and all harm but there are millions of rats in there. I didn't see them at first, I was just looking at the lovely coloured glass in the old doors and wondering if I could get it out and sell it. That's when I noticed the floor inside was moving. It was completely covered with them, all over each other, climbing up each other's shoulders like circus acrobats, to get up the walls into the floor above. Lord oh Lord there was a huge hole they were going through. I'm going to have to stuff all the holes in our place. I nearly got sick with looking at them. I wanted to scream with the fright I got. I could hardly get back up the wall and even then I had to sit on the roof for ages because Mrs Cunningham downstairs was right under the skylight gasbagging to Old Lyrics Cotter. If they once looked up they'd have seen me for sure.

British waters 1943. Nearly two years and the nightmares keep coming. Will I be forever walking down that terrible street? In my dream it's me holding a knife to his throat. One of the paring knives. I slice the skin very neatly and when I lift it away I get covered in blood. The little one comes running towards me, her arms out, screaming. She has the canvas holder in her hand and it's covered with blood as well. The woman at the window is laughing at us. Pointing and laughing.

I cannot think about it. I won't. I'm afraid to write home in case the police are still prowling around. I don't talk about home at all but nobody notices. There's a lot of hard feeling about Ireland's neutrality. I can't blame them, I'm beginning to feel the same myself. The cities here are getting a terrible pounding. The North Strand was, after all, a very small thing. There are hundreds of women and children getting killed every day of the week. Thousands. The cities are being bombed almost every night. Food is very scarce. The civilians are having a terrible time of it.

Two years and Martin is still asking about that night. What I saw. When did I do this or that or the other. He's annoying me. But I have to keep in with Rose or we'll have nothing to eat at all. I went down to Ringsend church and lit a candle in front of St Anthony's statue. I said that I'd be as good as gold for the rest of my life and not rob anything and look after Jimmy if only he found M for me. St Anthony's great for finding anything you lose. You just have to say three Hail Marys. That's what Rose said. I hadn't a penny for the candle but I lit one anyway. I said a whole Rosary. I thought that would do instead, but I suppose it was stealing. Fat lot of good it did me.

HMS Malaya 1943. We're training for something big, nobody says what, but I think we'll be leaving here soon. It's cold and wet all the time. We've been up in Scapa Flow. Now we're steaming south. I don't know how I'm going to keep going. Sometimes I'm so frightened I could scream. But we're men and we're sailors and we all put on a brave front. It isn't easy with your friends getting killed all the time. You only get to know them and they're gone. Peader bought it last month.

Ma's all out of sorts. Shouting and screaming the place down and slapping Jimmy every time he cries. I went at her with the sweeping brush. I swear to God I'll kill her if she hits him again. He's awful sick most of the time. He never stops crying. He's hungry, but the only thing he can keep down is milk. The Boylans downstairs keep complaining they can get no sleep.

I think of L all the time. I don't know when I realized I loved her, but I do. I remember the first time I saw her. She had the poor child in her arms. The first thing I thought was that she needed a good wash. I didn't notice how pretty she was until we were at the hospital and the nurse asked her was she the mother. Her pale face went rose pink – she looked like a little flower. I thought the child was hers as well. But it was the mother's all right. If you could call her a mother. And I know who the father is also. I can still see him coming at me when I said 'Why didn't you make it & SONS?'

Lyrics Cotter says we're all going to get thrown out of the houses, that they're going to be sold. He says we've to all stand together and have a lock-out. The traditional stand of the Irish people against their exploiters and suppressers. I hope I've spelt that right. Old Lyrics is full of himself. And he's a great one for getting everyone else to do his dirty work. They're getting up a committee God help us. None of them would talk to Ma. She was out all night. When I got up she was fast asleep at the table with a butt end in her hand. It burnt a hole in the table. Pity it didn't send the house up. She's gone again tonight. Jimmy's coughing awful bad. I'm afraid.

Will she tell anyone? Will she? How can I even think it? I still think of her as she was the morning I left. The holder clutched to her breast, her finger to her lips. She stood so still. Still as a statue. That is how I think of her. I wanted to run to her and take her with me. I am useless, useless.

I couldn't stick it, so I left. Anyway Jimmy's that sick I couldn't move him. I couldn't leave him. I don't know what we're going to do about the rent. Rose says to tell Mrs Reynolds I'll go back. Easy for her. What would I do with Jimmy? I thought Rose might offer but she can hardly manage Sean and the new baby with all the sewing. I wish I was dead. I don't want to spend my whole life scrounging and begging. That's what I did the other day. Took off me shoes and sat down in Grafton Street. A guard chased us away. Said he'd lock me up, next time. Jimmy was coughing something terrible. But I got three and fourpence in coppers. I swear to God I'd run away if it wasn't for Jimmy. Where would I go? What if I wasn't here when me Da got back? I'm not talking to that old St Anthony. I think I'll try St Jude. Patron saint of hopeless cases. Like me. I know me Da's never coming back. I just keep hoping is all.

I miss her so much. All the other lads talk about

their sweethearts all the time. Go to see them on leave. And what do I do? Skulk away in London. Sometimes I think I want to get blown to smithereens. When we get back I make up stories. About how my girl is driving an ambulance. I've managed it so far. I feel ridiculous.

Rose and Martin are trying for a corporation house. It's nearly in the bag. Martin says he knows someone with pull that can get them on the list. I'm not sure what list. He's out of the guards for ages, he drives a bread van for Boland's.

I'm learning to do french seams. Rose is making lovely nighties out of some old stuff her mother gave her. She says it's real linen. Looks like an old sheet to me. Anyway I'm doing the side seams. She said the other day that I've the nimblest fingers she ever saw. I love sewing with Rose. She's a bit bossy but she never shouts. I hope she never moves.

I think of her all the time. Did I ever think of her as a little girl? I don't think so, not from the first day when we were walking to the hospital. The sun came out for a minute and she smiled up at me with such trust as I've never seen. I've made a drawing of her face and I keep it with me all the time. She's nearly eighteen now. I wish, I wish. I think Mr Handl's dead. That means that L doesn't know if I'm alive or dead. There's something else. Something so terrible I can't think about it. I'll never see her again.

Ma's been gone for ages. Someone saw her way over in Amiens Street the other day. I won't repeat what he called her. She didn't like us but I miss her all the same. Jimmy's been awful sick again. He had me up all night with the coughing. M's ma is dead. I saw the funeral. They moved out of the house a while back. I never see them any more. Everything's changed. Father Union came up the road last night. He's new in the church. He says he's delighted to be back in Raytown, that's what some people call Ringsend. He's nice, always joking and laughing. Dolly Brennan says he's a great singer. She came over when he stopped to talk to me. Her that'd never give you the time of day. He gave us a bag of broken biscuits. They were lovely. I put them in hot water for Jimmy. He hasn't been able to eat much.

I went to his house again. Nearly three years. I took the tools. I feel he's nearer when I hold them. I know it's useless. I know he won't be back. He said goodbye didn't he? Just nodded his head. I swear I could hear him saying, keep them Lily, till I see you again. He will come back. I know he will. He has to. I just want to tell him how much I love him. I know he loves me. I know it.

LCT 461. 1944. We arrived in Normandy on the 6th of June, at seven in the morning. They gave us a pep talk about making history before we set out. We've been here for nearly a month, about a mile off Sword Beach shunting tanks in and out. We are filthy, exhausted. The noise is indescribable. Bodies. Oil. Black. I can smell fear. I thought it was a saying but it's not. And the screaming of men frightened half to death is terrible. I dream sometimes of a cool clean white place with no

noise. And sleep. I wonder how long we'll survive.
How long it will go on? What'll I do if it ends?

One of the Little Sisters came to the house. There
was nothing to eat. Mrs Heaney couldn't manage
more than half a loaf. I don't blame her, she's
awful good to us but she hasn't got much herself.
Sometimes I don't know what to do. I can't leave
Jimmy to go up to Rose for sewing. The nun said
that Father Union asked her to see could she do
anything for us. She was nice, not all holy. She sat
Jimmy on her knee and gave him a big spoon of
cough mixture. She put tuppence in the gas meter
and boiled some water to help me wash him. She
brought something for the tea as well. Now she
comes every day she says we have to get Jimmy
better so I can get some work. She's going to ask
somebody she knows. I was afraid she'd want to
take Jimmy away to Artane or somewhere, but she
says I look after him grand. She made me feel like
something, so she did. I notice there's a new sign
up on the printers. Raytown Press, it's called. They
say a gang of the workers are running it these days.
It looks terrible run-down.

I haven't filled this in for a long time. I haven't felt
like it. Too much going on. Too much fighting.
Too many people getting killed. I sometimes think
that when this war is over there won't be a single
young man left. I don't know how many I've seen
getting killed. I don't think of Buller any more.
That old bastard deserved to die but I don't intend
to carry the can for anyone. If I get out of this alive
I'm going to live my own life. I'm not going back

to Dublin. I'll send for Lily when I can. I want to take care of her and the child if he's still alive. I hope Lily doesn't move. I need to be able to get in touch. I wish Mr Handl was still around.

We were mined. Near Antwerp, in the river Scheldt – the Germans controlled Walcheren island at the mouth. There are mines everywhere, fearful casualties. The Canadian motor launches were wooden so when they were hit they caught fire. God. The stench of burnt flesh. The screams. I had a chest injury. My nerve is completely gone. I'll keep to my plan. I am scared half out of my mind. If I'm not on duty I'm learning French, Dutch, German, anything to keep me occupied. I've learned to intercept radio messages and sometimes I can translate them. My head feels as if it's on fire. Dear God don't let Lily let on she knows me. They'll get her for sure. What did she see that night? If she saw me drop the holder, what else did she see? I didn't know how much danger she was in. No wonder they couldn't wait to get rid of me. I'm going out of my mind with worry. My head is on fire. Stuffed full of death and pain and treachery. I woke up screaming last night. I don't know what I'm going to do.

1945. They've moved us out of number 8. They said it was infested. I had to laugh. It's been infested for years. We've a room over Mrs Heaney's shop until I find my feet. I wish old Mr Handl wasn't dead. I miss him still. I don't care what they say. He was a great man. He saved my life.

I'm nineteen. I feel as old as the hills, I found two grey hairs in the front of my head. Jimmy is doing all right but he's still very small. He never seems to grow any more. But he's very good and quiet. He can nearly say my name. No-one else can make it out, but I can. And he has the best smile in the world. I don't know what I'd do without him. Sister Clare still comes every week. But for her, we'd starve. Sometimes I think it would be easier just to walk along the seashore and out into the water and never come back. The word is that M is dead. I just heard it, casual, when I was standing in a shop in Sandymount. An old gasbag at the counter was counting all 'the Irish boys from the area who gave their lives for His Majesty.' West Brit. I wasn't paying any heed to her but then I heard his name. Listed dead. Listed. That's not certain, is it?

1948. For a dead man I'm doing all right. I had a breakdown after Belgium. One shelling too many, one leave too few. I just gave up. Went off my rocker for a while. I attacked one of the fellows from Belfast who was getting me down. I was in hospital for only a few weeks. They had more pressing cases than broken minds. I went to London and got a job in HM Stationery Office, digs in Pimlico. I went back into a nursing home – mad-house – a couple of months later. A V2 hit us the same night. So I lost a leg as well as my head. V2. Such an innocuous name for those silent deadly rockets. Ten people were killed, I was listed among them. Wonderful wasn't it? Dead and legless. If I wasn't already out of my mind, I'd go mad. The word went out and the bereaved families were notified. Which effectively closes the case against me, doesn't it? They can't chase a dead man. The only thing is a dead man is no good to Lily.

I didn't know about any of this until nearly a year later. I was quite badly injured. It took three operations to lop enough off the leg. Then there were complications like blood-poisoning. I missed other things as well. The terrible reports after they found the camps, Belsen, Auschwitz, Dachau. I thought of old Josh then and how little he talked about München. He had children there and grand-children.

It was almost two years before I was, so to speak, back on my foot, and another six months before I could manage to get and keep a job. Everything would be fine if only I could get in touch with Lily. I wrote to her at last, at Daedalian Road. I should have done it years ago. But I was afraid that whoever was the landlord now would get the letter. God knows what I thought. I should have had more faith in her. She wouldn't have given me away. I didn't use my address. I got a PO box number in London, just in case. The letter returned. House demolished, tenants resettled. No forwarding address. I knew it was useless. I wrote to Mr Handl in desperation but the letter was returned as well. Addressee deceased. I was right after all. Poor Josh dead. But then, so am I. I have to be sure where I stand before I do anything more.

May 1951. Ten years. M is dead, I have to believe it now. Sometimes I think I'm the only survivor. I'm twenty-five. I have a job in Cassidys on George's Street, doing alterations. I have a nice

236

little room in Harcourt Street. Jimmy's dead three years next month. He still looked like a small child, but he was nearly ten. I kept him with me for as long as I could. The place in Daedalian Road was desperate but we knew where we were there. The houses were boarded up when Mrs Reynolds left after the war ended. Nobody could tell us who the new landlord was. A solicitor from Merrion Square was in charge but he wouldn't have any truck with the likes of us.

Poor Jimmy couldn't settle when we moved to Mrs Heaney's. She couldn't get used to him crying either. After a few weeks I wheeled him back home to number eight. There were still people living there. Not everyone got out when they were told. He sank very slowly. It took over a year. I wouldn't have been able to manage without Sister Clare. He got another cold that winter and it never went. In January Sister Clare said we'd have to get him to hospital. He was in Baggot Street for a week and he seemed to be grand for a while after that, but soon the coughing started again and the long nights of crying. She came one day with a woman in a car and said she'd like to show me a place where they would be able to help Jimmy. I didn't want to go. I was that tired, I never got much sleep that time. The car was something gorgeous. We drove a long way, out Mount Merrion to Stillorgan to St Augustine's. The Colony it's called, run by The Brothers of St John of God. There's loads of boys like Jimmy there. They teach them all sorts. It's awful clean and the grounds! Beautiful trees, a huge monument, gardens. I never saw the like. Beautiful.

The Brother was nice, Feargal he's called. He sat with Jimmy for a long time and talked to him as if he was able to understand. They got a doctor to examine him. Jimmy didn't think much of that, I can tell you. He pissed all over your man. I nearly spilt my sides with the laughing. Before we left, Bro Feargal said Jimmy would be welcome, any time. I said I could manage, thanks very much.

About a month after that, I finally gave in. I should have done it years ago. They were that nice to him. Maybe if they'd got him sooner they might have helped him to walk or talk? I worry about that sometimes. That I kept him back. Poor little fellow was worn out with all he went through. An ambulance came for him. Caused a bit of commotion in Daedalian Road, I can tell you.

I'll never forget going in to see him the first time. He was in the infirmary. The Brothers were all in white and everything else was white as well. After our place it was like a snow palace. Little Jimmy was tucked up in a bed with beautiful white sheets right up to his chin. They washed his hair. It was shining like gold on the pillow. He looked like a little doll. He put up his arms for me. I could have slept in the bed with him it was that big and roomy and clean. So very clean. That's what I want. A house full of clean everything. Bright, white or beautiful colours. If I never see dirty green or brown again, it'll be too soon.

Sister Clare found a room for me near St Augustine's while Jimmy was sick. God knows who paid for it. I couldn't. I owe that woman my life. During the day while I sat with Jimmy, I did the sewing and mending for the infirmary. He lingered on for weeks, not getting any better but not getting any worse either. I think he was really comfortable for the first time in his life, poor little dotie, and he just didn't feel like giving it up. More power to him. Then just as the spring came and I thought he was out of the woods, he took bad again.

CHAPTER TWENTY

The Diaries
1951–1961

The doctor has become exasperated with me. He says that if I cannot talk, I must write. Write what is so painful, since I cannot speak of it. 'Keep a diary,' he said, 'you will find that things just emerge. No-one need read it, not even you. Try it.' I didn't tell him I'd always kept a diary, I didn't want to disturb his neat little theory. But the laugh is on me.

My life stopped that night. I should not have run away. It didn't help me, it made everything worse. I thought if I ran then, I would leave the memory behind. I might as well have packed it in my suitcase. Sleeping and waking it's been with me ever since. Sometimes in the night I go over it all again. Force myself to remember it, step by step. But I do not always remember it the same. Details elude me. Motives, reasons. Why did I run? I cannot remember just exactly why I was in Daedalian Road that night. I cannot recall how I got home. Nor where the idea to join the navy came from. Even at seventeen I was a pacifist. Well, not pacifist exactly; afraid.

I was born the year the treaty with Britain was signed, the end of the War of Independence. I was weaned on violence and talk of violence. There wasn't a man of my father's generation who wasn't in the GPO in 1916. He had the added good fortune to have been shot – caught in the cross-fire during a skirmish – during the civil war. It ensured his immortality, at least as the main attraction of the local public house. He wasn't a hero. My father's loyalties were always slightly suspect, but he knew a starring role when it hit him on the arm. Overnight he became Dev's man – well, not overnight precisely – he waited until after the winning team emerged before he started celebrating in earnest. De Valera's success ensured the demise of the family firm.

It started slowly, but within a decade, what had been a thriving printing business slid into near bankruptcy. And his family began the faster slide from affluence to near poverty. The house in Blackrock was sold, we moved to rented accommodation. Not bad at first, but with each move closer to the city, the houses got smaller and meaner. I was taken out of my private school to the national school. My mother simply opted out, becoming more and more vague. She'd always had maids, now she had none. She was neither fit for, nor interested in, keeping house. She became a martyr to her nerves, as we all did. In her imagination her poor husband was the victim of a gang of scheming, jealous thieves. She couldn't cope with the changes, so she pretended they weren't happening. I seem to have inherited these tendencies. My sister and I also inherited her looks.

She was tall, thin and dark, with a long nose and dark eyes. The Armada has a lot to answer for; she looked like a Spanish grandee.

My sister was the real casualty. She's eight years older than me. Clever, ambitious and wild to make her mark in the young state. Fate seemed to be on her side; she was born in 1916. She was a true patriot, she believed passionately in De Valera and believed passionately in Ireland. She wanted to go into politics. She wanted to go to university. She wanted to change the world. She could have, she had the ability, but she was taken out of school at fifteen and sent off to become a shorthand typist. I adored her, admired her, became her willing slave. She took the place of both my parents, cared for me, fought my battles. I followed where she led. I was the willing partner in her schemes. And her great scheme was that one day we'd salvage the family business from the worst of my father's excesses and rebuild the family fortune.

Nobody takes much notice of girls now, but it was much worse in the thirties. Unemployment was widespread and what jobs there were went to the men, the breadwinners. Whatever jobs she got – she was not a good secretary – were as charity from the friends of better days. She hated the jobs and she hated the charity. I left school at thirteen and was apprenticed to my father's master printer. At the same time, because she was out of work, my sister went to work with the bookkeeper. My father, faced with this evidence of his own fickleness – his children in such menial positions – went to pieces. We kept ourselves going with our own schemes. We reasoned that now we had a toehold, *there would be no getting rid of us. That, even if it was from the bottom up, we were learning the business. Then in 1937 my father acquired a partner. Buller Reynolds entered our lives.*

Acquire was the word. We never knew what kind of transaction passed between them, but whatever it was, Buller quickly gained the upper hand. Oddly enough, for such a greedy man, he made no effort to reverse the firm's declining fortunes. I've wondered since if it was the site he was interested in? It was just beside the dock-basin. Perhaps he gambled that with Britain at war, Ireland's neutral stand would collapse and that such a position would, in those circumstances, be very useful. Very lucrative. Maybe. Such sophisticated ideas didn't occur to us at the time.

Before you could wink, we were out on our ears. My sister because she had the temerity to question some account or other, me because I was my father's son. Poor girl was left to kick up her heels and plot revenge, in idleness. There was some wild talk about running off to Spain – for Franco, I suppose, knowing her – but mercifully it came to nothing.

I was rescued by Joshua Handl. He had a small private press and bindery behind his little bookshop. He produced rare, limited editions. I became his apprentice shortly before my fifteenth birthday. It was the best bit of luck I ever had. He was a good man, a gifted teacher. The work exactly suited me, then and now. Ringsend was a laughable place for such an enterprise, but refugees from Nazi Germany had few options in the thirties. Besides, he was an honest and distinguished man as was soon recognized by those who beat a path to his door. I told my sister, and myself, that I was learning yet another aspect of the printing trade. That it would be useful, in time we could also extend into publishing. That and only that made her consent to me working for a Jew. Like everyone else of her time and class, she was carelessly anti-Semitic.

My father drank himself to death. Within three years of that diabolical deal with Reynolds, he was dead. It happened a couple of months after war was declared. Now at last, we thought, we'll be able to get back in control. Technically, as the only son, I inherited the business. In reality, my sister and I had a pact that we'd be equal partners. She would learn how to run the business while I took care of the printing side.

We went, like lambs to the slaughter, to announce our plans to Buller Reynolds. When he stopped laughing, he gobbled us up and spat us out. We were in and out of his office in about two minutes flat. Plenty long enough for him to tell us that there was no partnership. Just Reynolds. It was what he wanted, what my father intended. End of story. The new name went up on the fascia board that same afternoon.

I have never had the stomach for fighting and I didn't fancy my chances against Reynolds. I suspected even then that we'd get nowhere with him and, like the coward I am, I accepted what had happened. I don't know how long it took my poor sister. But it was worse for her. All her frustrated ambition was centred on this one chance at doing something worthwhile, helping her family, of making her mark. She was wild with despair, *inconsolable. She raged against the fates, my spendthrift father and my poor silly mother who thought the world had ended because she could no longer keep an account in Brown Thomas. She was nearly insane with frustration.*

I knew she'd despaired when she took a job as a shop assistant in the underwear department of Clery's. A vast, no-nonsense emporium on the main street of the city. The pay was poor, the merchandise not to her taste. It seemed to be an exercise in humiliation. But I'd got it wrong. Within a month she was installed in the accounts office learning, she claimed, exactly how a large and successful enterprise was managed. She was magnificent.

1952. Rose came to see me the other day. She's opened a little shop in Wicklow Street, ladies' high class tailoring. Martin does the deliveries and the books, he left the guards years ago. He was too soft-hearted to be locking people up, poor Martin. Rose wants me to come and work for her doing alterations. I don't know. I was dead keen at first but now that I think about it, I'm not sure. Too many memories. She'd be asking about Jimmy and maybe even about M. If I hear the name Daedalian Road again I'll spit. Anyway she can't pay me as much as Cassidy's and God knows that's little enough. No, I'm not being honest. I was a bit put out that she thought I was only capable of alterations. If anybody else asks me to turn a coat for them, I'll fling it out the window.

I love the New Look. It's taken me a bit of time to catch up on the fashions. It came out in 1947. But mind you, fashions were far from my mind then, with Jimmy so sick and all. I've been copying some of those Dior dresses for the girls in work. They're gorgeous for dancing in, lovely swirly skirts. Much easier than tailoring suits. I have it in mind to get started on my own one of those days. Not yet but, I haven't the money. Me and some of the girls go to a hop once a week. They're teaching me to dance. They say all I need is a bit of practice.

I made a resolution not to mope any more. I think that while I was grieving for my little brother I must have been grieving for M as well. They say he was killed in the war, like thousands of other poor Irish boys. Funny, isn't it? I never felt he was dead.

1953. People have been dropping like flies with the Asian flu. My room has been as cold as ice all winter, I can't seem to get the place warm. Every time a bus goes by, the windows rattle. I wish I had a house of my own. I don't think I'll ever manage it. I'd have the best bathroom in the world, I would. It's what I hate most about digs, the bathrooms are ferocious. Cold, mouldy and smelly. I take the skin off my hands I use so much Vim on the bath. Even so, it's never clean. It's like getting in with half the household. And some of their habits I wouldn't like to mention. There are six bedsits in this house. I took a good look at it the other day. It isn't that much better than Ringsend, after all. I'm getting nowhere with my life. I'm twenty-seven, over the hill. Who'd want me now? The girls at work think I'm twenty-three. It's not much of a lie, is it? I met a nice boy at a dance last week. He's called Fagan. Hope he's there Saturday.

I've been doing alterations (no coats turned, by request!) for Rose after all. She still doesn't pay much, but I'm saving up. I have to get out of this place.

1956. The new children's hospital in Crumlin was opened this week. It reminded me of Jimmy, all those little nippers in their beds. There was a lot of pictures in the newspapers. I cut one out. It had a picture of a crowd of people on bikes. The caption caught my eye. *Pedal-Pushers for Paediatrics. £7500 raised for Tiny-Tots.* There was a very good-looking woman in the front of it, one leg on the ground, looking over her shoulder, smiling. Her clothes were great. Black ribbed polo-neck jumper and tight slacks to her ankle – pedal-pushers. It would suit me, though I've never in my life worn trousers. But I'm going to have a go. I cut the picture out of the paper. The woman reminds me of someone. I think she's one of Rose's customers. Anyway I thought I'd copy the slacks, they looked very smart.

1957. I've met a French girl. I think I've fallen in love with her. She is small and dark and full of fun, which is a change for me. She is so uninhibited, so exotic. I suppose I mean she's sexy. Sophisticated. She thought it very amusing that I am, was, a virgin. She didn't think there could be another ex-sailor in the world in such a predicament. She organizes my life for me. We met outside the shop about six months ago. She asked directions, I could hardly understand her English so I answered her in French. She burst out laughing at my accent. I said I didn't understand why, when she spoke appalling

English, her accent was considered charming and when I spoke grammatical French, my accent caused her much merriment. It was not the way I usually behave. Normally I don't say a word. She replied that to learn good French one needed a French mistress. Perhaps her English is not as bad as I thought?

June 1957. I've made up my mind to paint this dump, I'm that ashamed of it. No use putting it off any longer. I won't get anything better for what I can afford. I wish I could work for Sybil Connolly. Maybe I'll go and see her. In my hat.

June 1957. The past is behind me. I'm getting married, in France, next week. Claudine has gone ahead, she left a fortnight ago. Sometimes in the night, the old times return and I'm afraid again. I've told her nothing, what would be the point? She knows my nerves were shattered in the war but she is full of courage. Perhaps that is behind me as well? I haven't had a breakdown since I met her. She is so capable, strong. She doesn't mind the leg. She makes me happy. When she is not here, the darkness comes. We are going to live with her parents. They run a farm, I'm to help. C says that since she will never learn more than the twelve phrases of English she's memorized, then we'd be better off where both of us can speak. I will make a new life, make her happy. She thinks she may be already pregnant. I hope she is. That would really be a new start. I've prayed for the first time in years, that everything will work out for us. Sometimes, I am so afraid.

November 1957. I've been putting off thinking about it. All this time I never copped on. I'm so stupid. She's tall like a man. A big strong woman. She's one of Rose's customers. By chance Rose sent her to me the other night. God, I nearly died when she knocked at my room door. I was up on the table trying to get at the ceiling with the paint brush. When she got no answer she poked her head around the door. She conducted her business with me on top of the table and herself looking up at me. I bet she never looked up to anyone in her life before. It was only when I jumped down that I realized how tall she is.

'Rose Vavasour sent me, she said you'd do this job in a hurry.' She had a beautiful red skirt with her which needed letting down. She wanted it by the morning. I was so struck with looking at her that I promised to leave it into Rose's shop on my way to work. I'll kill Rose for letting her come to my place. There's little enough privacy. She didn't know me from Adam, thank goodness. I won't do any more work for her. This is it. Poor M. I don't believe he's dead at all. God I wish I had a better head.

January 1958. I found another room. It's on Haddington Road, further away from work but that can't be helped. I'm going to try for another job as well. I'm staying away from Rose. I ate the face off her for sending your woman to me. She thinks it's because I'm ashamed of how I have to live. 'You're too proud Lily, these people can help you.' Like hell. Anyway we're talking. I told her she could keep her old money. I know I'll never see M again. It doesn't feel so bad now that I know it wasn't me he was staying away from.

March 1958. I painted the new room. It's much nicer, livelier. I'm not that keen on white, but it was the cheapest and at least it looks clean. I'm going to make curtains next. Shocking pink, so there. Live dangerously, I say. There's only four bedsits in this house, the rest is two flats, so there's only four to share the bathroom. A slight improvement. At this rate I'll have my own by the time I'm forty. I wish I could meet a decent fellow. I never seem to be all that interested. I don't want to be an old maid, though.

1960. I went for an interview with the designer for Colette Modes. Miss Hayes she's called. I'm starting there in two weeks when I've worked out my notice. I'll be learning to cut patterns. I'm on top of the world. An extra eighteen shillings a week. I think I'll go mad and buy a bit of furniture. I could pay it off by the week.

April 1961. I haven't filled this out for a long time. I got another raise at work and these days I get to make frocks – sorry, gowns – for the clients. I love the work. I moved into one of the flats downstairs. It has a little bedroom, a bathroom and a kitchen dinette. It sounds grander than it is and costs more than I can afford but I wouldn't swop it for the world. I painted it all lovely and made more curtains. They match the others pretty well. I even covered an old sofa I got cheap from the second-hand shop down the road. Frank made me a lovely chest of drawers. I met him about a year ago. He's a carpenter, the cousin of a woman I work with, widowed about five years ago. He had his own house way out in Dun Laoghaire. It's great, just needs a good lick of paint. I could do it up lovely. He has two sons but I've never met them, they emigrated to Australia a couple of years ago. He's a mature man, fifty-three, but then I'm no spring chicken myself these days, thirty-five last birthday. But I don't look my age, I still answer to twenty-eight.

Frank wants me to marry him. He's a decent, kind, man and I wish I were in love with him, but I don't think I ever will be. He's not a bit like M to look at, so that's something. He isn't too tall, and has blue eyes and fairish hair. Maybe I could learn to love him? I like and respect him already. Can I expect any more than that, at my age? We agreed I'd think about it. I have to confess, I'd like a child of my own, more than anything. After Jimmy died I never thought I'd say that, he was like my own. I suppose I've always been a bit afraid that if I had a baby it would be backward like Jimmy. It's funny that, because it never mattered with him, I'd have died without him. He kept me going after Ma abandoned us.

Will I have to tell Frank all about that? About me Ma and all? I never did have a Daddy. I only made him up. I've stopped telling myself lies, so I wouldn't want to start life with Frank that way. I've too much respect for him. I'll give myself more time.

CHAPTER TWENTY-ONE

It was Maria who came up trumps and found the expert on bindings for me. Or at least the bookseller who pointed me in the right direction.

By the time I'd finished the diaries, my vague idea of trying to find Lily's friend had become both more focused and much, much, more urgent. I'd no idea of his name beyond M, but I knew, without doubt, that he was jointly, with my mother, the author of an amazing account of the same murder Arthur Reynolds had ranted about and, as far as I could tell, the same 'incident' that I'd found so starkly referred to in the newspaper archive.

No wonder the date had rung a bell. The murder on 31 May 1941 in Daedalian Road was the important thing. I couldn't understand why my brain had been so sluggish in making the connection. *Lily died in exactly the same place*. It blew my mind. She'd witnessed the original murder of Reynolds's father. Was it too much of a mental leap to conclude that Arthur Reynolds or his henchman Hanlon had killed her? And if they'd killed her, then surely that other witness, M of the diaries, was now in his line of fire.

I now knew, of course, what they'd been after. Somehow, they must have known of the existence of the diaries. How? They'd been so carefully hidden. I tried hard to train my mind along a single track, follow each thread to its conclusion. Yet doubts crowded in from all sides. Would Reynolds have suggested my mother had been murdered, if he himself had done it? Not unless he was deranged, as I'd glibly supposed him to be. He certainly knew something; was looking for something or someone. Who? What? If he wasn't the murderer then who was? Was he working with Hanlon? Who was next on the hit list? M? Or me, of course. But why? Why? Why?

Who would be interested in a fifty-year-old murder? M's sister might, but like everyone else she'd faded out of the picture, another victim of the rapacious Reynolds. There were lots of peripheral people but, having read the diaries, it was plain to me that the real dramatis personae had been on Daedalian Road that night. It was they, or their descendants, that I had to think about. And the fact that it was all so long ago. What would anyone hope to gain by knocking off a harmless old lady fifty years on? It wasn't as if Lily hadn't been there all the time. What was the big deal? It was an old crime; these were elderly people who, as Lily would have said 'would be better off saying their prayers.'

Of course the thought of her had me in floods. I covered my eyes and banged my head against the table with frustration. I could not bear to think about my poor mother lying injured and in pain, left to die slowly and alone on that ghastly road. I would find her killers. They would not get away with it, not if I had anything to do with it. I'd make the blasted Gardaí sit up and take notice.

No more shilly-shallying. M, that other witness in 1941, had to be found. It stood to reason, if Lily had been in danger, then so was he. And she must have sensed something, because she had taken meticulous care to leave no clues to his whereabouts; no mention of his name, no scribbled address, no phone contact. She had even attempted to rub out and scribble over the letter M in the diaries. It took me ages to work out. I eventually deciphered it by putting a hard surface behind her scribbled erasure and rubbing the (fortunately blank) back of the page with a soft pencil. Kid's stuff, but it worked. The M eventually appeared, faintly but unmistakable. As a clue it was pretty useless; he could be anywhere. The reflection of the red bus in the photograph was the slender thread on which I hung my conviction that he was living somewhere – it was like finding my way in a maze – somewhere with easy access to Heathrow. Lily had tried all the coaches because yours truly was continually urging her to broaden her horizons – or so I thought at the time. But she had her own agenda. Remembering the way I'd chivvied her, I was ashamed. Someone should start a society for the protection of parents from their bossy, up-tight children.

Almost from the start I began to link the mystery-man in the photo to the co-author of the diaries, to M. I suppose recognizing them outside the cafe led rather naturally to that conclusion. Since M had been an apprentice bookbinder, it was almost a QED that he'd bound their two diaries together. But when? Had they always been in contact or had they newly discovered each other?

Why were there only two? Why had they stopped in 1961? If there were more, who had them? There were a hundred questions, but perhaps the most interesting was, what significant point or fact was I missing? In the middle of a sleepless night I laced a cup of milky tea with a shot of brandy – one of Lily's old tricks – and sat, with a notepad, and worked out how best to proceed.

The two diaries sporadically covered twenty years: from when Lily was fifteen until she married my father, twenty years later. Much of the first volume – on her side – was about her life and about her poor little brother, whose illnesses sprinkled the desperate little entries. She'd obviously adored him and her sense of defeat when she finally gave him into care was poignant. His death, in her twenties, released her, but her childhood was gone. Not that she ever had much of one. The drunken mother, the pretend father, a severely handicapped brother. Dickensian was too mild a term – Little Dorrit's lover was on hand to deliver her, Lily's was not.

How could she have been so optimistic? Why hadn't she shared her past with me? There was so much to be proud of – she was amazing. Yet, until I read the diaries I'd had no idea that her beloved brother Jimmy had neither walked nor talked. She never once said anything about her mother abandoning them. Her sanitized version was that she and Jimmy had been orphaned young and that he'd died of pneumonia when he was nine years old. 'Sure who'd be interested, Chucks?' I could almost hear the laughing tone. How right she was. Had I ever asked?

She knew the Reynolds family though; she worked for the murdered man's widow and took care of baby Arthur – Baba in the diary. Did he remember her? He hadn't said so and he didn't strike me as a bloke who'd be slow in coming forward with his grievances. By her own account she'd nicked his food for her sickly brother. Yet Arthur claimed no memory of Dublin at all, so he can't have remembered Lily filching his grub.

Apart from her dubious relationship with the Widow Reynolds and son, Lily must have had a few other little scams going. Selling coupons alone can't have supported them. She was resourceful. What else might she have been up to? I scanned the pages eagerly again, this time with more care.

The diaries had been bound with Lily's pages randomly interleaved with M's entries. Dates were haphazard. Whereas her hand was childish and changeable, sometimes slanting forward, sometimes backwards, his was old-fashioned copperplate which hardly varied at all. Where was his sister? Who was she? What had happened to her? M obviously never got back in touch with his family. He never mentioned any of them by name. His entries gave the stark chronicle of his life during the war and being invalided out, minus the lower part of one leg, in 1944 in time for the V2 raids on London, when he was still in his early twenties. He obviously moved both job and house several times but, though he referred to his work quite a bit, he never mentioned the name of the towns he lived in after the war, nor anyone he worked with; it was as if he lived his life in a vacuum.

Second time around, the thing which struck me most was the contrast between the squalid poverty of Lily's childhood and – I took this thought very carefully – and the comfortable sum – by contrast huge – she'd managed to squirrel away, month by month, year by year. I had not tried to find out exactly when that steady flow had started but I wouldn't have much difficulty working it out. Less comfortable were the questions – who was paying and why?

'That would be telling, Chucks.' How many times had I heard her say that? In other words, mind your own business. But it was my business. If I did not know what was going on, how could I protect myself? From whom?

From whoever Lily, that sweet old, cheery old, harmless old lady was blackmailing. That's who. My brain hadn't gone entirely soft. I was beginning to wonder if the bloke in the photograph might be her accomplice. And that made him even more vulnerable. I wasn't making moral judgements, I'm afraid I had a sneaking regard for Lily's craftiness. I mean it beat suburban housewife, didn't it? But if Lily had been knocked off, it didn't take an enormous leap of the imagination to figure out that her handsome old pal would be next on the hit list. I avoided the question of why they might be interested in me.

I rang Maria as soon as I got up. She was in a meeting and she didn't manage to get back to me until after ten.

'Have I got this wrong or did you live near a

bookseller in Ealing?' My question came out of the blue and it was some moments before she could make head or tail of what I was on about.

'Yes, that's right. They lived, they lived ... crumbs, I can't remember what number ...'

'Name? Can you remember the name?'

'Yep. Hartwell, I think. I haven't seen her for ages. Grace Hart ... no not Hartwell. That's not right. I didn't know her very well. Hartford? No. Hart something. I'll think of it in a minute. She was very specialized, as far as I know. Why do you want to know?'

'I wondered if she might know something about the bindings, on my mother's diaries. You know? Identify who made them? I could go and see her this morning.' After days of inertia I was wild to be up and moving.

'Hartford? Her name is ... Hell, I'm not sure that's right either. Hartwell? Hart something. Look up Hart. I think the number is 219. Or 218 Khartoum Road. W13. She'll be in the book. Give her my best.'

No Hartwells on Khartoum but there was a Hartfield, RS, 218 Khartoum Road. No mention of books. Nor, more curiously, were there any Hartfields (or Hart anything) under Booksellers in the *Yellow Pages*; either new or antiquarian. When I tried the number listed for RS, there was no reply. But I was in no mood for delay, I wrapped the diaries carefully and went to call. It simply didn't occur to me that she might not be in.

It was easy to find the house because it was so close to Maria's old flat, in one of those long pleasant leafy roads about five minutes drive from

Ealing Broadway. There were two couples playing tennis on the courts as I turned the corner. In the sunshine it was pure Betjeman. A couple of Joan Hunter Dunns lobbing their balls blithely unaware of the passing years.

The Hartfield house looked a little run down. I almost fell over a broken tricycle lying across the garden path and the tiny lawn was completely overgrown. Looking at its carefully-maintained neighbours, I could almost hear the communal sighs of despair. The peeling hall-door was slightly ajar.

The doorbell was on the blink but when I banged on the wooden panel, a little boy, wearing pyjamas and grubby dressing gown, appeared in the opening. He was about eight or nine and was holding a TV remote control in his hand. I was obviously a welcome diversion. He beamed up at me.

'Hello.'

'Hello back.' I grinned. He was an impish little chap with huge brown eyes and dimples in either cheek. Just my idea of William. 'Is your mother in?'

He looked at me solemnly and slowly shook his head. 'My dad'll be back soon. At least, he said he would. He's just gone down to Sainsburys. What's your name?'

'Nell. What's yours?'

'Jamie. I've got chicken-pox. Well, I had it, now my little sister's got them. She's got spots everywhere.' He giggled. 'Even on her bottom,' he added daringly, watching for my reaction.

'That's interesting. You had them there as well?'

He ignored that. 'D'you want to come in? My

259

dad says it's really catching.' He seemed delighted with this challenge and watched with keen interest while I frantically tried to remember what childhood diseases I'd had. Every child gets chicken-pox, don't they?

'What about your mum?'

'I don't have a mum, my dad looks after us. We're a single parent family.' He looked up at me proudly, perfectly at ease with himself. He didn't look at all like a threat to Tory Britain. Vulcan Redwood could do with coming around here, I thought, and grinned back. My latest and best chum.

'Can I wait for your Dad then?'

'You certainly can! Any time.' Jamie's father came staggering up to the door with two plastic carriers in either hand. He dumped the bags at his son's feet and rubbed his numb fingers together to restore the circulation. I'm a bad judge of age but I thought he looked about fifty, very tall, well, big actually. Much too heavy but with the same bewitching 'help me' smile of his attractive young son. They were absurdly alike, but he could as easily have been Jamie's (young) grandfather as (elderly) father. He mopped his brow and held out his hand. He'd had a couple of pints, his smile was expansive.

'How do you do.'

'Nell Gilmore.'

'Reggie Hartfield. You looking for me?' He held on to my hand.

By this time Jamie was dragging the bags along the hall, presumably towards the kitchen, so I felt it safe to mention the missing mum again.

'Your wife, actually.'

'Ah.' He smiled ruefully. 'My wife or the mother of my children?' His irony didn't come off, he sounded quite wounded, apologetic even. I was just about to melt when I realized he was looking me over with rather more interest than seemed necessary. Attractive he might be; the pox was another matter. Anyway he was clearly in a worse mess than me and I'm not very keen on other people's children, so I ignored the pathos.

'The bookseller?' I asked tentatively, suddenly wondering if she was dead.

'Ah, Grace,' he replied tenderly. 'Alas, she doesn't live here any more, like Alice.' He held his head on one side waiting to see if I caught the reference.

'Good film, I'd love to stay and discuss it but it's quite urgent. Do you know where I can find her?'

'What's the date? Twenty third of August? You'll find her in Clerkenwell, I believe. For the moment. She's just come back from the States, but I think she may be moving quite soon. Can you give me an idea what it's about?'

'I want to ask her about some books. It's probably a long shot, it's just that my friend Maria, who knows her – knew her – suggested I talk to her … about some valuable bindings. I don't want to sell them, I just want to …' I stopped when he began to laugh at my confusion. Jamie was back, grinning up at me as well. They obviously thought I was a complete bimbo. Mr Hartfield held up his hands.

'Good grief, I don't need a potted history, I thought we could ring and find out if she's free to see you, that's all. You don't want to be haring all the way to Clerkenwell on a wild goose chase, do you? Besides,' he added conspiratorially, 'gives me an excuse to contact her. Find out what she's up to.' He beamed down at me, took my arm firmly and led me inside.

'Off you go, young James and make us all a cup of coffee,' he directed, as he picked up the hall phone. There was some delay after he asked for 'Grace' but when he'd spoken to her for a few minutes he handed me the phone. She was apparently going to be in her flat all day 'for reasons I would appreciate when I saw it' and would be happy to look at my diaries. I got the impression that it was 'diaries' rather than 'bindings' which interested her.

The coffee was espresso and excellent. Useful kid. The three of us sat happily chatting for half an hour until a beautiful, slim and extremely spotty little girl joined us. By which time I conveniently remembered that I'd never had chicken-pox and made a fast getaway. It was only a white lie; Mr Hartfield was coming on a bit strong. The helpless type can always spot a sucker. And for my money, one was quite enough. One too many, actually. I'd been there and had got more than the T-shirt.

CHAPTER TWENTY-TWO

It took me quite a time to find my way to Grace Hartfield's flat in Clerkenwell. It was, for me, a completely unfamiliar part of London. I don't suppose I'd been in that area more than a couple of times in ten years. The eighteenth-century street she lived in was only about half a mile from King's Cross. It was remarkably quiet and beautiful. Not even the background roar of traffic could spoil the effect. It reminded me, very strongly, of parts of Dublin. Or Richmond come to that, which is, I suppose, why I live there. One of the things I love about London is that it throws up these unexpected lovely surprises. Somehow that fleeting feeling of mild delight stayed with me and coloured my memory of my first meeting with a couple of strangers whom I knew, instinctively, would become friends.

The man who answered the door was American, about five-eleven with thinning pale hair, tortoise-shell glasses, blue eyes and an enormous welcoming, lop-sided grin. He had a raffish streak of dirt down the left side of his face and a lock of hair over his eyes. When he saw me, he held up two filthy palms and gave his friendly grin.

'Hi. I won't shake hands, I'm too grubby. We're packing up. I'm Murray Magraw, Grace's partner. She's expecting you.' He led the way up the staircase which was littered with empty removal cartons.

'We're moving on Tuesday, there's stuff all over the place, you'll have to watch where you walk. Careful,' he said and grabbed my arm as I stumbled over a large pile of books on the top step. We literally fell into Grace Hartfield's arms.

She was standing on the landing, serene, amused and startlingly good looking. I'm ashamed to say that my first thought was: 'She must have been a cracker.' But I quickly revised my opinion. She still was, she had the kind of classic looks which last.

She was about the same height as me, five-seven. Slightly thinner, better figure. Her grey-streaked black hair was held roughly in an untidy ponytail. She was dressed in an ancient pair of jeans, white T-shirt and white trainers, all scruffy and dirt streaked. There were stacks of books, clothes and odds and ends of furniture all over the place. When we introduced ourselves, she showed me into the almost dismantled sitting-room and cleared a space for me on a huge broken-down sofa.

'We were thinking of stopping for a beer and sandwich,' she said. 'Would you like to join us? Murray's going to fix something. I can look at the diaries once I've cleaned myself up.'

She excused herself and left the room. A minute or two later Murray put his head around the door and announced he was 'off to get something from the deli'. I sat wondering what was wrong with me; eyeing up the talent like an old pro. The world was suddenly full of amazingly attractive men. Perhaps my body was saying what my mind could not accept, that Davis and I were all washed-up. On the other hand maybe the fact that the 'Hartfield men' were both otherwise heavily and obviously engaged had something to do with it. The awesome attraction of the unattainable. I unwrapped the diaries and didn't hear Grace come back into the room until she sat down beside me.

'These are really lovely,' she said quietly, turning over the books. 'What can you tell me about them?' She made no attempt to open them but sat holding them on her lap, her hands playing gently over the surfaces. She had long, slim, rather bony hands with neatly clipped nails. She wore no rings. She had released the ponytail and run a comb through her shoulder-length straight hair. I think that's when I fully realized how striking she was. Her eyes were that strange washed-out grey-blue that people from the west coast of Ireland some-times have. She smiled when I interrupted myself and asked her suddenly if she had Irish connec-tions.

'Not just connections, I was born there. My family came to England when I was a child. I went back for the first time five years ago.' She looked wistful, a little sad, until she smiled again. 'I spent six very interesting months there in 1991. It was good for me.' I waited but she didn't expand; instead she began to leaf slowly through the diaries, all the time asking just enough questions for me to suddenly throw caution to the winds.

'They belonged to my mother, I've only just found them. But they're not just written by her, there are two diaries bound together. I have to find out who the other person is. Was? I have a hunch that the co-writer is also the binder. You see, she died, in very strange circumstances, about a month ago. I have a feeling that these diaries hold some sort of key – it sounds weird, I know – but there seems to be a connection between them and her death. I think. I may be wrong but I desperately want to find out who put them together.'

Her clear eyes didn't so much look at me as through me, into some other time or place. After a little time she swivelled around, her expression was withering.

'How very strange,' she said very softly, 'how very strange. I've been down a road rather like that myself. I'm sorry about your mother.' Her fingers lightly brushed mine. 'Do you mind if I ask Murray about these? He knows a good deal more about bindings than I do. Let's see what he thinks.'

While we waited, she explained that she'd been living in the States for the past couple of years, first in Minnesota working in a 'Special Collections Library' with Murray, then, when the climate got her down, she moved to Colorado. She spoke easily, with confidence; she looked very content.

'Our relationship was slow-growing, at least on my side. We finally decided we'd try to make a go of it together about six months ago. To commit, as they say.' She laughed and shook her head in disbelief. 'I can't imagine why it took me so long, it's good.' She suddenly sounded quite American, or was it her obvious happiness showing through? She grinned apologetically. 'You met Reggie? How did he seem? The children?'

'Dazed, was my impression. They're not yours, are they?'

'No, no, afraid not. Unfortunately I couldn't have any. Dazed? Is he all right?'

'I just mean he seemed to be a bit overwhelmed. The boy is smashing. I only met the little girl for a few seconds. They both had chicken-pox, spots all over ... I got out as fast as I could.' I shrugged. Grace threw back her head and laughed heartily.

'Oh, Lord,' she said, 'poor old Reggie. Still, it's what he wanted ...'

'He looked as if he could do with a bit of help.'

Grace stuck her tongue against the side of her cheek and looked at me archly.

'Reggie's stock-in-trade,' she said. 'I take it you didn't oblige?'

'That's right. I have a job. Is he alone?'

'Yes, at least for the moment. The children's mother has gone walkabout apparently. It happens from time to time, she has a complicated existence. Don't worry, she'll be back, she won't ever find anyone better than Reggie.' Oddly, she didn't sound bitter, or even hurt, just mildly affectionate. After my brief meeting with him I could, more or less, see why it might be so. They each referred to the other with the same fondness and respect. Whatever had broken them up had obviously been sorted. Lucky them.

Murray made a mean pastrami-on-rye sandwich. We ate them with sour-sweet gherkins and drank a cold lager apiece from icy bottles. The flat was stuffy and dusty and unbearably hot, with sunlight streaming in the open windows. Over lunch they told me, with a sort of amazed terror, that they'd bought a stone cottage in a village close to Oxford

267

and were moving the following week. Murray would be working at something called 'Bodley'. I assumed it was either a college or a library but didn't want to show my ignorance by asking. Grace planned to resuscitate her dormant bookselling business, this time in partnership with Murray, from home. The Clerkenwell flat would be modernized they said, and, if their move was a success they would rent it out. Presumably if the rustic idyll didn't last they'd use it themselves. They were clearly not short of a bob or two.

I watched them while they examined Lily's diaries, their two heads bent close together, consulting in inaudible murmurs. I envied them their obvious contentment, the equality of their interaction, their attractiveness. I could almost feel myself roll up in a little ball of loneliness and self-pity. Until I noticed Grace watching me.

'Do you have any idea who might have bound those books?' I asked her abruptly as Murray cleared the debris and went to make coffee.

'Murray thinks there is something familiar about the tooling – the decoration – though he's not sure what,' she answered doubtfully. 'That's what we were trying to figure out, though I've got to say it seems almost too much of a coincidence.' She spoke half to herself.

'You see,' Murray said tentatively as he handed me a steaming mug, 'I believe I saw something very like them recently. They're an excellent pastiche, which is why the memory lodged.' He stopped abruptly. 'A good pastiche is difficult to do. Either the binder has to find really excellent old brasses –

268

the tools for the decoration – or he has to make them, carve them, himself. Do you understand?'

I shook my head. He came and sat beside me and, taking my finger, ran it lightly over the decoration.

'Now look carefully,' he instructed. 'You'll see where the pattern is repeated. It's built up of these small diamond-shape blocks with the complicated swirls joining up to continue the patterns. Whoever did this,' he raised his glasses and peered myopically at the indented leather, 'knew what he was about. I'm pretty sure he cut his own tools. It's not a copy, it's in the style of – a pastiche – of an early nineteenth-century binding but the decoration has a much more modern feel to it. Witty. Do you see?' He put his face on one side and smiled his lopsided hopeful smile. 'And, of course, the leather is new. Looks French to me. The skin, I mean, not the tooling.'

'French? How can you tell?' The notion of 'witty' rather passed me by.

He laughed. 'That's the easy bit. The way it's cured and its perfection. Comes off a large skin, difficult to find in Britain these days. Hey! You don't want to know all this. It's the binder you're interested in, right?'

'Right. The diaries are dedicated to my mother from MM. For some reason I have a hunch that MM is also the binder – I explained why to, er, Grace.' This was stretching the point. Their eyes met. Grace gave a doubtful little shrug.

'Well, I think that's probably a long shot but it's the only thing you have to go on, so we might as

269

well give it a whirl.' She looked from one of us to the other.

Murray went off, unearthed a camera and took some Polaroid snaps of the bindings, both of the complete covers and close-ups of the detail. Then he examined both books, minutely, for a signature and, failing to find one, murmured that he had an appointment at two-thirty. I was mildly surprised that he took the photographs with him.

I spent the next couple of hours helping Grace to pack the contents of a large bookcase. She didn't ask, I offered. If I'm honest, I was feeling at a bit of a loose end. She was easy to talk to and became fascinated as I told her a little of what I'd learned about my mother from the diaries. Whereas Maria had been rather sceptical about my growing suspicions about the nature of Lily's death, Grace listened and, while she didn't encourage my morbid fears, she took them seriously. The account of the murder interested her most. When I told her it had happened fifty years before, she remarked enigmatically that sometimes the repercussions of evil take an extremely long time. I had the impression that I'd touched a raw nerve somewhere because she was quite preoccupied for some time afterwards. So long, indeed, that I began to feel uncomfortable and in the way. But when I made a move to go, she straightened up and asked the most unexpected question.

'Are you about thirty?'

When I nodded, she sighed. 'I inherited this flat from my niece. She was about your age when she died. Be careful, Nell. I did what you are trying to do now. I went back into the past and I got more than I bargained for, I'm afraid. Be very careful whom you trust.'

As she took me to the door she said, 'Nell, we'll do our best to find your bookbinder for you. I can see it's important. Unfortunately, it may take a little time. We'll ask around the trade. If necessary, I'll borrow the books from you . . .' She stopped short at my alarmed expression and touched me lightly on the arm. 'I'll be discreet. I won't mention your mother's name to anyone. Or yours. You mustn't worry, we'll help all we can.'

We exchanged phone numbers and addresses and she promised to be in touch as soon as possible. The shrill ringing of her telephone cut short the awkwardness of our goodbyes.

I felt flat as I walked down the front steps. I hadn't thought beyond trying to identify the bookbinder. I suppose it hadn't occurred to me that it mightn't be a simple matter. After all, people identify unknown paintings the whole time, so why not bindings? I realized that I'd half expected Grace to pounce on the diaries and say, 'Ah yes, undeniably the hand of dear old so-and-so,' or something equally pretentious. Of course I was delighted she wasn't a bit like that but I was, I confess, also a little disappointed. I'd assumed that the touch of the master would be unmistakable. As it turned out, my hunch wasn't far out.

I was almost at my car when I heard my name called. Grace came sprinting up the hill and, when she got to the car, leaned against it till she caught her breath.

'Crumbs, I'm out of shape! That was Murray on the phone. He remembered why the bindings were

271

familiar, remembered where he saw a match. You didn't say there were more?'

'There aren't.' I bit my lip in alarm. Why was my heart thumping? I could almost feel the colour draining from my face.

'He was at the British Library a few weeks ago. A friend of his is one of the keepers there. He's almost certain there was a binding like yours lying on the desk all the time they talked. Murray didn't actually remark on it, they were preoccupied with something else, but it kind of lodged in his memory. He's almost sure it was either a match or damn close to one,' she finished triumphantly.

'Can he find out?'

'Yep. He's on to it. His pal had just left when he called, but he'll get him at home later. Would you like to wait?'

I shook my head and told her I'd go home. I asked her to phone later. My thoughts were in turmoil. All at once my fear that I'd been watched in Dublin crystallized. My diaries had stopped in 1961. If there were more, where were they? Who had taken them? Or had I missed them somehow? Had Lily hidden them too well for me, but not too well for other, more experienced, searchers?

'What's worrying you so much, Nell?' Grace asked.

I couldn't answer. I babbled that I was all right, that I'd phone her, that she could phone me and God knows what else, and drove away before I made a complete ass of myself . . . I needed to think, to be alone, to blockade my flat and my mind against intruders, find out if anyone had been hovering around *Morgen Morgen*. I couldn't quite believe how stupid, how trusting I'd been, or how slow off the mark. While I was dithering, Lily's beloved was being sought by someone more determined, more able and a great deal more ruthless than me. Please God, I whispered, please Lily, let him not be dead. Let him not be dead because of me.

CHAPTER TWENTY-THREE

Jen Harper came around that evening to give me an update on the office politics. She took in the situation, disappeared for an hour and came back loaded down with a take-out Chinese and her laptop computer. She suggested I'd feel better if she took me through what had been going on for the past month, and she was right. She stayed overnight and the following afternoon decided to stay Saturday night as well. We watched *Quiz Show* on video and had another take-away. This time, she cajoled sushi from a new Japanese restaurant on the Twickenham Road. She liked it better than I did; it was all right at the time but afterwards I felt a bit sick. Or maybe it was the second bottle of Jacob's Creek – I hate their oaky Chardonnay – we drank while she regaled me about the hunk who'd started work in the cargo unit next to *Morgen Morgen* at Heathrow. They weren't yet on more than greeting terms but Jen's mind was made up; he was her man. After her fifth glass of wine she had them walking up the aisle. She made me laugh, but then she always can. I don't know how I'd have got through that weekend without her.

On Sunday we had a lazy morning in bed with the newspapers, followed by a long walk by the river. By the afternoon both my head and body were back into something approximating normality. For almost thirty-six hours I'd managed to stop

274

brooding and concentrated on getting back to my job on Monday.

Grace Hartfield didn't ring until quite late on Sunday night. Her news was disappointing: Murray's friend couldn't recall seeing the book described.

'Don't be too down-hearted, Nell,' she said kindly. 'I'm not really surprised. It is several weeks ago, and he's handling such a variety of stuff. Murray's arranged to see him tomorrow afternoon. I'm sure the photos will jog his memory. We'll be in touch as soon as we have anything. We're almost as intrigued as you are.'

I crossed my fingers that something would come out of the meeting. I'd not forgotten that Grace and Murray were moving house the following Tuesday which would make them much too preoccupied to think about my problems. If nothing emerged before then I thought I might take myself to Sothebys and see if their experts could help.

Both my spirits and my brain were back in low gear; I felt I was losing it. After a restless night, I got up very early the following morning and found, to my irritation, that I was completely out of supplies. Stale coffee and no bread. It was still only six-thirty when I set off for the airport so there was plenty of time to drop in to Terminal One for breakfast which I often did on my way to work. At least you can be sure of freshly squeezed oranges from the juice bar on the second floor.

The coach terminus is directly across the car park. Four coaches rolled out, one after another, as I waited at the nearby traffic-light. I scanned the destinations idly: Bath, Oxford, Reading, Cambridge. I had a piercing memory of the excited way Lily used to jump out of the car and toddle off on her travels. Often we'd set off early, as I was doing, and have a croissant and coffee together. Suddenly the scene seemed full of her. The irritated honking of car horns behind me broke my maudlin self-pity, but my appetite was gone. I bypassed breakfast and had a cup of instant at my desk.

The memory of the coaches continued to niggle, off and on, all day. Not that there was any time to dwell on it. I'd never before been away from the job so long which, I suppose, was the reason why I found it almost impossible to click back into work-mode. I disguised it as best I could, but I found the constant demand for quick decisions almost impossible to cope with. The phone never stopped ringing, people kept barging in either to say hello or to hurry things up. The fax machine ground out a steady flow. Obviously my old sparring-partner, Roger, had managed to stack things sufficiently to overload the schedules. I hadn't a single free moment all day to concentrate on anything but getting collections and deliveries back into optimum order and soothing disgruntled customers.

I dragged myself around the supermarket on my way home and was unloading the car when Maria stuck her head out her bathroom window and said a man had been looking for me about half an hour before. Her head was wrapped in a white towel; she looked very fetching.

'Murray Magraw?' I asked. She scratched her head and grimaced.

'Shit. I didn't get his name. Tall. Well, pretty tall

. . .' Maria's five-two, Steve is five-six. She's not very reliable about height.

'American?'

'Yeah, could be. I didn't quite catch what he said. I had shampoo running down my face. Sorry.'

'Did he leave a message, Maria?' I found it hard to control my rising irritation.

'Yeah, said he'd catch you at work tomorrow.'

I froze. I hadn't given the book-partners my work number. I made myself walk slowly over to Maria and forced myself to smile.

'Can you describe him, Maria, please?'

'Like I said. Tall, dark suit. Terrific smile. Snake hips . . . I must say, Nell, you don't waste too much time, you crafty old thing. Is that why Davis . . .' her voice trailed away. 'Nell? Did I do something wrong?'

I swallowed. 'No, honestly.' I bit my lip. 'Maria, was he at the front door?' The entrance to both flats are side by side. At the back they are separate, mine, on the first floor, by way of an outside iron staircase. I couldn't look at Maria while I waited for her answer; I knew what it was going to be.

'No, Nell, he was round the back, that's how I saw him, when he passed the bathroom window. Like you did. Oh hell.' Her hand shot to her mouth. 'Oh hell, fuck, it was a prowler, wasn't it? Damn! How could I fall for it? He said he was looking for you. He said "Is Miss Gilmore not home yet?" '

'Gilmore? He asked for Miss Gilmore? For heaven's sake, Maria, my name is on the doorbell. Oh bloody hell.'

I dropped everything and let myself into the flat, Maria followed hard on my heels in her dressing-gown. We dashed from room to room, examined the windows, but as far as we could see nothing had been disturbed. Except my peace of mind.

Steve arrived home as we went downstairs to retrieve the groceries. I must say he coped admirably with the pair of us and made us drink a stiff shot of brandy apiece. I resisted their offer of dinner and went back up to my flat as soon as I could. My appetite was gone.

The incident was just one too many. I was certain it was Hanlon – the description fitted – I was terrified. Since I'd been stupid enough to give him my work number, I had only myself to blame. I was too edgy to try to work out, calmly and rationally, what the hell was going on. In retrospect, I realize that the break-up of my relationship had a lot to do with how stupid I felt that night. Rejection is ugly even if you've more or less precipitated it yourself. I suppose, deep down, I had flung down a challenge to Davis and fully expected, desperately wanted, him to leap up on his white charger. He hadn't thought it worth his while. And if he didn't or wouldn't, then who would?

The way I kept wanting, worse, inviting, strange men to come on to me was deeply disturbing. It was pathetic. It was dangerous. They could all be Hanlons. But by far the worst thing was that my work, for the very first time ever, had failed to help. It didn't occur to me that I'd gone back before I was ready or able. I'm something of a linear thinker and I felt too pressurized to concentrate on the job when there was so much unfinished business rampaging around my head. At some level, I suppose, I was afraid that, having been found wanting as a lover, I might also be demoted at work. And isn't death the great, the final, rejection? My mother had not only died, she had transformed. I knew nothing about her or her life; I had loved an illusion. At least that is how I felt as I trudged up the stairs.

The answer-phone was blinking. I hesitated before flicking the play-back button, my eyes running restlessly over the contents of the flat. The vague sense of an alien presence I'd felt in Dublin was back, with a vengeance, but with a very significant difference. I didn't think Hanlon – I was certain it was he – had got inside. But deep in my bones I knew that somewhere in my flat there was something he wanted. Something I had overlooked. Something Lily had left. Perhaps I had already found it and did not realize its value?

Murray's laconic drawl was wonderfully soothing. 'Hi, Nell? It's Murray Magraw. I have some news. Not as much as we hoped, though. Still, it might help. Will you call me back?'

No disclosure, no phone number. Grace must have taken me very seriously. I marvelled at their discretion. Suppose Hanlon, or whoever, had got in? Suppose he'd got a message meant for me? I listened to the other three or four messages from concerned friends, while I dialled the Hartfield number.

Grace answered. 'Oh, Nell. Murray thinks you should go and talk to his friend at the British

Library. The bindings might jog his memory. One of us would take you but . . . the movers will be in tomorrow. I'm sorry, I know you're in a hurry. His name is Graham Stockport. We said you'd make an appointment to see him tomorrow. Here's the number.'

'Murray said there was some news?' I said as I jotted it down.

'That's it, I'm afraid. But I'll ring if anything turns up.'

She was as good as her word. About fifty minutes later she rang again.

'News?' I asked eagerly.

'Yes. Rather odd actually. The story is that someone came into the library about ten days ago and, just like you, asked if anyone could identify the binder.'

'Ten days ago?' I squeaked. Grace stopped in mid-track and only continued when she was satisfied I was all right.

'Graham was busy. His assistant, who handled the enquiry, suggested that the man leave the book. It was sent up to Graham's room but he set it aside because he was busy. It was still on his desk the following day while he was taking to Murray – they're writing a book together. Graham didn't manage to get around to the binding until the porter rang for it some hours later. So he had only time for a quick look. It was just like yours, in green morocco, same decoration. He said he had no idea who bound it.'

'But he had?' I asked more in hope than certainty.

'Nothing then, actually not until about twenty

minutes ago.' Her voice lightened triumphantly. 'He came around. They've just gone off for a drink. I said I'd ring you.' She laughed delightedly. 'Listen, Nell, you'll like this. Old Graham is quite a fusspot. He was caught out some years ago when some valuable books, which had been left for him to value, disappeared. So now his assistant automatically photographs everything that comes in for assessment, before it ever gets to Graham. After he looked at Murray's pics he had a backlog of films developed and bingo, there it was. He brought the photographs around to compare the two sets. They're delighted with themselves. They're in the pub celebrating.' She sniffed. 'Any excuse.'

'Do they know who did them?' I asked impatiently.

'No. But Murray's certain they match. And, something else . . .'

'What? Oh God, don't keep me in suspense, please.'

'Graham thinks he may have seen a similar binding some time ago.'

'Oh, is that all?' I could feel my heart sink.

'It's something. You've got them intrigued. I'm pretty certain if anyone can find your binder, they will. Look Nell, I'm not making difficulties. Graham and Murray can't identify him, but they know someone who almost certainly will. They're trying to get in touch with him. His home number's unlisted so they have to wait until tomorrow. Apparently he's *very peculiar* about his privacy. They'll have to try him at the library.' Assuming it was the British Library, I didn't ask what library she was referring to.

'But, but, my binder, my mother's friend, may be in danger . . .'

'Yes. But neither Murray nor I felt we could breach your confidence and say so,' she said calmly. 'Will you be at home all evening? I'll go and fetch them. We'll work out a plan and call you back.'

'Hang on, Grace? Could I come around now? I'll bring the diaries with me.'

She considered for a moment before agreeing. I hung up before she could change her mind. I checked the locks on the windows, primed the alarm and double-locked the doors. I dropped in on Steve and Maria and asked them to call the police if they heard any more prowlers. Then I drove, like a bat from hell, to Clerkenwell. Even breaking seven traffic lights, it took almost an hour.

Graham Stockport was a small elderly man with a pronounced stoop and bad teeth but what nature had stinted in looks, he made up with charm. He disarmed me immediately by apologizing for letting 'my' diary out of his hands. By now he'd convinced himself that his caller was 'a terribly shady customer, my dear' who had stolen the diary. For some unknown reason, Dr Stockport was extremely partisan in his belief of my claim to the books I'd brought with me. He took them from my hands with the same reverent care Grace had displayed the day before, and examined them minutely for a long time before handing them to Murray.

'You can see traces of the German influence, here . . .' And they were away. Grace rolled her eyes to heaven and went off to the kitchen to make some coffee while I sat listening to them, almost screaming with impatience. But even a child could see that Dr Stockport, once launched, was not to be hurried. In due time he raised his eyes from the diaries and beamed at me.

'These are really quite wonderful, my dear. I wish I could tell you who made these beautiful things, but I cannot. However, I think you must go and see an authority I know in Oxford. His knowledge of books and binding is encyclopaedic. Made it his life's study, though I believe he is entirely self-taught. I've written down the college number, because I'm ashamed to say, I can't remember the chap's name. It's embarrassing, but there you are. Just ask for the restorer, though of course, he may call himself the conservator, or archivist perhaps. I hope he will help you. Astonishing chap, but I have to warn you, he may take some persuading, he has something of a reputation as a recluse, besides . . .' and he was off again.

I did not notice Murray slip out. Dr Stockport rambled on for ages and he was impossible to interrupt. An hour or so later, I dropped him at King's Cross station, and drove slowly home, memorizing the college name and phone number he had written down for me before I left. When I stopped for petrol I lit a cigarette, burned the slip of paper and let the ashes float away into the night sky. I'd learnt my lesson at last.

I did not go to bed until nearly three, I was much too twitchy. Instead, I systematically went through the flat gathering together every single memento of my mother: her guide books, photographs, odds and ends of clothes and an old toilet bag I found in the hot press. I almost missed it, because it was wedged between a pile of towels and the wall. Inside there was, rather strangely, a stout, short-handled screwdriver. It was such an odd thing to find in the bag that I felt certain it was there for some purpose. I held it in my hand while I ran my bath, then I laid it between the taps and sank back in the deep perfumed foam. Why would Lily keep a screwdriver in the hot-press?

My brain slowly unscrambled. The great thing about long hot baths is that you can release your mind to wander where it will: hot-press, toilet-bag, screwdriver, bath. Screwdriver, bath. My hand edged lazily along the wooden side-panel of the bath, stopped as I traced the shape of a screw-head with my dripping fingers, first one, then another. When I came to a third, I shot out of the steam like a rocket and, wet and naked, knelt beside the bath. Eight screws, each capped in bright chrome, held the panel in place. I dried my hands and removed the caps, then took the screwdriver and unscrewed the wooden panel. On the floor behind it, inside a ziploc sandwich bag were two envelopes. The first contained a dozen or so photographs. I put on my bathrobe and dried my hands before taking them out. The contents of the second envelope immediately arrested my attention: neatly held together, with a pink paper clip, was a little bundle of used coach tickets, every single one a day-return from Heathrow to Oxford.

I took the photographs to the bedroom and spread them out on my bed. They were, obviously, from a single roll of film, taken on a beautiful sunny day. Half of them had my mother in the foreground but what interested me was the male, Panama-hatted figure, shyly posing in the others. In the last picture of all, he was sitting with my mother at the café table. It was not as good as my mother's framed copy, the figures were much more blurred but, oddly, the diaries were much clearer and also the name of the café, Browns. I went through the photographs again, this time more slowly. I thought I recognized at least one of the buildings; the much photographed Radcliffe Camera. I checked Lily's guidebook so there'd be no doubt in my mind.

All roads seemed to be leading towards the dreaming spires of Oxford.

CHAPTER TWENTY-FOUR

Dr Stockport beat me to the draw the following morning. He rang me at the office when I was on the point of phoning his contact in Oxford. It took me a few moments to make sense of his long-winded spiel but I eventually gathered that there was a hitch.

'Alas, I had forgotten that I shall be at a learned' (he pronounced it learn-ed) 'meeting most of today but if, my dear, you would wait until tomorrow evening, then I could quite easily accompany you to Oxford. I wish I could remember the poor fellow's name but you know, it has completely slipped my mind. I rang the college to say we would visit the library tomorrow. Had the secretary not been, well, my dear, she was rather officious, but *had* she mentioned it *en passant*, as it were, it would have ameliorated the situation considerably. Dear me, my poor memory.' He had a pedantic trick of almost audibly punctuating his clauses and sub-clauses which, even in my disappointment, I found highly diverting. I wondered how on earth he managed to talk to the secretary without eliciting the archivist's name. Though on second thoughts it was quite easy. Trying to get a word in with Dr Stockport was almost impossible. But I had a shot.

'Would you like me to pick you up?'

'By motor car?' He made it sound a very

delightful proposition. 'I had thought the train, my dear, but, since you so kindly offer, a motor-ride would be most agreeable. Such nice weather. An open-topped car, you say? How very delightful *that* will be.' He was really very sweet. We agreed I would pick him up at four the next day.

'I shall get away a little early, we must avoid the rush-hour,' he announced succinctly, with a surprising touch of practicality. I half expected him to suggest a picnic en route. He apologized again that 'we could not make our excursion today' but promised to be waiting for me the following afternoon. He reminded me to bring the diaries. There was nothing to be done but endure yet another delay. It seemed almost too much to bear.

My inability to concentrate seemed to be growing. I was literally dragging myself around trying to look as if I was in control but I don't imagine I was fooling anyone, least of all, Jen Harper.

'I think you should be at home, Nell.' She was standing at the window out of range of my glare. 'If you don't mind me saying so.'

'Why?' I asked belligerently.

'It's too soon. You look dreadfully tired. You've no energy. You need to lighten up. Will I go on?'

I was about to make some crack about her being my assistant, not my nanny, when she suddenly hissed: 'Psst, come and look, quick, tell me what you think.'

I wandered over to join her, preoccupied by the accuracy of her assessment and resenting it. She was right on every point.

'Quick, quick, you'll miss him.' She grabbed my arm and pointed to the tall figure striding towards the next office. 'That's him. That's ma ma-an!' she carolled. His back was to us. As he pushed back the concertina-door I couldn't quite see his face but the broad-shouldered, pin-striped back completely unnerved me. I thought I was going to be sick.

'Oh my God.' I stumbled back to my desk. Jen was at my side, all concern. I said nothing until I could control myself.

'How long has he been around?'

'He's not here all the time. He's designing a new computer package for North South Transit next door. He's a consultant. He's been in and out for about a month. Why, Nell? Do you know him?'

'Yeah.' My face was set. Hanlon. The bastard had been snooping around while I was still in Dublin.

'He didn't say.'

'He was asking about me?'

'Not really. I was telling him about my job. Your name naturally came up.'

'Have you been out with him?'

'Couple of times. Casual. Pub lunch, that kind of thing. Otherwise . . .'

'Otherwise?' I could feel the fury suffuse my face. 'Otherwise he drops by to chat you up? Right? You didn't mention the parcel I sent you by any chance, did you?' I said nastily. Poor Jen. If I hadn't been so recently bereaved I'm certain she would have told me what to do with myself. She looked very upset.

'Jen. I'm sorry, I don't trust Cormac Hanlon . . .'

'Who?'

'That guy you're so keen on, Cormac Hanlon . . .'

The tension flowed away. She drew back her head and humoured me with amused indulgence. 'Who in hell is Cormac Hanlon? That's not his name.' She indicated next door with a flick of her thumb. 'His name, since you asked so nicely, is Matt Craig,' she said sarcastically then immediately relented. 'Honestly Nell, what's got into you? Of course I didn't mention the parcel. How can you ask? Was there anything wrong with it?'

'No.'

'Of course there wasn't. I took it home the minute it arrived and I gave it into your own hands the day you came home. You didn't find anything wrong with it then, did you?'

'I know, I'm sorry. Forget it. I made a mistake. I thought he was someone I know.'

'I feel quite upset that you should even think I'd discuss it!' Jen turned away sulkily and busied herself shuffling papers around my desk. She wouldn't look at me. I felt mortified. After a discreet pause she went quietly back to her own desk and logged on to her computer.

I put my head in my hands and closed my eyes in shame. My obsession with Hanlon was out of hand. I was seeing bogeymen everywhere. Even a passing likeness – to his suit, for pity's sake – was enough for me to assume it was actually the man. If anything was guaranteed to demonstrate my state of mind, my uncalled-for attack on Jen was. That wasn't how we operated. We were completely open with each other. Now I had pulled the carpet from beneath her feet in the most autocratic way.

By the time I'd calmed down and opened my

eyes, Jen had disappeared and Dieter was coming through the door. He eyed me with some concern.

'My dear Nell! I've just got in from Milan. I'd no idea you were coming back so soon. Really it's ridiculous, I told you to take as much time as you want. You look so pale. What's the matter?'

What could I say? I'd always tried to keep my work and private life absolutely separate. At *Morgen Morgen* my image was cool, efficient, competent. I didn't get sick, I didn't ask for time off. No girlie stunts. Until now. The urge to pour my fears and half-fears into Dieter's sympathetic ear was tempting but not wise. We knew and liked each other in our professional guise. Perhaps his private life was as chaotic as mine but somehow I doubted it.

'I'm not sleeping terribly well since my mother's death.' I brushed his concern aside. 'And I've a touch of flu. I'll be all right.'

He regarded me silently for some minutes then perched himself on the side of my desk.

'I actually came to ask Jen for your Dublin number. There's something I wanted to discuss with you, Nell. I didn't expect you back for another week, at least. I thought that was what we agreed?' Though he spoke gently enough, in my embattled mood he sounded distant, offhand.

Strange how difficult it is to accept help or even concern from your friends. From people at work, even harder. I wondered why it was that the kindness of two relative strangers the day before had been so much less threatening than the affection and sympathy offered first by Jen, now Dieter. But there seemed to be no reasonable answer to that. Or not one that I could cope with.

I shrugged. 'What is it you wanted to talk about?'

He had his hand on the door-handle. 'It'll keep. I think you must now hand over to Jen and go home and rest. I insist, Nell. I don't want you getting ill.' His tone brooked no argument. 'Come and see me before you go. We could have lunch together, I'll send out for something. Give us time for a chat.' He was very formal. He shut the door quietly but remained in the corridor outside. For some minutes I could hear the soft murmur of his voice and Jen's.

Was I being given the boot? I sat stock-still, my paranoia rising. Jen put her head around the door, looking flushed and distinctly apprehensive.

'God, Jen, I'm sorry. I don't know what got into me.'

She hesitated for a moment or two before putting her arm around my shoulders.

'I do. You're so wound up, Nell, honestly. If you don't slow down you'll . . .'

'Crack up. I know, I know. I'm going home after lunch. I'll take another week or so, if you think you can . . .' My voice wobbled.

'It's OK honey, it's OK,' she soothed. We clung to each other until we'd both stopped snivelling. Then we sat at my desk, as we usually do, and sorted through the calendar for the following two weeks. Late August is a quiet time for freight movement. With a couple of temps, Jen could do it standing on her head but she was thoughtful enough to ask if she could phone me for advice should there be a panic. When we finished, I cleared my desk and packed my briefcase with the ominous feeling that I was leaving for good.

Dieter was standing at the door of his office, waiting for me. He ushered me in with more ceremony than I thought necessary but I kept my lip stiff. When I said that I'd sorted things with Jen and would take the extra leave he advised, he nodded. He pulled up a chair for me and he perched himself, as he usually did, at the edge of his desk and sat silently, swinging his leg, waiting. He looked uncomfortable, as if he was trying to work something out.

'I think,' he said finally, 'I think there's no other way . . .' He was interrupted by a discreet knock on the door. I swallowed but said nothing. What was there to say? Except that I desperately wanted Jen, not Roger, to take over my job.

A young lad strode into the office carrying a cold-box. Dieter moved silently to the window while the boy whipped out a white cloth and transformed the desk into an impromptu picnic table. Plates of smoked salmon and brown bread emerged from the box followed by a bottle of Moët and a half dozen flutes. Exit with style, I suppose, but God! I could do without it. The boy glided out and Dieter picked up a glass.

'Are we celebrating something?' I asked stiffly.

'Well, yes, Nell, as a matter of fact we are. I know you're not in the mood, but we've just appointed our new operations *director* for the UK.'

I closed my eyes and cursed Roger Mason to hell. Shafted. I was too furious to say anything. But I still had my dignity. I sat bolt upright in my chair, raised accusing eyes to my late boss and smiled frostily. Dieter seemed to be having some difficulty composing his expression. He carefully eased the cork from the bottle, looked straight at me and broke into a huge grin. I'll never understand the German sense of humour. I forced a smile, game to the bitter end.

'Will you accept?' he asked casually.

I gasped. 'But I thought . . . Me?' My voice was too loud and much too shrill.

'Yes, of course you. Who else?' He laughed and filled both glasses. 'Well, come on, Nell, will you?'

'Oh God, yes. Of course I accept,' I said and burst into tears. Dieter filled a couple of plates, and mercifully ignored the waterworks.

'I've asked Jen and Roger to join us. Before they come there are one or two things . . . I know you'd like Jen to take over your job, OK? Roger will be running the Manchester office. Officially the changes will be from the first of October, but I think Jen can start right away, if you agree. You're to meet the full board on September twenty-fifth. I'll travel with you to Hamburg. When we get back, I'll ease you in for a couple of weeks before I go to head office where I'll be your direct contact, which, I must say, I'm delighted about.' He waited for me to agree and I did, enthusiastically.

'Good. You'll need to recruit a few extra staff, Nell, but we can go through the budget later. That all suit?' He shook my hand and then, rather shyly, hugged me. 'Our first woman on the board! Oh Nell dear, I'm so pleased.' He looked quite bashful.

I was overwhelmed. Bless him, but I don't think Dieter had any idea what had been going through my mind or how insecure I'd become. I raised my glass, took a long swig of cold wine and thanked him. He had, from my first days with *Morgen*

Morgen, made sure the glass ceiling never slid over my head. I had barely time to tell him how much that meant to me before Roger Mason and Jen joined us.

I couldn't quite believe the salary I was offered – and accepted – I wasn't that de-railed. I could almost hear Davis's squeal of pain all the way from Hong Kong. Directorships had been on his agenda, not mine. According to him, I wasn't the right stuff. Stuff him, I thought crudely, but while the elation lasted I felt almost normal. Normal and quite nasty, actually. Vis à vis my late lamented lover, that is.

I drove home in a daze, slowly. The champagne was playing roller-coaster with my head and my empty stomach. I wasn't entirely sober but I managed the journey without incident, then lay down to sleep it off. I had just dropped off when I was woken by a persistent buzzing of the doorbell. I must have looked a sight when I groggily opened the door. The stranger on my doorstep seem to notice.

'I'm sorry if I've disturbed you,' he said politely. 'Is your name Gilmore?' His voice was soft, educated and just the slightest trace foreign.

'Yes. Who wants to know?' I asked suspiciously.

'I do,' he said and switched on the most amazing smile. Maybe it was the champagne – and the empty stomach, of course – but I beamed right back. The new director may even have giggled. Then I remembered, a fraction too late, *beware strangers*.

He was probably in his mid to late thirties. Thin and very tall and, if not exactly handsome, nice looking. Dark almost black eyes, curly blue-black hair, sprinkled with grey, a rather prominent nose. As I appraised him he openly appraised me. I've no idea what he thought. Probably nothing very complimentary. I was rather dishevelled, my make-up long since cried away. Fear and suspicion must have vibrated from me but I was rooted to the spot, unable to move.

'You are,' he checked a slip of paper he was carrying, 'you are, er, Lily Sweetman's daughter?'

'You knew my mother?' My mouth opened like a distraught goldfish.

'Alas, no, not really. I met her once, just briefly. My father and she . . .'

His alarming black eyes hypnotized me, I could not look away. My head kept nodding up and down, then it began to swim. His voice seemed a long way off.

'My name is Daniel Garnier,' he said, pronouncing it *à la francais*. 'My father sent me. He is ill and would like to see you. May I come in and explain?' He sounded exasperated.

I gripped the door for dear life. Another stranger. Another personable stranger claiming to know Lily Sweetman, wanting to get inside my house. I was all alone, Maria and Steve still at work, as were the next door neighbours on either side. Fear and suspicion must surely have shown on my face, because he stepped towards me and put out his hand. I backed away, then I did the girlie thing and passed out.

I came to on the sofa with my caller pressing a glass of water to my lips. I spluttered and tried to jump up but my legs wouldn't obey. I must have looked as ridiculous as I felt because he seemed awfully amused. Not unkindly, just, well sort of friendly, as if something quite pleasant had occurred to him. It never before struck me that humour is a hell of a good antidote to fear. Next thing he was taking my pulse.

'It's all right, I'm a doctor.' He was full of surprises. 'When did you last eat?'

'Lunch time?' Then I remembered how I hate smoked salmon, or at least the nasty slimy variety the caterer had supplied. I like it Scotch and slightly dry and crumbly, none of your old super-market kipper. 'Last night? Sometime yesterday. I'm not big on food at the moment.'

I bent over and pressed my throbbing head to my knees and only realized he was not beside me when I heard the kettle being filled in the kitchen. That's the other antidote to fear; domesticity. I knew if, at that moment, my smiling intruder brought me a cup of tea, I'd let him have whatever he asked. He came in with the tea and a small plate of lightly buttered bread – just as well I'd done the shopping – and sat over me while I sipped and swallowed. He did the talking.

'I'm sorry to have frightened you. I beg you to believe I mean you no harm. I'm here because my father is very ill and keeps asking for you. It has taken me several days to locate you, he wasn't very coherent about where you live. Morgan at the airport is what he kept saying. I eventually worked it out. Your secretary pointed you out as you left the car park. I followed you home but it's taken me a little time to gather my courage to ring your bell.'

As I struggled for control, I weighed him up. He seemed genuine enough; the most obvious thing about him was his embarrassment. If he'd wanted to take advantage of me he could have done so when I fainted. But it would have been stupid to take him too readily at his word.

'Did you say you're a doctor? Where?' I asked briskly.

'In France.'

'GP or hospital?'

'Hospital.'

'OK, what's the phone number? Quick, no thinking.'

He reeled it off. I went to the phone and dialled the long string of digits and got the Hôtel Dieu in Carpentras – wherever that is. It seemed genuine enough, I could hear ambulance sirens in the background.

'*Je voudrais parler à Monsieur Daniel Garnier.*' There was a short delay while I was put through, presumably to his secretary. When she came on the line she regretted that Monsieur le Docteur was away and offered the services of a '*confrère*'. M le Docteur looked a trifle bemused when I rejoined him.

'That's quite a trick,' he said.

'What is?'

'Your memory. Will you remember the number?'

'Not for long, unless I write it down.'

'I hope you will.'

I coughed. Enough of the banter. 'Well now I know your name but I'm not any the wiser.' I eyed him steadily. 'I'll give you exactly five minutes to explain exactly who you are and what you're doing here. Oh, and by the way – where the hell is Carpentras?'

'In Provence. I'm an orthopaedic surgeon at the regional hospital.' He took off his watch and laid it elaborately on the coffee table. Then he cocked an eyebrow at me and began to talk.

'My father lives in Oxford.'

I held up my hand. 'Hold it, right there,' I said. 'What's his name?'

'Myles Garnier.'

M? My heart sank. The diaries were dedicated by MM. 'Garnier? He's French?'

'No. His name is really McDonagh, Garnier was adopted for convenience.'

So. Myles McDonagh. MM. This was more like it. Was I getting somewhere at last?

'And you're his son?'

'Yes.' He smiled. He was enjoying my discomfort.

'And your name is Garnier? How come?'

'Five minutes, you say? I'll try to explain. My parents met when my mother was in England as an au pair. She's French. After they married they lived in France for ten years. My grandparents have a small vineyard in the Ventoux, about ten miles from Carpentras. When my parents married, they helped run it. People there found it difficult to pronounce McDonagh so they used my mother's family name. Eventually, I believe, Papa changed it legally.' Gallic shrug. 'I've always been Garnier. After a few years my father became ill, depressed. They were not very happy. Eventually they separated. My father returned to Oxford when I was ten years old. I was at boarding school there, so I've always seen a lot of him. I went to university in Aix. My mother still runs the vineyard with her partner, a Frenchman. OK, that explains the names. Three more minutes,' he said, and took a deep breath.

'They kept in touch, my parents. They get on better long distance. My father prefers to cope with his illness alone. Sometimes my mother visits, since my father no longer leaves home. Never. That is how I knew your mother meant so much to him. He travelled to Ireland for her funeral.'

'Just a minute. If he was there, and he wanted to see me, why didn't he talk to me then?'

Daniel Garnier shook his head sadly. 'If I understood his behaviour, I might be able to help him, but I cannot. My poor father is a sad and frightened man. I have never known why.' He sighed. 'Your mother understood him, I think. He seemed comfortable with her.'

'How do you know that?'

'It's a long story and it probably won't make sense because you don't know him. About eighteen months ago, I was at a medical conference in Oxford and I saw them together, quite by chance. He didn't know I was in town. I was walking up the Woodstock Road towards Green College, when I spotted him sitting in the sunshine, outside Browns restaurant. He was with a woman and they were chatting like happy children. I have to tell you I was astonished. Papa never goes to restaurants. Never. I was even more surprised when he invited me to join them. Unfortunately, I was already late for a lecture so I could only delay for a few minutes. It was wonderful, they were so much in love . . .' He smiled at me ruefully. 'Too French, eh?' he asked archly. I gave a weak smile.

'She had a camera beside her on the table. She asked if I would take their picture. She looked so . . . so . . . *gaie* . . .' More gallic shrugs. I couldn't stand it. I went off to my bedroom and fetched the envelope of photographs and silently laid them before him.

'Ah, you have them!' He pulled them out, studied them all carefully and looked at me excitedly. 'Good, now you know I . . .' He shuffled through the photos then divided them into two neat lines on the coffee table. 'These are very interesting, don't you think? They say so much about the two of them.' I followed his eyes but did not understand what he meant.

'Look. These taken by my father – see, he focuses on the buildings, your mother's image is slightly blurred. Now look at hers – he is in sharp focus, the buildings not.'

'You think he was more important to her than she to him?'

'If I had not seen them together, but just these pictures, then perhaps I would think so.' He spoke gently. 'But I did see them. No, my father is afraid. Afraid of life and afraid of people. It is habitual with him. That is what these pictures show. He is too old to change. He loved her. I would swear it. But perhaps even she could not help him enough.' He pushed the photos away and passed his hand over his eyes.

'After he came back from the funeral, he became ill. I think he stopped eating. He also stopped going into college. But he did that sometimes, so it wasn't remarked on. In any case it's vacation time, there were few people about. His absence wasn't noticed for over a week. The librarian raised the alarm when he went to the college to collect some restoration work and found my father wasn't around. They sent someone up to his house but it appeared to be abandoned. The neighbours weren't able to help, they hardly know my father. After his third or fourth try, the librarian rang me in France.

'I came at once. I found him collapsed in his study, fully clothed. He was very ill. He asked me to leave him be but the college secretary, who was with me, phoned emergency. Father had a heart attack as they were getting him into the ambulance. He isn't recovering well. Every time he comes around, he asks for you. I beg you to come. Please.'

There are moments in your life when you know that if you make a move it will be irrevocable. This felt like such a moment. I remained immobile for so long he must have thought me catatonic. Could I trust this stranger? I'd read the diaries so I wanted his father to be M. It was he, above all, I longed to meet; the kind and gentle boy who had loved my mother. Garnier had merely identified the man in the photograph. Was it enough? Was this another ruse? Was he another envoy for Hanlon or Reynolds?

I told him to wait for a few minutes. I washed quickly, stuffed the diaries in my bag and rang Dr Stockport. Mercifully, he was not at home. When I recovered from my astonishment that he had an answering machine, I politely cancelled our appointment for the next day. I hoped he knew how to play it back, it seemed a dangerously modern contraption for so old-fashioned a pedant.

'Is your father a bookbinder?' I asked abruptly when I joined Dr Garnier.

'Yes,' he said.

We left for Oxford shortly after seven. I insisted on following Dr Garnier in my own car. Even though my instinct was to trust him, I thought it safer to hedge my bets a little. I'd had enough trespassers in my private space. Lily would have been delighted with him, though. The French are very patriotic about their cars, even the half-French; his was an obscenely large Citroën. He drove like a maniac. I had difficulty keeping up. I wasn't sure whether I believed his explanation about his name. Not that I was interested. All I wanted, and I wanted it passionately, was to get to the bottom of my mother's death. Everything else was a diversion.

Dr Garnier had talked hard and persuasively but what made me trust him most was that he appeared to be as perplexed and nervous as I was. Though I tried, I couldn't remember seeing his father at the funeral but, having read the diaries, I was already partisan about him, specially if he really was the boy who'd loved my mother. But people don't die of love, do they? I'm not French or particularly romantic, it just didn't seem reasonable. Strange and frightening things had been happening to me since Lily died. I had plenty to think about on the journey. As I sped along the M40, I forced my mind back over every detail of the funeral: my first sight of Reynolds, then of Hanlon. Slowly, from the edges of my memory, came the shadowy figure of a tall stooped man limping towards the gate of the cemetery. I moved the three men like chessmen. They had seen me. Had they seen or recognized him?

He limps ever nearer the gate, I go to talk to the sexton, my head bent against the rain. When I come out, Hanlon is in the porch with his umbrella. We hurry out to the car. No sign of the old man. We stand there. Something happens as we stand there. What? Water splashes our legs. A big black car passes us. A Mercedes. Dark windows. That car. I saw it again somewhere. Where? Where? I try and try but the images have faded.

CHAPTER TWENTY-FIVE

The John Radcliffe Hospital in Oxford – a series of vast, white, modern cubes – is situated on Headington Hill, on the eastern approach to the city from London.

The roads were mercifully clear, and we made it in just under an hour. Daniel Garnier's father was on the seventh floor in the cardiac ward which ran the whole length of one side of the building. It was divided into multiple four-bed cubicles which opened on to the corridor.

I recognized him immediately, he was so like his son. But whereas the son was thin, the father was emaciated. His bed, with a surrounding battery of monitors, was in the central unit, nearest the nursing station. He looked dreadful, his complexion a deathly greyish-white. Tubes from his nose and wires from his chest and arms were connected to the complexity of winking machines behind the bed-head. Visiting time had ended and lights had been dimmed by the time we got there but for the really sick, or the dying, time schedules did not seem to apply.

The old man was asleep, his breathing shallow and rasping. Every now and then a dreadful tremor ran through his body. Within a minute or two of our arrival, Dr Garnier went to consult the young houseman and nurse at the desk while I sat quietly beside the bed. I had the weirdest feeling that an agitated Lily was hovering somewhere close by, trying to get a word in.

Was this the M of the diaries? How could I tell? He was certainly the man at the cafe. I took the photo from my bag to check image and reality: the beautiful long slim hands were not pale, as in the picture, but a sickly blue-white. Though the fine lined face was much thinner, the abundant grey hair was the same. His son was not as handsome, but I hoped he was happier. Even with his eyes shut, the father emanated sadness. Though perhaps I was being fanciful.

As he woke he moved his head restlessly, back and forth, on the pillow. I studied his side view and with a shock recalled again the drifting memory of that slim, grey-haired figure limping towards the cemetery gate at Lily's funeral. I closed my eyes, the better to fix the image. Once again I moved the mourners, the watchers, into place; the neighbours, the friends, Hanlon, Arthur Reynolds, me, M. I could see him moving off towards the exit before I lost him. Where did he go? Had he a car? Had Hanlon and Reynolds been watching to see . . . to see what? It suddenly seemed obvious. They wanted to see who would make contact with me. But wily M had kept well away. They had missed him. Or had they?

Was there someone else watching . . . watching him? Oh yes, I thought, oh yes. There was someone lurking in the back of that blasted black Mercedes.

He was trying to say something. The flutter of his fingers over my hand broke my reverie and when I leaned over the bed I saw that his eyes were open, pleading.

'Closer,' he mouthed and his eyes drooped with the effort. The pulse counter leapt to 106 then dropped back to 62. As it danced up and down, it exerted a fearful fascination. I tore my eyes away and held my ear to his cold lips.

'Nell?' He whispered, clutching my hand. 'Lily's girl?'

'Yes. I'm Lily's daughter, Nell. Are you, er, M?'

His eyelids flickered. 'Milo.' A breath rather than a sound and Lily's Milo drifted out of consciousness. I sat back and watched him until he began to stir again. He fought his demons gallantly, poor man, but the effort was appalling. I took the two diaries from my bag and placed them under his right hand. I tried to warm his poor fingers with mine and, after a little while, they began to move lethargically over the top cover, identifying the tracery. The eyes remained closed. He slid his hand from under mine as if he was searching for something. Then he began to claw at the bedcover. I could almost feel the effort he was making to open his eyes again, but he was too weak.

'Milo?' I whispered in his ears. It seemed so natural to call him that, as if I'd known him all my life. 'How many are there? Milo? How many diaries did you make?'

There was another long pause as he drifted off again. When I put out my hand to take his again I noticed he was holding three fingers outstretched with the little finger and thumb curled under his palm. His eyes were still closed.

'Three? Were there three diaries, Milo?' I held

306

my head close to his on the pillow. He smelt of dried apples.

'And ... box ... letters. Box.' The words, though faint, were quite clear.

'You made a box as well? A box for Lily's letters?'

'And mine,' he rasped. His head lolled sideways and he gave a deep, juddering sigh. The heart-rhythm patterns danced a mazurka and the numbers on the monitors fluctuated wildly. Behind me, a nurse talked rapidly, urgently. Daniel returned and sat at the other side of the bed. He touched his father's forehead with the tips of his fingers.

'Papa? Lily's girl is here. Papa?'

'Danny.' The word was barely audible but I had never heard a name uttered with such love. Milo's eyes blinked open, a faint half-smile stretched the parched lips. His son took a cotton swab from a glass on the bedside table and held it to his mouth. The effort it took to suck the moisture was agonizing. I felt the fluttering fingers clutched at my sleeve.

'Lily ... love ... Lily ... life ... killed ... re ... Nell ... ledge ... danger ... us ...' The sounds came between long painful pauses while the lips made sentences of the silence surrounding the seemingly unconnected words. Ten words. I did my number trick and committed them to memory. *Lily, love, Lily, life, killed, re, Nell, ledge, danger, us.*

Though I leaned closer and closer as his lips continued to move, I could not catch the word he kept repeating. Us, us, us. Us? His? Use? House? It might have been house.

307

'House? Are you saying house, Milo?' He made a supreme effort and gave an almost imperceptible little nod of his head.

'Whose house, Milo? Yours or Lily's?'

He didn't respond. The number of one of the monitors suddenly began to slide backwards, hesitantly at first, then with increased rapidity. I was mesmerized by those dancing green lights: 98, 74, 53, 38, 26, 12, 4. Milo's hand rested on his chest, his forefinger outstretched. There was a piercing, insistent bleep, the bed was surrounded by nurses and doctors and I found myself being eased gently out into the corridor by Daniel. He led me rapidly away, gripping me firmly by my elbow. Involuntary rasping sobs came from my throat.

'We both need a cup of coffee,' he said shakily. We headed towards the lift.

'What happened?'

'Probably another myocardial infarction – a heart attack, he's been having them since he came in.'

'Is he? Is he . . . ?'

'Going to die? Yes.' His voice was flat, lifeless. 'Probably in the next few days. But I think not tonight.'

I looked up at him but for the life of me I could not ask him why he sounded so certain. I didn't need to, he answered anyway.

'He has fought too hard, he is too determined. It is, I think, something to do with you. Or your mother. He wants to . . . God knows what he wants . . .' He ran his hand through his hair and looked down at me. In the close confines of the lift he seemed even taller yet, touchingly, much

308

younger, more vulnerable. As we rode downwards I jotted the ten disjointed words on the back of my cheque-book and stuffed it back in my bag.

Neither of us spoke again until we found the canteen. It was empty of both staff and customers and served only by a hot and cold drink dispenser. Of course, the moment I saw there was no possibility of food, I became ravenously hungry and desperate for a cigarette.

'I'd like to stay another hour or so. Until he settles down. It won't be too late to eat, if you can wait till then?' Daniel said suddenly.

'I should get back home . . .' I felt awkward, in the way. I also felt that I was partly responsible for his father's dreadful agitation.

'I hoped you would stay, see him tomorrow?' He tried to keep his tone light but it was a plea nevertheless. I swallowed hard and looked at him. 'I mean it,' he said.

'I'll come back first thing in the morning, early.'

'It may be too late. Can't you stay?' He spoke gently but insistently.

I looked at my watch. It was only twenty past nine but it felt like the middle of the night. 'Yes, of course, if you think . . . I don't suppose you know a hotel I could . . .'

'I stay in a very good bed and breakfast close by, there's a room there.'

'Fine.' I didn't ask him how he knew, I was too embarrassed. I wanted to go yet I'd promised to stay. I was so sorry for him. It was outrageous that with so much going on, he felt compelled to look after me as well.

'Dr Garnier? Does your father have a limp?'

'Yes, he lost a leg during the war.' He lowered his head, suddenly overwhelmed by grief. He interlocked his agitated fingers and rubbed his palms back and forth nervously. His hands were quite unlike his father's; square, strong with rather stubby fingers which didn't match his tall slim frame. After a while he noticed me staring and spread them out before me.

'Farmer's hands.' He forced a wry smile. 'Like my mother's and grandfather's. As it happens, very practical for an orthopaedic surgeon. Strength is useful. All those overweight arthritics.'

It almost broke me up, the effort he made. My own thoughts were haywire, all over the place, flitting from Lily to Milo to . . . What? Danger. He said danger.

'What'll you have?' Daniel broke in on my thoughts.

'Two-seven,' I answered without thinking.

He looked bewildered. 'Two-seven?'

'Black coffee, no sugar. You'll have to press two-seven on that machine to get it. We have one like it in the office. It's what I call the stuff that comes out, it's certainly not coffee. I'll get them. Two-seven for you as well?'

He watched listlessly while I wrestled with the coffee machine. In the event, neither of us drank the filthy stuff, we just stared moodily into it until one of the nurses called 'Danny' back to his father's bedside. While he was away, I phoned Maria and told her I was staying on in Oxford. When I told her I'd found the man in the photo she was agog, but mercifully restrained herself. Perhaps I sounded more upset than I realized.

'How long will you stay, Nell?'

'As long as it takes. He's very ill, Maria. He looks dreadful, poor man.'

I promised to ring her the following day and had just put down the receiver when an ashen-faced Daniel reappeared. He stumbled in, threw himself down at the nearest table and buried his head in his hands. The room was so still that the faint click of the electric clock was audible. He wept inconsolably, with great juddering heaves of his shoulders. I didn't know what to do. I desperately wanted to comfort him but inspiration failed me. Doesn't it always? I waited till the storm subsided then joined him at the table. I don't know how long we sat there, facing each other, looking but not seeing, our thoughts turned inwards.

A young doctor broke the spell; he looked half-dazed with fatigue. Ignoring me, he touched Daniel on the shoulder and beckoned him to one side. They conferred in whispers for a short time then they went away. After about ten minutes, Daniel came back looking considerably relieved.

'It's OK, he's come out of it.' He smiled. 'He's resting now. He'd worked himself into a fearful state, looking for you. I promised to bring you around in the morning. I hope that's all right?'

'Yes, certainly. But,' I hesitated, 'I won't make him worse, will I?

'No. He's been holding on for you.' He smiled down at me.

'He'll be all right alone? I can easily find a hotel if you want to stay with him overnight?'

'No. He'll sleep now, he's exhausted. I'd be in the way.' He smiled again and for a moment looked almost happy. 'Now, I don't know about you, but I am ravenous.' He threw back his shoulders. 'OK? Let's go and eat.'

CHAPTER TWENTY-SIX

We drove in convoy to Mrs Power's B&B. It was stylish, airy and meticulously clean. I wasn't entirely surprised to find that Mrs Power was a Frenchwoman who fussed and clucked over '*cher* Daniel' like an adoring mother. I parried her more personal enquiries as she led me up to a delightful little suite under the eaves. By the time I rejoined Daniel downstairs my knowledge of his way of life had grown a little.

'The Papa' was a little eccentric. This was not her opinion but what other people said. So strange, he lived just a tiny walk away, yet she never saw him except when Daniel stayed. And not often then. Daniel had been coming to her house since he was a boy – half-terms, weekends, holidays. He was like a son. She and ''is maman' came from the same village in Provence. She was very proprietorial, well nosy, really. I remembered why I usually avoided guest-houses.

When I eventually escaped, Daniel drove me across the town to a small Italian restaurant. He seemed to be well known there as well.

Which table for '*il dottore*?' What would Dottore like to eat?

'Special tonight, we have the fantastic sea-bass, the fantastic asparagus, the beautiful saltimbocca . . .' The waiter fussed over him, offering choice but in fact choosing both food and wine for the two of us. It was exactly what we needed.

We ate the sea-bass and asparagus, it would have been churlish to do otherwise. Fantastic might have been pushing it a bit, but the food was good and the service excellent. We both needed cherishing and the waiter filled his role to perfection. We drank a crisp, fruity Corvo and ate heartily. Neither of us said very much during the meal. The intimacy of the small restaurant had made us shy, I think, but by the time we'd finished the meal we'd begun to relax.

'Those books you showed my father, what are they?' he asked, as he refilled my glass.

I fished them out of my bag and pushed them across the table. He turned them over in his hands several times before flicking through the pages. He looked up at me.

'My father's writing, I think. Yes?' So French suddenly.

'Yes, and my mother's. They seem to have both kept diaries since the forties. Your father bound them together. I don't know when. In the last few years, probably.'

'My father?' He sounded astonishing. 'My father made those? Such beautiful craftsmanship. I had no idea. How strange.'

'But you told me he's a book-binder . . .'

'Yes, of course but he only works on very old things. More a restorer. I didn't know he could do work like this. Why do you have them? Why did you bring them to him?'

I answered him with another question because something was puzzling me.

'Did you know that my mother had been in love with your father since she was fourteen or fifteen? They lived close to each other.'

Daniel sat back in his chair and stared at me, a look of complete bafflement on his face.

'In Oxford?'

'No, in Dublin.'

'In Dublin?' He squinted up his eyes. 'My father lived in Dublin?'

'He was born there,' I said quietly. The poor man was flabbergasted.

'*Non*. Surely, I would know? He would have said.' He tried to smile. 'It is something to be proud of, to be Irish,' he added gallantly. '*Non*? Why would he hide it?'

'Daniel,' I said it as gently as I could, with all the pain and regret I felt for those two sad lovers, his parent and mine, 'I don't think your father was hiding the fact that he was an Irishman; I think he was, quite simply, *hiding*. For most of his life.'

I explained as best I could, telling him everything I knew. How I'd found the diaries and read about the murder. What witnessing that awful crime had done to them. I could not explain why Milo's reaction had been so extreme, because I had not worked it out. But I was able to convey my growing certainty that their fears, their instincts, had been right, by telling him of my growing certainty that Lily had been knocked down deliberately.

'*Mon Dieu*,' he said. 'My father . . . I can't believe. This is terrible. Poor unhappy man.'

I pulled my cheque-book from my bag and we tried to work out what Milo had struggled to tell

315

me. It was hopeless. It was already plain to me, and probably to Daniel, that danger was coming from more sources than one. I ended, rather lamely, by making a poor fist of describing my strange adventures with Reynolds and Hanlon. And that was when we began to make headway.

'Re?' Daniel raised his eyebrows at me.

Sometimes you can't see the wood for the trees. 'Oh, how stupid of me. Of course. Reynolds.'

'Father or son?' he asked softly.

'God knows,' I said, then something struck me. 'But let's suppose the son. He gave me the complete creeps.'

'He was in touch with your mother. What about my father?'

I shrugged, my mind had gone haywire again. Something he'd said in the flat had been niggling at me all evening; now it surfaced. 'Your father has a phone?'

'Of course.'

'Does he use it much?'

'No, hardly at all. He regards it as something for emergencies.'

'Ex-directory?'

He shrugged again. 'Of course.'

'What's the dialling code?'

'Zer-one-eight-six-five, why do you ask?'

'There's no trace of it on her phone bill. She must have used a public phone.'

Daniel Garnier laughed heartily. 'There was no need for her to do that, I think. The Irish code must be, let me see,' his eyes mocked me, 'Zero-zero-three-five-three? Yes? Well then, my father phoned her at least once every day. I paid his phone bill a few days ago. It was so high I checked it through and every call, but three, was to the same number. I knew immediately who it must be. They last talked on the twenty-ninth of July. I remember, because it was a much shorter call than the rest.'

'She was killed on the twenty-eighth,' I said softly. 'He must have spoken to Mrs Dwyer. I wondered how he knew she was dead.' I stared into the abyss. I might so easily have spoken to him myself. He might have been spared so much. We all might.

'The murder was so long ago. That is what I don't understand.' Daniel broke in on my thoughts.

'Nor me,' I said fervently, 'nor me.'

That was the heart of it. The absurdity of fifty years of retribution didn't bear much contemplation, it was outlandish. I knew that, and so did Daniel. But we also knew that Milo's anguish was real, not imagined. We'd witnessed it with our own eyes, felt his terror, almost touched his anxiety.

The waiter brought us a grappa with our coffee and then, because the restaurant had almost emptied, he lingered a little. His mood was light, he pulled Daniel's leg about '*la bella signorina.*' It was obviously a regular routine. He changed our mood. I think we were both relieved to set our worries aside for that brief time. We were reluctant to leave. When the waiter was called away, Daniel laid his hand on mine and called me by my name for the first time.

'Nell? May I read the diaries?'

'You can read those two.'

'There are more?'

317

'I think so. Your father was trying to tell me . . . another diary and a box of letters. I think he was trying to tell me where the box was or is. He kept repeating "ledge" and "us, us" I figure he was saying "house". But not which house, unfortunately.' I shrugged.

'Aren't there only three possibilities? His, Lily's or yours.' I was relieved he took me seriously. 'We can look in Papa's house tonight or tomorrow. I have the keys. But what about the third diary?'

'That was stolen. I'm almost sure it happened while I was in Dublin. After Lily died. It's one of the things that makes me nervous, I'm pretty certain it was either Reynolds or Hanlon.'

I told him about Dr Stockport and it dawned on me that it must have been Milo whose name that pompous man had not been able to recall. The way he'd said 'conservator' made it sound either humble or dubious – perhaps both? He described him as an expert on bindings, not a maker of them. Strange that neither he nor Daniel had realized Milo was such an artist. I felt a faint thrill of satisfaction that I'd got so close on my own, with only Lily's tickets as clue, before he sent Daniel to me.

'Have you not seen his work before?' I asked.

'Never.'

'That's astonishing, isn't it? I mean, if I could do stuff like that, I'd want people to know about it, wouldn't you?'

'Ah,' he replied enigmatically as he raised an eyebrow, 'but then, you don't know my father, do you?'

I sat looking at him for a long time, teasing out

my rather different interpretation of Milo's secrecy.

'Suppose,' I said slowly. 'Suppose your dad wanted to obscure the fact that he was trained as a binder. Dr Stockport said that work of that quality would be instantly recognizable – once you'd identified the binder. Milo might have regarded it as a sort of marker. So if he was trying to lie low, he wouldn't want his signature, as it were, in circulation, would he? But, at the same time, he had to earn a living . . .'

'He could have retrained. He was invalided out of the war. Lots of war veterans did.'

'When he lost his leg?'

'Yes, of course.'

I didn't reply to that. He would find out soon enough that a V2 rocket was responsible for the leg. I wondered if he knew his father had had his mental breakdown first.

'That must have taken a long time – learning to walk and so on?'

'He was in hospital for months then, of course, he had to have the orthosis fitted – the false leg. It gave him a great deal of trouble over the years – infection, badly fitting appliance . . . He hardly ever wore it in the house, he preferred crutches.'

'Is that what got you interested in orthopaedics?

He nodded, with a rather preoccupied smile. All at once I felt too discouraged to think, much less talk, about the past. I sensed he would prefer to come by his father's story the way I did my mother's – alone and in private. I pushed the diaries towards him.

'You take them. Do you mind if we go now? You must be shattered. I know I am.'

319

'Yes, I am suddenly. Will you stay in Oxford for a few days?' he asked.

'If Mme Powers will allow it.'

'She will.' He grinned. 'I would like to read the diaries and talk all this over again tomorrow, when we are less tired,' he said and added hesitantly, 'we might see if we can find anything in Papa's house. I wish I knew . . .' His voice trailed off.

'Why didn't you stay with your father?' The question had been on the tip of my tongue all evening and at last I couldn't suppress it. He looked faintly puzzled, as if he'd not thought about it much. He ran his finger around the rim of his ear and looked straight at me.

'Strange, isn't it?' He shrugged. 'I don't really know. I never do, I never have. I always stay with Marie-Claire. She is a remote cousin of my mother, they've been friends since childhood. And, of course it was easier when I was a little boy – food, washing and so on.' He shrugged. 'My father likes . . . who knows?' He held his hands up, palms outward, all French again. 'It is how he is. Very, very private. No intimate friends. Few people even know where he lives, or anything much about him. I have never seen visitors in his house, it is his private world.' He gave a rueful little snort. 'And, as you know, even I did not know where he was born.' He sounded hurt. I was ashamed of having let my curiosity get the better of me.

'They had that in common,' I said. 'My mother never entertained either. People rarely came to the house and certainly not for meals. I'm ashamed to say,' I added ruefully, 'I assumed it was a class thing.' Our eyes met, not very comfortably.

'It did not affect our relationship, you know,' he said, very seriously. 'I have always loved coming to visit him. Even as a child, he took me seriously. He has many interests, great courtesy. Remote, yes, but he always treated me as an equal. He is such a contrast to my mother who is fussy and likes to know everything that's going on; the secrets of your soul. Sometimes it's too much, I too, run away. My father is more tactful. Even as a child I liked that. Got used to it. He let me go my own way, make my own decisions. Perhaps he was uninterested. I just thought he trusted me.' Another shrug. 'Whichever, it suited us well.'

'He seems very, er, gentle,' I said lamely. I almost said sad, bruised, but that didn't seem accurate either.

'I hope I didn't, em, embarrass you at the hospital? Crying. Funny, isn't it? I feel like a child there. I am a doctor yet I am as bewildered as anyone else. I know what's going on, but it doesn't seem to matter. Or help. I cannot relate my knowledge to my emotion. He is my father and I love him. I don't want him to die. Specially not now, when there's so much . . .'

So of course I thought about Lily. But I thought about something else. I thought, how lucky this man is to know *before his father's death* how much he loves him. I had to wait until after Lily died to find out the depth of my feeling for her, the finality of my loss. I envied him the knowledge and I envied his simplicity of expression. I looked at him with different eyes and I liked him well. There wasn't much bullshit about Daniel Garnier. Which was something of a novelty for me.

321

It was late when we left the restaurant. The car was parked some way away and, after a moment's hesitation, Daniel linked his arm in mine. The moon was new, the night dark but mild as we strolled along the narrow street. We had almost reached the car when he suddenly threw back his head and laughed.

'We too, have something in common. If things had been different, we might have been brother and sister?'

I hoped it was dark enough to hide my blushes. 'Parents,' I countered, as we reached the car. 'Parents, who'd 'ave 'em?'

As he opened the passenger door, he dropped a light little kiss on my forehead.

'Not French-English,' he hooted. 'French with a touch of Irish. What do you think about that, Nell Gilmore?'

'It's fine by me,' I answered.

CHAPTER TWENTY-SEVEN

It took me ages to get to sleep. My dreams were busy and anxious, full of snarling androgynous figures who swirled around me full of menace and spite; each face an ever-changing composite of all those who had bombarded their way into my life since Lily's funeral. I sensed, in the way you do in dreams, that Milo and Lily were there, just out of sight, keeping watch while I struggled. The scene kept shifting. One moment I was hauling myself out of the sea, the next, crashing through under-growth, great clawlike branches grabbing at my eyes. Then I was watching the murder. I could see the figure of a man crashing to the ground while the two kids from Daedalian Road did their strange, ritualistic little dance around him. Their fingernails were blood-red talons and they were waving a weird banner made of the green and gold dress. When they disappeared it was left hanging in mid-air, like a lifeless wraith on a gallows.

I must have slept deeply at some stage, because I woke just before six, feeling reasonably rested. The room was very bright, the white walls shimmering with light. Below I could hear the sound of passing cars and, every now and then, ambulance sirens. As I lay dozing, in that pleasurable midway state between sleep and consciousness, the cogs in my brain slipped imperceptibly into place and began to grind away. The clues were already there, I just had to work them out.

I started with the supposition that my mother was killed because she had witnessed that long-ago murder. With my eyes closed, I conjured the scene she had described: The victim (Reynolds), the boy (Milo), the gunman in the garden, the cyclist, the woman at the window, the little witness (Lily). Why had Milo not stood his ground and defended himself? Had he, too, seen the gunman in the garden? Could he identify him? Lily had believed, for fifty years, that she alone had seen the assassin. Yet Milo had run and kept running. He left Dublin a couple of days later – as far as I could work out – and never saw his family again. They believed him dead in the war. They pretty well disappeared from the picture after those first accounts of the murder.

Why did Milo never contact Lily? There was a side to Milo which worried me. Tough or terrified? Was he not trying, as best he could, to protect her? According to Lily, Milo was innocent. She knew, because she believed that she alone saw what happened. But, according to what they'd both written, *he didn't know that*. They had not compared notes – until when? When had they made contact again? A year ago? Two, three? The missing diary would show the date, wouldn't it? Damn, damn, damn.

I drifted in and out of sleep, but all the while, at some level, I kept chipping away. And then I remembered that Lily left another clue: the Oxford coach tickets. I had only flicked through them, the revelation of where she'd been going had been so startling that I hadn't thought to examine them closely. But my memory for numbers is good, I could remember exactly how many there were – twenty-two. I worked slowly back over her visits, the last less than a month before she died – March, October '94, August, May and so on until I got to 1989. If I got my numbers right and I usually did, I reckoned that Lily and Milo had found each other either in April or June of '89. 1989? Something wrong there. Lily hadn't discovered the coaches until after I went to work for *Morgen Morgen* in '91. I worked out that she'd made about fifteen visits to me in the four years from autumn 1991 until her death. Depending on when she'd caught up with him, she could have made seven further visits to Oxford. Without telling me.

Sometime during those visits they would almost certainly have matched what they'd seen. Was it not, after all, the reason they'd parted so long ago? So. They compared notes on the murder . . . *and nothing came of it*. They had carried on their ecstatic ding-dong for three years. Secret and safe. I stopped short, running the possibilities through my mind. Why hadn't they trusted their only children enough to share their happiness? Why had they kept it hidden?

Something was out of kilter. I knew Lily – or I was still labouring under the illusion that I did. Lily would want to care for the man she loved. She would want him by her side. At home. So what or who did Milo still fear, that prevented him returning to the place of his birth with the woman he loved? Unless of course he didn't want to leave his comfortable niche in Oxford? That seemed reasonable enough. So, if that was the case, why didn't she up sticks and move in with him? It would have been easy, apart from losing her business, her income. I was already settled close by in London. By her own admission, she'd always loved coming over – even before the love affair. I would have welcomed her living nearby. In many ways it would have been ideal. So why not? Had Lily been nervous of losing her independence? It just didn't seem enough, somehow.

I was getting nowhere. I went back and discarded the what ifs and the wherefores and reduced my theory to its simplest element: Murder.

1. Lily and Milo make contact after fifty years. How?

2. Assume they still love each other. Want to be together.

3. But Milo is terrified of something or someone. And perhaps Lily is too?'

4. When they meet again, each of them thinks he knows exactly who killed Buller.

5. He thinks it's the cyclist. Lily knows it is not.

Start from there: she tells him about the gunman. But he is still afraid. Why? Why? Why? Because he knows something that she doesn't, or didn't. That the cyclist and gunman were in cahoots. It sticks out a mile. The cyclist attracts Buller's attention, the bloke in the garden plugs him, then disappears through the house behind.

6. What she tells him frightens him more than ever. But he is too scared to tell her why?

Continue from there: Suppose Lily works it out

for herself? Tries to figure out some way to protect him? She wasn't subtle, Lily. But she kept her thoughts to herself. Or in the diary. She wrote everything in her diary. They continue meeting. *Nothing happens . . . until when?*

7. What happened, just before she was killed, that put her back in danger?

Did she discover that the murderers were still alive? *Or did they discover Lily?* And through her, Milo?

Oh what a dumb fool I was! Who, oh who, came to stir up the dead embers? Who found Lily Sweetman?

'I saw her a few weeks back. She knew my father. A long time ago, in Ringsend.' *The grim avenger himself, Arthur bloody Reynolds.*

It didn't take long for my next terrified thought to surface: if he'd led the killers to Lily, then he could also lead them to me – and Daniel.

I got up quickly and dressed, too wired-up to stay in bed. It was twenty-five to seven. I crept softly downstairs and let myself out of the house. I hesitated at the entrance and looked carefully up and down the road. The morning traffic was moving past the end of our quiet little road but the pavements were deserted of pedestrians or snoopers.

While I hesitated, an early-morning jogger came out of a house a few doors away and swayed past. My shoes were wrong, but what the hell, I followed at a brisk trot. She turned left at the main road, past a hospital whose rambling buildings were in stark contrast to the modern Radcliffe, then left again, and increased her pace. The sign at the corner told me I was on Old Road. I could not keep up but I kept her in my sights. We eventually crossed a high bridge over a motorway and climbed steeply up to – according to the sign – Shotover Hill.

At the top, a wide grassy avenue stretched into the distance in front of me and an obligingly placed framed map showed a huge wilderness off to my right. A large factory complex lay below us. The sun was bright and the smoke rising from the power-station chimneys in the distance made it all rather like a Lowry industrial landscape. Only the tiny figures were missing from the scene, but they were behind me, giving their bow-wows early morning walkies.

I followed the arrow towards Horspath and walked halfway along the avenue where I rested on a giant boulder. I was relieved that I felt no sense of danger. Too many fat dogs, too many sleepy owners. It was all too peaceful, too ordinary. Or so I thought, as I sat in the sunshine and watched a woman race a couple of greyhounds. She had a tiny butterfly tattooed crudely on her right temple. It struck me as a wonderful, dotty, eccentricity. Suddenly, I wanted to wipe away everything that had happened since Lily's death. I wanted, oh how I wanted, things back to normal, the way they used to be. I wanted to be in control of my own life, not floundering around like a baby seal.

'I'd bet on the grey,' I remarked when the woman reined the hound in from the nosy investigations of a couple of Labradors.

'She won last Friday. Seven-to-four.' She beamed. 'First time out as well.' She moved off just as my jogger came staggering past. She was easier to keep up with on the way down.

Marie-Claire was sweeping the porch when I got back to the house. We exchanged greetings and when she offered to dry off my dew-dampened shoes by the furnace, I took them off and handed them to her. I wouldn't want wet shoes on my pale blue carpet either.

'Would you like a cup of coffee?'

'That would be lovely, but it's hardly worth it. I'll be down shortly for breakfast, if that's all right?' I went back upstairs. The early morning air had been too chilly for my light sweater and pants, I felt rather shivery. I undressed quickly and stood under the steaming-hot shower until my circulation was restored. When I stepped out, I was mottled some fine shades of pink. I wrapped one of Marie-Claire's fluffy white towels tightly around me, turbaned my head with a smaller one and went to cool off by the bedroom window.

I had an excellent view of the whole of the short street and beyond. The area seemed to be full of hospitals. The Nuffield Orthopaedic Centre, so close I could read the sign I'd missed earlier, on my walk. I wondered vaguely if its proximity had been another influence on Daniel's choice of career. As my eyes ranged to and fro, I realized uncomfortably that I was checking for unwanted snoopers. I was relieved to see none.

There was a soft tap at the door. I swung around as Daniel stepped into my room with a cup of coffee in his hand. It smelt wonderful. He started back at the sight of me and half the coffee sloshed into the saucer.

'Oh, I'm sorry. Marie-Claire said you were up and dressed. Sorry.'

'It's OK. I got cold on my walk and warmed up in the shower. Is that coffee for me?'

He looked at it ruefully and then back at me. 'What's left of it.' I was amused to notice how mortified he was, at my predicament and his, and wondered why it didn't occur to him to scarper. I took in his grubby too-small track suit. He was showing a good four inches of hairy ankle and calf. The shrunken sleeves were halfway up his arms.

'You've been out as well?' I asked. *Oh tall and sweaty one.*

'I went running. Around to the Radcliffe and back. My father had a good night, we talked a little.' He smiled shyly. 'I said we'd both go back later. About noon, if that suits you?'

'Yes, of course, if you think I won't tire him?' I wanted to ask if he'd read the diaries but couldn't quite manage it.

'He asked for you. Nell?' He became serious. 'I couldn't read the diaries. I wanted to but, well you know ... God, you look good.'

I'm sure he didn't mean, or want, to say what he'd said. He looked as surprised as I felt.

We stared at each other, then he backed against the door and looked me up and down. As if he were seeing me for the first time and liked what he saw. I didn't move. I couldn't. You don't choose when or how you fall in love, do you? Our timing was atrocious. He was beside himself, preoccupied with his dying father; I was terrified of being followed, attacked, knocked-off. Yet we couldn't tear our eyes off each other. He was too tall, too thin, his nose was too long and his thick black hair was standing on end. I could have eaten him. I felt like dropping the towel and flinging myself at him.

He broke the air-lock. 'I'm almost thirty-seven. I'm reasonably well-off. I was with someone, for almost six years.' He spoke rapidly, the words tumbling out too fast. 'We broke up eight months ago. She wanted something more permanent. She said I was incapable of committing myself, of sharing. I'm not. I've just never wanted to before.'

Before? He stopped. I waited. I could hear his breathing, as he could mine. I felt as though I was being strangled.

'Nell, are you free?'

'Yes,' I whispered. My heart did a little somersault.

He laid the coffee cup on the bedside table and came to me. We stood close, but did not touch. I could feel the warmth of his body through the thickness of the towel. He bent down and touched my lips with his.

'Not here, not now. It is too important. We can wait. You will wait with me, Nell?'

He won me with that 'with'. I cupped his face in my hands, then, with a force that almost knocked me off my feet, he locked his lips to mine. He was a spectacular kisser. I clung to the towel, but I lost my head.

And my heart too. 'Yes, I'll wait. Daniel.' I

pulled away and smiled up at him. Dammit, he was tall. 'Until after breakfast, anyway,' I added flippantly. The air was too electric, we both needed to cool off. 'Now I think I better get dressed.'

We laughed. God, I felt so happy.

'Me too. But first, for me, a very cold shower. Nell? Oh, Nell?' He didn't say what was in his mind. Perhaps he'd forgotten. He looked as dazed as I felt.

He paused at the doorway, fumbled nervously with the door-handle before he spoke again. 'Will you come with me to Milo's house after breakfast?' he asked softly. I nodded. 'I'll read the diaries later, after. I find I can't bear to now. It's hard to explain . . .'

'You don't have to, Daniel. You don't have to. Not now. And you don't have to take me to the house until you're ready. You know that.'

'Oh, but I want to. I want you to see him as I see him, as well as . . .' He shrugged and, after a moment's hesitation, he loped back into the room and took me in his arms.

We clung together, for comfort, not passion, like orphans in a storm. Which is, come to think of it, pretty well what we were. Our emotions were all over the place, out of control. It was hard to know whether to whoop for joy or burst into tears. Too little sleep, too much pain, too much grief, too much fear. Too much adrenaline.

When he left, I had another shower, this time a cool one. Otherwise I might have been forced to make a spectacle of myself at the breakfast table.

CHAPTER TWENTY-EIGHT

'I've been offered a job there,' Daniel pointed across to the orthopaedic hospital as we left the B&B. We were on our way to his father's house.

'Will you take it?'

'I'm thinking about it.'

'Would you like to work in England?'

'I've worked here before, did some of my training. Two years in the Nuffield, one in the Radcliffe on Accident and Emergency. Good places.'

'So you'll take it?' I tried to keep my voice light, I'm not sure how successfully.

'That depends.' He grinned down at me. He did need a haircut. 'There are some unknowns in the equation. Now.'

'For instance?' Oh God, why couldn't I leave it alone?

'You for instance,' he teased. 'Is Oxford too far from Heathrow, do you think?'

I'd asked for that, but I didn't answer. Not from flirtatiousness but because my mood was as unpredictable as my emotions. One minute I could put Lily and my own fear out of my mind, the next, the whole disaster crowded in on me. Daniel was the same. He was putting himself out for me nobly, when what he wanted most was to be at his father's bedside. It didn't seem possible for either of us to act normally. I'd almost forgotten what normal was.

'I want to explain,' Daniel broke in, 'I intended to read the diaries, but I couldn't bear to go beyond the first few lines. It wasn't possible for me to deal with having my feelings for him, my knowledge of him, disturbed. There have been too many shocks. Do you understand? It's the wrong time for me. Later, it may be possible. But it doesn't seem right, just now. I'm sorry.' He sighed. 'You must have felt like that too, about your mother?'

'I still do.'

'I'll help all I can. You know that?'

'Yes. But later. There'll be time later, Daniel. Now, there's your father.'

He took my hand and brought it to his lips.

'Let me,' he said, shaking himself, 'show you Quarry, I'm very fond of this part of Oxford.'

He took me on a roundabout ramble, ostensibly to give me a little guided tour. In reality, I think he was postponing the moment when he'd have to enter Milo's house. He kept up a running commentary as we walked.

'Quarry is one of the byways of Headington. It's where the stone for the early Oxford colleges was quarried until it ran out in the mid-eighteenth century.' He pointed to where the pits were still traceable in the varied levels of the houses. A warren of narrow alleys and lanes ran every which way. Some of the oldest houses and cottages were of the local cream-coloured stone, the grand and the modest set together hugger-mugger. There seemed to be no discernible patterns, no order, in the arrangement of the short streets. If ever I saw organic growth, this was it.

We didn't go to the house directly, Daniel clearly took some pleasure in leading me through one pedestrian alley after another. Or perhaps he was psyching himself up for what he might find? He was preoccupied and nervous. Eventually we climbed up out of a hollow and out to the open forecourt of a beautiful old pub, where I was amazed to see a motorway a few hundred yards away from us. The short road leading to it had a magnificent stone wall on one side, cottages on the other. The roar of the traffic apart, we might have been in a rural village, wandering through the past.

'Is that the road to London?' I asked, trying to get my bearings.

'More or less. There's a roundabout a couple of hundred metres away which leads to it.' He pointed to his left.

'Convenient.'

'Very. Even by coach. It stops at the round-about.'

'From Heathrow?' I asked, in surprise.

'Yes, indeed it does.' He looked at me, his head on one side, as if he was following my line of thought. But I wasn't thinking of myself.

'My mother travelled by coach,' I said shortly. Indeed she did. Lily never ceased to amaze me. I didn't know whether to laugh or scream. What fun she must have been having. At my expense? I pushed the thought aside. I had begun to appreciate how little I figured in her arrangements with the beloved.

'Then she didn't have far to walk,' he said, 'as

335

you'll see. We're almost there.' He drew me into a narrow lane off to our right. It ran along the back of a long stone house which looked as if it might once have been a row of cottages. At the other end, we crossed another short curving road and turned into the second of a pair of unsurfaced lanes which were signposted to Shotover Hill.

'All roads leads to Shotover,' I remarked, and told Daniel about my morning walk.

We were back in the middle of the country. The cottages obviously predated the lane which snaked around them as best it could. Not a single one of the five or six houses pointed in the same direction. The small gardens were full of flowers, there were trees everywhere. I thought it was lovely and said so.

'Well,' Daniel replied laconically. 'It is and it isn't. It's too close to the by-pass. It's noisy, specially in the summer, with the windows open. But you're right, I do think it's the best bit of Quarry. Here we are.'

We stopped outside the last entrance on the lane, the only one with a high screen of trees, which entirely hid the house. When we walked through the gate, I realized it was like everything else about Milo – secret. He'd found himself a beautiful, secluded little hidy-hole.

It was a tall, pretty cottage, rather like a child's drawing, with the hall door in the middle, a window on either side, three above. A low-pitched roof, the walls washed white, the woodwork painted a dark, blackish-green. An ancient wisteria, its long branches resting on a series of thin metal arches, formed covered walkways along the sides of the house. The garden was neglected and past its best – it was the end of August after all, and the summer had been hot, with no rain for almost two months. But in a normal summer, I thought, it must have been heavenly. If the house was like a child's drawing, the garden was a dead ringer for the Secret Garden. Lily must have adored it.

While Daniel struggled with the door locks and turned off the burglar-alarm, I walked around the back. There was no demarcation between front and back garden. It was as if the house had simply been set down in a small patch of land which backed on to a graveyard. The other houses on the lane were close by, but the only building visible from Milo's garden was the church. A solid, narrow wooden gate led out on to the little lane, only a few steps from the graveyard entrance. I lifted the latch and tried to open it but it stuck after a few inches.

Inside, the house was small, two rooms up, two down, with a single storey extension at the back, on the ground floor. I never saw a neater house. Nothing was out of place. A sitting room on the right of the tiny hall and, on the left, a book-lined study which looked as though it had once been a dining-room; it had an open serving hatch on the back wall, looking into the kitchen. Both rooms were about fifteen feet square with surprisingly tall ceilings – close on seven feet, I estimated. Which was just as well, given the height of both father and son. The exquisitely clean modern white galley kitchen led into a pretty conservatory large enough to hold a small oval table and two chairs. A couple of potted shrubs, an orange and lemon, gave off the most gorgeous perfume.

It was all beautifully appointed, but it struck me, with some force, that it must have been quite a daunting house for a visiting child. When I looked up, Daniel was watching my reaction. I think he understood my reservations because he led me back into the study and pointed to a pair of crutches beside the fireplace. Our eyes met. Damn. I had forgotten Milo's disability. Everything was arranged for ease of movement. Taken in that light, the house regained its charm.

There was a huge, wooden contraption in the right-hand recess of the chimney-breast. It was obviously a press of some sort, but it put me in mind of a guillotine. Its heavy wooden frame supported a couple of cross-beams. Suspended from the centre of the upper beam, a heavy wheel-driven screw held a vast square of wood, at least eight or nine inches thick. At the base of the press there was a wooden cube on which rested a series of much thinner boards holding folded white cloth between each pair. It wasn't quite as tall as Daniel, but it was close.

'What is it?' I asked.

'It's a French standing press – for bookbinding, originally. As you see, Milo used it for pressing his sheets.' He smiled at me ruefully. 'Though perhaps also for binding diaries, would you say?'

'French?'

'Yes, but I think they were also made in England. Actually, there are a couple like it in his college. This one is actually French. It comes from a small town near where I live.'

'You brought it over?'

'Yes, it comes apart. We found it at an antique market and thought Papa would enjoy it. I don't think I ever saw him so pleased. He loves it. He said his first teacher had one like it.' He smiled, remembering.

We. We found it. We. The exclusive we. The sharpness of the stab of disappointment took me by surprise. I turned away for fear he would read me too easily. We were still singular, after all. I did not tell him that Josh Handl was the name of that first teacher. There didn't seem any point.

'I don't know where he keeps his letters or diary, but there aren't all that many places. As you see.' He put his arm around my shoulder, drew me to him and buried his face in my hair. 'These two rooms, his bedroom upstairs. Nell?'

'I will go upstairs myself,' was all I could say. I felt more alone than ever. Excluded. Neither of us could face the intimacy of the bedroom, both because of the parents but also, I suspect, for ourselves. There was a sort of madness between us, of wanting to fall, fall, fall into a passion that would obliterate the need to confront the passion of our elders. And our ignorance of it. For myself, I knew, but could not share, the certainty that ignorance was sucking me closer and closer to danger. Since I'd come into the house I'd been afraid. In the study the menace was almost tangible. Or was it only jealousy?

Daniel had suggested a cup of coffee when the phone rang in the front room. I wandered into the conservatory while he answered it.

'That was the hospital,' he said quietly when he

339

joined me. 'I'm afraid I must go, at once.' He sat down at the little table and took my hand. He looked worried. 'Come in an hour or so, will you, Nell? Please, I think I'll need you then.'

'I'll be there.' I checked my watch. 'At twelve?' As he handed me the keys he squeezed my hand.

'Daniel, I'm not sure I can find my way back,' I said uncertainly.

He drew me to the window and pointed out the back gate. 'Go through the graveyard. That's the way I'll go. There's an avenue on the other side. It's more direct than the way we came. And quicker.' He drew two little maps and wrote down the burglar alarm number at the side of it. 'It'll take about seven minutes to walk to Marie-Claire's on Gathorne Road.' He pointed to the second map. 'The Radcliffe is a five minute drive from there. I'm sorry I can't help. I hope you find what you're looking for.' He sounded strained and preoccupied, I noticed he didn't seem to be able to say his father's name or call him 'Papa'. He was only barely under control, but his good manners held.

'He spends most of his time here or in the study. There's just one bedroom and a bathroom upstairs.' He smiled bleakly, then he left.

I locked the door after him. With Daniel around I gave no thought to prowlers; with him gone, I could think of nothing else. I pulled out my cheque-book and looked at the list I'd jotted down the day before. I concentrated on just two words: 'ledge', 'us', or house, as I now believed it to be.

Ledge could have meant anything – shelf, mantelpiece, window-ledge, etc. Rather than scurrying around I decided to search in as orderly a way as possible, taking one room at a time. I went into the study and ran my eye over the books in the bookcase. I suppose I thought that one book would be most easily concealed among many. But I'd overlooked Milo's passion for order. His books were arranged by author and he had obviously taken a great deal of pleasure in amassing collected editions. Some were hardback, some paperback, the odd single stood out a mile. I concentrated on those but nothing remotely like the diaries caught my eye. I pulled down books at random and examined the space behind. If anything was hidden behind the books, I could not find it.

The wall-to-wall carpet was oatmeal in both colour and texture, the curtains were heavy white linen. A narrow refectory table stood against one wall on which were a couple of small, abstract, sculptures and three or four pieces of old silver: A bowl (full of paper clips), a couple of small jugs (stamps in one), an elaborate branched candlestick with four candle-stubs. Three sombre, dark-framed still lifes on the walls. I peered behind them but drew another blank. And that was about everything, except for a couple of comfortable armchairs with a small, circular, occasional table between them. On it were a reading lamp, a beautiful jade-coloured china bowl and a couple of books. I flicked through the pages hoping something – a letter or a note even – would fall out, but nothing did. I glanced idly at the titles. One was by Swift, the second was a biography of Wilfrid Owen.

I detected Lily's influence in the sitting-room. A beautiful blue and pink oriental rug had been laid over the oatmeal. The walls echoed the pale terracotta of the rug. Bookcases covered two walls, but in the alcoves on either side of the chimney-breast were two enormous landscapes, in brilliant summer colours, hanging above two beautiful matching antique chests of drawers. There were loose covers on the soft furniture – a chesterfield and armchair – which matched the broad striped blue and white curtains. Austere Milo had allowed himself to be taken over, with some force. The bookshelves looked as if they were about to migrate elsewhere. I wondered if he'd ever used the room when Lily wasn't there.

Even before I started my search, I knew I wouldn't find anything in the sitting room, and I didn't. It would, of course, have helped had I known what I was looking for. I pulled out drawers, felt behind pictures, down the sides of chair cushions. I made a half-hearted attempt at the bookcases as well but I'd already decided that I would have to go through all the books one by one. But later, not now. Time was marching on, I had promised Daniel I'd join him at the hospital. I felt increasingly nervous. Every sound I didn't make myself made me jump. When the church-bell tolled at eleven I almost jumped out of my skin. It sounded as if it was in the next room.

Perhaps it was that thought which sent me back into the study. Something, vaguely out of kilter, bothered me. I leaned on the door post and allowed my eyes to travel slowly around the walls, the furniture. The book on the table. I leaned over and picked up the Swift. Lily's house was on Swift Terrace. I scrambled through the pages, opened it

back on itself and peered into the spine cavity –
nothing. It had to mean something. But what? I sat
bolt upright on Milo's chair, trying to guess where
his eye might have fallen. The base of the French
press. And there it was.

I turned the screw-wheel and yanked the boards
out. I laid the sheet and the boards on the floor and
pulled out the wooden cube on which they'd
rested. No wonder it rang bells. It was exactly the
same sort of old butter-box that long ago Milo had
used to make Jimmy's chariot. I sat on the floor
and turned it slowly over. There was no lid. An
empty hollow box. I closed my eyes and swayed
back and forth with frustration. Milo had been
trying to tell me what I already knew. Where I
would find Lily's diaries; the matching box in Swift
terrace. I turned the box over and examined each
side, absentmindedly, rather than because I
expected to find anything, otherwise I might have
missed the tiny printed label stuck inside. *Property
of Draper College.*

Yet Daniel said he'd given Milo the press.
Why would the college claim ownership of an
old butter-box? The ways of institutions are
indeed strange, but surely not *that* strange?
Hadn't Daniel said something else while I was
sulking because he'd referred to his girlfriend?
There are a couple like it in the college. Not ledge;
col-lege. Milo's box was hidden in one of the
college presses. I wasn't going to find it in his
house, clearly.

I decided to look in the bedroom on the off-
chance that I might find something else. Or maybe
it was simply that I wanted to confront it while I

still felt strong enough. Without Daniel. I was glad he wasn't with me. There were more demons to kill than one.

I put everything back where it had been, including the well-pressed linen. I picked off the college label and stuck it in my pocket and climbed the stairs, languid with disappointment. I could barely put one foot in front of me. It was straight and steep. I only half took note of the chair-lift which ran up the wall to the landing.

The two rooms upstairs must, at some stage, have been gutted and then rearranged. The bedroom was about one and a half times the size of the sitting-room and the bathroom which led off it was, in consequence, much smaller. I peeped at it from the wide doorway. And here again I was confronted with Milo's disability. There was a sort of hoist affair over the bath and several waist-level rails attached to the walls which were white-tiled. The floor – no danger of slipping – was cork. It was functional rather than luxurious and, like the rest of the house, immaculately clean. Two white towels were draped on the radiator. I fingered them idly. Draped, I thought, and my mind went into overdrive.

Draped. Drapier. Swift. Drapier College. Swift Terrace. *Drapier's Letters*. Who wrote *Drapier's Letters*? Why Jonathan Swift. Not the college, the bloody books? I crashed down the staircase into the study. The collected Swift was on the second shelf from the top, just out of my reach. I dragged a chair from the kitchen and took down *Drapier's Letters*.

I gagged when I recognized Lily's writing. There were three pages, closely written on both sides.

12 April 1993. A year ago today, my dearest love. I never thought to write those words, never thought such a miracle could happen. I feel as if a whole sky full of stars has burst over my head and rained down on top of me, on top of us. I feel foolish with love. Greedy for you. I close my eyes and see you. Feel your dear arms around me. I feel as if we're part of each other, I never knew what 'flesh of our flesh' meant before, now I do. You've been in my head so long, I am dazzled by the real you. It was never so good in my imagination. Now we're complete – head and body. I know you, your voice, your smile, your touch. Oh Milo, I have to write it down. I have to make it real. Scribbling was all I had for so many years, the writing down, the making believe, that one day, in some place, I would see you and you would say – Oh Lily, Lily, what took you so long?

And you did. That's what I can't believe. Those were the very words you used. I thought you might look up and see this silly old woman but you didn't. You saw me as I was, and I saw what you saw. Isn't that the miracle? I saw young Lily Sweetman, and saw that she was grand. You made me see that we were just like we ever were. Young lovers. That for each other we would never change. It's what we are, beloved Milo, one.

I know this is the anniversary of the day we finally met again, held each other. But secretly, you know, I keep that other anniversary too, of the day

I first happened to see you. When I think of how easily I might have missed you. A second or two more, and you'd have been gone. Thanks be to God that child stepped out on the road.

It was my second time to Oxford and I only came because I missed the bus to Bath. Think of that! I was sitting looking out the window at the Liberty shop when you came out of the bank. I remember every move, I was riveted to the window for fear you'd disappear. You turned your head when the coach screeched to a stop. You stood for a second, looking up at the rain, turned up your raincoat collar and went down the side street as the bus began to move again. The limp almost put me off, but your dear face was exactly the same. I ran up the bus, shouting for the driver to stop. I said I was going to get sick. I couldn't think of anything else that would make him open the door. I left my best hat behind, but you'd disappeared. I went down the length of Alfred Street and then either way along Bear Lane, King Edward Street, around by Christ Church. By the time I got as far as Merton Street, I knew I'd lost you. I nearly went mad, asking people if they'd seen you. They thought I was off my head as well. Then I had a cup of coffee and put on my thinking cap. It was as well that you never gave up the books, otherwise I'd have been rightly banjaxed. I started finding out about colleges and libraries and writing to them. It was weeks before I thought of asking which colleges had bookbinders or restorers. Indeed to be honest, it wasn't me that thought of it at all but that nice man in the Bodleian Library. He said that there was no-one of your description working there but he pointed me in the right direction all the same.

A year. And never a day when I haven't heard your lovely voice. I worry sometimes about your phone bills. A whole lovely year and we're only beginning to know how far it's possible to be headed. Imagine. The things I didn't know! The things I would have thought impossible. Our bodies amaze us, don't they? We're like young lovers. Sometimes I want to jump up and shout for sheer, mad, wild, joy. I want to stand up in a public place, the bus or somewhere equally stupid, and make a right exhibition of myself, shouting. Who says love is only for the young? Sure what would they know about it? They haven't the time. And we have both. The time and the inclination. Lover of lovers.

That blessed day I first saw you. You kept asking me when, how I got to you? And then you kissed me so hard, I couldn't say. I lost my head as well as my power of speech. You make me feel so beautiful. Like the song. So young. I love the way you make me laugh and then tell me it's the most exciting thing in the world for you – but I can't say what you say. You know it already. Where did we learn all this? How to give each other so much pleasure?

Did we talk at all that first day? All I remember was you taking off your specs and lifting me up to you. I kept saying – Thank God I found you – but I don't suppose God was anywhere in sight. He would have been blushing if he was. Say what you like about that oak table.

How did we get to your house? I was in such a

daze I can't remember. Did we take the bus? A taxi maybe? One minute we were making love in your workshop, the next on your bed. I don't remember getting there at all. And I don't remember a single word we said, except you asking me why it took me so long.

I've wondered a lot since, about all that time that passed. Sometimes when I'm inclined to feel sad about it, and regret the passing of the years, I cheer myself up with the thought that now we are both free and we've learned to take each day as it comes. Doesn't it amaze you sometimes, that our feeling for each other never changed, in all that time? That it grew and grew until that day we met again and the explosion happened. Funny when you think about it. An explosion parted us and we made our own explosion when we got together.

I sometimes feel all-powerful. That with you, nothing can harm me. Do you ever feel like you want to tell everybody that you're the greatest lover in the world? You are, Milo mio, you most definitely are. I feel like writing a song about you and getting Peggy Lee to sing it. I know you'd prefer Kiri whatshername, but believe me, old Peggy'd have smoke coming out of their ears.

I haven't told Nell. I know I promised, but I haven't told her that I'm thinking of coming to live with you. Not thinking. Decided. I'm not asking if you still want me, I know you do. But I feel selfish about it. When you said you'd talk to Danny I suddenly knew that I didn't want to share you yet. That's why I asked you to wait. You have lived in my head so long, the habit is too strong for me. I know it is for you as well. I know it.

I had to laugh when you confessed you'd find it hard to say anything to Danny. You said what I'm saying back to you now, that it's all too precious. Ours. Private. To tell the truth, I'm not ready to have our love looked at through youthful eyes. We see what we see. I don't want to know what other people choose to make of us. It is too precious, too fine a thing for that. And I don't want our children to think that what we do to each other is undignified or smutty or anything else. It's nothing of the kind.

I don't know how I'd begin to go back to thinking about those times. It still frightens me, even now. Ringsend. Even the sound of it wakens the past. There are so many explanations. We both understand why you did things as you did. You know what sort of household I came out of, but I don't think my lovely Nell would be too happy with knowing what her grandmother was. I never knew what happened to her, never really wanted to. Poor Jimmy. I was so afraid when I was carrying Nell that she'd be afflicted the same way. It'd be a lot for her to have to think about. She doesn't need that kind of anxiety in her young life.

I think your idea of putting the diaries together and then letting Nell and Danny read the whole thing, in their own time, is the best way forward. I'm bringing all the old notebooks and jotters with me when I come. Anyway, my dearest Milo – and I can hear you laughing and saying what a little schemer you are, Lily – the time it'll take you to bind them up gives us our time and our privacy for a while longer.

I'll see you tomorrow, my dearest love. I'll come

straight from the airport on the twenty past five coach and back the same time on Sunday. I don't intend to set foot outside the door. Maybe not even downstairs. Nell is in Germany on business but in any case, she doesn't know about my little excursions. I don't know why, but it seems to add to the enjoyment. Your Lily.

CHAPTER TWENTY-NINE

I turned slowly to face the pale blue bedroom. I kept my eyes under firm control, concentrating on the impersonal. Heavy cream-coloured curtains, handsome white-painted, built-in cupboards on either side of the blocked-up fireplace. A white wicker chair, an old blanket chest on one side of the bed, a chest of drawers on the other.

The bed, where they had made their ecstatic love, was vast. It had been stripped, the covers neatly folded, stacked beside four pillows. The room smelt musty. I almost ran.

I opened the wardrobes, one had hanging space, the other shelves. I was all right until I realized that three of the shelves were Lily's. I closed my eyes and ran my fingers through her things. I released nothing but a faint whiff of her perfume, no papers came to hand, no trinkets, no messages from beyond. Then I spotted two of Lily's suits amongst Milo's sombre tweeds. I sat down on the floor with a thump. I forced myself to look again and I found myself facing, among a neat row of shoes, a man's leg.

I stifled a scream, but I couldn't stop shaking. It looked so pink, so hairless, so thin, so artificial. Poor Milo, I thought, what a passion-killer. And then I laughed. There was I, all mopey and sentimental, but the thought of going to bed with a one legged-man had me in stitches. Hysterical with mirth. When I finally calmed down, I picked up the leg gingerly. It was surprisingly heavy. The bottle-green velvet slipper on the long slim, lifeless foot looked incongruous, absurd. It might as well have been labelled, *Love from Lily*. It was the kind produced for the Christmas market. You know – an emperor in your own home – type of thing. Daniel said his father always took the leg off in the house. I gave a little snort. Not always, I thought, not always.

I held the leg against my own and estimated that Milo was over six foot, and if the artificial matched the real, he was very thin. Which of course set me thinking about him and Lily again. I hastily put it back beside the matching slipper, among the shoes, and looked at the sad little collection. One of each pair looked like new; long, narrow and uncreased. The matching partners were sorry sights; worn, misshapen, down on one side. I knelt down and checked Milo's shoe size. Eleven (b). I caressed the green velvet slipper with the flat of my hand. Smooth, gleaming, a silly little gold crown embroidered on the upper. Long and narrow.

Oh God, oh God, Lily, I cried, what the hell were you up to? I closed the door quietly, deliberately, and went downstairs.

I threw myself down on the armchair in the study, lay back and tried to stop the breathless pumping of my heart. I closed my eyes to shut out the terrible images that came back from my dream to haunt me. How much I'd noticed without realizing, after all. What else had I seen which had not yet floated to the surface of my memory?

Where was the danger coming from now? Who? Why? After all this time, Why?

I put Lily's letter back between the leaves of the book. This was not what Milo wanted me to find. This was his secret touchstone. His reality, not mine. I wished I hadn't read it. She was more his than mine. I was alarmed by my prudishness. Ashamed. I should have had the generosity to rejoice for them but I wasn't ready. I did not want to acknowledge such passion, such abandon in my own mother. I could not. It was obscene. I hated him for leading me to it. Yet I knew in my heart that desperation and grief had driven him. He wanted me to know, to see that he'd made her happy. Most of all, he wanted his son and her daughter to understand their love. But I resented him deeply for taking the risk. How dare he disturb me?

As I was returning the book to its shelf, I noticed that there was another, odd, volume of Swift two shelves down. I pulled it out. It seemed to be a short miscellany, bits and pieces from the great works. The dust jacket had three titles printed on the front cover: *Tale of a Tub, A Modest Proposal* and *Drapier's Letters 1–5*, underlined. I flicked through the pages from the back. Between pages twelve and thirteen I found a flimsy slip of paper, with Lily's car registration and the word *malle*, written in Milo's hand.

Malle? malle? I stared at the message, willing inspiration. The only Malle that came to mind was the film director Louis Malle. Babar! I laughed out loud. I can't remember which of my friends at college had worked out that *malle* was French for trunk. We used to call Louis Malle, Babar. Thought we were dead smart. Milo's message meant that there was something hidden in Lily's car – in the trunk, the boot.

I started to pray as I dialled the garage in Dublin where I'd left Lily's car.

'Michael? Nell Gilmore.'

'Ah, you got my message then,' he said, and my heart sank.

'Nooo,' I said slowly. 'What message?'

'I got an offer for the car, a good one. Nell?'

I swallowed hard. 'Have you sold it, Michael?'

'Of course not. Not without telling you. You said you might want to sell it though, didn't you?'

'Yeah,' I started hesitantly.

'You haven't changed your mind, have you?'

'Not exactly. Michael?'

'It's all right, keep your hair on. The guy wants it immediately. That's why I rang. He's been in three or four times. But I didn't want to close without talking to you. It's still here.'

'Thank God,' I said fervently. 'Michael? Would you please do me the most enormous favour and go and look for something my mother left in it? It's in the boot.' I crossed my fingers.

'Where? What am I looking for?'

'I'm not sure. A box? A package of some sort. Just look, would you? Please.'

'Could it wait till the afternoon? I'm up to me oxters.'

'Michael!' I screamed. 'Just do it, would you? It's important.'

I had an agonizing four minutes before the phone was picked up again.

'It's a package, Nell. A small package.' He laughed. 'It must be worth something. It was hidden under the wheel. Did she win the lottery or what?' It took about two seconds for him to remember Lily was dead.

He coughed. 'I'm sorry, Nell. I forgot myself there for a minute. What do you want me to do with it? It's addressed to you. In Richmond.'

I thought quickly. Would it be safe in Richmond? In the post? As safe as anywhere.

'Michael, you still there?' I asked him to put it in a padded envelope and register it express to Maria at the airport. 'I'll catch the twelve post, Nell. Promise. The post office is only across the road. I'll go immediately. Now, what about the car?'

'Michael, I'm sorry, but I've changed my mind. I'm not selling. Do any work that's needed on it. I'll talk to you in a couple of days.'

'Game ball.'

'You don't mind?'

'I don't mind at all, Nell. It's up to you.'

'Michael? The guy who wanted to buy it. What does he look like?'

'Big fellow, well set up. Broken nose. I was surprised he wasn't going for something bigger to be honest.'

My heart sank. How could I have been so stupid? 'You didn't let him have a test drive, did you?' I asked as casually as I could.

'By himself? Indeed and I didn't. I've been caught out by that one before now. I would have taken him out myself, but I was too busy. I said I'd do it this evening. I'll take the wife to the pictures instead.'

'Take her out for a meal. On me. Don't let anyone in that car till I come, please Michael. I can't tell you how important it is.'

I cradled the phone, praying that I'd done the right thing. I tried to concentrate, to recall if I'd looked in the glove compartment, before I put the car in the garage. Then I remembered we'd checked the log. I'd pulled out at least six or seven tapes before I uncovered it. There was nothing else in the compartment, except the tapes. Had she recorded something? Some message? That thought set me off again, threatened to drive me mad. There were so many possibilities. Things I'd overlooked, not recognized, seen and forgotten. I was beginning to have a profound respect for detectives. The professionals, not the amateurs.

One thing at least. If it was Hanlon who'd tried to buy the car, and it sounded very like him, I had foiled him. But only by the skin of my teeth. Who said you couldn't trust car-salesmen? Lily had bought each of the three cars she'd owned from Michael. The woman was a sound judge.

The church bell rang. As it died away I thought I heard a tap on the window. I jumped with fright, but it was only a breeze blowing a branch of the wisteria. I tore up the slip of paper and sent the tiny fragments of paper swirling down the kitchen sink. I looked over the study to make sure I'd left it as I'd found it, fluffed up the cushions, checked that the bookshelves gave nothing away. I even replaced the two books exactly as they'd been on the table. It was just after quarter to twelve. I wouldn't make it to the hospital by twelve but I hoped I wouldn't be out by too much. I looked around for the last time, checked Daniel's maps, picked up my shoulder bag, set the burglar-alarm and let myself out.

I remember thinking, as I walked under the pergola to the back gate, how hot and sultry it was. I squeezed through the gap in the gate, tugged it closed after me and crossed the narrow lane into the churchyard. I normally like graveyards, like wandering around them but I didn't feel comfortable. Not unsafe, just uncomfortable. It was peaceful and well-kept but I suppose it was just too soon after Lily. The bell continued to toll as I hurried past the church porch. It went on and on. The bell had an unpleasant, flat tone, as though it were cracked. Through the open doorway I glimpsed a figure in a neon shell-suit pulling the bell-rope. I tittered. An unlikely Quasimodo.

I followed the path around the back of the church to a double wrought-iron gate leading to a beech-lined avenue. It was quite short, about a hundred yards. I was relieved to see cars passing along the road at the end of it. I set off at the double. The shade of the trees was lovely because there wasn't a puff of wind.

And that was my last thought, or nearly my last. There was not the slightest trace of a breeze. Yet the hanging branch of wisteria had been swinging gently, back and forth, back and forth when I'd looked through the window. The bell stopped ringing. Behind me, I heard the churchyard gate squeak. Quasi going home for his dinner, I thought, but I quickened my pace. I was half running when I glanced over my shoulder. My head exploded.

CHAPTER THIRTY

I woke up in hospital with a splitting headache. Daniel was fast asleep in a chair beside the bed, his head thrown back, his mouth wide open. Just as well he had such a nice set of teeth. His hair was standing on end again; he'd obviously been tearing it out. I noticed he did that when he was at a loss. Endearing, if dramatic. He snored gently. I was getting the full picture and I wasn't quite ready. I felt extremely fragile.

When I shut my eyes it felt as if someone was running a sharp knife over my head. I opened them again. I couldn't move my right arm. My left obeyed, though it weighed a ton. My head, my poor throbbing head, and my right arm were encased in bandages. There was a syringe in the back of my hand with a transparent tube attached to a blood transfuser. I tried not to think about Aids. Instead, I fretted about how long Dieter's patience would hold out with his immobile director-elect.

Not that I wanted to think about such mundane problems. I had matters of life and death on my mind. I felt as if I was going to die. Now. Within the next few seconds. I hate being out of control. I wanted to bawl the place down.

I moved my head gingerly and looked around. Small, single, side ward. The door was wide open and I could see people passing along the corridor.

The lights were on and it was dark outside. I turned my head to the window too quickly, and gave an involuntary little scream of pain. Daniel shot upright as if he'd been stung on the backside.

'Oh thank God, you're all right,' he said.

'I'm not a bit all right. Every bone in my body is on fire,' I said as a nurse stuck a thermometer in my mouth. That shut me up. Daniel cupped my good hand in his and held it to his lips. The nurse shone a light in my fiery eyeballs and pronounced satisfactory progress. I was about to argue, then my memory came flooding back.

'Oh God, Daniel. Your father? How is he?'

'He died just after eleven this morning.'

He looked shattered. Neither of us spoke again for a long time. He held my hand until I stopped crying. Truth to tell, I wasn't sure who I was crying for – Milo, myself or Lily – but I had a terrible feeling it was low-down, wallowing, horrible, self-pity.

Milo saved my life. And Daniel's mobile phone. That's not hysteria. I was bleeding very badly when Daniel found me. When I hadn't turned up at the Radcliffe by twenty to one, he rang the house. When he got no answer, he rang Marie-Claire, who told him that my car was still in her car park. He assumed I was on my way and hung around for another fifteen minutes before alarm bells began to ring. He drove straight to Milo's house. He didn't tell me until next day that it had been comprehensively trashed.

He found me unconscious about halfway down the church walk. I'd been hit on the head with something sharp and heavy, a rock appropriately enough, seeing it was a quarry. My right arm was very badly gashed. My bag, of course, with Milo's door keys, was gone. And everything else with it. I'd even obliged with the burglar-alarm number and a handily little map of exactly where I was headed. I could think of more convenient routes to the hospital.

'The books in the study?'

'Most of them on the floor.'

'The press?'

'Still in one piece but the sheets and boards were scattered.'

'The books, Dan,' I said. 'Swift's *Drapier Letters*. Inside, to your . . .' I suddenly couldn't seem to remember the words. I began to cry again. A nurse came in and gave me an injection.

'Hush, little one, sleep. You've had a terrible time.'

'You, too,' I started, then I dropped off the edge of the world.

I woke up several times in the night and each time was pumped full of painkillers and urged to rest again. Sometimes when I opened my eyes I thought he was there. But then, there seemed to be a regular army pounding through the room. Everyone I'd ever known. At one stage I thought Dieter was perched, like a giant bird, on the bed rail. But it turned out to be a sleepy young German doctor taking my pulse.

'*Morgen Morgen nur nicht heute*,' I said loftily. He laughed uproariously. His reaction seemed a trifle extravagant so I asked for a new translation.

He chortled merrily. Whatever it was they were giving me for the pain was extremely entertaining.

I was much better by the morning. My eyes didn't need propping when I opened them, though my head still hurt like hell. And my vanity, when I realized that all my hair had been cut off. Daniel looked in at about ten. But he was preoccupied and didn't say much, or not anything that I could remember. That he came was enough. He had insinuated himself into my life so thoroughly that every time I saw him, it was as if I was simply catching up, or reminding myself of things about him I couldn't possibly know, but felt I did.

A policeman came at some stage to take a statement. I wasn't much help. I hadn't seen anything. I knew my assailant wasn't an opportunist bag-snatcher, as he opined, but I didn't offer any theories.

He was a cheery soul. 'We've had three or four very serious incidents in the Headington area this summer. An old lady died last week as a result of the same kind of attack, just across from the hospital grounds.'

I listened with only half an ear as he instructed me about when and where to carry my bag, and how dangerous it was to walk down deserted lanes by myself. I was about to protest that there was at least one person in the church as I passed. But I buttoned my lip when it occurred to me that my attacker must have hidden in the church. Was it he, in the shell-suit? Had he watched Daniel leave a couple of hours before? Followed the route he took? Checked that I was still in the house? Then waited patiently until I walked straight into his trap? Whoever was stalking me was a good deal cleverer than me but then, he knew what he was after, and I didn't.

I kept myself reasonably calm until the policeman left. Then I went spare. If he'd seen us go into the house, he must have followed us from London. If he followed us, he knew where we were staying. He knew about the hospital; he probably knew about Milo's death. He certainly knew where I was now.

By the time Daniel came back, late that afternoon, I was up to high doh. My temperature soared, I was screaming at the nurse, poor concerned woman that she was, that I didn't want to sleep. I had to, had to, stay awake.

I heard her click her tongue and mutter something about delayed shock, as she went out. Daniel closed the door after her, then came and sat at the edge of the bed. He held up a restraining hand when I began to babble.

'Hear me out, Nell. I'm as frightened as you are. I've worked it through, exactly as you have. We have to get you out of here. Have you private health insurance? Tell me, yes or no. No speeches. I don't believe in it either.'

'Yes. *Morgen* carries it for us.'

'Right. Tell me who to call there.'

'Talk to Dieter Ross. Don't say anything to Jen Harper, please. Just Dieter.' I gave him the telephone number and then, in case Dieter was in the German office, that too.

'You close your eyes and sleep for a while, there's something I have to do.' He was out the door before I'd time to blink. I don't know how long he was gone, I didn't seem to be able to stay awake. Next thing I knew, I was given a jab in my arm and lifted bodily onto a stretcher. Daniel was standing by the door as they wheeled me out to the lift. He held his finger to his lips and whispered, 'Trust me.'

For one awful, world-stopping, sickening minute, I lost faith and wondered if, after all, he was on my side. In my feverish state I worked out that he, Daniel, had had ample opportunity to bash me up. He knew where I was, the route I would take. But then I came to my senses again. He could have bashed me up any time in the previous twenty odd hours. But he hadn't. He hadn't even ravished me. That's the moment when I realized I was on the mend. Sex is the great leveller.

Daniel was looking after me all right. Over the next few hours, my reliance on him grew, my trust in him strengthened. He rode in the ambulance with me to a private clinic in London. To this day, I don't know whether it was he or Dieter who arranged the transfer, I guess they were both involved. I lived in a protected bubble for the next week, waited on hand and foot. My only visitors besides Daniel were Maria and Dieter. It wasn't that I didn't trust Jen, but I was still afraid. How could I be sure exactly who her new man was, unless I met him? I certainly wasn't up to that.

Milo's funeral was delayed until the end of the following week. On Monday morning Daniel, hopping from one foot to the other, announced that he had to get back home, that afternoon, to catch up on his operation list. It might have been true but I had the feeling he needed time on his own, to climb his mountain, to grieve for his father. He promised to be back on Thursday or Friday and exacted all sorts of promises of good behaviour from me. Since I was guarded like a prize racehorse, there seemed little chance of anything else. In any case, I'd rather gone off the hands-on approach. Chasing around hadn't done me any good. I had a better chance of working out who my murderous attacker was if I sat and thought about it hard enough. And I was in exactly the right place to do it.

The dressing on my head was changed on Monday afternoon and I had my first shocked view of the bald me. It was not a sight I'd recommend. I gave Maria a ring to see if the package from Dublin had arrived.

'No, not yet. I checked with the post. They say it should be here tomorrow or Wednesday. I'll whizz in as soon as I get it. I'll see you this evening, anyway. Rest, Nell. Rest.'

I told her about my hair and asked if she'd like to spend a fortune on a selection of wacky hats. She came around at seven with two boxes full. While we kitted me out with four of the best, I picked her brains. My own was still sluggish, the temptation to curl up in a ball and forget everything was almost irresistible. But I couldn't stay in hospital and safety for ever.

'Maria, if you had a guest house in Brighton, what would you call it?'

'This a game?'

'Yeah, sort of.'

'What kind of person am I?' she asked, joining in the fun.

'A film buff – thirties to fifties.'

'Brighton Rock? Brief Encounter? Hey, that's good for a B&B.' She giggled.

'I'm not sure about humour. Try romance. God, my head hurts.'

'Casablanca?'

'Casablanca,' I said, 'Casablanca.' Then I began to cry. I didn't want to go the next step, didn't want to make any more decisions.

'Can you tell me about it?' Maria asked gently.

'I'm trying to find someone, in Brighton. Arthur Reynolds. I rang directory enquiries, but he's not listed.'

'He has a guest-house?'

'Had. It may have been sold.' I shrugged, defeated. Maria looked at me for a minute, then picked up the phone.

'I've got a pal who does night-shift on directory enquiries. Let's see if he can help.'

It took exactly ten minutes for him to call back after Maria told him what we wanted. There was one Casablanca (private hotel) listed. I held my breath when Maria asked him whose name it was listed in. She listened to his reply, then beamed up at me.

'Symons. Oh, dear. What? That's great. Late Reynolds? Arthur? Oh, Mrs Maisie? Hang on.' She raised her eyebrows at me, I gave her the thumbs-up. 'Yes, yes, yes. Get the number. And the address.'

She managed to get both, but not without a lecture on telephone ethics.

'Who's the romantic then?' she chortled. 'Casablanca, Sebastopol Road. A name like that, I'd stay there myself.' She dialled the number and passed me the receiver.

I was about to hang up when a high-pitched, *refained*, voice announced: 'Casablanca, can I help yew?' I almost said, 'Play it again, Sam.' Instead, I took a deep breath, and, in as firm a voice as I could, asked for Arthur Reynolds.

There was a pause before she replied. 'Who's calling, please?' she asked suspiciously.

'My grandma and Arthur's mother were very old friends, during the war. Mum asked me to look Arthur up when I got here. Is he at home?' I held my breath, avoiding Maria's theatrical amazement.

The woman coughed. 'I'm afraid yew've got the wrong number. Mr Reynolds moved last year, when my husband and I bought the premises. I'm sorry. You know old Mrs Reynolds died? Oh you did?'

'Yes, that's why I'm calling.' I sniffed. 'Poor grandma died the other day. I thought Arthur would like to know. The funeral, you know.'

'Oh dear.' The voice dropped to a husky whisper. 'I can see you haven't heard. Poor Arthur Reynolds died two weeks ago.'

'Oh my God,' I whispered. This time, I was sincere. 'What happened?'

'Oh, it was dreadful, a dreadful shock. In London he was. Out for the day, poor man. He liked travelling about. Took to it when his old mum died. He was thinking of buying a car.' I pricked up my ears. 'Poor Mr Reynolds.' She lowered her voice piously. 'He had an accident. Did you not read about it? It was in all the papers. He fell under a train at Piccadilly. Nothing anyone could do. What did you say your name was?'

I hung up and began to shake.

'I've got to get out of here,' I jabbered. 'They're all dead, Maria. They're all dead. Lily, Milo, Arthur Reynolds. I was meant to die. Maria, they're going to get me. What am I going to do?'

Maria sat beside me with her arm around my shoulders, trying to calm me. But I was way beyond fear now. Sometime in the night, when I was in my drugged sleep, someone would creep in and finish the job they'd started on Friday.

'Nobody knows where you are,' Maria said sharply. 'Nell, stop this instant. Watch my lips. Nobody knows where you are. Except Dieter, me and Daniel. Calm down.'

'Daniel. They've probably got Daniel. How could they miss him, he's so tall.'

'Yeah, yeah. What d'you think they'll do? Carry around a ladder? Come on Nell, Daniel can look after himself.'

'They've been after me all the time. I thought Reynolds was one of them. He tried to warn me, Maria. I wouldn't listen. The poor man. He tried to warn Lily. She didn't listen either. And they got her.'

'Hush, Nell, hush. This is doing you no good, and it's frightening the hell out of me. Would you like to tell me everything? See what we can work out together?'

I must have looked like a madwoman. I scrambled out of bed.

'Nell, stop for God's sake!' Maria grabbed my arm and pulled me backwards. 'I'll stay with you tonight. But there's no way anyone can get past that heavyweight on the desk out there. They just won't let you in unless your name is on one of their lists. Look, they're used to dealing with loopy pop-stars. You'll be OK. OK?'

I lay back and closed my eyes. My arm had started bleeding through the bandages. I looked at the blood and began to weep, silently, hopelessly. There wasn't anything anyone could do, either to avenge those three deaths or to stop the killing. They were too clever at staging accidents. I knew there must be a thousand ways I could die by accident in hospital. No matter how closely I was guarded.

The nurse gave me and Maria a piece of her mind when she saw the mess of blood on the bed. She changed the dressing and changed the bed, then stormed out in a fury. Five minutes later she came back with two huge, brimming, tumblers of gin and tonic. With a slice of lime apiece.

Maria stayed. Heaven knows what she said to the dragon-nurse who put up a day-bed for her and allowed us to lock the door. I don't know if it was the gin, or the combination of gin and painkillers, or total mind-numbing fear, or a cocktail of all three but I went out like a light.

'Nell?' Maria whispered, as I was drifting off, 'Nell? You know who the killer is, don't you?'

'Yes,' I murmured, 'yes. I know who . . .'

CHAPTER THIRTY-ONE

One of the sweetest blessings of the private hospital (apart from the gin) was that they didn't feel compelled to hand out breakfast at dawn. I slept until nine, by which time Maria had left for the airport. She rang at twenty-past, to say the registered package had arrived and was already on its way to me, by courier.

My overwhelming feeling was not relief but fear and dreadful, incapacitating, weariness. I'd slept heavily, dreamlessly, yet all I wanted was to close my eyes and sleep again; sleep for ever. I had no urge to confront my future or lack of it. I was sick with worry that whatever Lily had left for me would draw me further into her terrified awareness of what was in store for her. As long as it wasn't actually spelled out, I could avoid thinking about it too closely.

I emptied my mind, shut off feeling and went into retreat to prepare myself for what she wanted me to know. The nurse who changed my dressings soon tired of persuading me to talk and left me to my blues. The long gash on my arm was still raw and angry. It ran from above my elbow almost to my wrist where I'd landed on a jagged piece of rusty iron. Mercifully, I couldn't see the crisscrosses on my head. The nurse didn't encourage mirrors until she'd set one of Maria's hats, at a jaunty angle, on top of the bandage. I looked like a tragedy queen; gaunt and white. The flesh on my face had melted away. But the sight of my Friar Tuck hair-do raised a watery smile. I had a ring of short pale curls, artfully escaping from under the bandage. If I'd had the courage, I'd have done a Sinead O'Connor and shaved the lot. But I hadn't her face. Or her bottle.

'A bit of make-up, honey, you'll look fine,' the nurse cajoled, and offered to send for the resident make-up *artiste*. 'She'll make you feel wonderful.'

I doubted it. 'I'll wait till tomorrow,' I said sourly. 'I wouldn't want all my treats in one day.'

'What about a massage? The physiotherapist is very good. Have a go. You'll feel better.'

Massage on offer as well? No wonder the rich look good. I wondered how much the company was paying for it all. But I kept my thrifty thoughts to myself. Truth was, I had hardly enough energy to sit up, much less have some terrorist running up and down my spine.

'Tomorrow,' I said and turned away. When she tip-toed out I sat up again but it took a much greater effort of will for me to pick up the phone.

Fortunately, Dr Stockport, who was on his way to a meeting, was unusually taciturn.

'Ah, Miss Gilmore, I'm so terribly sorry, I'm afraid poor Mr Garnier – the binding expert, I remembered his name, finally – has died. Suddenly, last week. The very day, my dear, we were supposed to see him. I don't know if I can be of any further help.'

'Dr Stockport, I know you're in a hurry, but do you mind if I have a word with your assistant? The person who took in the binding? It would be a great favour.'

The assistant, Tom Rowall, sounded much younger, less formal. He caught on quickly when I explained what I wanted.

'Well, I wouldn't normally remember so clearly, but of course Graham has been quizzing me. The person who came in was, in any case, rather striking.'

'In what way?'

'Tall, thin and rather dramatically dressed. Black Cecil Beaton hat,' he laughed. 'Long, cream silk raincoat, belted. Very Armani.'

Tall and thin. Not Arthur, Daniel, I thought, for one heart-stopping instant.

'You said person, were you just being PC?' I asked.

He laughed again. 'You're pretty sharp. No, not PC. I simply don't know. Could have been either, I didn't take all that much notice. Antique dealer I thought, a lot of them are somewhat, er, flamboyant. But I don't know. Very reluctant to leave the binding – that was unusual.'

'Because an antique dealer would be used to doing so?'

'Yes, the honest ones anyway. They aren't all, of course, which is one of the reasons we photograph everything, as I'm sure Graham told you?'

'At length,' I said, without thinking.

He gave a little snort of laughter. 'And ninethly, eh?'

'Quite.' We both giggled.

'Did you happen to mention any other experts he might consult?' I asked quickly.

He didn't answer at once. I could hear the rustle of paper in the background.

'Well, now, I'd forgotten that. I believe I suggested the Bodleian in Oxford. There are several experts there.'

I swallowed hard. 'Did your antique dealer have a cat?' I asked.

'Nor a broomstick,' he laughed. 'Was my description that good?'

'Spot on, I'm afraid.' I cradled the phone softly, lay back and went fast asleep.

Lily's package was on the bedside table when I woke up, and two huge bouquets. Pale pink roses, with love from Daniel; white lilies and carnations, fondly from Dieter. The room smelt like a garden. Thank goodness there were no chrysanths. I'm at one with Oscar Wilde on the subject of serviceable flowers; I can't stand the smell of them.

I admired my flowers for as long as I could put off opening the package. I was impatient yet listless. Finally, I picked at the sellotape, eased off the paper and slowly uncovered Milo's beautiful, creamy, vellum box. It was about the size of a cigar box. The lid was ornately decorated with gold. Lily's name looked as though it had been written in his own hand, framed with a lace filigree design. The box was locked.

I picked it up and found an envelope underneath. When I slid my trembling fingers under the flap and it eased open, a small key dropped on the bedcover. I felt as though I was floating on the ceiling looking down watching, but detached, as I eased the letter out of the envelope.

I was interrupted by a knock on the door, I

slipped Lily's things under the covers as one of the young nurses came into the room.

'My, aren't you popular. What beautiful flowers. And a French letter,' she said, handing me the post. When I tittered, she blushed and put her hand to her mouth. 'Oh lord,' she said, 'I meant it was from France. Sorry.' She looked at me apprehensively.

'Don't be. Nice thought.' I forced a smile. 'If a bit optimistic.'

She fussed around, tidying the room, fiddling with the flower arrangements.

'Your hair will grow, quicker than you think,' she said encouragingly, with a smile. 'I shaved mine off, for a dare, last year. Nearly lost my job. But look at it now.' She twirled around, showing off her short bob. 'And it's much stronger too, easier to manage.' She grinned. 'I like the hat, blue suits you. Same as your eyes.' She winked as she went out. She was almost as good as the gin; she gave me a tiny reprieve. I opened Daniel's letter.

I don't know how to address you, Nell, because I don't know where I stand, or where we stand. I know how I feel, but I don't know if I have the right. I think you know why I ran away – I am my father's son, after all. It wasn't only to work. I needed to clear my head.

I wasn't entirely honest with you. I read the diaries. And, before my father died, the day before I met you, I read the enclosed letter. It was this rather than what he said that persuaded me to find you. What he said was a shock. I don't quite know why I pretended ignorance to you. I suppose I was looking for either denial or confirmation from you, though I can't honestly say, even now, which I'd have preferred. To say my feelings for my father are confused would be to seriously understate the case.

I am sending his letter because it's as much for you, as for me. I hope you'll read it before we see each other again. Covering-up, running away, lying, was disastrous for our parents. And very nearly for you. If there is to be a future for us, and I hardly dare hope for one, then I wouldn't want to repeat those mistakes. Nor start, if there is to be a start, that way.

You talked in your delirium, while I sat beside your bed. I think you know more than you've said. I think you aren't sure who to trust. I'm overwhelmed by your courage, and by much else besides. I am afraid of losing you, afraid I may not even be within reach.

This is not what I meant to write, nor what I want to say. I'll come to the hospital on Thursday evening. The funeral is on Friday, Daniel.

I took Milo's thick letter from the envelope, turned it over, opened it. But I couldn't read beyond the first few lines.

I killed Lily Sweetman. I wasn't there, I didn't drive the car that ran her down but I might as well have done. And now I no longer want to live. I'm not fit to. I loved her, how much I loved her. She had become my life, and I am responsible for her death . . .

I slowly folded both letters and slipped them back in the envelope. A nurse came in to check my temperature, the dressings, my blood pressure. She doled out my pills, suggested I drink more water, encouraged me to take a little walk along the corridor. The hospital routine was relentless, healing. It expanded to fill the time, to fill the spaces in my head. I didn't resent the speed with which I was becoming institutionalized, I surrendered to it.

For about five seconds. I waited for the nurse to go, then I pulled Lily's package from under the bedclothes. I unlocked the box first and riffled through it. It looked like a random collection, pages torn from copy-books, letters from Milo, newspaper clippings. I left them as they were, re-locked the box and pushed it to the back of my pillow.

Then, with a leaden heart, I slowly unfolded my mother's last letter. I read the first three words over and over, cherishing the unfamiliar tenderness of her greeting. Never before had she used anything but Dear Nell.

Nell, my darling girl. The past caught up with me today and I am frightened. He caught me unawares. I don't know how he found me, I didn't think to ask. I couldn't squeeze a single word out, my mouth was that frozen with fright. Oh Nell, my treasure, I'm so afraid. You are the only one who could have helped me. If only I'd trusted you, taken you into my confidence, told you everything. Oh my dear, I am very sorry.

I'm so confused and sick with fear for you and me and ... oh God, even now I can't write his name. We've been covering up and lying for too long. Something is stirred up now and I don't know where to turn. I can feel it, I can feel it deep inside me, the same as all those years ago, when those heavy footsteps came slowly, slowly up the stairs and I pulled the old grey blanket over our heads so we wouldn't hear. Oh God. He never really went away at all. He's been there all my life. I am out of my mind with fear.

I knew him at once, for he's the spit of the old devil, his father. Flabbier, smaller, no body to him, but the same horrible leering smile, as if he'd only to put out his hand and you'd melt away into it. I couldn't take my eyes off his floppy bow-tie and I could see, as if it was yesterday, the blood pouring out of old Buller Reynolds's head.

I was walking Spud along the pier. Right at the end we were, watching the new Sea-Lynx churning up the waves. There wasn't a stir otherwise, the heat was something terrible. There weren't many about. I sat down on a bench to catch my breath when this man sat down beside me. Too close. I edged away, slowly, so as not to be too obvious, but as I moved, so did he. I was already nervous before he spoke, I nearly jumped into the sea with the fright, when he did.

'Lily Sweetman?' His voice was higher than Buller's, a kind of horrible whine. I could feel my mouth opening but no word of denial came. I knew him. I knew him. Oh God, I wanted to run but I couldn't move.

'What?' I whispered.

'I've been doing a little detective work, it took me a while but it's all coming together now. I know all about you. You married Francis Xavier Gilmore in 1959. Daughter, Ellen May, born in 1964. Your husband died in 1983. Once you know where to start, it's easy . . . I've got quite into it. I traced every name in the rent-books. Funny though, everyone else seems to be dead. I expect you were the youngest.'

'I don't know what you're talking about.'

'Oh, I think you do. I think you do.'

'Who are you?' I could hardly hear my own words.

'Arthur Reynolds is my name. I believe you knew my father, long ago.' I could feel my head nodding up and down, up and down like a doll. *Six times six thirty six, five fours twenty, Janey Mack me shirt is black. Sweet Star of the Sea help me. Nine times, seven times . . .* But still I said nothing. Spud began to sniff at his shoes. He bent down and patted him. 'Who's a good boy then?' he said. I tried to pull the dog away but my hands wouldn't work.

'I wonder if you could help me?' he asked and waited. I looked into his face for the first time. He was biting his lip, like he was nervous too. His forehead was covered with tiny drops of sweat.

'No. No. I don't know you. No. Leave me alone.' I stood up to go. I wanted to fly, fly back down the pier, as far away as I could get. He knew my name. Lily Sweetman. How long is it since anyone called me that? Except for my own dear love. How did he know my name?

'Please. I don't mean to upset you, I just need . . .'

'I have nothing for you. I don't know you. Get away from me.'

'I only want to show you something. Please, I'm not here to cause trouble, just to find out . . . to satisfy myself . . . About my father. You knew him.

You must have. Just give me five minutes. There's something I want to show you. Please?' He fiddled at the catch of a small attaché case he was holding on his lap. He looked for all the world like one of them Mafia fellows in the films. That's it, I thought, he's going to shoot me. He had a funny, greasy lock of hair plastered across his bald pate. I stared at it but what I kept seeing was Buller's head, like a broken egg, bleeding all over the path.

Who put him on to me? Not Milo. Who then? Nobody else knew anything about all that. I never told anyone. Not ever. So who sent him? Who knew?

I sat down again when, oh my Nell, I should have run. I should have kept on running.

He opened back the lid of the case and took some papers out. And a little faded red cash-book. I could feel the sweat pouring down my back.

Number eight, Daedalian Road was written in purple copying-ink pencil on the cover. He pronounced it die-dalian. 'My father died on that road,' he whispered, then whipped around and stared into my face. 'Didn't he? Wasn't he murdered on that road?' he hissed. 'The road you lived in as a girl?'

My head began to nod again, I couldn't stop it. I knew what was coming. I braced my back against the bench.

'My mother died some time back,' he said in a more normal voice as if he was trying to get on the right side of me. 'Wonderful age she was, over ninety, and sharp to the end. I found a lot of stuff when I was clearing the house. Rent books, plans of the houses he owned. The printing-works.

That's what I'm really interested in.' He snorted. 'Not that anyone will tell me anything about what happened to the printing-works. We were shafted. We were robbed. I'm going to get what's due to me.'

'I know nothing about any printing-works.' It was almost true. 'I can't help you.'

'How could you? You can't have been more than a child at the time. That's not what I wanted to ask you about.'

'What then?'

He pulled something else out of the case, closed the lid and laid it on top. My eyes nearly popped out of my head when I recognized a tiny model made of match-sticks of the row of houses Buller Reynolds owned all those years ago. It was as if they'd never been knocked down. I was back, I was back . . . I could feel myself being sucked backwards.

'Who made that?' The words were out before I could stop them. 'Who did it?' It was the spitting image. The dead arose. I closed my eyes; I could not bear to look. When I opened them he was smiling at me with a terrible glint in his eye. He's mad, I thought, he's mad.

'I did. I found pictures and the plans. I made them. It's a hobby. I usually make ships but houses are much easier, fewer curves, not so much chopping up. You know those houses, don't you? Knew them? It's where you lived, isn't it? Isn't it?'

'For a while.'

'Anastasia Sweetman and two children, Lily and James. That's right?'

I shook my head. To hear my little brother's

name read out like that was terrible. My poor dead Jimmy.

'I know the names of everyone on that effing street,' he said. 'I could recite them in my sleep. I sometimes do. Cotter, Doyle, Kelly, Vavasour. Now, there's an unusual one.' He cocked his head on one side and watched for my reaction. I held my breath, I didn't move a muscle. Vavasour. Easy to trace. Rose's name over the Wicklow Street shop. All he had to mention was Sweetman. Rose and Martin were long gone but their daughter Sinead . . .

'Your mother never paid any rent, did she?' he said nastily. 'My father must have been a very tolerant man.' He leered, his pink tongue slid across his wet lips.

I almost choked. 'Yes, he must.'

'So why was he murdered, Lily Sweetman?'

Four fives twenty, two twos four, nine eights, nine eights, nine eights . . .

'I was a child,' I whispered, my tongue dry in my mouth. 'I was a child when it happened . . . I know nothing.'

He grabbed my hand and squeezed it tight, drawing it towards the little model.

'Oh, I think you do, I think you do. Top floor. That's where you lived, isn't it? Number eight. See there.' He poked my finger against the fragile gable end and it shot through a tiny gap. 'A window. You're not surprised, are you? I found it on the plan. I missed it at first, thought it was just some fancy brickwork. But you knew it was there, didn't you? So, what did you see, Lily Sweetman?'

Close your eyes and pray to God. Ten times ten.

Nine times, nine times . . . Blessed Mother keep us from harm. Four times four is sixteen, five fives . . . Don't go near him Lily, and for God's sake, don't let him near you. Keep little Jimmy with you. Always. Don't let go of him. Don't you know he's afraid of the child? He thinks he'll put the evil eye on him. I'll get you out of there . . . I'll get him away from you . . . I'll get the knife . . . I'll give it to him . . . between the eyes, Lily . . . Right between his filthy eyes . . .

'It's too late to do anything about the murder, Lily Sweetman. You're in no danger from me.' He put his horrible face right up to mine, his lips were bared, but he was still sweating like a pig. 'It's the print factory I'm interested in. Who took it over?'

I pushed him backwards with all my might and ran to where there was a crowd of people. But he keeps following me. Everywhere I go, he's there. I don't see him but I can feel him.

And now, I can't find my diary. I hunted high up and low down but there's no sign of it. I know I had it a few days ago. In my sewing room, just like always. But it's gone. Nobody would steal a diary, I can hear you say. But they would, Nell, I know they would. It had very little in it. I could hardly bear to spoil the lovely creamy pages. It wasn't taken for what was in it, Nell, it was because of the cover. Milo's beautiful work . . .

He must have found out about the press, how big it's got, who's still in charge. If he did that, if he showed them the rent books and my name, then I'm a dead woman. And after me, him.

CHAPTER THIRTY-TWO

Milo to Daniel:

I killed Lily Sweetman. I wasn't there, I didn't drive the car that ran her down but I might as well have done. And now I no longer want to live. I'm not fit to. I loved her. How much I loved her. She had become my life, and I am responsible for her death.

Why? Because I did what I've always done, I ran away. I hid my face. I closed my eyes to what was going on. I shut out the past and by doing so, thought I had it under control. I was wrong, of course. The past has had me by the balls all my life.

If I'd had the courage I would not have let you read this before I died. I thought I could slip away, and with me gone there should be no danger, no-one else for them to kill. But oh my son, I long to see your beloved face again. I need forgiveness from someone and you are the one I choose. You won't thank me for that. You won't thank me either, for sending you on one final errand.

I want you to find Lily's girl. I want you to take care of her. Don't let her start asking questions about her mother's death. Whatever she does, don't let her ask questions.

I hope this is not too late. I'd hoped the whole damned business would be buried with me but I

*was at Lily's funeral and I saw Arthur Reynolds
approach the girl. I knew from Lily that it was he
who opened the Pandora's box. Danny, you've got
to find Nell Gilmore. She works for some sort of
freight company at Heathrow. Morgan, I think it's
called. Find her and talk to her, tell her what I said,
beg her forgiveness for me.*

*Lily and I witnessed a murder in 1941. I was
accused of it. I ran away and kept running. And
those who should have known better did not tell
me I was exonerated. I knew I was innocent but
I'm afraid I guessed who the real murderer was.
And, eventually, realized I knew who the murderer's accomplice was also. That is the worst part.
Lily, on the other hand, saw both murderer and
accomplice but, mercifully, could identify neither,
at the time. At least I don't think so, but I'm no
longer sure. She was so used to protecting me, she
may have tried to protect me from that too.
Fortunately the murderers had no idea she existed,
much less witnessed the killing. The policeman
seems to have gone to considerable lengths to
protect her. But you would, for Lily. She was
exceptional.*

*No-one was charged. Eventually it was all
forgotten. Swept under the carpet. As long as I
stayed away and no-one knew about Lily, we were
safe.*

*It was wartime. Like many Irish boys of my age,
I joined up – Oh yes, I am Irish, another thing I
omitted to mention – The Royal Navy, as it
happened. Theirs was the first recruiting office I
happened on in Belfast, five days after the murder.
I was in Portsmouth three days later. Within six*

months, I was shipped off to Scotland and obscurity. I covered my tracks as best I could. I trusted no-one, said nothing. I didn't write or contact my family from the time I left. I knew where they were, that was enough. They could not contact me, I made sure of that. Nor anyone else through them. I felt safer that way.

I was invalided out of the Navy in 1944 with nervous exhaustion – my first mental breakdown. I lost my leg when a V2 rocket dropped on the hospital. I was ill for nearly two years so I didn't know I'd been listed dead. Clerical error, I believe it's called. At first I was angry, but I soon realized that it was precisely what I wanted. My family believed me dead. I left it that way. I had no intention of returning to Ireland. I knew I would be killed the moment I re-appeared. My mother died in 1943, of pneumonia. She'd been ailing for years. Now, I think she would have been diagnosed as having pre-senile dementia, then she was seen as a dim-witted old woman. She was only fifty-six.

I got a job as a bookbinder in Salisbury. I had no indentures, but even then I was a skilled printer and wasn't above making the odd forgery. My first employer had trained me well and after the Salisbury job, there was no difficulty getting others. I moved to Cambridge in the mid-fifties and met your mother soon afterwards. I was glad to go to France. It opened up life for me. Your grandparents were tolerant, found jobs I could manage. Almost without noticing I became the second M Garnier. What Frenchman could pronounce McDonagh? Garnier was fine by me. I set up the vente directe *from the farm. We were a little before our time, the package tours and amateur wine buffs hadn't yet taken to the road like they do now. Even so, the vineyard was too small to support a passenger. My old leg made me useless as a farmer. I eventually got work at the library in Avignon. They used every skill I had, and taught me more. The French have respect for craftsmen, they gave me a profound interest in the history of bookmaking and print. I should have stayed in France, but when the marriage turned sour, I ran away again.*

You did not know my family had owned a printing-works in Dublin. It was always assumed I'd take it over when my father died. I was apprenticed to his printer, Jack Reilly, when I left school. No, my dearest boy, I'm not going off at a tangent. It is relevant.

My father hated the press, thought it beneath him. He'd read history at Trinity and fancied himself a gentleman. As had his father before him. Neither of them had any interest. It skipped two generations. My sister was mad to get her hands on the business, she saw possibilities our parent couldn't. I just loved printing. She was extremely intelligent, I was not. I only really began to develop when I got away. My sister was rather overwhelming, though I adored her. My mother was very remote, my sister was the only one who had any time for me. A sister to die for, as they say these days.

My father was a heavy drinker. He ran the business into the ground and when he did, he sold – or virtually gave away – half, to a man called Wilfrid Reynolds. He was cheated, or thought he was. We moved into rented accommodation, my sister and I were taken out of our private schools. We kept moving lower down the house market, into poorer areas. My sister gave up all hope of university and went off to learn shorthand and typing. She resented it deeply. I was taken out of school at thirteen. When he saw his only son as a printer's apprentice, my father was horrified. I think that was when he realized just how bad things had become. The final straw was when my sister persuaded his book-keeper to take her on as a junior clerk. We felt we had to learn the business somehow but my father accused us of humiliating him in front of his workers. He died in a drunken stupor when I was fifteen; choked on his own vomit. That's when my mother really began to go downhill.

The first thing Reynolds did, when he took over the press, was to throw my sister and me out. It would take many pages to explain why we were powerless against him, so you'll have to take it on trust. Because that is when our real trouble began. My sister conceived a scheme to get back the family firm. I was rescued by Joshua Handl who had a small private press and bindery at the back of an antiquarian book shop nearby, in Ringsend. You cannot know what a laughable place that was for a book shop, but Jewish refugees from Nazi Germany, in the thirties, had few options. He was an honest and distinguished man. He taught me everything and I revered him.

On the night of 31 May 1941 Buller Reynolds was murdered on Daedalian Road. For reasons that are not important now, I had followed him from the printworks. It was very dark. I was on one side of the road, hidden by the shrubbery. He was opposite, a little ahead of me. I heard a faint noise behind me. I turned my head and saw a cyclist. I pressed myself further into the bushes as the bicycle passed me. It stopped just behind Reynolds, and, in front of my eyes, the cyclist raised a gun and shot Buller dead. As I stood, paralysed with terror, Reynolds's head exploded and he fell. I lost sight of the bicycle as I stepped out of the shadow. I was too shocked and frightened to cross the road, too terrified to run. At that moment a woman threw open a window, in the house opposite, and screamed out, pointing at me, 'I saw you, murderer!' I ran then, all right.

I ran because I was traumatized. Reynolds's head was practically blown off in front of me. Murder close up is not so neat as it is on film. I ran because I was accused by Mrs Brennan who claimed to have seen me do it. I knew who she was, I thought she must also have recognized me. I ran because I was frightened. Two things I did not know might have saved me, but I doubt it. Lily saw what happened. She didn't recognize the cyclist, but she didn't think that was important. Because she saw that it wasn't the cyclist, but a gunman behind Buller, who fired the fatal shot. Unfortunately for me, it was fifty years before she could tell me.

After I got home that night, my sister discovered me in a state of collapse. She took charge immediately, as she always did. She saw the predicament I was in. I had seen a murder. I had been accused by a witness. I had a motive: Reynolds was the enemy of our family. I was near him. I dropped my tool-holder, including two sharp knives, at the scene; further evidence that I was there. I would be charged. On the other hand if I put the police on to the real killer – the cyclist, as I thought – and they identified him, I would be in different, but equal danger. Whichever way I turned, I was stumped. The only thing was to run like hell and hope that, in time, the police would track down the killer themselves, without my help.

By next morning my sister had hatched a scheme to get me away. A group of us would take a spin out to the seaside on Whit Monday. They would return. I would not. I would keep moving north to Belfast. We would only communicate through the small ads in the Irish Times. My sister would eventually let me know when I could safely return. It was a good plan and I agreed. But as we left, two things happened.

Monday, 2 June 1941, the second worst date in my life. Ten or twelve young people showed up at about eight o'clock. How it was organized, I cannot recall. I was the last to pull away from the house. My sister was sharing a tandem with a friend of mine who rather admired her. They were larking about, drawing attention from me, I think, and everyone was laughing. She was wearing a pair of my old trousers. I'd never seen her in trousers before and she looked wonderful, like a dark Marlene Dietrich. She was always very striking looking, that morning she looked radiant.

It was beautiful weather, unusually warm and sunny. Just as I pulled away I saw Lily standing like a little statue in the porch of an empty shop a *few doors from our house. We didn't speak, but as our eyes met she held my tool-holder to her breast and put her finger to her lips. My head was in a whirl. If she'd seen me drop the tools, she'd witnessed the murder. Was I off the hook? Could she give me an alibi? I hurried to catch up with the others. My sister heard me call and stopped the tandem. She dropped her leg to steady herself, pulled a beret from her pocket and clapped it on her head. She turned to smile at me. I closed my eyes in horror as I recognized the cyclist.*

Remember, I did not know about the real gunman so I thought I had recognized the murderer, not just the decoy. It didn't matter that I was innocent. If my sister was charged then I would be seen as her accomplice. It was just another reason to run. I could not deal with or even think about what Lily was trying to tell me. A more horrendous fear was eating me up, filling my head. My adored, my beloved sister had set me up. If she had not done so deliberately, she had seized an opportunity when it presented itself. I told you she was clever, quick-thinking. I was her little brother, but I was in her way. My mind began to fragment. I bent my head and pedalled furiously as the group surrounded me like the equipe in the Tour de France. There was no way I would ever go back.

We move now to 1992, when Lily tracked me down. I did not mean to fall in love with her. I did not seek her out, she found me. I did not want her, but when I saw her again, so little and so hopeful and oh so loving, I could not help myself. I am weak. But I am not stupid. Allowing myself to become part of Lily's life was both.

Shall I excuse myself by saying I was celibate too long? That I'd always loved her? That I owed her my life? That is true and much more besides, but I've thought about it long, my dearest boy, and I've thought about it hard. I loved her because with her I was me. I've been adrift all my life. I cut myself off so effectively, I became a recluse, but it was never really to my taste. I was safe in Oxford. Who would find one library, one old bookbinder, among so many? I would have been safer in France, of course, but well, you know Claudine and I were not happy. She was too bright, too intelligent. She knew, early on, she could never get near me. How could she? I only existed by my own invention. The man from nowhere, always looking for obscurity. Jean-Paul was much better for her, I knew, but it didn't make it easier to bear. Both of us wanted to protect you. In that, at least, we were at one. The solution we worked out was the best we could devise.

Lily and I didn't talk about the murder for some time. And even then we talked around it, rather than about it. If you have buried something so long, and at such cost, it is not so easy to disinter. I didn't have to pretend with Lily. She soon realized how ill I was, how mad I could be. One day, though, she asked me if I had seen what she called 'the real gunman'? We danced a sort of pavane around each other, feeding out titbits of information. We matched the diaries but we never really matched our stories. I couldn't, even after so long, bear to tell her I'd been sacrificed by my own sister.

I suppose that is why I've been in and out of the Warneford so often over the years. I never faced the real reason for my madness. Couldn't. Much easier to pretend that my nerves were shattered in the war. The old leg was great supporting evidence, if you'll forgive the pun.

The beginning of the end was the fifth of May this year, another date that is etched on my memory. So short a time ago. I will try to write it as it happened. I hadn't seen Lily for several weeks, I'd been in one of my black clouds and hadn't properly emerged. She'd come over for the week-end but from the moment she arrived I noticed she was unusually quiet, troubled. She could always make me feel relaxed, happy, but this time it didn't work, perhaps we were both trying too hard. I can't quite remember what led up to it, but suddenly Lily let drop that she was my sister's dressmaker. I saw red.

'Why didn't you tell me?' I asked sharply. I could feel an attack coming on. I wanted to climb up to my room and shut myself in. I didn't want her with me. I began to weep, I desperately wanted her to stop talking, to leave me alone. But Lily had too much courage, she took my hand in hers.

'I hate having secrets from you. I've been wanting to tell you. Milo, listen to me. I didn't seek her out. Rose Vavasour put her on to me, years ago.'

'Do you talk about me?' I asked fearfully.

'Never. How can you ask?' She laughed grimly, rubbing my hand in hers. 'Your sister is not like you, darlin', she doesn't notice small things like me. I'm her dressmaker, that's all. For her, I do not exist otherwise. Oh Milo, I promised you never to say anything. Do you not trust me? Milo? You

*need to talk. It's been too long. We need to clear
the past away. We need to free ourselves.'*

*I couldn't say anything. I was rocking to and fro
when she came and stood behind me. She put her
hands on my shoulders, trying to make me still. I
couldn't see her face.*

*'My love? Milo? It was your sister on the bicycle
that night, wasn't it?'*

*I went on rocking. After a few minutes, she tried
again.*

*'I never told you who the gunman was, did I?
Milo, are you with me? Do you know who it was?'*

*I shook my head. Her hands gently massaged my
neck. You could have heard a pin drop in the
room. I didn't want to know.*

*'It was Dolan Hanlon,' she said quietly. 'Tony,
his brother, was in it as well.'*

*'How could you possibly know that? You didn't
even know the Hanlons, did you?' I was savage in
my anger.*

*'Not then. That's what confused me at the time.
You remember when the lorry dropped you, after
you all came back from the North Strand? I was
watching, as it came up the road. It stopped to let
Jack Murphy out. I thought it would go on, no-one
else from our part of Daedalian Road went over
that night. I was amazed when the Hanlons
jumped down, had a few words with the sergeant
and then, cool as you like, walked into number
eleven. They pulled the string holding the key out
of the letterbox. They knew it was there. Nobody
else was paying much attention to them. The driver
was talking to Sergeant O'Keefe. Milo, they knew
the key was there.'*

'A lot of people kept their keys like that.'

'I know. But Milo, number eleven was the house the gunman used.'

'I don't understand. Why would they draw attention to it? It's mad, it's stupid. You're dreaming. You've remembered wrong.' I didn't want to hear any of this. I'd been at school with the Hanlons. Their father was the foreman of the press, he took care of my sister and me. The two boys worked there as well, they were our closest friends. I wanted her to stop. I wanted to be left alone.

'Not mad, Milo, clever. Diabolically clever. They didn't underestimate O'Keefe. They must have known he'd eventually work out where the gunman hid. There were three or four fellows their age living in that house. They were causing confusion. They certainly confused me. I couldn't figure out what they were up to at all.'

'But you have now?'

'I reckon they went in for the gun, and left the back way. It had to be something like that.'

We looked at each other for a long time. I think we knew that the thing which had cemented us together was beginning to pull us apart. In the end, we were afraid of being honest with each other.

'Milo, they took the press over from Reynolds. I didn't realize it for years. They made a great business out of it, but it was kept as shabby as ever on the outside. After the war ended, it must have been after Maisie Reynolds went back to England, the sign was taken down. The Raytown Press, it was called then. People said the workers were running it, but they weren't, your sister was. Her *and the Hanlons. She married Tony. He became a TD, died of a heart attack when he was forty-six. Then she took on Dolan. She outlived them both.'*

She pulled a chair up and sat beside me but I wouldn't look at her. She poured us both a stiff whiskey.

'When did you work it out?' I asked, after a long time. I took her hand in mine. It was warm, soft, but full of her strength. She sat very quietly, so calm. Lily had this strange, wonderful, quality of stillness. To look at her you'd think she was always quick, mercurial. But she could calm me like no-one else.

'Not for years. 1981. Every tenth anniversary of the North Strand bombing, there's an article in the paper. Small. I used to cut them out, I'm not sure why. It always started me thinking about it all again. And you. A small indulgence, maybe.' She smiled ruefully.

Something about her voice made me look at her, but her eyes wouldn't meet mine. She had veered away from what she'd intended to say and I didn't, couldn't, wouldn't, save us both by drawing her back.

'I think that's when I finally worked out why you never came back and I began to hope that maybe you weren't dead after all,' she said lamely, and gave another small, sad smile. She rubbed the back of my hand gently, over and over. She looked so tiny, so forlorn. Somehow, I knew that my determination to protect myself had defeated her for a second time.

CHAPTER THIRTY-THREE

I put away Milo's letter, tucked it back in the envelope with Daniel's. I wished I hadn't read it, wished I didn't know that Lily's dream had exploded. Yet perhaps it hadn't? She had no illusions about Milo, she had always cherished him for himself. Surely, it would have taken more than that one incident to shake her love for him?

In the middle of the night, when I couldn't sleep, I took out her box again. I wasn't looking for solutions this time. I was fairly sure that I'd worked out most of the story. What I wanted, at last, was to know exactly what it was Milo was doing in Daedalian Road that night? What was the real reason for Lily's unshakable devotion?

I read the papers in order, working from the top, as she had arranged them. So I came to what I was looking for, stealthily, as she'd intended, jotted on the loose copy-book pages. I found what Lily couldn't bear to remember, even with her lover. Yet she wanted me to see. Why else would she have gone to so much trouble to preserve that little box for me?

The first thing I found was the cutting from the newspaper (1956) about the opening of the Crumlin Children's Hospital. There was a note pinned to it.

* * *

I didn't mean her to see this, but she did. She was flattered when I said she looked like a young girl. She did, too. She said she'd been cycling since she was a youngster. I don't know why, but that's when the penny dropped. I think I expected her to say, myself and my brother or something like that. That's when I knew why he never came back. When I began to wonder if he was still alive, after all.

1980. Frank is awful bad these days and very low in himself. He's never been a reader so he doesn't know what to be doing with himself. Pity he doesn't like the TV better. Sometimes, late at night when we can't sleep he asks me about things. I could never talk about it at the beginning but now I can. He's been a good man for me, no-one could have been kinder. He was the right husband for me, the right father for Nell. In a strange way I know that if I'd married M there wouldn't have been enough room for a child. I wonder sometimes why I think that? Maybe lovers are too inward-looking to be parents? In the years I've been married to Frank, my regard for him has grown into love. Not passionate, but steady. And Nell has all his best characteristics, reliable, sure, her feet well on the ground, and her lovely, blonde looks. What she gets from him anchors the flighty bits. People think he's got no imagination, but they'd be surprised. He knew why I kept putting off the wedding, why I was afraid to let him touch me. God bless him, but he never asked me right out; he let me tell him in my own time. Never forced himself on me, let me come to him in my own way, my own time.

I made a vow before the wedding that I would put M out of my mind for ever. And on the whole, I've kept to it. Sometimes though, when I least expect it, some little memory takes hold of me. Like now that Nell is talking about attending the university and I haven't got the money. And Frank needs more help than we can afford. He needs to stop worrying about my future for a start. I wish I could take him away for a holiday. I'll take on more work. I wish it paid better.

1981. Forty years. A bigger bit than usual in the paper, commemorating the fortieth anniversary of the North Strand bombing. Nell's just finished her Leaving, the nuns say she's going to come out top of the class with honours in everything. She's only seventeen, I don't know where she got her brains. Frank had another little stroke last week. I was racking my own brains thinking what more I can do and suddenly it hit me. It's been staring me in the face all along. It may be dangerous. Have I the courage? How can I protect myself? I've got to get this right.

I went through one of my shoe boxes until I found what I was looking for. The day she was due for a fitting, I placed three or four of the North Strand articles around the table in the sewing room, as if I'd been studying them. I put the 'Pedal-pushers' photo underneath. I waited till the door-bell rang then I took the phone off the hook. I let her into the hall and said I was on the phone, would she go the sewing room and wait? I gave her a full five minutes before I went in, as noisily as I could. She was looking out the window, but I could see the papers had been disturbed. I made sure she realized I'd noticed before I bundled them all up and put them in a drawer.

'My daughter's doing a paper on the North Strand bombing, for history,' I said casually. She didn't say a word. She just tried on the dress and left. When she came to collect it a couple of days later, she gave me an envelope with exactly twice what she usually pays me.

'You've put in too much,' I said.

'I don't think so, Mrs Gilmore, do you? You mustn't undersell yourself.'

I got what I wanted but my stomach has been upset for days. Why do I feel that she's way ahead of me? Like a cat playing with a mouse.

1983. Frank is at rest at last. He had a terrible couple of years. I never saw such frustration when he was trying to tell me what he wanted. It was a relief when he gave up the struggle, most of all for himself. Poor man, I'll miss him. Nell was a tower of strength throughout. She never says much but I can always rely on her. The two of us are very tired. I feel as if I could sleep for weeks but I'm still getting up, making cups of tea at four in the morning. Nell's the same. Sometimes we talk till dawn.

The night he died, I finally told him what had happened. I'm not sure whether he could hear me. It must have been about three o'clock in the morning, his face was growing cold. I was sitting holding his hand while he slipped away. I wanted him to know how grateful to him I was. How much I loved and trusted him.

It happened about ten days before Buller died. I

398

made the mistake of going out on the landing when me Ma screamed. He was standing in his stocking feet with only his shirt on. It was all unbuttoned. He came at me with his big thing sticking out in front of him and grabbed me. 'Kiss me cock, Lily,' he laughed, pushing me to the floor. I couldn't move with the weight of him. He kept pushing, pushing into me, I thought I would tear asunder. I could smell him all over me. His filthy tongue filled my mouth. I didn't make a sound. There wasn't any point. When he moved off me, I grabbed his hand and bit into it till the blood ran, then I took off down the stairs with him bellowing like a bull. I ran and ran all the way to Mrs Heaney's. She didn't answer the door. It was after eleven. Mr Handl looked out of his shop to see what the commotion was. He took me in and gave me shelter. He had an old blue knitted shawl around his shoulders he took off and wrapped around me. He warmed some milk for us and sat with me, without asking a thing until I was ready to tell him. I couldn't stop crying, I was that ashamed. I felt filthy dirty with the smell of him and blood all down my legs. I thought Mr Handl would think the worse of me, but he held my hand and cried too. Then he heated a lot of water and filled an old zinc bath and went out of the room while I washed myself down. He didn't come down the stairs till I called him.

'Is there a lock on the room door, Lily?' he asked.

'Yeah, like that one,' I pointed to the kitchen door, 'but it's all rusty. The key is stuck solid.'

He got out a screwdriver and showed me how to

take off the lock. He even put a few drops of oil in a little bottle for me to loosen the screws. He told me to get the lock off when me Ma was out and bring it to him.

'The boy will mend it. He can do anything with those clever hands of his, my dear. He'll put it back for you. You'll have to let him in when there's no-one about. Can you do that? I would give you shelter if I could, my dear, but people talk. I would not be forgiven. But I will help you all I can, you know that? Now you must go, my child, before anyone sees you.'

'Do you never sleep, Mr Handl?'

'Not much, these days, my dear, I am too old for sleep.'

Before I left he talked to me about how it is between people who love each other. He said I would find a good honest man someday who'd make me happy. That all men were not like Buller. Nobody had ever talked to me like that before. I wished and wished he was my daddy. Afterwards he said something funny, but it proved to be the best bit of advice I ever got. 'For the moment, my dear, keep yourself looking as shabby as you can, Lily. Don't wash your hair or your face. Keep your head down. You're too pretty for your own good, my dear. What about the child? Does he harm him?'

'He's afraid of his life of Jimmy, thinks he's bad luck.'

'Then keep Jimmy with you, always. He's good luck for you, Lily. A little blessing.' He made me keep the shawl. It came in real handy for Jimmy. Ma was asleep when I got back, Jimmy was snivelling, as if he'd been crying for hours. But Buller was gone, thank God.

I got the lock off next morning. It took hours. Ma was snoring like a pig, dead to the world. She didn't notice. I got it down to Handl's in the chariot with Jimmy sitting on top, screaming blue bloody murder with the key sticking into him. My legs were like jelly, I felt sick and sore all day but I stayed well out of me Ma's way. She took off for Gerrity's, about eight. She wasn't talking to me for what I'd done. She told me I had to be nice to Buller. She didn't even ask was I all right.

M came with the lock at about ten. I waited for him on the steps. We crept up and I kept watch while he put it back on the door. I don't know what we'd have done if me Ma and Buller had come back. He put a bit of twine through the key when he finished and showed me how easy it worked. He didn't say much, just that I was always to come to him for help. He talked so gentle. I kept the key in my pocket except for when I locked me and Jimmy in.

They saved me, the pair of them. They didn't think I knew M was outside the house every night after that, in case I needed him. He hid behind a bush on the railway side, waiting until after Buller left. I used to watch from the high window. That's why he was there that night. Because the night before, Buller tried to rape me again.

1985. I've tried to stop working for her. There must be a million other, better, dressmakers but she'd have none of it.

'We understand each other so well, don't we?' says she.

401

These days I go to Mount Street. I go in the basement door and am kept waiting, like a beggar, until madam bestows herself on me. Even the prices she gives me wouldn't make up for the insult, nor buy one of those designer things she wears. Her money was great while Frank was sick and Nell in college. Now I don't need her, I can't get rid of her. One of these days she's going to pounce. Like those cats of hers.

June 1995. I haven't seen Reynolds for a week or so. He was always hanging about wanting to talk. Last time he was waiting on the doorstep. He said he just wanted five minutes, he'd come to warn me. I told him he could say what he had to out in the open. I didn't want him in my house.

He told me how he'd found the press in Ringsend and talked to an old man who'd worked there for years. The next day a young man came to his B&B. Introduced himself as Hanlon, general manager of the Raytown Press. Very polite, asked if he could help with his enquiries. Reynolds fell for it. Told him about his father and how he once owned the press. Hanlon laughed and said there must be a mistake, that the press had been owned by the McDonagh family for several generations and that his uncle had married the last of the McDonaghs. Since then, the Hanlons had run it, though his aunt was chairman of the board. He said that none of them had ever heard of a Reynolds being involved. That Reynolds must be thinking of some other press. Like Handl's, which was one of several presses in the Ringsend area in the thirties and forties. Perhaps that was the one?

He offered to help Reynolds investigate and casually asked how he'd got on to the Raytown Press? Reynolds said he just walked around Ringsend until he discovered it. That he knew its approximate location, his father had owned a row of houses on Daedalian Road and he guessed the press was within walking distance. Hanlon immediately said that of course it was Handl's then, because it used to be just beside the church in Ringsend, less than a quarter mile away.

Hanlon was so sympathetic Reynolds showed him the rent books and the model of the houses. Told him how he'd traced the only tenant still living. Told him my name, my maiden name. Told him exactly where I lived. Told him about my daughter. The stupid bastard. I was shaking so much I couldn't say a word.

'Mrs Gilmore,' Reynolds said, 'I told him too much. I didn't cop on fast enough. When I told him everything I'd found out, his manner changed, he laughed and said that I should run away home to England. The way he said it was very menacing, an unmistakable warning to mind my own business. I knew then that I'd found the right press all right but I wasn't going to get anywhere. If I tried anything, Hanlon would see me off. I shouldn't have mentioned Daedalian Road. It stuck a chord, I could tell from his face though he tried to hide it. I shouldn't have mentioned your name either. I wish I'd listened to you that first day. I've come to warn you. I feel very frightened. He was really tough. I should have listened to you. I'm sorry Mrs Gilmore.'

I screamed at him to go, that I'd have the police

on him for molesting me. I didn't know what to do. I still don't. I've a terrible feeling I'm being followed, that a trap's been set and I've walked straight into it. The cat will pounce for sure now. I can't ever go to Milo again. It's him she wants. I can't go to Nell either, in case I put her in danger. I'll ask her to come here. When she comes back from holidays. I'll tell her everything. Nell will know what to do. But is it safe?

I put away my mother's box and cried myself to sleep.

CHAPTER THIRTY-FOUR

Hospital gowns, like straitjackets, open at the back and keep you in a dependent mind-set. When, on Wednesday afternoon, my bandages were replaced by much simpler dressings and the movement of my arm was restored to me, I got the nurse to help me change into my own pyjamas. I'd had enough of being looked-after and of everything else to do with hospitals. I wanted out.

Early next morning, with my injured arm held out of harm's way by a very patient, damp, nurse, I had my first bath. When I viewed myself in the mirror in all my glory, I realized why I'd ached – and slept – so much. My body was a mass of bruises, black, blue and every other colour of the rainbow. Quite a comic sight, really. I laughed though I'm not sure why. Probably nerves. As I hobbled back to my room I wondered if I would ever be able to move without effort again.

It took ages to get into my clothes, even though Maria had thoughtfully brought a light button-through dress. It was cream and blue silk and felt wonderfully soothing next to my bruised skin. It was something to feel feminine again. I was absolutely determined not to get back into bed. I didn't want to interview a single other person, nurse, doctor or visitor, lying on my back. I felt at too much of a disadvantage, or so I told myself. I didn't want to admit that it was Daniel I had in mind. It's hard not to act like a wimp when you're being looked down upon from on high. By noon, I was ready and waiting, nicely displayed in an armchair.

I had plenty of time to gather my thoughts, make my plans. That was important to me. I couldn't run forever, not if I wanted to live a normal life. And I did. I needed to get back to my job, my flat and anonymity, as soon as possible. I didn't want to be another Milo. I had no intention of offering myself as a punch bag, or allowing my aggressors to choose the time and place of my disposal. Nor was I inclined to meekly follow where Daniel McDonagh Garnier masterfully led, much as I liked him. Lily had led me into danger, but Lily had left me the means of getting out. If, that is, I had properly understood the information contained in the box. Nothing in Milo's letter caused me to change my mind. It was he the killer wanted all along. Lily had saved him, once certainly, twice probably. Perhaps it was my fate to sort out Daniel.

I ate a little lunch, staggered up and down the corridor by way of exercise, watched an old Fred and Ginger movie on the box, dozed, had another little walk. By five o'clock I decided he wasn't coming, that I might as well go back to bed. I was standing by the window watching the rush-hour traffic gather on the road below when I heard my name. I turned around slowly.

'Have you ever seen a field of flax?' he asked surprisingly. I shook my head.

'Your eyes are the same colour. You look better, Nell.'

He stood with his back to the door, as he had at Marie-Claire's the previous Friday. He was holding a battered old briefcase and was formally dressed in a dark suit, with a cream shirt buttoned to the neck, no tie. He'd had his hair cut. He looked tired.

'Even without the hair?' I patted my blue beret.

'You should always wear hats, even in bed. They suit you.' He smiled wickedly. 'How do you feel?'

This could go on for ever. 'Fine, thanks,' I said shortly. 'You?'

'I've just been to see the funeral people, in Oxford. Gruesome. It's all arranged for eleven tomorrow morning, in the church next door to his house, then the crematorium.'

'Will your mother come?'

'Yes. She flew back with me. She's already in Oxford, staying with Marie-Claire. It's been one hell of a day. I could do with a drink.' He took a bottle of Domaine Garnier from his briefcase. 'Doctor's orders. Will you join me?' He grinned.

He had a couple of glasses in the case as well. He set them down on the table beside me and fetched himself another chair. Neither of us said anything while he poured the wine.

'You read the letter?' he asked.

'Yes, both yours and Milo's.'

'You already knew, didn't you?'

'Yes. I think I knew even before I met you. I just didn't realize it until next day.'

'When?'

'When did I know for certain? When I was alone in Milo's house. When I saw the slipper on your father's appliance – it was in the wardrobe. He had unusually narrow feet. It was the first thing I noticed about her as well. I met her in Dublin.' I looked up at him.

'You know my aunt's name?'

'Hanora Hanrahan. She looks like Milo. And a little like you.'

'I could do without that, I think,' he said heavily and took a long swallow of wine. 'You also know why she killed your mother?'

'Had her killed. Yes, I do. Because Arthur Reynolds suggested to her henchman, Hanlon, that Lily had witnessed the murder as a girl. He also told him precisely where she lived at the time.'

'Will you explain?'

This is what I'd been preparing for all day, all week. Someday, perhaps, I would let him see the complete set of Lily's papers, but that day it seemed important not to mention Lily's blackmail scam. Was it because I didn't want to acknowledge that the woman who had arranged my mother's murder had also contributed to my education? That had I asked questions at the material time, I might have somehow prevented what happened to my mother? I suspect it may have been. All I knew for certain was that it was my problem, to deal with in my own time.

'Your aunt only knew Lily as her little dress-maker, Mrs Gilmore. It seems crazy, but I guess Lily couldn't quite bring herself to lose all contact with Milo's memory. Whatever. It hardly matters now, except it meant that Hanora used to come to our house. At some stage she must have seen the diary – the missing one – but only realized its significance when Reynolds identified Lily Sweetman for her. After Buller's murder, Lily worked briefly as a maid for Maisie Reynolds. Arthur didn't remember her, but I guess when Hanora's memory was jogged, she did. She must also have had some inkling of the Milo/Lily connection. Maybe Mr Handl or Dolly Brennan mentioned it? I simply don't know.

'Shortly before Lily's death, the diary went missing. Hanora must have taken it, or got Hanlon to do so, probably the latter, she's much too canny to compromise herself. She would have seen Milo's work when he was an apprentice. All she needed was a prompt to recognize it again and Reynolds provided that. But of course, Lily's diary was both recent and dated. I'm afraid your aunt put two and two together and realized that your father was still alive and recently in touch with Lily. All she had to do was flush him out.'

I looked straight at Daniel for the first time, I wanted him to understand fully the depth of my anger. He held my gaze, without moving, as he absorbed the implication of what I'd said.

'My God, Nell,' his voice was a husky croak, 'my God, you can't mean it?'

'Oh, indeed I do. I suspect she arranged old Arthur's quietus as well. He conveniently fell under a train at Piccadilly Circus. So I won't come to Milo's funeral, if you don't mind. I wouldn't want to get in the bitch's way. It's you she'll want now.'

'Me? Why me?'

'Well, apart from the fact that we both know all about her, you are her brother's only son. She has no children. I don't suppose it's a latent maternal instinct that's driving her so maybe she's looking for an heir? She's loopy enough for anything.'

409

Daniel thought about that for quite a while. One of his best qualities was that he didn't feel compelled to voice all his thoughts. I waited while he worked it through. He listened too carefully not to fully understand where I was heading. He nodded slowly, unravelled himself and got heavily to his feet. He blundered halfway across the room before he turned and faced me again.

'Not loopy, terrifying. What will you do, Nell?' he asked softly. He looked completely shattered. 'Can you have her charged?'

'With what? My mother's "accident", Arthur Reynold's "mishap"? Your dad died of natural causes.' I shrugged and slowly shook my head. 'I don't think so. It's all surmise. The ramblings of a little old lady and her grieving daughter. Hanora Hanrahan has powerful friends. She'd make mincemeat of me.'

'So what'll you do?'

'With your help, Daniel, I thought we'd have a stab at making mincemeat of her.'

We talked for hours and, though he spoke no words of love, I knew he ached for me as much as I did for him. He left at about nine, after he'd helped me to bed. I kept my hat on the whole time, I didn't want to catch cold.

The following morning, on the dot of eleven, I discharged myself from the hospital. Daniel and I reckoned that Aunt Hanora and Hanlon would be at the funeral, which gave me a couple of hours to make my escape. I hired a taxi for the day and headed straight for my bank in Richmond where I deposited the diaries and all the rest of Lily's and Milo's papers. After that I went to my flat, packed a suitcase and headed for a spa hotel on the outskirts of Aylesbury. We'd made reservations the night before. I checked in under the name of James, out of sheer superstition. Jimmy had protected Lily, and we were in dire need of protection. Daniel rang at one o'clock to make sure I'd made it.

'Was she there?' I asked.

'Yes, she was there.' He sounded subdued. 'She wasn't hard to spot, she looks so exactly like Milo. A more together version. Elegant, hard. I studied her carefully.'

'Was Hanlon there?'

'No, not that I could see.'

'Did you speak to her?'

'Yes, as we planned. Just as we were leaving the graveyard I fell back and introduced myself. Asked if we were related. She handled it well, no blips, admitted she was his sister. She said he had been reported killed during the war and that she'd only very recently discovered he was still alive.'

'She expected you to swallow that?'

'I rather think she was fishing but I kept up a front of polite interest. I showed absolutely no hostility. I treated her like a fragile old woman and pretended to be concerned about her leaving the graveyard by the avenue exit. I said there had been a number of attacks there recently. I mentioned yours as happening to someone from Milo's college. Said you were collecting some stuff from the house when it happened. Sorry, my darling, but I pretended I wasn't terribly involved, or interested.'

'Well done. Were you nervous?'

'No, I suppose I was surprised at how old she

411

looked. She didn't make me nervous, she made me feel vicious. I kept remembering the things she's done. To you, to Lily, to my father.'

'Did you manage to wangle an invitation?' I asked.

Daniel chuckled. 'Oh yes, indeed. As I walked her to her car, we talked about Dublin. I let drop I was collaborating with someone in St Vincent's and that I'd be visiting next week.'

'She fell for it?'

'Like a lamb to the slaughter,' he answered. 'Asked if I'd like to come to one of her *soirées*? Next Thursday evening all right for you?'

'Almost a week. Perfect. She's gone?'

'Yes. The college put on a reception but she didn't turn up. A large number of the fellows came to the church. I was very touched. Milo would have been amazed at how highly he was regarded.'

'And liked. People don't come only out of regard, do they?'

'No, probably not, but it's nice of you to say it. I'll get to the hotel as soon I can. Nell? Rest.'

My flight had almost wiped me out, but I managed to make a few phone calls. Then, satisfied that the groundwork had been laid, I slept most of the afternoon, in a huge, comfortable, canopied bed. It was growing dark when I was awoken by the sound of the door opening. I lay frozen with terror, unable for a moment to remember where I was. 'Nell, it's me,' Daniel said softly. 'May I come in?'

I couldn't answer, my heart was still pumping too painfully. Gradually, as my eyes got used to the gloom, I saw that he was in his usual position, standing with his back to the door, uncertain of his reception. I struggled to sit up, every muscle in my body crying out in protest. I groaned. Oh, the advantage of long legs. He came across the room in a couple of strides and took me in his arms, so tenderly, so carefully, I could have wept. We clutched each other for what seemed like hours, and we might have stayed like that for ever, but for another polite tap at the door. I jumped sky high.

'Hush, it's only room service. I ordered some wine.' He pulled open the door with a flourish. 'Oh, and dinner too. I didn't think you'd feel up to the dining-room.'

The man was a genius. 'I'm not sure I could even make it to the top of the stairs,' I laughed.

'You won't mind if I stay?'

'For dinner? Of course not.'

'No,' he said slowly, 'I was thinking of, well, a little longer?' He twisted his head to one side and eyed me quizzically.

'Like the night?'

'Like for ever, actually.'

'Do you mind,' I said demurely, 'if we take it one night at a time?'

He busied himself pulling out the cork and pouring the wine. He brushed his lips lightly against mine as he gave me the glass.

'I wasn't quite straight with you the other day . . .'

'About reading the diaries? You said.'

'No, something else. I'd already accepted the job in the Nuffield. I start at the end of October. Before that, we both need a holiday. In the sun if possible.

You need recuperation.' He took my hand. 'So, will you marry me, Nell Gilmore?'

'Yes, Daniel Garnier,' I said. 'I will.'

We made love for the first time that night, if you could call it love-making or dignify it with the word. Poor Daniel, I spent more time trying to protect my aching arm than pleasing my lover. Worse, in the middle of proceedings I took a fit of the giggles at the notion of Lily with her one-legged lover and Daniel with his one-armed, bald bandit. When he eventually coaxed the cause of my mirth out of me, we both had hysterics. It was wonderful; healing, soothing, but most of all, bonding. Afterwards we decided that if we could survive the absurdity of our present predicament, we could survive anything. He made me feel wildly, wonderfully happy.

We stole that week, away from the world, away from fear. We kept to our room, spoke to no-one save the staff and each other, walked, and within a couple of days when my cuts had fully closed, swam, in the warm, empty pool. Otherwise we learned each other by making love. What can I say? We made each other laugh? We were completely at ease? Well yes, that too. But there was much more. He was a gentle, considerate, knowing, exciting lover, but he was also delightfully, unrestrainedly sexy. We started gently enough, out of consideration on his side and self-protection for my bruised body, on mine. But by the end of our stay, we were effortlessly, completely in love.

We flew to Dublin the following Wednesday and checked into the Shelbourne Hotel. From there we were within easy distance of Mount Street.

CHAPTER THIRTY-FIVE

The first time I'd met Hanora Hanrahan, on that hot summer day, I'd worn a short, skimpy white linen skirt with a navy and white tank top. Bare legs, flat scruffy sandals. I was tanned and freckled, my hair tied up in a pony tail, I must have looked about eighteen. For the party, it was essential that she should not recognize me.

I made up my face carefully, full war paint, with not a freckle in sight. Hot red lipstick in stark contrast to my pale skin. With a black, dévoré velvet turban, the effect was pretty good. Without it, I looked like a rather sad clown. The criss-cross of stitches on my head looked like miniature rail tracks. Against the blond stubble – my hair was growing out paler than normal – the livid, purplish scars were shocking.

I dressed all in black silk crepe – tailored jacket, long slim skirt – which had cost me a small fortune in Brown Thomas that afternoon. It was worth it, I have seldom worn anything so flattering. With a pair of deadly, high heeled, black grosgrain pumps I was nose level with Daniel. He did a double take when I emerged from the bathroom.

'Wow,' he said. 'You look stunning. So beautiful, I'm afraid to touch you.' He held me at arm's length and pirouetted me around. 'Perfect. Straight out of *Vogue*.' He cocked his head on one side and raised an eyebrow. 'French *Vogue* of course.'

I ignored the chauvinism. 'You look pretty sensational yourself,' I said.

He was got out to the nines in a hired dinner jacket. He held up his arm in mock self-protection.

'Not pretty. I protest. Sexy, lecherous, randy but never pretty.'

'Pretty sensational, I stick to my guns,' I laughed. Then we got serious for a few minutes and went over our plans before calling a cab.

Mount Street was lined with cars. We asked the taxi to drop us a little way from the house. We were both very nervous and needed a few moments' walk in the cool evening air before facing the fray. As we approached, we could see the sparkling chandeliers of the first floor drawing room. People, men for the most part, were chatting by the tall, uncurtained windows. It looked wonderful, the sort of party you long for. Daniel squeezed my hand. We took a deep breath and mounted the steps.

The door was answered by the ancient retainer, who ushered us into the hall. The Burmese cat was still sitting at the bottom of the beautiful staircase, licking his chops. Hanora was at the top of the stairs, dressed in a shimmering burgundy dress, cut on the bias. She wore golden slippers and stockings and a heavy gold necklace and bracelet. For her age she looked amazing, but then she had an excellent dressmaker.

Daniel clasped my elbow as we climbed towards her. She stood waiting for us as a queen would her subjects. For style, élan, panache she was the nonpareil. We exchanged glances as she put out her hand to him.

'My dear boy, my dear Milo's boy, welcome.' She turned to me with her eyebrows raised. 'And you've brought a friend? How nice,' she said vaguely. She extended her hand to me briefly then led the way into the drawing room, without asking my name. A man's woman clearly. I didn't mind, I was satisfied she hadn't recognized me.

The room was huge and lofty and crowded with the glitterati of Dublin, togged out in their best. Even at the doorway I recognized a dozen politicians, several journalists and a couple of well-known actresses. There must have been a hundred people in the room and the level of talk was oppressive. A waiter handed us each a glass of champagne as we entered. We quickly separated, as planned. Daniel allowed himself to be led into the crowd by his aunt, I made my way to the central window where I'd glimpsed my quarry from the street below.

Surprising what a black hat does for a girl. It obviously lent an air of mystery I don't normally possess. Or perhaps it was that I neither wished to impress or be impressed by the company for I knew I would never see any of them again. I felt aloof and in control for the first time since my mother died. But I kept reminding myself of her and why I was there. I avoided mentioning my name, parrying enquiries about who I was and what I was doing in such company, as deftly and with as much grace as I could.

Des Murphy-Clarke had hardly changed since our college days. He'd been one of the crowd I hung around with, though even then I'd been wary of him. I think we all were; the general feeling was, more or less, better to have him on your side than against you. But he was always entertaining, I've never known anyone with such an endless fund of scandal and titillation. He was also highly adept at prising stories out of everyone else and his gift had made him one of the most successful, and feared, journalists in Dublin. I didn't much like the look of him now, the tan was too yellow, the hair too black, the incipient paunch desperately trying to escape the grip of his waistband. But it didn't matter, he was a real ferret once he'd got the whiff of a story. I could almost see his nostrils twitch as I hove into sight.

God bless him, he pretended not to know me. He did his lecherous have-I-got-thrills-for-you act, as he allowed a sweet old senator to draw him into conversation with me. From time to time I noticed Hanora looking our way but she didn't intrude, Daniel saw to that. We stayed by the window for about an hour, making conversation with passing guests. Eventually, as the party was thinning out, we talked only to each other.

'You come to these bashes often?' I asked, not quite casually enough.

'Often enough to be able to turn up when it's convenient. For me.' He laughed. 'Though the lady thinks it's only her convenience I think of.'

'Imagine that,' I said. 'Aren't you the clever one.'

'And aren't you the cracker?' He grinned wolfishly. 'Nothing changes. Except you get more beautiful. The get-up is bloody electrifying, girl. But then, you always had style.' He paused and moved closer. 'Is it time?'

I nodded and with as much visibility as I could, passed him a folded slip of paper. Then I put my face close to his ear and told him a story.

Daniel and I were the last to go. We followed my little senator down the stairs to where Mrs Hanrahan was bidding her guests goodbye. She signalled Daniel to wait and when she closed the front door she turned to us with her most dazzling smile. It terrified me.

'Stay for supper, will you? I haven't really talked to you, Daniel. And you haven't introduced me to your friend.'

'My fiancée,' Daniel said curtly. 'I'm afraid we can't stay. Prior engagement, Aunt.'

'You make an extremely handsome couple,' she said grandly and held out her hand to me. I ignored it.

'We've already met, Mrs Hanrahan,' I said, as Daniel moved in behind me and put his arm around my shoulder.

'Surely not?' She peered across at me short-sightedly. Daniel whipped off my hat and tipped forward my head to allow her an unexpurgated view of the scars.

'I'm Nell Gilmore. Surely you remember, Mrs Hanrahan?' I straightened up and looked into her eyes. She backed away from us but she couldn't tear her eyes from the scars.

'The little dressmaker's girl?' she whispered.

'The little dressmaker you had killed,' Daniel said softly.

'I beg your pardon?' She gave a hollow little laugh, as if she couldn't believe her ears.

'It's Nell's pardon you should beg,' Daniel said roughly. 'You know why we've come, don't you?'

'I suppose so,' she answered slowly, 'but I prefer if we don't go through a full rehearsal, if you don't mind. Just tell me what you want,' she said, attempting to regain control.

'Nothing,' I said. I took the envelope of money she'd given me at our previous meeting from my purse and handed it to her.

'This is yours. You made a mistake, you'd already paid my mother,' I said blandly.

She considered me silently as she flicked it against her wrist. 'You weren't in on it?' she asked softly.

'No.'

'You didn't know?'

'Not then. Your other mistake,' I paused, 'was mentioning Ringsend. My mother never did.'

'I see. He wasn't meant to be on that bloody road, that night,' she burst out. 'How was I to know he was involved with that whore's child?'

'My mother, you mean?'

She shrugged. 'Facts are facts. I never meant him to stay away. I would never harm my little brother. He knew that.'

'I'm afraid he didn't.' Daniel said roughly. 'His mind worked more slowly, less ambitiously than yours, when his mind was working, that is. Tell me, was it worth it?'

She laughed in his face. 'I've had my moments.' She looked straight at me. 'As did your mother, no doubt?' I blushed. Daniel looked at me quizzically, but mercifully said nothing.

Hanora closed her eyes and sighed. 'If only I'd known poor Milo was alive. If only that horrible little man Reynolds hadn't blundered in. If only, if only. Oh well. There we are.' She smiled grimly. 'I am rich, childless . . .'

'So you are,' Daniel said. 'But Lily is dead, and Milo and Arthur Reynolds.'

'I had nothing to do with Milo's death, I wouldn't hurt either of you.'

'You had everything to do with his death. You had everything to do with his ruined life, as well.'

She looked at him questioningly but said nothing. Daniel turned to me and took my hand. 'Nell?'

'The diaries you didn't find have a complete account of the murder,' I said. 'Complete. I also have letters, notes, newspaper cuttings from May 31 1941 right up to the present, compiled jointly by my mother, and Milo. It's being held in a bank with a covering letter from Daniel and me which will be sent to the police and my solicitor if ever anything happens to either of us.'

She looked at us mockingly, pityingly, as if she thought we were pitiably out of our league.

'Or,' Daniel added, 'if ever Hanlon gets up to any more of his murderous tricks.'

'But there is no longer any need, is there, my dear Daniel?' She pushed me away. Her eyes were bright, sparkling, mad. 'Now that I've found you. You will take your father's rightful place. It is what we planned so long ago. Of course, my dear, you will have to drop that silly French name.'

'No,' he said, emphatically. 'No, I will not.'

Hanora looked at him under her lashes, mischievously, and for a moment it seemed possible that we had only imagined the evil she had done.

'What about Hanlon,' Daniel repeated.

'Hanlon is surplus to requirements, my dear. He will not trouble you again, or anyone else. I've sent him to London. I'm surprised you didn't know.' She looked straight at me but I didn't allow myself to flinch. 'You see,' she smiled languidly, 'I've promoted him beyond his capability so he'll manage his own decline. Stupid man. Not a worthy successor. Too little thought, too much action.' She laughed softly.

The Burmese cat slunk around her feet, mewing loudly. She pushed him aside gently with the tip of her shoe and the cat languidly returned to his pals on the stairs. I noticed, with alarm, that they all had their unblinking eyes turned towards their mistress. I felt oppressed, as if I was going to faint as I caught the whiff of them for the first time. I clutched Daniel's finger tightly and he moved closer to me. We were both shaking a little as Hanora threw back her head and laughed.

'So you'll go to the police? Or to your solicitor?' She snapped her fingers in my face. 'Fat lot of good that'll do you.'

I bent my head again and pushed it in her face. 'No,' I said. 'That would be too kind. I changed my mind. I thought of something much more effective.' I straightened up, put my hat back on and smiled at her. 'I didn't think you'd know anyone from *The Sunday World*. It was really very nice of you to invite Des Murphy-Clarke. He's an old friend of mine. From university.' I looked at her sideways

422

and watched the dawning fear in the intensity and viciousness of her glare.

'What?' she roared.

'Oh yes. An old friend. I rang him and asked if he'd be at your party. He only came to see me.'

'How dare you? You were with that fucking journalist all evening. In my drawing room.'

'That's right. He was terribly interested in what I had to say,' I said smoothly.

'That scum wouldn't dare.' She spat the words. 'That rag. Nobody believes that rag.'

'I thought you might say that. I think you're wrong of course, but just in case, I alerted the chaps from *The Irish Times* and the *Independent* as well. So many journalists at your party, I didn't quite get around to them all. But it doesn't matter, I gave Des the exclusive.'

'You little bitch!' She launched herself at me, but Daniel was too quick for her. He grabbed hold of her wrists and held them gripped in his strong hands.

I stepped adroitly past, threw open the door, and turned to look at them. The cats were gathering at Hanora's feet. Daniel pushed her backwards and joined me.

'Your mother kept my brother from me,' she screamed. 'She had no business doing that. All those years.'

I glared at her. 'Three years is what we're talking about, Mrs Hanrahan. She only found him again three years ago. If she was able to find him, so could you. You had better resources, after all. Trouble is, he didn't want you to find him. He was terrified of you.'

'I did nothing. They can't libel me. I'll sue. I'll destroy the lot of them. I'll destroy you.' She was defeated now and blustering and we all knew it. The cats prowled round and round her legs, their backs arched, tails waving.

'I don't think so,' I said. 'You could try, though. Des would like that. He really wants to create a stir. He says it's the best story he's had in years.'

'Only if I'm still around,' she snarled, 'to be humiliated.'

'That's right,' I said. My throat felt dry, raw. 'You've got two days.'

She banged the door behind us, but even with it shut, I could still hear the dreadful cackle of her laughter. Daniel and I clutched each other in the darkness. We were both shaking. Revenge is not sweet.

FINALE

The story broke the following Sunday, by which time Hanora Hanrahan had disappeared. The headlines were lurid. *Unsolved Murder Basis of Printing Fortune. Dublin's Leading Political Hostess Vanishes.* Des Murphy-Clarke dug deep and dug dirty. He was much too canny to make any direct allegations. It was neatly done but it was all innuendo.

There was hardly any mention of Cormac Hanlon. It was all Hanora. His article spread over four pages complete with pictures of her with several leading politicians. The common thread, as Des subtly pointed out, was that they had all, at some time or other, been involved in notorious financial scandals over just about everything: beef, property, insider dealing, government contracts. Hanora had her finger in many pies that I knew nothing of, I had merely handed him a hook to hang his facts – or theories – upon. I didn't feel particularly proud of myself.

Once he'd got his teeth into the story Des couldn't let go, he wanted it to run and run. The following week, while we were packing to go to France, he unexpectedly turned up at my flat in Richmond. He was like a dog worrying at a bone.

'Just tell me one thing, Nell, did your mother know all that was going on?'

'I've no idea. There was no mention of it in the diaries but . . . I wonder . . .'

'She was very smart, your mother,' Daniel said suddenly. 'She might have guessed. And if she had she would probably have discussed it with my father. They could have worked it out.'

'What makes you think that?'

'Well,' he said slowly, 'you both say that at least some of those scandals were well publicized.' He shrugged. 'She read the newspapers, didn't she? If everyone else was speculating, why not her?'

Murphy-Clarke, suddenly realizing that I was hiding something, looked at me sharply. I turned away, afraid he'd read my mind and start digging. Whether Lily knew or guessed the whole of what was going on was best left a matter of conjecture. Without realizing it, Des had indicated why her scam had been so effective. Hanora Hanrahan could not permit the slightest hint of dirt to sully her image. She couldn't afford to, there was too much at stake. As casually as I could, and with my foot firmly on Daniel's, I changed the subject.

'I don't quite understand just how Raytown Press became so big?'

'First of all, the war. Printing contracts that had previously gone to big outfits in England, had to be met at home. For some reason they had huge stocks of paper. Paper became very short so they were able to mop up printing contracts that would have gone to more important firms in Ireland.'

'They were lucky to have had the stock,' I said insouciantly.

'Luck?' Des snorted. 'Luck had little to do with

it. Someone was very, very smart. Prescient, I'd say. Listen, they couldn't lose . . .'

'What if Ireland had joined the Allies, gone into the war?' Daniel asked.

'How do you mean?' I started.

'Think of the site,' Des interrupted. 'Man, it's right beside the deep-basin dock. They'd have really been quids in then. The Brits were desperate for the Irish ports.' He laughed. 'No wonder Reynolds was knocked off. Once they gained control, the press got stuck in and fairly gobbled up government contracts, used them to expand and expand, at home and abroad.'

Nor was that their only line, he told us. Raytown Press had a huge slice of the international science and medical publishing market. Des was not slow in pointing out startling operating similarities to the empire of the late great Maxwell.

I could only wonder that Lily had survived so long having tweaked at the lid of that Pandora's box. She could not have known what danger she was in even though she'd been aware that she was mouse to Hanora's cat. Was she more? An amusing little mascot providing a tantalizing frisson of threat? A little fun for the great lady? To be kept sweet while she discovered just what Lily thought she knew? Or did Hanora, at some level, fear – or hope – that Milo was alive and that Lily would lead her to him? Maybe. Or maybe I was only extrapolating with hindsight.

Murphy-Clarke cleared up some other mysteries under Daniel's skillfully naive pumping – his French accent became quite thick, I noticed, as he asked about his aunt. Hanora married –

alliteratively – twice, widowed twice. Her first
husband – Tony Hanlon – had been her entree into
politics. At the time of Reynolds's murder his older
brother, Dolan, was her lover. Until another of his
conquests 'had got herself pregnant'. Des Murphy-
Clarke's words, not mine. That marriage lasted
for only a couple of years, until the nameless
one conveniently took herself off with baby
Cormac. Dolan and Hanora resumed their affair,
Tony became a TD. Murphy-Clarke described
the trio as inseparable – the salacious implications were rather laboured – until Tony died
from a heart attack as did his brother, Dolan
about ten years later. After that she married her
second husband, Hanrahan, who was also a
politician, a member of the Senate. Both marriages
were childless. Murphy-Clarke also insinuatingly
listed five or six 'good friends', a police
commissioner amongst them. His name meant
nothing to me.

'So she was effectively running the press alone?'
Daniel couldn't bear to say her name. I think he
hated her more than I did. Hated being related to
her.

'Oh yes. At least for the past fifteen years,' Des
Murphy-Clarke replied. 'It was all hers.'

So she was entirely responsible. I felt sick as I
watched Daniel's colour rise.

'What about the nephew?' he asked tersely.
'When did he reappear? What was his position in
the company?'

'Not sure,' Des replied languidly. 'Not yet.'

'Have you been able to find out anything about
him?' I burst out.

I wished we hadn't mentioned him as Murphy-Clarke's eyes slid slyly from one of us to the other and back again. He really was the most awful sleaze-ball.

'I'm still digging,' he said ominously. A slow satisfied smile spread across his face. He left shortly afterwards.

Over the following few months, Daniel and I did our own largely unsuccessful, sleuthing on Arthur Reynolds. I felt sorry for him in the end, poor, sad man. He was a loner, recently bereaved, with few friends. For those reasons and because they had no evidence of anyone else involved in his fall to his death, the police presumed it to be suicide. As far as we could gather this was on the basis of a fairly ambiguous note he'd written, six months before his death, to the couple who had bought his mother's guest house. We went to see them, posing as long lost friends of the Reynolds's but learned little more. What he'd been hoping to gain in Dublin remained conjecture. If his canny mother had not been able to press her claim to the printing press fifty years before, he could hardly have hoped to be successful, could he? With his mama dead, was he just a lonely, unattractive man in desperate search of the loving father of his dreams? Perhaps the poor man had at last discovered just what a monster had fathered him. Perhaps the police were right after all. Perhaps he had killed himself.

I try not to think about Cormac Hanlon. One good thing at least, he wasn't Jen's boyfriend. I met Matt Craig when I finally went back to the office. He was not dissimilar in build but that was all. My overheated imagination had been at work the day I thought he was Hanlon. Sometimes it is still. My fear of him remains.

Which leaves me. I had set out to avenge my mother's death by destroying her destroyer. I thought it would make my loss easier to bear. It didn't. But in the process I learned something about her life which only made it harder.

When I was about ten, one of the nuns at school had a powerful line in spooky stories. My favourite was about a young, dark-haired priest exorcizing devils. The punch line was that he always staggered out of the room, after the ordeal, with his hair snow white. The strange thing is that it's happened to me. My hair didn't grow back a paler shade of blonde. It grew out pure white, exactly like Lily's. It has the strange effect of making me look much younger. Daniel seems to like it, I'm less sure. It looks quite startling on a six-months pregnant woman.

THE END